The Callahans

Marilee Bonnell

iUniverse, Inc.
New York Bloomington

The Callahans

iUniverse books may be ordered through booksellers or by contacting:

iUniverse
1663 Liberty Drive
Bloomington, IN 47403
www.iuniverse.com
1-800-Authors (1-800-288-4677)

ISBN: 978-1-4401-0482-4 (pbk)
ISBN: 978-1-4401-0483-1 (ebk)

Printed in the United States of America

iUniverse rev. 12/04/2008

Chapter One

Samantha Callahan stood before her full-length mirror, taking a long, critical look at herself. Dressed in a pair of faded blue jeans and a checkered flannel shirt—with her long hair stuffed under her floppy hat—somebody could easily mistake her for one of her father's cowhands. Her eyes were one of her best features, Samantha thought. Like her younger brother James, she had inherited their father's incredible blue eyes. But her best feature of all was her unusual hair. Nearly reaching the back of her knees, her honey-gold mane was an inherited trait on her mother's side; all the Thomas women had extremely long hair. She'd heard that her great-grandmother Thomas's hair had touched the floor.

Samantha flung her long, thick plait over her shoulder, and left her room. She proceeded down the hallway, and, as she descended the wide-banistered stairway, already she could smell the wonderful aroma of freshly brewed coffee.

When Samantha entered the kitchen, her mother was standing at the counter preparing breakfast. Her father was seated at the table, drinking his morning coffee. She noticed his face was wrinkled in a thoughtful frown.

Samantha plopped into her chair, plucked her hat off her head, set it on top of the table, and casually remarked, "You look mad enough to spit nails, Pa."

His frown deepened.

"Will somebody please tell me what's wrong?" Samantha was looking at her mother.

Her father finally replied, "Guess who was waiting inside the barn this morning when your brother went out to do his chores."

Samantha immediately knew *who* her father was talking about. Her brother James and his best friend Jake Martin had been getting into fist fights lately. Nobody knew why.

"Luckily Amos heard the commotion and broke up the fight this time," John said. "I just don't understand what's gotten into Jake. He and James are supposed to be best friends."

"Well something certainly is troubling that boy," Rachel said over her shoulder at her husband.

She turned her attention back to her task as she thought about her son. At nearly nineteen years of age, James was considered a man now; he was no longer her little boy. James was looking more and more like his handsome father every day, Rachel mused. Her men were close to the same height, well over six feet. They shared the same piercing blue eyes; their hair was the same medium length and black as midnight. Except her husband's was now beginning to gray a little around the temples. It was getting harder to tell father and son apart.

"I think those eggs are scrambled, Rach."

She stopped what she was doing and turned to face her husband. "Don't you think it's about time you had a talk with Jed about his son?"

"I think talking to Jed might make matters even worse. Best let the boys try and work out their own problems."

Rachel poured the egg mixture into a skillet on the stove and tossed the empty bowl into the sink. "We can't allow these fights to continue, John . . . it's been going on long enough."

"Just out of curiosity, who won the fight?" Samantha wanted to know.

"There's no winning a fight, Samantha," Rachel scolded her daughter as she set a huge platter of flapjacks on the table, along with a large bowl heaped with scrambled eggs. She then took her seat across from her husband, and frowned. *How can John sit there enjoying his meal when their son was getting pummeled several times a week*, she thought with exasperation. Okay, maybe pummeled was a slight exaggeration.

Still, something had to be done. And, if her husband wasn't willing to do anything about it, then she would.

"I could always talk to Ester about Jake," Rachel suggested.

"That would be even worse," John replied with his mouth full of food. "Give the boys a chance to settle their own differences . . . let's wait and see what happens."

Rachel nearly spewed her coffee all over the table when she heard her daughter's mumbled opinion of Jake Martin in a few very unladylike words. "Samantha Callahan, you watch your language, young lady!"

"Where did you learn such vocabulary?" John demanded to know.

"From you, of course," Samantha said in a teasing tone.

Rachel's scowling expression was now focused on her husband.

"Hey . . . she didn't learn language like that from me," John assured his wife. Then he turned to his daughter with a scowling expression of his own. "I never want to hear anything like that come out of your mouth again, Samantha!"

"Yes, Sir." Samantha then inquired about her brother. "By the way, where is the champ?"

"Finishing his chores . . . which reminds me . . . Rach, we need to hire another hand. Charlie Bates quit yesterday."

"That's because Charlie would rather hang around the brothel in town than do an honest day's work," Samantha bluntly stated what everybody knew was fact.

John threw back his head and laughed.

"Samantha Callahan, you're beginning to sound like your father's hired hands," Rachel chided her daughter, then turned away to hide her grin.

Inside the barn Amos stood watching James, who was running a brush over his horse's hide, obviously still angry over his fight with Jake. He'd been with the Callahans ever since John and Rachel had first moved to Bear Creek. Rachel had been expecting James at the time, and Samantha had been about a year old. John had hired him on the spot; and after only a few years had promoted him to foreman. So he really felt like part of the family.

Amos wondered if he should try to speak to the boy, but not having any experience with children of his own, he really didn't know what to say that might help ease the boy's frustration. Maybe he'd better think of something to say though. The way James was going at the poor horse with that brush, the animal soon wouldn't have any coat left.

Amos heard the barn door creak open. He let out a sigh of relief when he saw John walking toward him. He gladly took his cue and hurried out of the barn.

John grinned at the way Amos practically ran past him to get out of the barn. His foreman could easily handle a bunch of rowdy cowboys all day, but when it came to family matters, it was a completely different story.

As John stood observing his son, he thought he was looking at himself, nearly twenty years ago. He frowned when James turned and tossed the brush into an empty bucket and noticed the newest bruise on his son's other cheek.

"You're beginning to look like a raccoon." John started forward.

"How long have you been standing there, Pa?"

"Not long." John stopped and reached out to touch his son's swollen cheek. "Don't you think it's about time you told me what's going on between you and Jake?"

"I'm not exactly sure myself," James admitted with a slight shrug of his shoulders. "I didn't have any clue at all, until this morning. Apparently Jake has a problem with . . . he told me to stay away from his sister, but he didn't say why. He didn't seem to have a problem with me and Sarah before. Why the sudden change . . . your guess is as good as mine."

"You're involved with little Sarah Martin?"

"Pa, Sarah is almost *my* age . . . where have you been?"

John rubbed the back of his neck, mumbling under his breath to himself, "I must be older than I thought."

"There's something you should know, Pa." James had been meaning to tell his parents how he felt about Sarah Martin; it just never seemed to be the right time or place. Now was as good as time as any. "I've asked Sarah to be my wife."

"You did what?" John bellowed. "Are you crazy? You're both way too young—"

"You were my age when you married Ma!"

"That was different!"

"How?"

With the shocking news his son just gave him, John wouldn't be surprised if more gray hairs had just sprouted on his head. He began to pace back and forth. "Does Jed and Ester know about you and Sarah?"

"No—not yet anyway." James didn't want his father to know that he was a little leery about asking Jed for his daughter's hand in marriage.

John turned to face his son. He chose his words carefully. "I know you're a man now, James. I'm not trying to tell you what to do, but getting married is a huge step . . . all I'm asking you to do is give this some serious thought. Then, if you still insist on marrying Sarah, I think it would be wise if we told Jed together."

"Thank you, Pa."

Samantha stood at the sink, washing the breakfast dishes, while Rachel sat at the kitchen table, quietly observing her daughter. As usual, Samantha was dressed in her customary attire: a pair of old faded blue jeans and a flannel shirt. Her chestnut-colored hair was fashioned in a thick plait that hung down her back to her knees.

Rachel had long ago accepted the fact that her outspoken daughter would much rather be out riding the range and rounding up cattle than helping her in the kitchen. Samantha could be downright stubborn at times once she got her mind set on something, but she had a bubbly personality and an enormous sense of humor. Rachel could remember many past winter days when the whole family had been stuck indoors because of the snow and how Samantha had kept them laughing with her witty remarks. She had grown into such a lovely young woman too, Rachel mused. And she oftentimes wondered if there would ever be a man suitable for her only headstrong daughter . . .

Rachel snapped out of her thoughts when she heard what sounded like several riders approaching the house. "I wonder who that could be," she said more to herself, scooting out of her chair. She walked over to the window and looked outside.

"Ma, who is it?"

"Looks like Jed and—some of his ranch hands."

For some reason Rachel had a bad feeling that this wasn't a social call. Just in case there was trouble, she hurried to the cabinet where

John kept his rifles. After grabbing one, she crossed the kitchen to the backdoor.

"Ma, what's wrong?"

"Stay inside, Samantha." Then Rachel slammed out the door.

From inside the barn John and James had also heard the unexpected visitors. As father and son approached the small group of men astride their horses, John started to suspect that something was wrong when Jed remained seated on his horse. He began to feel even more uneasy when he got a glimpse of Jed's somber expression. He was about to send James inside the house when Jed suddenly drew his gun.

"Your son defiled my daughter, Callahan!" Jed shouted in a furious rage.

With lightning speed John launched himself at Jed, knocking the gun from his hand, then he jerked him off his horse, grasping him by the throat. "Tell your men to throw down their weapons!" When Jed refused to comply, he tightened his grip. "I won't tell you again!"

"Do as he says, Jed!"

John looked over his shoulder to shout at his wife, "Get back inside the house, Rachel!"

"I'm not going anywhere, John Callahan!" she shouted back, holding her rifle steady. "Do as my husband says, Jed! Tell your men to drop their guns!"

Seeing Rachel standing there, Jed struggled with his emotions. He'd never intended for things to go this far. His wife had just informed him that morning about their daughter being in the family way . . . naturally he'd gone berserk. And even though Sarah had adamantly sworn that James was not the father, who else could it be? So when he saw James, he'd lost his temper.

Now as Jed looked into the eyes of the man who'd been his friend for more than twenty years, he knew he shouldn't have come here, not until he'd had a chance to calm down. And what if Sarah was telling the truth? Besides, he could never hurt Rachel.

"Drop your weapons," he finally ordered his men.

Immediately John released him. He then picked up his gun, emptied the chambers, and handed it back to him. Jed nodded, and slipped his gun inside its holster.

"Now what's this all about?" John demanded to know.

Jed could feel his temper rising again. He pointed an accusing finger in James's direction and angrily shouted, "Sarah's in the family way and I believe your son's the father!"

With all eyes now trained on him, James was just as stunned about this unexpected news as everybody else. Sarah hadn't said a word to him about . . . ! If it was true, it couldn't be his because they had never . . . ! James really didn't know how to respond, so he said nothing.

"Why don't we go inside the house and talk about this," John suggested to Jed.

Samantha had been watching the confrontation from the veranda. She lowered her rifle, and let out a sigh of relief. She hadn't wanted to shoot anybody, but she would have to protect her family. When she saw her parents and James, along with Mr. Martin, all walking toward the house, she knew her family would not be needing her assistance. Samantha turned and entered the house, hoping no one had noticed her . . . .

Rachel preceded the men into the kitchen. Wordlessly she walked directly over to the stove to heat some coffee. She couldn't believe that her son could possibly be responsible for Sarah's condition. There had to be some kind of mistake . . .

"Have a seat, Jed," John said. "You too, James."

Suddenly feeling like an old man, Jed dropped heavily into an empty chair. He removed his Stetson and set it on top of the table, ran a hand through his hair. "John, I guess I should apologize for coming over here in such a fit of fury, but how would you react if your wife told you that your daughter was . . . ?" Jed couldn't even say it. He glared at James.

"Mr. Martin, I swear I never touched Sarah!" James looked beseechingly at his father. "Pa, you have to believe me!"

"I believe you, son, but let Jed have his say."

Over John's shoulder Jed could see Rachel leaning against the counter, staring at the floor. He didn't want to hurt her, but this had to be said. "Sarah broke down last night and told her mother about the baby. I know your boy there and my Sarah's been spending a lot of time together."

"That doesn't mean we were . . ." James could feel his face flush with embarrassment. "I didn't even know Sarah was . . . we've never . .

. look, I swear the baby's not mine. But I will tell you this, Mr. Martin. I love Sarah, so it doesn't really matter if she's . . . what I'm trying to say . . . I want to marry your daughter."

Rachel gasped. "You're both way too young to get married!"

"You and Pa were already married at my age," James reminded his mother. He gently added, "Ma, in case you haven't noticed, I'm a grown man now."

"James is right, Rachel." John knew this was hard on his wife, but she had to accept the fact that her children were grown.

Jed studied the young man seated across the table from him. He believed the boy was telling the truth. "If the baby's not yours, then who's is it?"

"I have no idea, Mr. Martin." James had been wondering the same thing himself. He knew Sarah loved him. It just didn't make any sense.

John was watching the different emotions flicker across his son's face. It was obvious that James wasn't ready to make a rational decision yet. Even though he was deeply concerned for Sarah, the fact remained the girl was carrying another man's child and he didn't want his son (grown man or not) to do something he might later regret.

"I'm truly sorry about your daughter, Jed, but I won't allow James to marry Sarah . . ."

"Pa . . ."

"Let me finish!" John's warning look told James that he'd better hold his tongue. Which he wisely did. Then he looked back at Jed. "What I was going to say is . . . I won't allow James to marry Sarah until after the baby's born . . . you never know what can happen between now and then." To James he said, "Then if you still want to marry Sarah, you'll have your mother's and my blessing."

James didn't seemed very pleased, but he didn't say anything.

"I agree with your pa, boy," Jed said.

"Please listen to your father, James," Rachel added, seating herself at the table.

"Apparently everyone thinks I'm still a boy!"

"Then don't make a boy's decision!" John sharply told his son.

"Jed, have you given any thought about the possibility . . . what happened to Sarah . . . might have been against her will?" Rachel couldn't seem to think of any other logical explanation, though she didn't want to believe that any man was capable of such a horrible crime.

From the shocked expression that came over Jed's face, it was obvious that it hadn't crossed his mind. Rachel noticed that her son looked stunned, too. She hoped that she wasn't about to make a bad situation even worse, when another thought occurred to her.

"Does Jake know about Sarah?" she asked Jed.

"Sarah's always been real close to her brother, so," Jed shrugged, "I would imagine that Jake probably knows. Which might explain the boy's mean temper lately," he added more to himself. "Why do you ask?"

"No wonder Jake's been taking punches at me," James suddenly stated. "He must assume that I'm responsible for Sarah's condition."

Jed took a closer look at the bruises on James's face. He hadn't really given them much thought, until now. "Did my son give you those bruises?"

The boy's silence was answer enough.

"Would anybody like some coffee?" Rachel asked, hoping to ease some of the tension around the table.

John quirked a dark brow at his wife. "Maybe a shot of whiskey would be more appropriate about now. How 'bout it, Jed? Care for a drink?"

"I could certainly use a drink."

"I think I could use a drink myself," Rachel muttered under her breath.

Rarely did his wife partake in any hard liquor or the *devil's brew* as Rachel called it. And John wasn't going to warn his wife how awful the so called *brew* might cause her to feel; she would find out soon enough.

After a quick jaunt to the liquor cabinet, John poured them all a drink from a bottle of his finest whiskey. Rachel gave him a disapproving frown when he set a glass in front of James, but she held her tongue.

"It appears I owe you and your family a huge apology, John."

"Forget it, Jed . . . I understand. I have a daughter of my own. If there's any thing that Rachel and I can do to help, please don't hesitate to ask."

Jed shifted uncomfortably in his chair, now feeling terrible for the crazy way he'd acted. He quickly downed his drink, before replying, "That's very kind of you, John, but I think this is something me and Ester will have to work out for ourselves." He picked up his hat, positioned it on his head, and stood out of his chair. "I took up enough of your time already, I'd best be going."

Jed started toward the door, abruptly stopped and turned to James. "Jake took off early this morning and I haven't seen him since. Do you have any idea where he might've gone?"

When James didn't respond, "Well, answer the man," John said to his son. "Do you know where Jake could be?"

That was a question James really didn't want to answer. But he couldn't lie, especially to his own father. He reluctantly replied, "Jake probably went into town." That was the truth. He just didn't say *where* in town Jake more than likely was, and he hoped that Jake's pa would accept that as an answer.

He didn't.

"There's something you're not telling me, boy," Jed said suspiciously.

John was sensing the same thing. "James?"

James wished he could ask his mother to leave the room, because there was no tactful way to put this. Might as well just come out and say it. "Jake's probably at the brothel."

Rachel gasped.

"What would my son be doing in a brothel?"

James wasn't about to answer that.

Suddenly Jed's face became flushed with fury. "How long has this been going on?" He held up his hand. "Never mind . . . it doesn't matter." Without another word Jed twirled on his boot heel and slammed out the door.

John, Rachel, and James hurried to the window. They stood there, watching, while Jed mounted his horse and then took off at a gallop in the direction of town.

His men followed close behind him.

"I certainly would not want to be in that boy's boots," John remarked.

Samantha had been on her way to the kitchen and had overheard the last part of the conversation. The instant she realized that Jake was in serious trouble with his pa, she tiptoed back through the house and out the front door, then raced toward the barn to fetch her horse. She might be angry at Jake for the way he'd been acting lately, but she still considered him a friend, and she knew what Jed Martin was capable of when the man was in this kind of a rage.

Chapter Two

Wade Chandler rode at a steady pace, still heading west. That old prospector had told him to follow this dirt road about twenty more miles. Although he wasn't very familiar with this part of Montana, surely he'd already traveled the estimated distance. He was beginning to wonder if Bear Creek was another one of those remote little Western towns where if a person blinked they might pass right by it.

Chandler pulled his Stetson lower over his eyes to shade them from the bright afternoon sun. It sure seemed hot for late June. He hoped that town was around here somewhere, because he was hungry and was tired of hunting his own food; and he could sure use a decent bath.

Finally Chandler spotted what looked like buildings up ahead through the trees, and let out a sigh of relief. He nudged his stallion at a faster pace . . .

Bear Creek was small indeed, Chandler noted. The entire town consisted of maybe a dozen scattered buildings on either side of the widened dirt road. As he rode past Ike's Mercantile Store, there was a tall, skinny man sweeping the front porch, watching him with suspicious eyes. Chandler politely nodded at the gentleman. But the man only glared at him, then stepped inside the store and slammed the door shut.

"Mighty friendly town," he muttered under his breath.

The next building Chandler passed by was a bank. Ironically the sheriff's office was located right next door. There was also a boardinghouse and restaurant. He was grateful for that. Across the street was a blacksmith shop and livery.

But there was only one particular building he was looking for, and every town, no matter how small, always had one of these. He finally spotted it at the end of the road.

Chandler halted his horse in front of the shabby-looking building, and dismounted. Actually this place was a hurdy-gurdy house, he noted, that also served as a saloon. He hastily looped the reins around the hitching rail, slapped his dusty hat against his leg and plopped it back on his head, before stepping through the swinging doors.

Worried that Jake's father would beat her to town, Samantha ran poor Daisy nearly the whole way. Her eyes darted back and forth as she trotted along the street. So far, there was no sign of Jed or his men, and Samantha breathed a sigh of relief. But as she approached the brothel at the edge of town, she began to feel a little apprehensive about going inside such a place; not counting the heap of trouble she would be in if her father ever found out about it.

Samantha frowned in disgust when she spotted Jake's chestnut gelding tethered in front of the building right along with the other *fornicators'* horses. She slid gracefully from Daisy's bare back and hurried toward the batwing doors. There was never any need to tether her horse, because the mare would not wander very far without her.

Standing on her tiptoes, Samantha peeked over the top of the double doors. Loud boisterous laughter filled her ears as she carefully scanned the inside of the crowded room, trying to locate Jake. She wondered why so many men visited these kind of places. It didn't look like much; basically there was a bunch of rowdy cowboys sitting around the tables, drinking and playing cards, while scantily dressed women hung all over them.

Samantha wrinkled her nose at the pungent smell of cigar smoke and cheap perfume. She took a deep breath and let it out slowly, trying to gather the courage to go inside . . .

Seated at a small corner table, nursing a bottle of whiskey, Chandler noticed the top of the woman's head peek over the doors. All he could really see were her eyes, which were a brilliant shade of blue. She appeared to be looking for somebody, a husband perhaps? When she slid through the swinging doors and he got a good look at her face, Chandler was struck by the woman's beauty. She was dressed in mens' clothes, and the faded blue jeans outlined her backside like a second skin, giving him a clear view of a well-shaped bottom.

And he'd never seen hair so long. She wore it in a single plait that hung nearly to her knees! The color was unusual, too, like dark honey mixed with red and gold. Her flawless skin was slightly tanned, so he assumed she must spend a lot of time outdoors.

Chandler began to notice there were several men ogling her. Why that should infuriate him, he didn't know. And he felt a sudden overpowering urge to protect her. Didn't she realize what kind of place this was? She was asking for trouble just being here . . .

Samantha finally spotted Jake. He was seated at a table playing cards with some rough-looking men she'd never seen before. Why would Jake even step foot inside such a place? He should have better sense than that. She was tempted to turn around and walk back out the door and let Jake's father catch him here.

Hoping nobody would notice her, Samantha started walking in Jake's direction. She hadn't gone very far when a man grabbed her around the waist and pulled her on top of his lap. The smell of whiskey nearly made her gag. She immediately began to fight him.

"Get your filthy hands off me!" Samantha hissed.

"Come on, honey, just one little kiss," the man slurred.

"Let go of me!"

Samantha kept struggling to get away, but the man had a grip like a vise. She glanced around the table at his friends, hoping one of them might come to her rescue. But it was soon obvious that not a one of them were going to rush to her defense. Nobody else seemed to notice her dilemma, or maybe they just didn't care.

When Samantha realized she was on her own, panic began to take hold of her senses, causing her to fight like a wildcat. "Let me go, you overgrown ox!" she furiously spat.

"Let her go, Ralf!"

Relief washed over Samantha when she heard Jake's voice. Ralf seemed to loosen his grip on her and she twisted around to see Jake standing there. His fists were clenched tightly at his sides, and his eyes glittered with a vicious hatred she'd never seen before. The way Jake looked frightened Samantha even more than Ralf.

"I said let her go!" Jake snarled.

Ralf stood out of his chair, dropping the woman on the floor at his feet. "Are you talking to me, boy?"

"Are you deaf?" Jake angrily retorted.

Samantha shot to her feet and stepped in between both men. "You gotta get out of here, Jake . . . your Pa's on his way to town!"

"Did ya hear that, sonny boy? Papa's on his way . . . better run on home."

Jake glared at Ralf, before turning to Samantha. "You never should've come here. I want you to leave . . ."

"The lady ain't goin' anywhere just yet," Ralph sharply interrupted.

"The lady was just leaving," a deep voice loudly intervened.

The room suddenly went still.

Samantha turned to look at the tall, handsome stranger who was standing beside her, like a giant guardian angel. Save fŏr the black Stetson covering his head, he was dressed entirely in buckskins; knee high moccasins hugged his feet. He wore matching pearl-handled Peacemakers strapped low on his narrow hips. Reaching the top of a pair of wide shoulders, his hair was black as a raven's wing. His dark, penetrating eyes dared the other man to argue with him.

Samantha thought that Ralf looked like he was about to faint.

Ralf was considered a big man, but he felt small in comparison to the tall Indian standing before him. It didn't take him long to decide that maybe he'd better back down. After all, he wasn't stupid. Still, he didn't want to look like a complete coward in front of his friends.

"Look, mister, this ain't no concern of yours."

"It is now," the stranger replied in that same deep, threatening tone.

Ralph looked toward his friends for help, and scowled, when they quickly resumed their card game, pretending that nothing was out of the ordinary. *Cowards!* he inwardly fumed. He then thought about his options: He could challenge the Indian to a gunfight, but figured the man probably knew how to use those weapons strapped to his hip. His only other option was to let the woman go.

"She ain't worth it," Ralph finally said, then sat back down at his table.

Now that she was out of trouble, Samantha immediately reminded Jake, "You have to get out of here, before it's too late."

Jake knew Samantha was right. He turned to the stranger still standing at her side. "I appreciate what you did, mister. I know you've done enough already, but do ya think you could see that Sam gets home safely?"

"Who's Sam?" Chandler asked.

"I can speak for myself, Jake Martin!" Samantha angrily informed him. "And I certainly don't need no escort . . . !"

Chandler arched a brow as he listened to the heated discussion taking place between *Sam* and the young man called Jake, wondering if he might be the woman's husband? But that didn't make any sense . . . why would Jake ask him to escort his own wife home. Besides, he didn't see a wedding ring on her finger. Perhaps Jake was her brother then? though he couldn't see any family resemblance.

Sam huh, Chandler thought to himself. Well—whatever her name was, he'd been mistaken about the *defenseless little woman.* He couldn't believe the language that spewed from those lovely lips . . .

"Look, kiddies," Chandler finally interceded, having heard enough. "You can stop your arguing . . . I'd be happy to escort Sam here home."

Grumbling under her breath about stubborn men, Samantha suddenly twirled on her boot heel and marched toward the batwing doors, because she knew Jake wouldn't leave this place until she agreed to allow the man to escort her home.

Once outside, Samantha didn't say anything when Jake hastily pecked her good-bye on the cheek. She watched him vault onto the back of his horse and gallop away, before turning to the stranger. She had to admit, the man certainly was handsome.

"I suppose I should thank you for rescuing me from What's-his-name."

"I believe it was Ralf."

"What ever. Look—there's no need for you to escort me home."

Chandler pushed back his Stetson and gazed into eyes that were such a striking blue. "I always keep my word. I promised your friend that I would take you home and that's what I intend to do. By the way, my name's Wade Chandler, but I prefer to be called Chandler. I assume *Sam* is not your real name, Miss . . . ?"

Rolling her eyes, Samantha placed her thumb and forefinger between her lips, then let loose with a whistle. A moment later, she heard Daisy's soft familiar nicker as the mare rounded the corner of the building.

"What's that?"

"I believe it's called a horse," Samantha sarcastically replied.

She called that swaybacked, mule-looking thing a horse? Chandler had never seen a sorrier sight for a horse in his entire life. "You can actually ride that thing?" He had spoken his thoughts out loud.

"Don't you know that it's not polite to insult a man's . . . er . . . woman's horse?" Samantha hoisted herself upon Daisy's saddleless back, and clicked her tongue.

Chandler watched the woman gallop down the street, shaking his head. "Helpless woman indeed," he grumbled under his breath as he hurried toward his stallion.

Samantha wasn't surprised when she heard the sound of hoofbeats coming up behind her. She knew who it was before the big buckskin stallion appeared alongside her mare. She expected some sort of tongue-lashing from the man, but he said nothing. He stared straight ahead, obviously preferring to ignore her, which suited Samantha just fine.

The handsome Indian rode tall and straight in the saddle, Samantha couldn't help but notice with admiration. In the sunlight his coal-black hair had a bluish hue. His facial skin was dark and smooth, completely free of hair . . . probably due to his Indian heritage. Samantha remembered hearing somewhere that Indians never had to shave . . . apparently it was true. Something else she remembered very clearly was that his eyes were as black as his hair and that he had lashes that were way too long for a man. And his lips were full . . .

He suddenly looked at her, grinning. "Do you like what you see?"

Samantha's cheeks instantly grew warm, but she tried to hide her embarrassment by giving him an unladylike snort.

Chandler chuckled. "You never told me your name?"

"It's Samantha," she grumbled in reply.

"Sam suits you better."

Samantha frowned at him, not sure whether she had just been complimented or insulted. Not that it really mattered. "I don't remember asking for your opinion, Mr. Chandler."

"You can drop the mister."

"My parents taught me to respect my elders," Samantha haughtily replied. She burst out laughing at his scowling expression.

"I'm not *that* old."

"If you say so."

His frowned deepened, then he shrugged. "Jake—is he your husband?"

"Not that it's any of your business, but I have no husband. Jake's just a friend."

Chandler didn't understand why the fact that she wasn't married should please him. After today, he would never see her again . . .

"Look, Mr. . . ."

" Just Chandler."

"What ever!" Samantha snapped impatiently. "At this snail's pace, it'll be dark before I get home and my Pa's gonna skin me alive as it is. You've escorted me far enough . . . if you'll excuse me, I haven't got all day." Then she let out a shrill whistle.

Chandler's mouth flew open when her mule-like horse suddenly shot off like a rocket. Who ever would have guessed the *mangy mare* could run like the wind. If he hadn't seen it with his own eyes, he never would have believed it.

With a bewildered shake of his head, Chandler turned his stallion around and headed back toward town, glad to be rid of the troublesome woman and her odd horse. Then he started thinking about 'Ralph the ruffian'. It was very possible at this very moment, Ralf could be waiting somewhere to ambush the unsuspecting young woman . . .

Grumbling under his breath, Chandler swung his stallion back around and took off at a full gallop after *Sam.* It was unlikely he would ever catch her, but he had to try. As he raced across the grassy prairie at breakneck speed, he prayed that his stallion wouldn't step in some unforeseen gopher hole. If he ever found the woman, he had a half of mind to turn her over his knee for scaring the daylights out of him!

His rising panic made him think of another day long ago . . .

"Graywolf, you got it!"

"Yes, Little Bear." Graywolf ruffled his little brother's hair. "Now let's get this deer to our Uncle's tepee. You can carry my bow and arrows." He handed his brother the quiver, then he hefted the heavy animal over his horse's withers, picked up the reins and they started walking back toward the village.

"When will you teach me to hunt, Graywolf?"

Graywolf glanced down at his little brother. He chuckled at the way Little Bear was trying to keep pace with him, while struggling to carry his quiver. The quiver was longer than he was tall. "I think you need to grow more first, then I will teach you."

"That's what you always say," Little Bear complained.

"You can't shoot a deer if your arms are not long enough to pull back on the bow. Now stop chattering like an old woman, before you scare off all the game."

Suddenly Graywolf stopped in his tracks, giving his little brother the signal for silence. He listened carefully for any unusual sounds. And that was the problem; the forest was *too* quiet. Something wasn't right . . .

Graywolf hastily discarded the deer in some nearby bushes, covered it with several tree limbs he found lying on the ground. He then hid his little brother inside a hollow tree stump. After giving the frightened child a reassuring smile and telling him to brave, he vaulted onto his stallion's back and galloped toward the village . . . .

Graywolf blinked back scalding tears as he stared in horrified shock at what remained of a once peaceful village. Nearly every tepee was now nothing more than smoldering embers. *Who could have done such a terrible thing?* his mind inwardly raged. He started running through the village like a madman, searching for his father and uncle, shouting their names . . . but neither man answered, nor was there any sign of them. In fact, it was as if the entire tribe had simply disappeared!

With tears streaming down his cheeks, Graywolf raised his face toward the heavens and screamed his agony at the top of his lungs.

Suddenly remembering *Little Bear!* Graywolf ran to his horse and vaulted onto its back, then he raced through the forest to the place where he'd left his little brother.

But Little Bear was gone . . . .

Snapping out of his turbulent thoughts, Chandler urged his stallion faster, now determined more than ever to find the girl, even if it took him all night.

It was nearly dusk when Chandler finally happened upon a large ranch which boasted of several buildings. Surrounded by a small thicket of tall cottonwoods was a house . . . a really *big* two-story house, with four giant pillars that held up a covered porch which extended nearly the entire length of the front of the house. Whoever owned this place probably reeked with the smell of money, Chandler figured, the so called *well-bred* folks. He wondered if *Sam* could possibly live here? Then he remembered the way the woman had been dressed, the way she had spoken like a cowhand, and ultimately decided that he must have the wrong place.

Halting his stallion, Chandler sat there staring at the house, debating whether the young woman could possibly be the daughter of one of the hired hands. He was in such deep thought, he didn't hear the man sneaking up behind him, until it was too late.

"Don't move, mister," a voice warned him. "Keep those hands where I can see 'em and get down off your horse, real easy like."

Twisting slightly in the saddle, Chandler saw a gray-haired man standing behind him with a rifle tucked under his arm. Raising his hands in the air, he swung his long leg over his horse's head and dropped lightly to the ground.

"Don't get trigger happy, gramps."

"You just keep your hands where they are and we'll get along just fine."

"Now what?"

"Toss your weapons toward me."

"I thought you told me to keep my hands where they are."

"Just do it!" Amos sharply commanded.

Chandler did as told.

Amos carefully picked up both guns and shoved them inside the waistband of his britches, then he made a gesture toward the house with his rifle. "Start walkin' and keep those hands . . ."

" . . . where you can see 'em, I remember," Chandler grumbled.

"Don't get mouthy, son."

Chandler rolled his eyes as he started walking forward. When they reached the front door, the older man shoved him inside the house and shouted, "Hey, Boss! I found somebody sneakin' around outside!"

"I wasn't sneaking!" Chandler angrily snapped.

Standing in what he supposed was a foyer, Chandler saw a tall man with upper arms like tree trunks come out of a room along the hallway and walk toward him. Assuming this must be the man of the house, he said in a not-too-friendly tone, "Mister, would you mind telling gramps here to get that cannon out of my back?"

"What's going on, Amos?" John demanded to know.

"I found this man sneakin' around . . ."

"I wasn't sneaking!" Chandler hissed at the old man. "I was looking for somebody."

"Who?" John asked.

Chandler noticed the man who stood before him was slightly taller than himself. And there was something familiar about the man's eyes that he couldn't quite put his finger on . . .

"I'm John Callahan. You can lower your hands."

"Thanks." Chandler's arms dropped at his sides.

"I wouldn't trust him."

"I think I can handle it from here, Amos," John told his foreman. "You can go on back to the bunkhouse now."

"May I have my guns back?"

John's arm stretched out toward Amos. Amos hesitated a moment, before placing both pearl-handled Peacemakers in John's hand. "I still wouldn't trust him," he grumbled as he slammed out the front door.

"You said you were looking for someone," John reminded his uninvited guest as he handed him back his weapons. He figured the Indian was probably a drifter. But when he saw the way the man expertly slipped his guns back inside the holster, it made John wonder if he could possibly be a gunslinger. Either way, the man seemed to have an honest face. *Maybe he was looking for work,* John thought hopefully, because he certainly could use another hand.

"I suppose I should introduce myself. The name's Wade Chandler, but you can call me Chandler." He held out his hand.

John firmly grasped Wade Chandler's outstretched hand. "You can call me John. You must forgive my foreman . . . sometimes Amos is a bit—overly cautious, but he means well. Now—who is this person you're looking for?"

Chandler was about to explain the circumstances which brought him here when he noticed the slender woman emerge from a room at the end of the hall and gracefully walk toward them. At first glimpse, he thought it was *Sam* from the hurdy-gurdy house dressed as an elegant woman . . . well . . . it was her . . . but . . . just an older version . . . except for the color of the eyes.

And suddenly it clicked.

Now Chandler knew why John Callahan's eyes had seemed familiar. So these people must be the young woman's parents . . .

"John, who is this man?" he heard the woman softly ask.

"Says his name's Wade Chandler." John now eyed him suspiciously. "You acted as though you knew my wife. Care to explain that?"

"I'll give it a try."

"Maybe I should explain," came a female's voice.

Chandler turned around. At the top of the wide-banistered stairway stood *Sam* from the hurdy-gurdy house. Still dressed in the same mens clothing, he watched her slowly descend the steps, looking even more beautiful than he remembered. She also wore an angry scowl which was obviously directed at him.

Samantha was almost to the bottom of the stairway. She could clearly see the stern expression on her father's face, and inwardly groaned. He was going to be absolutely furious at her when he found out that she'd gone to the brothel to warn Jake about his enraged father. She would've gotten away with it, if it wasn't for the *pea brain* standing beside him. She glared at the man. She never dreamed he would actually follow her home. Now she had no choice but to tell her father the entire truth.

John's eyes narrowed on his daughter as she halted on the bottom step. "Evidently, Samantha, no introductions are necessary. Apparently, you already know Mr. Chandler. You mind telling me *how* you know him?"

When she didn't answer, John angrily demanded, "I want to know exactly where you were this afternoon and don't tell me you just went for a ride!"

Samantha looked toward her mother for help.

"John, maybe we should talk about this later."

"Stay out of this, Rachel." Then he turned to Samantha. "I want an answer, young lady, and I want it now!"

"Excuse me, Mr. Callahan, but maybe it would be better if I explained." Chandler couldn't help but feel some sympathy for the girl.

"Why don't you mind your own business!" Samantha snapped.

"If I were you, Samantha Callahan, I would not say another word unless spoken to . . . you're in enough trouble already!" John calmly then said, "Go on, Mr. Chandler."

Chandler could feel Samantha's eyes boring into him, but he wasn't about to allow that to influence what he was about to say. *Sam* could get mad if she wanted to, but he wasn't about to lie to the girl's father. Besides, now that he'd had a chance to think about it, her father had a right to know exactly where his daughter was this afternoon.

"How can I tactfully put this," he said to himself.

"Just come out and say it," John told him.

Chandler shrugged. "Let's just say that I changed a man's mind about ravishing—Miss Callahan here."

Rachel gasped.

"That was well put!" Samantha hissed.

"And just *where* did this happen?" John questioned his daughter who was now staring at the floor, refusing to meet his eyes. He turned back to their guest. "Well?"

"The brothel in town," Chandler bluntly admitted.

Another loud gasp escaped Rachel's lips. Then an unexpected burst of laughter erupted from the other room.

"You can come out now, James!" John hollered out.

Chandler saw a door open and then a young man who was the spitting image of John Callahan came out of the room. He was obviously *Sam's* brother. And Chandler wondered how many more *delinquents* this couple might have? No matter, the parents certainly had his sympathy. Especially the poor mother, who looked about to faint.

"James, maybe you have some light to shed on the subject?" John said.

"I almost wished I did." Then he burst out in laughter.

Samantha scowled at her younger brother.

"This isn't a laughing matter, James Callahan!" John snapped at his son.

"I guess it depends on how you look at it."

"I would advise you to get out of my sight before I lose my temper!"

"Yes, Sir."

Chandler grinned to himself when the young man suddenly turned and dashed up the stairs. A moment later, he heard a door slam shut.

"I would advise you to go to your room too, young lady," he heard John say. "And don't come out until I tell you."

"But, Pa, I . . ."

John held up a hand for silence. "Don't you *dare* say a word."

Chandler saw Samantha's shoulders slump in defeat, then she turned and climbed the wide stairway to her room. He almost felt sorry for her.

"Looks like I owe you, Mr. Chandler."

"Just Chandler. And you don't owe me anything, Sir. I'm just glad I was there."

"So am I," John muttered under his breath.

"Would you care for a cup of coffee, Chandler?" Rachel asked.

"I'd sure be much obliged, ma'am."

Seated at the kitchen table, John and Rachel listened intently, while Chandler related the entire 'brothel story'. He ended with, "That's what I was doing outside when the old man found me." He shrugged. "You know the rest."

"I'm so glad you were there, Mr. Chandler." Rachel didn't want to even think what could have happened had this nice man not intervened.

"Please call me Chandler, ma'am."

"Samantha never should've gone there in the first place," John angrily said to his wife. "She was just lucky that Chandler was there. That daughter of yours is way too independent for her own good, Rachel. One of these days Samantha's going to get herself into a predicament and there won't be anybody to get her out of it."

Independent was a mild way of putting it, Chandler thought.

"John, why is it when Samantha pulls a stunt like she did today that she's my daughter and the rest of the time she's yours?"

John didn't reply.

"Are you from around these parts?" Rachel then asked Chandler.

"No, ma'am."

"Do you have any family?"

There was a slight pause, before he answered, "No, ma'am."

"What about a wife?"

"Rachel, stop pestering the poor man with personal questions," John gently scolded his wife. Then, "Where are you staying, Chandler, if you don't mind my asking?"

"Actually—I just got into town today, so I don't have a place to stay just yet. I'm looking for work, if you happen to know of anybody who might be hiring?"

"It just so happens that one of my wranglers up and quit on me yesterday . . . know any thing about ranching?"

"I've done my share."

"Then it looks like you just found yourself a job." John held out his hand.

Firmly grasping his new employer's outstretched hand, Chandler replied, "Then you just hired yourself a new wrangler."

"Good," John said. "Tonight you'll stay in our guest room . . . it's too late to put you up in the bunkhouse. First thing in the morning, I'll personally give you a tour of the ranch."

"I hope you'll feel at home here, Chandler," Rachel said with a warm smile. "I bet you're tired." She rose to her feet. "Come on . . . I'll show you to your room."

The next morning, while Rachel stood at the stove, preparing breakfast as usual, she felt a pair of strong arms suddenly slip around her waist. She looked over her shoulder to smile at her husband, and giggled, when he playfully nuzzled the back of her neck.

"John, stop that . . . somebody might come in," she whispered. "Now go sit down at the table like a good boy. Breakfast will be ready soon."

"I'm not hungry for food, woman." John then let out an exaggerated growl and playfully nipped at his wife's exposed neck.

"Go sit down, John," Rachel said, laughing, "I'll bring you some coffee."

Hearing somebody clearing their throat, John and Rachel both turned around. Rachel inwardly groaned when she saw Chandler casually leaning inside the kitchen doorway, wondering how long he'd been standing there.

A dark brow rose inquisitively. "Am I interrupting something?" Chandler asked.

"Certainly not," Rachel hastily replied, giving her grinning husband a stern look. "If you gentlemen will take your seats . . . breakfast is just about ready."

Chandler couldn't remember the last time he'd seen so much food, thinking, if this woman could cook as good as she looked then he was in for a real treat. Eagerly he heaped his plate with several fluffy hotcakes, a bunch of sausage links, along with a generous helping of scrambled eggs and fried potatoes.

Hearing a giggle, Chandler looked up and saw Rachel smiling at him. John was grinning at him, too. He felt himself blush.

"Did I mention last night that part of your pay includes free room and board, plus meals?" John said. "But maybe in your case, I should reconsider the free meals."

"My husband's only teasing," Rachel laughed.

"Of course I'm teasing," John said, chuckling. "You're a big man, Chandler, with a healthy appetite . . . there's nothing wrong with that. A word of caution . . . if you're going to survive on this ranch, you'll need a sense of humor."

"Could you please pass the syrup?" was Chandler's reply.

Several helpings later, Rachel was beginning to wonder if Chandler would ever get enough to eat. The man had a voracious appetite. And when he finally did push himself away from the table claiming "he couldn't eat another bite", Rachel had the feeling he was only being polite.

"More coffee, Chandler?" she asked.

"Please, ma'am."

As Rachel refilled Chandler's cup, she started thinking it rather odd that neither James or Samantha had come down to breakfast yet. While the men began to talk business, she excused herself from the table, then went to find out what was keeping her children . . . .

John and Chandler were heading out the back door when a loud shout from Rachel stopped them in their tracks. "Samantha and James aren't in their rooms," she informed her husband, slightly out of breath.

"I don't believe it!" John loudly bellowed. "And this . . . !" he angrily hissed, waving a hand through the air, "after what she pulled yesterday!"

"Please, John, it won't do any good to lose your temper."

"I haven't begun to lose my temper!"

Rachel calmly reminded her husband, "Do you remember what you said to me just the other day—that James and Samantha are no longer children and I should try to accept it? You were right, John. We simply can't order Samantha . . ."

"Tell me, Rachel, when was the last time there was anything *simple* where Samantha was concerned?"

As Chandler listened to John and Rachel's heated discussion, he was glad he didn't have any children of his own. Still, he couldn't help but feel worried about 'the little minx', knowing the kind of trouble she was capable of getting herself into . . .

"Do you have any idea where they might've gone?" Chandler hoped he wasn't making a mistake by sticking his nose where it didn't concern him.

"I have a feeling that James went to confront Sarah's father," Rachel answered, "and Samantha went with him."

"After what just happened with Jed, I can't believe they would go there," John said.

"Your son's determined to marry Sarah."

"But I told the boy not to go over there without me!"

"Haven't you heard a word I've been saying, John? James is a man and he wants to handle Jed on his own." Rachel then said to Chandler, "I'm sorry you had to hear this . . . we really don't want to involve you in our troubles."

Chandler's smile held sympathy. There was probably always trouble in some form or another where the spitfire was concerned. If it were up to him, when he found Samantha he would turn her over his knee, grown woman or not.

"Guess I'd better ride over to Jed's," John grumbled more to himself. Then, "Chandler, I'll have Amos show you around the ranch while I'm gone. I probably won't be back until late this afternoon."

"If you wouldn't mind, I'd like to ride along?"

"Maybe I should warn you . . . there could be trouble. And more than likely, if Samantha's involved," John sarcastically added.

Chandler grinned. "I'll take my chances."

"John, promise me you won't lose your temper?" Rachel pleaded with him.

He let out a sigh. "I promise I won't lose my temper." There was a brief pause, before he added, "Unless it becomes necessary."

"That's not funny, John Callahan!"

"My wife seems to be losing her sense of humor in her older age," John said, winking at Chandler. He chuckled when Rachel punched him on the shoulder. "Guess we'd better get going, while the gettin's good." He kissed his frowning wife on the cheek, then he and Chandler headed out the back door.

Rachel stood at the kitchen window, watching John and Chandler as they walked toward the barn. She noticed the determination in her husband's long strides. Whether John realized it or not, he was every bit as stubborn as James and Samantha.

Chapter Three

Chandler studied his new boss who rode quietly alongside him, looking like a man on a mission. He guessed John Callahan was probably somewhere in his mid-to-late forties. Whatever the man's age, there was no question he was in excellent physical condition, a man obviously still in his prime. With a daughter like Samantha, he was surprised that John wasn't completely gray, Chandler thought, chuckling to himself, for the poor man certainly had his hands full where the wildcat was concerned. If John were a smart man, he would marry his outspoken daughter off just as soon as possible, to any man that would take her off his hands . . . .

John was deep in his own disturbing thoughts. How often had he chastised Rachel for treating James and Samantha like children. He probably should learn to start practicing what he preached at his wife, because James and Samantha were plenty old enough now to start making their own decisions. Still, he couldn't help feeling protective of his children, especially of Samantha. He feared that one of these days her sharp tongue would get her into serious trouble, the kind she couldn't so easily get out of.

Needing to occupy his mind, John started a conversation with Chandler. "Why don't you tell me a little something about yourself."

"What would you like to know?"

"You said you had no family."

"That's right."

"Your parents had no other children?" John hoped he wasn't prying too much.

Chandler really didn't care to discuss that part of his past, it was just too painful. He didn't say anything, hoping John would take the hint.

John was curious why Chandler didn't want to talk about his family, but he respected the man's wishes. Again hoping he wasn't poking his nose where it didn't belong, he asked, "You ever been married before?"

"I was engaged once."

"What happened . . . if you don't mind my asking?"

Chandler shrugged noncommittally. "She married somebody else."

Apparently that was a touchy subject as well, John thought, sensing the man's reluctance to answer the question. "Then I assume you have no children," he muttered more to himself. "Trust me, they can age a man faster than a nagging wife."

Chandler chuckled.

"The Martins' spread is just over that rise up ahead," John announced. He kneed his horse to a faster pace, worried about what he might find once he reached Jed's.

As John and Chandler approached the ranch, John noticed there seemed to be some sort of ruckus taking place inside the main corral. When they got a little closer, he mumbled an oath under his breath as he leaped from his horse and took off at a run.

After hastily securing both horses, Chandler hurried toward the corral, wondering what John had seen to make him run off the way he had . . .

Samantha stood glaring at the big brute who'd tried to manhandle her last night, wanting to slap the smug expression off his bearded face. It figured Ralf worked for Jed! "If you ever touch me again, mister, you'll be sorry you ever stepped foot in Bear Creek."

Ralf didn't remember much about last night he'd been so drunk, but he remembered this woman. "No proper lady would ever be caught in a place like that," Ralf shot back. "And it's obvious that you're no lady . . . not with a mouth like you got. Your pa ever teach you any manners, girl?"

"Why you rotten, lowdown . . ."

"Samantha Callahan!" a familiar voice suddenly boomed behind her.

She whirled around. "Pa! What are you doing here?"

"I was about to ask you the same question, young lady. I thought I told you to stay in your room." His eyes swung toward the bearded man standing near Samantha. "Who is this man you're talking to?"

"This is the man that . . . who tried to . . . to . . ."

"So you're this gal's pa. Ya know, mister, your daughter has a mouth like a . . ." The punch came at Ralf so fast he didn't know what hit him. Like a felled tree he fell backward, landing flat on his back on the hard ground, out cold.

John glared at the men who stepped forward to help their friend. "Get him out of my sight!" he snarled in rising fury.

"What's going on here?"

John spun around at the sound of Jed's voice. "I was just teaching your hired hand some manners!"

"What did Ralf do?" Jed wanted to know.

"He tried to put his hands on my daughter!"

"If you're referring to the incident last night, I heard what happened. Samantha had no business being in a place like that. Maybe if you'd keep a tighter rein on that daughter of yours, there would be no future misunderstandings."

"Samantha, go wait over by Chandler."

"Yes, Sir."

John held his tongue until his daughter was out of earshot, then he angrily told Jed, "We've been friends for a long time, but if you ever speak that way about Samantha again, you'll get the same as What's-his-name."

"Are you threatening me, John?"

"Take it any way you like."

"I would advise you to get off my property." Jed started to walk away then turned abruptly to add, "And, John—don't ever bring that Injun here again."

"That Indian has a name . . . it's Chandler."

"I don't care what his name is. I don't want him on my property ever again."

Watching Jed's departing back, John was beginning to wonder if he really knew the man at all. His fists clenched tightly at his sides, remembering his promise to Rachel. If it wasn't for his wife, he would have knocked Jed flat on his backside for that Injun remark . . . .

Chandler observed Samantha as she slowly walked toward him, noting the slumped shoulders and bowed head. He grinned to himself. Apparently she must have received a pretty good tongue-lashing from her father. He watched her slip agilely between the lower rails of the fence, then she was standing beside him.

She stared straight ahead. "I wish I could hear what my father and Jed were saying."

"So do I."

Samantha looked at him then. "What are you doing here anyway? I thought you'd be drifting into the next town by now."

"Your father hired me."

Samantha snorted.

"You sound disappointed."

"It doesn't matter to me whether my father hired you or not. What are you smiling about?"

"You have dirt on your face."

"Where?"

Chandler reached out to wipe the smudge of dirt off her cheek with his thumb. Neither of them were aware of the young man who stood nearby, watching the tender scene with jealous hatred glittering in his eyes.

"I hope I'm not disturbing anything!"

"Oh, Jake, I didn't see you," Samantha said, feeling a little embarrassed.

Jake glared at the Indian, before snapping at Samantha, "If you're not too busy tomorrow, I thought we could go for a ride?"

Samantha was curious about Jake's rude behavior, but she didn't say anything. "After today, I doubt my father will let me out of his sight."

"A likely excuse!"

"It's not an excuse, Jake Martin!" Samantha fired back, hands on her hips.

Without another word Jake spun on his heel and stormed away.

Chandler's dark brow rose. "Your beau?"

"Jake and I are just good friends. He's always been more like a brother to me." Samantha laughed nervously, then told him, "When we were children my parents used to tease us about getting married someday . . . 'course it was just a joke."

There was no doubt in Chandler's mind that Jake Martin had more than brotherly feelings toward Samantha. He hadn't missed that 'stay away from her' look the kid threw his way just before he stomped off. Chandler wondered if Samantha realized that Jake was in love with her? Probably not. Personally he didn't care much for Jake: there was something not quite right with the young man. He didn't want Samantha anywhere near him, either. Now why should it matter to him if Miss Callahan hung around her crazy neighbor?

"I'd like to apologize for Jake's rude behavior."

"Do you always apologize for his temper tantrums?"

Samantha thought it was her duty to defend Jake, even though she felt in this case he didn't deserve it. But he was still her friend. "You just don't understand Jake, he . . ."

"Here comes your Pa." Chandler was glad for the interruption. It prevented him from saying what he really wanted to say. It irked him to no end that she would try to defend Jake!

"Pa looks madder than a hornet," Samantha commented, noticing his rigid expression. She inwardly cringed, hoping that anger wasn't directed at her.

"Where's your brother?" John snapped at Samantha as he slipped between the fence rails.

"James and Sarah went for a ride. Pa, what's wrong?"

"Let's get out of here." John was already heading toward his horse.

Chandler and Samantha looked at each other, and shrugged.

As they rode away at a fast pace, the corners of John's mouth lifted into a self-satisfied grin, remembering the way Jed had looked as he flew through the air. His knuckles still smarted a little, but it had been worth it. The only think that bothered him, he had broken his promise to Rachel. But maybe in the future Jed would think twice about calling Chandler an Injun. There were some very disturbing facts that he'd learned about his so called 'friend' these past several days. He'd known Jed Martin for almost twenty years, but evidently he didn't know the man as well as he thought.

John turned to Samantha as she guided her horse alongside his. "I don't want you going anywhere near Jed's, until I say different. And so help me, Samantha Callahan, this is one order you had better obey."

"What's going on, Pa?"

"Just this once do as you're told without any questions!"

"Will you at least tell me if this has anything to do with Jake?"

"Not at the moment." Without another word John then kneed his horse into a slow canter, putting an end to the conversation.

Why would her father order her to stay away from Jed's? Samantha wondered. He had sounded so serious when he'd said it, too. She let out a sigh of frustration, knowing it would do no good to pressure her father for more information.

Samantha turned and frowned at Chandler who caught up with her then. She was in no mood for his sarcastic remarks. He was grinning at her again with that irritating curling lip. And that was something else that bothered her . . .

"Do you always go around with that silly smirk on your face?"

"Can't a man smile at a pretty woman?"

"Spare me the flattery."

"Trust me, I wasn't trying to flatter you. Woman, you sure can be cynical at times."

Samantha rolled her eyes.

"Looks like John's having trouble with his horse," Chandler said with a nod of his head.

"What is it, Pa?" Samantha asked, halting her horse beside his.

"I think Buck threw a shoe," John grumbled in annoyance. "I'll probably have to walk him from here. You and Chandler might as well stretch your legs a bit."

Samantha immediately slid off Daisy's bare back, then she went to locate a bush.

"Any thing I can do?" Chandler asked, dismounting.

"You don't happen to have a spare horseshoe on ya?"

Chandler chuckled. " 'Fraid I'm all out."

When Buck started to act a little jittery, John talked soothing to the horse. "What's the matter with you, boy?"

"John, don't move!" Chandler suddenly called out in warning. "There's a big rattlesnake over by that rock . . . a few feet to your left."

Slowly John turned his head. His eyes widened in alarm, when he spotted one of the biggest rattlesnakes he'd ever seen, coiled and ready to strike. The snake was so close, he could hear the deadly rattlers. Now Buck was beginning to prance nervously in place, shaking his head. John was trying his best to calm the frightened animal when, all-of-a-sudden, Buck let out a loud whinny and then bolted in the direction of home.

"Don't even blink an eye, John," Chandler warned him. "I'm going to try and shoot it."

Easing his gun from its holster, he cautiously moved forward, stopping in his tracks, when he heard the snake protest. He could actually see the snake's body coil even tighter, and then the sound of its rattler grew louder. Taking careful aim, Chandler muttered an oath, when he realized that he still didn't have a clear enough shot. If he missed, the snake could easily strike John before he got off another shot.

"Shoot the blasted thing already!" John snapped impatiently. "What are you waiting for . . . the snake's permission?"

"You're in my way," Chandler replied.

"Well I would move if I could!"

From the corner of his eye Chandler noticed a slight movement. He let loose with several choice words under his breath when he saw Samantha moving toward her father. *What did she think she was doing?* Chandler wondered. Didn't she realize the danger she was putting herself in? When this ordeal was over, he was going to take his hand to Samantha's lovely backside and not even her father would stop him!

Chandler was about to yell at Samantha to get out of the way when he saw her reach down and pull a knife from her boot. *She had to be kidding,* Chandler thought. Then she sent her knife sailing through the air and hit her target with the speed and accuracy of even the most seasoned warrior.

His mouth agape, Chandler stood there, staring, in complete shock and disbelief. The blade of her knife had actually embedded the snake's head to the ground. He'd seen it with his own eyes and he still couldn't believe it!

"Pa, are you all right?" he heard Samantha holler out as she hurried toward him.

"I'll let you know . . . soon as my heart stops pounding." John wiped the sweat off his brow with the back of his hand. "Remind me to thank Amos for teaching you how to use that thing."

Now that Chandler had finally gotten hold of his senses, he holstered his gun as he walked toward John and Samantha hollering, "Woman, do you always put yourself in harm's way without thinking or is getting into trouble just your forte?"

Samantha tromped over to the reptile, removed her knife and carefully slipped it back inside her boot. "I had to do something while you were busy playing with your gun."

"I couldn't get a clear shot!"

"You had just as clear of shot as I did."

"And what if you had missed?" Chandler hissed.

"I always hit what I aim at," Samantha haughtily replied. "You might keep that in mind."

Chandler scowled at her. "I'll try to remember that."

"Could you two argue about this later," John loudly intervened. "If we're lucky enough to retrieve our horses we just might make it home before dark."

Grinning mischievously, Samantha proclaimed, "Finding my horse should be no problem for me." She then let loose with an ear-splitting whistle.

"Daggone it, Samantha, can't you warn a person when you're about to pierce their eardrums," John complained.

"Sorry, Pa."

A few moments later they heard the little mare's soft nicker. "Here comes Daisy now," Samantha happily announced.

"Daisy . . . you gotta be kidding," Chandler muttered to himself.

Samantha's face suddenly split into a huge grin. "Looks like Daisy's got company. It appears that at least Chandler's horse knows how to treat a lady."

Chandler turned around, and frowned, when he saw his stallion prancing alongside the ugly mare like an obedient puppy. "Obviously Ranger has no taste in women," he grumbled under his breath.

John and Samantha burst out laughing.

Because John's horse had taken off, he had no choice but to ride double with Chandler. Samantha burst into peals of laughter at the hilarious sight both men posed, perched as they were, on top of Chandler's stallion.

"I'm glad you find this amusing, Samantha. Just wait until we get home, young lady."

"You would still punish me, after I just saved your life?" Samantha teasingly replied.

John couldn't help but chuckle. "That might make a difference. But don't think that you're entirely off the hook."

"If you need any suggestions for discipline . . . ?" Chandler offered.

"I don't recall my father asking for your opinion, *Mister* Chandler." Samantha had purposely emphasized the word mister, because she knew he didn't like it.

"Since I've met you, *Miss Callahan*, my life's been put in danger on more than one occasion, so I guess I feel I'm entitled to an opinion."

"If you hadn't interfered in my business that first day, your miserable life never would have been put in any danger to begin with," Samantha angrily retorted. "So you can't hold that against me. And if you hadn't . . ."

"Am I gonna have to listen to you two yammerin' all the way back to the ranch?" John grumbled crossly. He shifted around on Chandler's horse's hard rump, trying to find a more comfortable position, which wasn't helping his mood any, either. "What does this animal have for a backbone . . . a hunk of iron?"

Chandler threw back his head and laughed.

It was nearly dusk when they finally reached the ranch. Samantha noticed the lines of fatigue clearly etched in her father's weary face. She, too, was exhausted. But Chandler didn't seem to be the least bit phased, which seemed to irritate her for some reason. Samantha told her father she'd be in later for supper, then headed directly toward the barn to take care of her horse. After all, the little mare had worked hard today and she deserved some pampering . . .

As Chandler halted in front of the house, his eyes lingered upon Samantha's stiff back as she trotted away on her mule-like horse. He knew she was angry at him; she'd hardly spoken a word to him on the way home. He shook his head. Never in his life had he ever met a woman more stubborn or determined than that blue-eyed minx. He swung a leg over his horse's head and dropped lightly to the ground, then stood there, waiting for his riding companion to dismount.

When John made no immediate effort to move, "Need a hand down, old man?" he teasingly asked with a lopsided grin.

"You try riding on this horse's iron rump and see how fast you move." With a low groan John carefully slid to the ground.

Chandler chuckled.

"John, are you hurt?"

He turned at the sound of Amos's voice. "I'm okay . . . just a little stiff and sore from riding on that stallion's hard rear. We had ourselves a little trouble on the way home . . . Buck got spooked by a rattler." He didn't mention that the rattler nearly struck him. Amos would start questioning him and he wouldn't have a moment's peace the rest of the evening.

Amos eyed the newest hired hand suspiciously, still not quite sure what to think of the man, before informing his boss, "We all got worried when your horse came home without ya. I was just rounding up some of the boys to start a search party."

"Then I'm glad I got back when I did. Say Amos, would you mind tending to Chandler's horse . . . we've all had a long day. Oh, and Buck threw a shoe . . ."

"Ernie already took care of that, Boss." Amos then led the big buckskin stallion away.

"John!"

When he turned around, Rachel leaped off the front porch into his arms. He hugged and kissed his wife, before setting her back on her feet.

Rachel acknowledged Chandler with a bashful smile and a nod of her head. "Where's Samantha?" she asked her husband.

"Looking after Daisy." John chuckled. "You can stop looking for injuries, Rachel, I'm just fine. Buck threw a shoe is all." He wasn't going to tell her about his close call with the rattlesnake, knowing how she'd react.

"I bet you're starved," Rachel said. "Come on . . . I've got supper waiting." She smiled at Chandler. "Won't you join us?"

"Much obliged, ma'am." Chandler removed his dusty hat, slapped it against his leg, before following John and Rachel inside the house.

Rachel quietly sipped her coffee, while the men finished scarfing down their meal. She didn't want to burden her husband with yet another problem, but she had no choice, because there could be more trouble with Jed.

"John, Sarah might be staying with us for a spell."

From the expression on his wife's face, John could tell that something was wrong. "What is it, Rachel?"

"Jed beat his own daughter," she informed him. "James brought Sarah here. He didn't know what else to do. I hope you're not angry?"

His jaw muscles tensed; and inwardly he was shaking. In spite of the rage now churning within him, John's voice sounded calm when he answered, "James did the right thing, and as long as Sarah's here, I guarantee Jed won't be laying a finger on the girl. Where is James?"

"He's helping Sarah get settled in the guest room."

"Good."

"I know it's really none of my business, but is there any thing I can do to help?" It infuriated Chandler that a man would beat a female for any reason, even if that female happened to be the man's own daughter.

"I think the only thing we should do is keep our distance from Jed . . . least for a while," Rachel replied. She turned to her husband. "Don't you agree, John?" Rachel frowned, noting the look that came over his face. She didn't need an interpreter for *that* particular expression. "John, promise me you won't do any thing foolish?"

No response.

Rachel decided to wait and discuss the matter with her husband in private when Samantha entered the kitchen just then. "I kept your plate warm on top of the stove, dear." She noticed her daughter's dirty and disheveled appearance. "You look like you fell in the mud."

Samantha grabbed her plate off the stove, then dropped into an empty chair at the table, looking toward her father. Apparently he hadn't told her mother about the fight she had with Ralf. She remained silent, hoping somebody would change the subject.

"Samantha?"

"She slipped and fell in the mud," John finally said to his wife.

A delicate brow arched at her husband. Rachel was certain there was more to the story, but she shrugged it off, for now. Later, she and

John would be having a serious talk. She turned her attention back to their guest. "Chandler, did you save room for dessert?"

"Yes, ma'am," came his enthusiastic reply.

"Maybe I should have baked you a pie of your own," Rachel teased, remembering the man's voracious appetite.

Chandler smiled.

Samantha was curious about the sadness that always seemed to be lurking inside the depths of Chandler's dark, compelling eyes, even when he was smiling, like now. She wondered what could have happened to make a man like Chandler always seem so sad? When Samantha suddenly realized that she was staring at the man, she quickly lowered her eyes, pretending to shove her food around her plate.

"Are you all right, dear? You seem a little flushed."

Samantha inwardly groaned. "I'm just tired, Ma. I think I'll turn in for the night." Without another word, she scooted out of her chair and hurried from the room.

"What was that all about?" John asked his wife.

"I'm not sure," Rachel replied, a puzzled frown creasing her brow.

Chandler had noticed the way Samantha had been watching him. The corners of his mouth lifted into a smile. He was experienced with women enough to know that she was attracted to him. Though she would never admit it, probably not even to herself.

"It's been a long day . . . think I'll turn in myself," John announced, standing out of his chair. "Chandler, how 'bout I walk you to the bunkhouse and introduce you to the other men, before it gets too late."

Chandler rose to his feet. "Supper was delicious, Mrs. Callahan."

"Please call me Rachel. And I'm glad you enjoyed it, young man."

Samantha tossed and turned restlessly upon her bed, unable to fall asleep. She knew it was late, because she'd heard her parents retire for the night quite some time ago. But she just couldn't sleep. Every time she closed her eyes, a certain handsome face appeared before her. With a frustrated sigh, she rolled over on her back, blinking up at the ceiling. *What was wrong with her?* Samantha wondered. *Why couldn't she get that drifter out of her mind?* He would probably be gone by the end of the week and she would never see him again. Besides, she wasn't some silly adolescent girl any longer, even though she still lived at home.

Sometimes it was depressing that all of the girls she'd gone to school with were now married, Samantha thought, frowning. And most of them already had families of their own. Except for her best friend Sarah. Not that Sarah was lacking in marriage proposals. Why just this past year alone, there had been a couple of young men who had asked for her hand in marriage. But Sarah had refused them. Because, since about the age of fifteen, Sarah had been in love with her brother.

Sighing wearily, Samantha closed her eyes. It was well into the early morning hours before she'd finally drifted off to sleep . . . .

Chapter Four

The lacy white curtains at the window gently fluttered in the morning breeze, allowing beams of sunlight to filter inside the room, casting flickering shadows upon the plush carpeted floor. Hearing voices outside her bedroom window, Samantha pulled the covers over head, trying to drown out all the loud noise. When her belly rumbled in hunger, she let out a defeated sigh. Tossing her covers aside, she got out of bed, walked over to her vanity, plopped down into the chair to brave a look in the mirror. Just as she had feared, there were dark circles under her eyes. Not usually one to worry about appearance, she hastily ran a hairbrush through her long, thick mane, and tied it back with a leather thong.

Rising, she dressed in a hurry, then left her room.

Rachel was seated at the table, flipping through a magazine, when Samantha entered the kitchen. She looked up and smiled. "Well, well, sleepy-head . . . so you finally decided to join us today. Are you hungry?" She was already heading to the stove.

"Famished," Samantha said as she dropped heavily into a chair.

When Rachel set a plate of food before her daughter, she noticed the dark circles under her lovely blue eyes. She then remembered Samantha had been acting a little peculiar last night, plus her daughter was normally cheerful in the morning—not somber like now.

"Didn't you sleep well, dear?"

Samantha shrugged, before stuffing a huge bite of food into her mouth.

Rachel frowned. Obviously that was about as much information as she was going to get for now. She poured herself another cup of coffee, then sat back down at the table. Rachel figured that now was probably as good as time as any to inform Samantha about their newest guest. She casually stated, "Sarah's going to be staying with us for a while."

Samantha looked questioningly at her mother. "What happened?"

"Let's just say—Sarah had a disagreement with her father."

"Who hasn't lately," Samantha grumbled to herself. She began to push the food around her plate. "Ma, how old were you when you married Pa?"

So that's what's bothering her, Rachel thought. "Samantha, there are lots of girls that aren't married at your age."

"You know that's not true . . . most girls *are* married at my age."

"Well—barely your age," Rachel added with a smile. "In answer to your question, I was a little younger than you are now, when I married your father."

"I knew I was an old spinster," Samantha said in despair.

Rachel pressed her lips together to hide her grin. "You're not an old spinster, Samantha. You just haven't found the right man yet."

"And I probably never will, because what man would want a wife he can't order around like his slave."

"All men aren't that way, Samantha. Your father's certainly not."

"But Pa's not like most men."

"Do you think your father's the only man who treats women with respect?"

"We are talking about the men here in Bear Creek," Samantha sarcastically replied. "From some of the men I've encountered lately," she went on to say, remembering 'Ralf the barbarian with octopus hands', "I would rather be married to a wild Comanche. I hope you and Pa are prepared to be stuck with me until I'm old and withered."

Rachel laughed. "I think you'll find a man to marry you before that happens."

Samantha wasn't so sure. Feeling a little depressed, she suddenly lost her appetite. "Ma, do you think Pa would mind if I rode out to the pond today?" She always felt better after a ride to the pond. It was a beautiful place; plus it would give her some time alone to think. "Or do I have to spend the entire day in my room?"

"I don't think your father would care if you took Daisy for a ride. Long as you keep out of trouble, dear," Rachel teasingly added. "I'll tell your father that I gave you permission when he comes in for lunch, so if he does get angry, he won't be mad at you."

Scooting out of her chair, Samantha walked around the table and hugged her mother and kissed her on the cheek. "You're the best." She headed for the door, throwing over her shoulder, "I'll be home before supper."

Samantha was almost to the barn when the sound of mens' laughter caught her attention. Inquisitive by nature, she took a quick detour toward the corral. The men were branding calves today, which was a grueling chore she didn't even like to watch, though her father insisted the calves couldn't feel a thing because of their thick hides. Unfortunately, sometimes when her pa was shorthanded, she had to help with the offensive chore, but thankfully that was rare.

When Samantha reached the corral, she immediately discovered what all the uproarious laughter was about. She giggled, watching her father trying to wrestle a stubborn calf to the ground, while Amos stood by ready to put the Callahan brand on its hindquarters.

But the little rascal wasn't cooperating . . .

"Amos!" John hollered. "Would you mind watching where you're putting that dang-gone branding iron! You're suppose to brand the calf not me!"

"If you'd hold the critter still!" Amos could barely keep a straight face.

"That's what I'm trying to do!"

The bawling calf again slipped through John's hands and when he tried to grab the fleeing animal, he tripped over his own feet and landed sprawled out on the ground.

The men all doubled over in peals of laughter.

John got to his feet, brushing the dirt off his britches. "Let the varmint go, Amos," he called out. "After that wrestling match, the little fella deserves a reprieve."

The calf was forgotten when Samantha spotted Chandler on the opposite side of the corral, casually leaning against the fence, his muscular arms folded across his broad bare chest. Towering over the other men, Chandler stood out like a sore thumb. He wasn't wearing a shirt, and his smooth, copper-colored skin glistened with a fine layer of perspiration. In place of his big black Stetson, a beaded leather headband kept his shoulder-length hair away from his handsome face. Dressed only in a pair of buckskin pants and knee high moccasins, Wade Chandler looked every inch an Indian today.

Mesmerized, Samantha couldn't seem to take her eyes off Chandler, thinking, he was *by far* the most handsome man she'd ever seen . . .

"Enjoying the view?" an angry voice suddenly snarled.

Samantha whirled around. "Jake Martin, how dare you sneak up on me like that!"

"You would've heard me coming if you hadn't been so engrossed with that . . . that heathen!"

"I'll have you know that *heathen* as you call him is more civilized than most of those *ruffians* who work for your father!" Samantha angrily spat. She tried to walk away from Jake, but he grabbed her roughly by the arm and then swung her around to face him. "How dare you manhandle me that way!"

"I'm warning you, Samantha, stay away from that Indian! I haven't waited all these years for nothin'! And I won't allow some Injun to take what's rightfully mine!"

"What do you mean what's rightfully yours?" She glared at the offensive hand still holding her arm in a viselike grip. "And kindly take your hand off me this instant!"

When Jake refused to comply, several unladylike words spewed from Samantha's lips as she jerked her arm free of his grasp.

"I won't stand for my future wife using foul language!"

"Your future *wife*," Samantha repeated incredulously. "Have you lost your mind, Jake Martin?" Planting both fists firmly on her hips, she added, "And since when did my *foul language* start offending you?"

"Decent women don't talk that way!"

"Are you suddenly deranged?" Samantha snapped at him.

Jake's smoldering brown eyes bore into her furious blue one's. "I mean it, Samantha! Stay away from that Indian!"

Without another word Jake twirled on his boot heel and strode toward his horse. He climbed into the saddle and angrily spurred his horse into a gallop. His thin lips twisted into an ugly sneer. *One way or another, Samantha Callahan, you will be mine.* But she was well-worth waiting for, Jake thought. Samantha was such a rare beauty that any man would be lucky to call her his own. Plus, there was the little added bonus of becoming John Callahan's son-in-law—who just happened to be the richest man around this part of Montana. Once he and Samantha were married, then everybody in town would respect him; no one would dare call him a spoiled brat ever again!

Samantha was both confused and angry as she watched Jake ride away. *Just like his father,* an inner voice warned her. In all the years she had known Jake Martin, she'd never seen this possessive side of him before. There had even been a time when she'd seriously considered marrying Jake, hoping that someday she would grow to love him. It didn't take her long to realize that she could never love Jake, except as a friend.

Finally convincing herself that there must've been some sort of misunderstanding, Samantha headed toward the barn to fetch Daisy. A ride to the pond was just what she needed to help lift her further sinking spirits . . . .

Chandler's eyes followed Samantha as she raced across the field on her horse. Having witnessed the heated confrontation between her and Jake Martin, he'd come awfully close to leaping over the fence and grabbing the kid and giving him a sound thrashing he would never forget. None of the other men had seemed to notice, and Chandler decided that it might be best to keep what happened to himself. Besides, John had enough on his mind right now without burdening the poor man with yet another problem. One thing was for certain though, he would be keeping a much closer eye on Samantha when Jake Martin was around. Something Chandler could not get out of his mind, the way Jake had looked at him yesterday . . . there had been a kind of insanity glittering within the depths of those dark brown eyes.

As Chandler got back to work, he thought about the way Samantha had been watching him, until Jake arrived and spoiled everything. An amused grin twitched the corners of his mouth, thinking that *gawking* would be a more appropriate word. As headstrong as Samantha Callahan appeared to be, she wore her emotions on her sleeve. Chandler was glad that none of the other men had noticed the way Samantha had been watching him or he'd never hear the end of it. Funny, but, he had sensed her presence the moment she was standing there, and had been thoroughly enjoying her appraising look, too, until that crazy kid showed up . . . .

Samantha always felt better coming to the pond; this beautiful place always did wonders for her occasional foul moods. Sometimes she came here just to be alone with her private thoughts. Daisy loved it here, too; there was plenty of grazing for her horse and lots of shady trees to ward off the summer heat.

Seated on a flat boulder, dangling her bare feet and lower legs into the cool water, Samantha looked out across the pond in wondrous awe. Surrounded by ancient oaks and towering birch trees, *the pond* was actually a rather small lake. Various kinds of bushes and shrubs also grew around the outer edge. Wildflowers dotted the nearby grassy meadow with splashes of bright yellows and purples and pinks. This entire area on her father's property was absolutely breathtaking; there was no other way to describe it.

If she listened close enough, Samantha could hear the gurgling sound of the clear mountain stream that fed the pond, a short distance away. Leaning back her head, she sighed contently, gazing up at the cloudless blue sky. If she ever married, this would be the place where she and her husband would build their home—with her father's permission of course. Then a picture of Chandler carrying her across the threshold flashed through her mind. Samantha inwardly scolded herself for even thinking such a ridiculous notion. Wade Chandler obviously was not the marrying kind. Besides, she could barely tolerate the man.

Noting the position of the sun, Samantha could tell that she had been here for quite some time already. My, but, how the time seemed to fly when you were enjoying yourself. She sighed, knowing she would have to start back home soon.

Samantha looked over her shoulder when she heard Daisy nicker. The way the little mare's ears twitched back and forth was a sign that warned her that 'something or somebody' was coming. Listening more intently, she heard the faint nicker of another horse, which was immediately followed by Daisy's answer.

When Samantha saw Chandler emerge through the trees on his big buckskin stallion, she angrily scrambled to her feet, wondering how the man had found her. Her brows furrowed into a deep scowl as she watched him dismount and tether his horse to a low-hanging limb.

As Chandler approached Samantha, he noticed that she had unbound her knee-length hair and the gorgeous wavy mane sparkled like spun gold in the late afternoon sun. A wry grin appeared upon his face when he next noticed that Samantha had removed her jeans. Unfortunately, the flannel shirt she wore was long enough to hide most of her shapely legs from his appreciative view. His smile widened. Never had he seen a more desirable woman . . .

"How did you find me?"

Her demanding tone immediately snapped Chandler to his senses. His smile disappeared and was replaced by a frown of his own. "I'm an Indian, remember?"

"If I'd wanted any company, you *dimwitted buffoon*, I would have invited you to ride along," she angrily threw at him.

Chandler's frown deepened. She was the most aggravating female he'd ever had the displeasure of meeting. "Your mother sent me to find you."

When several choice words spewed from her lovely lips, his frown deepened even more. "Does your father always allow you to speak like a hired hand?"

"Why should it matter to you how I speak?"

"It doesn't."

"Good."

"Look—I didn't come here to argue."

Grumbling something under her breath about infuriating men, she turned her back on him and plopped down on the flat rock, plunging her feet into the water.

Chandler sat beside her Indian style. "Evidently your pa wasn't very pleased that you took off without his consent." When she looked at him with a troubled expression, he quickly assured her, "Don't worry . . . your ma claimed full responsibility, so you're completely off the hook. I was just sent to tell you to come home."

There was a period of silence.

Chandler watched the brooding woman surreptitiously, wondering *what* or *who* had put such a bee in her bonnet. "We probably should be going."

Samantha let out a frustrated sigh that came out sounding more like a hiss. Chandler had been the last person she wanted to see. This man was the reason she'd come here to be alone in the first place. "Now that you found me, you can leave."

"I promised your mother I wouldn't come back without ya. Now you wouldn't want me to break a promise, would you, Miss Callahan?"

"I suppose not," she grumbled.

Chandler thought this might be the perfect opportunity to question her about her crazy neighbor. On his way here, he'd spotted Jake Martin on his horse, and every fiber of his being told him the kid was up to no good.

"Is Jake usually aggressive toward women?" he suddenly asked.

Samantha's head swung toward him. "You saw us arguing?"

He nodded.

It was a little humiliating Chandler had witnessed that fight with Jake, but what bothered Samantha the most, there was enough animosity between her father and Jed Martin, and, if Chandler were to say anything, he could make an already bad situation even worse. So what she said next came out sounding like an accusation, but in reality was frustration.

"Are you spying on me now?"

"I was simply observing," Chandler defensively replied. It seemed like all women had a talent for twisting a man's words around.

"Isn't that basically the same thing as spying?"

Not in his book it wasn't, but Chandler refrained from saying so. He rose to his feet. "How 'bout we call a truce and head back to the ranch?"

"Turn around."

"What for?"

"So I can put on my pants."

"Okay, I'm turning."

Samantha reached for her pants, hastily slipped them on, pulled on her boots, then she strode past Chandler toward her horse without so much as a backward glance at the annoying man. She didn't know Chandler was right behind her, until she felt his hands slip around her waist and then she was dropped unceremoniously onto Daisy's bare back.

"I don't know how you manage to stay on that nag without a saddle," Chandler muttered to himself as he vaulted onto his own horse.

"You're not using a saddle," Samantha irritably pointed out.

"My horse doesn't have a back so swayed that it looks deformed."

"Daisy can't help the way she looks." Samantha lovingly patted her horse on the neck. "Seems like I'm always having to defend you, huh girl?"

Chandler rolled his eyes as they started toward home. He had to chuckle at the way Samantha sat so proudly perched upon Daisy's swayed bare back. He couldn't resist teasing her. "At least a saddle would provide you with some kind of cushion."

Samantha frowned at him. "I don't need a cushion. And would you kindly keep your insulting remarks about my horse to yourself."

"I'll try."

"Mr. Chandler, do you enjoy purposely irritating me?"

"If I am irritating you, Miss Callahan, I'm not doing it on purpose." *It certainly doesn't take much to rile the woman,* Chandler thought.

"It must just come naturally then."

"If you say so."

"Are you mocking me?" Samantha demanded to know.

"I wouldn't even consider it."

The man was laughing at her!

But Samantha didn't get a chance to respond, because at that moment a ground-shaking clap of thunder suddenly rumbled over their heads. Neither Chandler or Samantha had noticed the thick, black clouds that were rapidly gathering in the darkening sky. The wind was already picking up speed, a telltale sign of a much more powerful storm to come. Even the horses seemed to sense what was about to happen and began to nervously prance in step.

Samantha had to shout at Chandler over the howling wind. "We need to find shelter fast! Follow me . . . I know a place!"

Squinting his eyes against the stinging wind, Chandler pressed his heels into Ranger's belly and raced after Samantha across the prairie . . . .

John paced outside on the back veranda that ran along the entire length of the house. He stopped long enough to turn and bellow at his wife, "There's a storm coming and my daughter is still out there somewhere!"

"I'm sure that Chandler's quite capable of taking care of Samantha. I believe she couldn't be in better hands."

"Maybe you're right," John said more calmly. Again he began to pace back and forth, adding more to himself, "But if they're not back soon . . ."

Rachel didn't tell her husband (call it woman's intuition) that she felt Chandler would protect their daughter with his life. When Chandler had volunteered to go after Samantha, she had read something in the man's eyes that was much more than just concern . . . .

By now the wind was whipping wildly and the rain was coming down in torrents. Both Samantha's and Chandler's clothing was drenched clear through. *Just a little farther*, Samantha thought, praying she was headed in the right direction. But she couldn't be sure. It was raining so hard she was having trouble seeing where she was going.

Finally Samantha spotted the familiar small thicket of trees just up ahead. She and Chandler halted their horses in front of the tiny weather-beaten cabin, sliding to the ground. They turned their horses loose, figuring their mounts would stand a better chance of finding their own shelter, considering the only form of shelter for the animals was an old rickety-looking barn that looked like it was about ready to collapse.

After they were safely inside the cabin, Chandler slammed the door shut and hastily secured the latch. While Samantha searched for a couple of blankets, Chandler found some wood and matches, and got a fire going inside the old potbellied stove. Shivering, he removed his saturated shirt and draped it over the back of a chair; there wasn't much he could do about his pants. He thanked Samantha when she handed him a blanket, then began to dry off his upper body.

"Who's cabin is this?" he asked.

"I really don't know," Samantha replied through chattering teeth. She wrapped the blanket more snugly around her shoulders. "Jake and I found this place by accident one day when we were out riding . . . that was several years ago. There wasn't anybody living here then and nobody's been here since . . . least that I know of."

Just the mention of Jake's name sparked Chandler's temper. "Do you and *Jake*—" he practically hissed the name, "come here often?" Seeing the hurt expression on her face, he immediately regretted his words.

"You don't like Jake much, do you?" Samantha bluntly asked. Though it had been more of a statement than an observation.

"Now that you ask, no I don't."

"But you don't even know him." Samantha didn't want Chandler to have a bad opinion of Jake who'd been her friend since childhood. "Normally Jake is a rather likable fellow. I know the two of you got off on the wrong foot, but—the person you met the other day *was not* the Jake that I know."

"Maybe that person *was* the real Jake," Chandler suggested with growing agitation. It angered him that she was always defending the crazy kid.

Wordlessly Samantha stepped over to the window, and quietly stood there, gazing outside. She couldn't really dispute Chandler's words, because she, herself, didn't know what to think of Jake anymore. Maybe what Chandler said was true. Again that inner voice warned her: *Just like his father. But Jake was nothing like his father*, Samantha inwardly argued. Sometimes Jed Martin could be a very aggressive man. Even her own father didn't know just how violent Jed could become at times when he didn't get his way; or when somebody didn't do exactly what the man wanted and precisely how he wanted it done. And there had been several times when Samantha had seen Jed take that anger out on his son.

"I think the worst of the storm has passed already," she remarked, noticing the wind had calmed quite a bit. "We probably should head for home . . . my parents will be worried."

"Samantha?"

When she looked at Chandler, again she was struck by the man's eyes. The longest lashes she'd ever seen framed a pair of eyes that were as black as night. His eyes were simply too beautiful for a man . . .

"Just be careful around Jake," Chandler finally said. "I wouldn't go off with him alone anywhere, either."

Chandler had stepped closer to her. Standing this close to Chandler caused Samantha's belly to do strange flip-flops. And it was suddenly hard to breath. Samantha thought about one time when Jake had kissed her, what she had felt then didn't even come close to the unexpected emotions churning within her now . . .

Gazing into eyes that were the purest blue, Chandler was beginning to feel things for Samantha that he didn't want to feel. It had been so long since he'd felt so strongly about a woman—not since his days as a warrior—not since *her*. Remembering his solemn oath that '*never again would he allow a woman to break his heart*', Chandler's voice sounded rather harsh when he told her they should get going. He wasn't really angry at Samantha; he was more angry at himself. Because if he were a smart man, the very instant he got back to the Callahan ranch, he would collect his gear and hightail it out of town just as fast as he could. Chandler frowned. Unfortunately, he didn't always do the smart thing.

Before Chandler realized what Samantha was doing, she suddenly tossed her blanket on a nearby cot and then she strode out the door without a word or a backward glance. A moment later, he heard that familiar high-pitched whistle.

Grumbling under his breath, Chandler grabbed his still soaked shirt off the back of the chair and hurried out the door after Samantha, knowing she would take off without him. *And so might that lovesick, jug-headed horse of his.* He realized the sooner he got Miss Callahan home to her parents, the better. And if he did decide to stay, he was going into town tonight . . . a drink was just what he needed to help put him back in his right state of mind.

Luckily Ranger hadn't taken off. He stood just outside the cabin, prancing anxiously in place, looking at him, as if to say: *hurry up, they're getting away.*

Chandler vaulted onto the back of his stallion and then charged after Samantha and that *cannon ball* she called a horse. Already she was way ahead of him. He could see her long hair waving out behind her like a banner. He had to admire her horsemanship. Samantha Callahan could ride as well as any Indian. But what amazed Chandler even more was, how a horse that looked like it could barely stand on its own four legs could run like the wind.

Chandler could feel Ranger's muscles straining beneath him as the stallion struggled to catch up with the mare. He said out loud, "Face it, old boy, you'll never catch that lightning streak, so you might as well save your strength."

Samantha glanced over her shoulder. A satisfied grin curled her lips. Chandler was so far behind, she could barely see him. Gently easing back on the reins, she gradually slowed her horse to a walk to wait for him to catch up with her.

When Samantha heard the sound of approaching hooves, she turned and smiled triumphantly as he eased his stallion beside her mare.

"What do you feed that animal . . . gunpowder?" It annoyed Chandler that his stallion was breathing hard and most of his body was covered in lather from the exertion, while *Daisy* appeared to be totally unaffected.

"I guess that only proves that you can't judge a book by its cover . . . er . . . in this case you can't judge a horse by its looks."

"I just don't get it," Chandler muttered to himself, shaking his head in bewilderment.

At Samantha's burst of laughter, he looked at her, frowning. "You really find this amusing, don't you?"

"Well—I guess I'd be lying if I said I didn't. But if it makes you feel any better, there's not another horse around these parts that can outrun Daisy."

"That don't make me feel any better at all," Chandler grumbled.

"I suppose then a race is out of the question?" Samantha teased him.

"I wouldn't even consider putting my stallion through such humiliation."

"What if I gave you a head start?"

"You've got to be joking."

The way Chandler was scowling at her, Samantha couldn't help grin. Funny how a grown man's pride could be so easily bruised, especially when it came to his horse. "Since you refuse the challenge . . ." she shrugged. "I wouldn't want you to over stress your horse, but—I'd like to make it home before dark, so guess I'll see you at home."

Samantha then made a clicking sound with her tongue and both horse and rider immediately shot ahead, leaving Chandler and his stallion quickly behind . . . .

Chapter Five

Samantha peered across the breakfast table at her stern-faced father who still hadn't said a word to her yet. Apparently he was still angry at her this morning. She let out a sigh. She really couldn't blame him. According to her mother, after yesterday's storm her father had spent the rest of the afternoon out looking for her and Chandler. It had been dark by the time her pa had returned home, drenched clear through his clothing, cold, tired, and hungry.

"I'm sorry, Pa," she finally said.

John leaned back in his chair, folding his arms across his chest, his bright blue eyes narrowing in anger. Ironically, it was the exact same thing his daughter did whenever she was angry about something, had he only thought about it.

"Do you think we could possibly get through today without another catastrophe? The cattle drive is less than a month away and I still have a lot to do. I can't keep chasing you around the countryside. So—until I say otherwise, young lady, you can only exercise Daisy in the field next to the house."

"But . . ."

"You'd dare argue with me under the circumstances?"

Samantha's mouth snapped shut. "May I please be excused?"

"But you've hardly touched your breakfast, dear," Rachel noticed.

"I'm not very hungry."

"You may be excused," John said. "And remember what I told you."

The instant Samantha was out of the room, Rachel turned to her husband. "Don't you think you're being rather harsh?"

"How do you figure?"

"You know how much Samantha enjoys her rides with Daisy."

Helping himself to some more coffee, "Did you have a better punishment in mind?" John inquired of his wife.

"Well . . . no . . . but . . . to restrict Samantha from her daily rides, you might as well lock her inside her room."

"That's the whole point, Rachel. Wait—" John slapped himself on the forehead, "why didn't I think of this before . . . ? How 'bout we take away something she really detests instead?" he sarcastically suggested. "Boy that'll teach her."

Rachel giggled. "Okay, you win."

"I knew you'd see it my way. I was only joking," he said at his wife's disapproving frown.

"It didn't sound like you were joking."

"You know, it's a sad day when a man can't tease his own wife. Honestly, Rach, what's happened to your sense of humor this morning?"

Her frown deepened.

"Guess I'd better git while the gittin's good." John downed the remainder of his coffee, then stood out of his chair. He reached over and pecked his scowling wife on the cheek. "I'm not sure I'll be home for lunch." Then he disappeared out the back door.

Samantha stood gazing out her bedroom window deep in thought. Because she had disobeyed her father *again,* she would probably be stuck inside this room for life. Though she hadn't exactly disobeyed him. After all, her mother did give her permission to ride out to the pond, but apparently her mother didn't have the authority to overturn her father's decisions. She would have to remember that in the future. Which was the reason why she was never getting married. She didn't want some man dictating her every move; not that her father actually bossed her mother around. But Samantha was determined that no man was going to tell her what she could or could not do, not ever. At the very least, a husband meant restrictions.

Samantha heaved a sigh. Now she was stuck exercising Daisy in the small pasture; she might as well not ride her horse at all. She wondered if her father would still allow her to accompany him on the cattle drive. It was the one thing she looked forward to every summer. Then, again, with that new hired hand going along, maybe it would be better if she stayed at home . . .

A sudden knock on the door startled Samantha out of her thoughts. She looked over her shoulder, and smiled, when Sarah peeked her head inside the room.

"Mind if I come in for a while?"

"Of course not." Samantha was grateful for some company.

Sarah closed the door, then she crossed the room and sat in the chair at Samantha's dressing table. "I've been doing some thinking."

Samantha noticed the way that her friend kept nervously folding and unfolding her hands in her lap. She walked over and plopped down on the edge of her bed. "What is it, Sarah?"

"I think it would be best for everyone if I went home," she replied in a voice so soft it was barely a whisper.

"Did you talk to James about this?"

Sarah shook her head.

Samantha could tell there was something that Sarah wasn't telling her. She began to question her friend. "Why do you think it would be best for everyone if you went home?"

Sarah shrugged.

"Did you and my brother have a fight?"

"No."

"Then I don't understand."

When Sarah's chin began to quiver, Samantha knew that something was seriously wrong. Rising, she stepped over to the chair to give her best friend an encouraging hug. "Whatever the problem is, Sarah, you can trust me."

Her slender shoulders began to shake with huge sobs. And Samantha felt a cold chill run down her spine. "What is it, Sarah?"

"James deserves an undefiled wife!" she suddenly cried.

"I'm not sure what you mean?"

Sarah looked at her then. "James didn't tell you—"

"Tell me what?"

When Sarah didn't say anything, Samantha boldly started to say, "You mean you and my brother . . ." but couldn't finish the sentence.

Sarah vigorously shook her head.

The reality of what Sarah was trying to tell her finally sank in. Samantha's body began to shake with mounting anger. Now it was becoming perfectly clear; the signs had been there all along. *Oh why had it taken her so long to see it!* And just the thought of what this gentle girl must have endured. It was almost too painful for Samantha to fully comprehend.

"Who did this to you, Sarah?" she bluntly asked.

Instantly Sarah's eyes widened in alarm. "I can't tell you!" she shrieked in hysterics. "He said he would hurt James if I told anyone!"

Samantha wasn't sure what to do. Should she tell her brother? *No!* her mind immediately shouted. She couldn't tell James what happened to Sarah . . . he'd go absolutely berserk! This was something she would have to try to handle on her own . . . least until she had more of the facts. She took Sarah firmly by the shoulders and forced her distraught friend to look her in the eyes. "Whoever did this horrible thing to you, Sarah, might do the same thing to some other poor unsuspecting innocent girl. And I promise you this man can't hurt James . . . it was only a threat to keep you from saying anything."

Sarah still refused to speak.

Something suddenly occurred to Samantha. "This man, to threaten you the way he did, it must be somebody you know . . . am I right?"

"Please, Samantha, I can't tell you his name!"

So she did know him. The panic-stricken expression on Sarah's pale face told Samantha more than words that it was true. Her mind reeling, she began to pace the floor, trying to figure out who this horrible monster could be, when something else occurred to her. *It all fit perfectly.* She swung around to face her friend. "It was Charlie Bates, wasn't it?"

Sarah didn't have to say a word: the answer was there in her terrified pale blue eyes. Samantha began to shake with an inward rage she'd never felt so strongly before. But her voice sounded calm when she reminded her friend, "You have to believe me, Sarah, that Charlie won't touch James. It was only a threat to keep you quiet. Besides, even if Charlie tried to carry out his threat, I have every confidence in my brother's ability to handle himself."

Samantha walked over and put her arms around Sarah and she held her friend, while she cried her heart out. She gently patted the top of her head, crooning to her. "Always remember that James loves you, Sarah, and what Charlie did certainly won't change his feelings any. I think it would be best if you didn't go home right now, unless that's what you really wanna do?"

Sarah shook her head. "I'd rather stay here," she sniffled. She loathed the thought of having to go home. She couldn't stand the way her father looked at her now with such shame in his eyes. And her parents were fighting worse than ever these days.

Now that Sarah seemed much calmer, "Why don't you go rest for a while," Samantha urged her friend. She found a clean handkerchief in her dresser, and tenderly wiped the tears from Sarah's red, puffy eyes. "Don't you worry about a thing . . . we'll work this out somehow. And, Sarah—there's no need for you to be afraid of Charlie Bates anymore."

Forcing a brave smile, Sarah rose to her feet and quietly left the room.

The moment Sarah closed the door, Samantha walked over to look out the window. She blinked back tears of rage. *How could Charlie do such a despicable thing! Well—he wasn't about to get away with what he'd done to Sarah!* Samantha walked over to her dressing table, jerked open the top drawer, grasped her knife by the pearl handle, and carefully slipped it inside her boot. She knew just where to find Charlie Bates and what she was going to do to the man when she found him . . . .

"You just cheated!" Jake snarled at Charlie.

"Boy, I'm gettin' real tired of you accusin' me of cheatin' at cards!"

Jake glanced around the table at the other men, and scowled, when he noted the doubtful expressions on their faces. He was absolutely certain that Charlie had just cheated, even if the others didn't see it. And he wasn't about to lose another hand, especially to a cheater. Besides, he'd already lost too much money for one day.

"I know what I saw," he persisted.

"Maybe you're just a sore loser," Charlie tauntingly retorted.

"I have no problem with losing!" Jake snapped back. "It's cheatin' that I have a problem with! And, Bates, if my pa hadn't given your sorry hide a job, you wouldn't have the money to be sittin' here rattlin' your mouth!"

"Calm down, Jake," Jess Merdock intervened.

"The bet's to you, Martin," another said.

"I'm out of this hand!" Jake angrily slapped his cards on the table.

Nobody noticed the tall Indian who slipped through the swinging doors and casually sauntered over to the bar. He carried himself with an unmistakable confidence that demanded respect; so did the matching Peacemakers strapped low on his hips. Save for the knee high moccasins that hugged his feet, he was dressed entirely in black. Even his hair was black as pitch, which he wore in a single long plait down his back. His black Stetson was pulled low over his eyes, shading most of his face.

After ordering a bottle of whiskey, the Indian ambled across the room over to a small corner table, and seated himself in a chair with his back facing the wall.

Jake finally noticed the newcomer. He thought the Indian looked like a gunslinger. And although he could not clearly see the man's face—which was mostly concealed by a wide-brimmed hat—somehow the man seemed familiar. He remarked to the other men, "That Indian over there . . . any of you ever see him before?"

"If I did, it was probably on a Wanted poster." Just looking at the intimidating fellow caused Jess to inwardly shudder.

"I ain't never seen him," Ralf remarked.

"I don't like Injuns," Charlie grumbled under his breath.

"I doubt they would like you either, Bates," Jake sarcastically retorted. He wished his Pa had never hired the man; Charlie Bates was nothing but trouble.

Sarah knocked louder on Samantha's door, but there still was no answer. Thinking her friend must have fallen asleep, she opened the door just wide enough to peek her head inside the room, and frowned, when she found it empty. Suddenly Sarah felt sick to her stomach, because she knew in her heart where Samantha had gone. *She never should've told anyone about Charlie,* she inwardly berated herself. *Especially her hot-tempered friend. Now if anything happened to Samantha it would be all her fault.*

White men—they were all the same wherever he went—avoiding him like the plague—like he was less than human just because he was Indian. But it didn't bother him anymore. In fact, he preferred they leave him alone. He'd come to this town for two reasons: and they were sitting across the room playing poker at a table. He didn't even know their names, but in his line of work it really didn't matter much. These men were different though, because he had a personal score to settle with them.

Morgan had been searching for these two outlaws for the past several years. A few years back he'd almost had them, but a gunfight that nearly took his life allowed them to get away.

But before this day was through, he would reveal himself. *And they would remember him.* Morgan wanted them to remember him, because he'd never forgotten them. Sometimes their faces still haunted his dreams at night.

Morgan was close enough to hear their conversation. So . . . the heavier set man's name was Charlie. *He'll be the one who suffers the most.* He then slammed his empty glass down so hard on the table, it drew some curious stares from several men inside the room. He glared at them, then smirked to himself. Just as Morgan figured, they immediately looked away, completely ignoring him after that.

Morgan poured himself another drink, then casually leaned back in his chair . . . .

John and Chandler raced toward Bear Creek, hoping to catch Samantha before she reached town. John still couldn't believe that Charlie Bates was the man responsible for Sarah's condition. He knew the man could be obnoxious at times, but to actually be capable of something so evil. Though he had to admit there had always been *something* about Charlie Bates that he couldn't quite put a finger on. The man had been mostly a loner and usually kept to himself, and the other ranch hands had avoided him whenever possible. He also knew that Charlie's favorite pastime was visiting the hurdy-gurdy house in town. Sometimes the man would be gone for days. John thought if only he'd listened to his gut feeling and fired Charlie months ago, maybe he could have prevented a terrible tragedy. Now—because of his bad judgement his own daughter might suffer. But God help the man if he dares harm one hair on Samantha's head . . .

Realizing he was about to run his poor horse to exhaustion, John slowed to a walk.

Chandler guided his stallion alongside John's horse. He could easily read the man's disturbing expression. "It wasn't your fault, John. There's nothing you could have possibly done to prevent what's happened."

John looked at Chandler and seriously said, "I just might kill Charlie for what he's done to Sarah. I'll do it slowly, if he lays one finger on Samantha."

"Do you think she'll actually confront this man?"

"Samantha would confront a gang of armed robbers if they harmed someone she loved."

That didn't surprise Chandler. "What about Charlie?" he then inquired. "What do you think he'll do if she does confront him?"

"I've been giving that some thought and—I really don't have an answer. Obviously Charlie's not in his right mind. A man like that, it's hard to predict what he might do."

Samantha halted in front of the hurdy-gurdy house, then gracefully slid from Daisy's bare back. She was trembling as she boldly stepped through the batwing doors. Her piercing blue eyes carefully scanned the room, narrowing into furious slits, when she found her quarry. Charlie Bate's was playing cards at a table with that other vermin Ralf—some other man she didn't recognize—and Jake. Samantha's brows knitted together in a deep frown. She hadn't thought about the possibility of Jake being here. Now she would have to approach the situation with some kind of strategy . . . Jake would go berserk if he discovered that Charlie was the man responsible for Sarah. And Jake was in enough trouble already.

But she'd better think of something quick, Samantha thought, because there were several men already staring at her and she was in no mood to be manhandled . . . .

While keeping a close vigil on the man called Charlie and his partner in crime, Morgan had nearly consumed an entire bottle of whiskey, though he wasn't even close to being drunk yet. Already he'd been propositioned by several *ladies* of the establishment and had regretfully declined their offers. He wished they would leave him alone though, because all this female attention he was getting seemed to be drawing the wrong kind of looks from a few drunks in the room. Not that he cared if they were angry at him; it was just that when a man had too much to drink it made him more reckless and willing to start a fight . . .

Morgan noticed the young man who'd just slipped through the swinging doors. The kid didn't even look old enough to shave yet. *They're starting awfully young these days,* Morgan thought in disgust. He felt like marching over there and tossing the lad out on his ear and sending him straight home to his mama.

When the kid happened to look Morgan's way, his eyes widened in surprise to discover that *he* was actually a *she* who had the face of an angel. A smile curled the corners of his mouth. *How could he have mistaken such a beauty for a young man.* If he'd only been looking just a little closer, you could definitely tell there was a female hidden inside those snug-fitting jeans. He wondered what color her hair was, but it was hard to tell completely tucked beneath her hat.

Morgan began to notice the young woman seemed to be interested in the same table that he'd been surveying most of the afternoon . . . .

The longer Samantha stood there watching Charlie Bates, the more filled with rage she was becoming. Now her mind was playing a horrible scene inside her head: she saw her best friend Sarah struggling with Charlie, trying to break free from the monster's clutches . . .

Scalding tears began to blur Samantha's vision, but she quickly blinked them away. As if in a trance she reached inside her boot and withdrew her knife; then, with her hate-filled eyes still focussed on Charlie, she slowly drew back her arm . . .

Her wrist suddenly grasped from behind, Samantha dropped her knife on the floor. She heard a low voice whisper against her ear . . .

"He ain't worth it, darlin'."

Samantha twisted around to give the man who had dared to interfere a piece of her mind, and gasped in complete shock. *It was Chandler, but it wasn't!* Her last conscious thought was that her mind must be playing a trick on her, before spiraling toward the floor . . . .

Something kept tickling Samantha's nose, so she swatted at the annoying object only to have it return again. She snuggled her cheek against her pillow, frowning. It felt hard, not soft and cushiony. And why was her bed moving . . . ?

When Samantha's eyes fluttered open, she discovered she wasn't in her bed but was riding on a horse and a man was carrying her in his arms. The annoying object that had been tickling her nose was the man's long hair. The last thing she remembered . . . oh yeah . . . she'd been about to hurl her knife at that black hearted Charlie Bates and somebody had stopped her . . .

"Chandler?"

He flashed her that familiar smile. "Did you sleep well?"

Struggling to a sitting position, Samantha angrily said, "Why did you stop me from giving that . . . that low-down rotten snake exactly what he deserved?"

"What are you talking about?" Chandler was beginning to wonder if Samantha might have hit her head on the floor harder than they thought. His arms tightened around her protectively. He frowned when she kept wiggling in his arms.

"What are you doing?" he finally asked.

"Feeling for my knife."

Samantha was even more confused when she discovered that her pearl-handled knife was safely inside her boot, because she couldn't remember putting it there. "Wasn't that you who grabbed me around the wrist?"

Chandler was really becoming concerned; she wasn't making any sense. "I honestly don't know what you're talking about, Samantha. Look—when your father and I found you, you were passed out on the floor. Nobody could tell us what happened . . . apparently you fainted for some reason . . . that's all I know."

"How did you and Pa know where to find me?"

"Sarah told your folks about Charlie," Chandler replied in a sympathetic tone of voice. "When she couldn't find you in your room, she was afraid you went looking for Charlie . . . obviously your friend knows you quite well. This might not be the best time to say this but—do you have any idea of the kind of danger you put yourself in?"

"I guess I wasn't thinking about that."

"I guess not."

"Didn't you say that you and my father found me?"

"That's right."

"So where's my father now?"

"He went after Charlie."

Immediately Samantha began to grab for the reins. "We have to go back!"

Guiding Ranger with one hand, Chandler struggled to hold on to Samantha with the other, while trying to keep them from falling off his horse. "Would you stop fighting me!"

"Let go of me!"

"Your father asked me to take you home and that's exactly what I intend to do! I don't know what's got you so riled all of a sudden, but John strikes me as a man who's perfectly capable of taking care of himself! That crazy stunt you pulled . . ."

"Is none of your business!"

Samantha continued to fight Chandler for control of the reins, but he had both her wrists in a viselike grip and wouldn't let go. When they nearly toppled off his horse, several unladylike words spewed from her lips.

Chandler could not believe the strength this woman had. He finally had no choice but to squeeze her wrists even tighter, until she let go of the reins.

"Release me this instant!" Samantha hissed.

"Not on your life, sweetheart." Still holding her wrists in his hand, Chandler nudged Ranger into a faster gait toward home. It proved to be a rather difficult task cantering across the prairie while hanging onto a woman who was fighting him at every turn.

"Let me go . . . you . . . you . . . *heathen!*"

"I've been called worse."

Realizing there was no use fighting Chandler, because the man had the strength of an ox, Samantha ceased struggling. She angrily demanded, "Did Jake happen to go with my father when he went after Charlie?"

"Jake was there?"

Samantha looked over her shoulder, glaring at the infuriating man. "He was playing cards with Charlie and Ralf," she said, exasperated. "Didn't you see him?"

"Jake must've left before your father and I got there."

"And what about the man who grabbed me?"

"What man?"

"What does it matter," Samantha sighed.

She was now beginning to think that she had dreamed the whole thing . . . no wait . . . the man had spoken to her, Samantha remembered . . . had called her *darlin*. Feeling more confused than ever, she laid her head back against Chandler's broad shoulder, closed her eyes. His muscular arm automatically tightened around her. Somehow Samantha felt completely safe wrapped in the cocoon of his strong embrace. She felt his warm breath tickling the sensitive curve of her neck, sending little shivers of delight throughout her body . . .

Chandler fought to ignore the unexpected feeling of desire that began to course through his veins. His heart had lain dormant for so long, he thought he was incapable of ever feeling anything for a woman again. He hadn't allowed himself to feel, not since—*no!* he refused to even think about Morning Star.

Chandler concentrated on the woman in his arms, pulling Samantha more closely against his chest, breathing in the clean, fresh scent of her hair. When he felt her body stiffen, he immediately relaxed his hold.

"Sorry, guess I was getting a little carried away."

"It's okay. It's just that I . . ." Samantha suddenly clamped her mouth shut. She couldn't just blurt out the fact that she had never allowed a man to touch her in such an intimate way before—which was probably obvious enough, especially to an experienced man like Chandler—assuming that he'd had a lot of experience with women. So she wouldn't embarrass herself any more than she already had, she tried to completely change the subject by saying the first thing that came to mind.

"Why don't you tell me about your family?"

When Samantha heard his sudden burst of laughter, she sat up straighter and twisted around, frowning at him. "What's so dang funny?"

"You are." Chandler found Samantha's bashfulness amusing.

Feeling she was somehow the brunt of some joke, "Maybe I should ride my own horse," Samantha irritatingly suggested.

"No way."

"Why not?"

"Because I promised your father I wouldn't let you out of my sight."

"We'll see about that." Knowing Daisy was somewhere close by, Samantha let out an ear-splitting whistle.

Chandler inwardly groaned, because he knew that ugly nag would soon come running like a docile pup. Already he could hear the mare's answering nicker. Before he had another fight on his hands, Chandler pressed his moccasined heels into Ranger's belly and the stallion lunged forward, leaving Samantha no choice but to hang on.

Morgan had been tracking Charlie since late afternoon; it was now getting near the evening hour. He figured he'd catch up with the man sometime tomorrow. Morgan thought again about the beautiful young woman who'd fainted in his arms. He'd hated leaving the poor girl lying on the floor the way that he had, but he couldn't allow this wretched man to get away from him—not this time. Morgan wondered what Charlie had done to the woman to make her want to hurl a knife at his heart. He might not have interfered, had he not wanted the pleasure of seeing the white man pay for what he'd done. And when he got through with Charlie, he would go after his cohort. Although the other man never actually participated, he could have stopped Charlie or at least have tried. So—far as Morgan was concerned, the other man was just as guilty, even though he wasn't the one who actually pulled the trigger . . .

"Pa, two men on horses are coming."

Samuel looked up from his task at the sound of his son's voice. "Where?"

"There," Morgan replied, pointing.

Shading his eyes against the glare of the sun with his hand, Samuel couldn't tell who the men were from this distance. He was getting on in years and his eyesight just wasn't what it used to be. Not just his eyesight was getting worse; he moved a lot slower these days. He'd been trying to repair this old shed for almost two weeks now and was starting to doubt that he would have it completed before winter set in.

"Son, run and tell your Ma we'll be having guests for supper."

"Yes, sir."

Morgan raced to do his father's bidding, excited to be receiving visitors. Living this far out, it was rare they ever got any company. He was thrilled just for the chance to hear the sound of another human voice; and he was anxious to find out what was happening in town.

But as Morgan burst through the front door of the little cabin and proceeded to tell his mother about their unexpected guests, the sound of gunshots exploded outside.

"Ma, hand me the rifle!"

"What is it, son?" Martha asked as she reached for the weapon.

Peering out the only window, Morgan couldn't see either man, but he knew they were out there somewhere. He took the rifle from his mother's trembling hands, then quickly checked the chamber, grumbling under his breath, when he discovered the rifle wasn't even loaded. He was heading toward the cupboard for some bullets when the door suddenly burst wide open and the two men stepped inside the room, each holding a gun.

"Put the rifle down, boy," the larger man warned in a threatening tone of voice.

"Please do as he says," Martha urged her son.

Morgan looked at his mother who by now was visibly shaking, and immediately lowered his weapon, carefully leaning it against the wall. Besides, what good would an empty rifle do him now. When his mother began to cry hysterically, Morgan walked over and wrapped his arms protectively around her.

"Shut that old woman up!"

"What do you expect?" the skinny man said. Which earned him a hard slap across the face that knocked him to the floor.

"Don't ever talk back to me again!" the larger man furiously spat.

When Martha suddenly bolted toward the door, shouting her husband's name, a loud gunshot split the air. Morgan let out an agonizing cry of pain and rage as he watched his mother's lifeless body crumple to the blood-splattered floor. Then a savage scream erupted from his throat as he charged the man who shot her . . . .

Morgan didn't know which man had butted him in the back of the head with his own rifle, but it had taken him several agonizing days to recover from his head wound. He could barely walk when he buried both of his parents behind the little cabin. Then, for some unexplainable reason that he still didn't understand, he set fire to the shed that his father had been working on. He remembered standing there in a complete daze, watching the shed burn, until it was nothing but smoldering ashes. He couldn't bear the thought of destroying his parents' cabin and had left it untouched. He had painstakingly planted his mother's favorite shrubs all around the grave sight, vowing that, no matter if it took him the rest of his life, he would hunt down those two men.

Morgan could hardly believe that he was so close to finally achieving his main goal in life. For nearly ten long years now, he had waited for this day. When it was all over, he was thinking about going home for a while. He'd managed to save enough money over the years by hunting down outlaws, and was seriously considering a different profession. Maybe he would become a rancher. At the very least, he would take a long vacation. He wasn't sure if he was ready to quit his job just yet, because he took great pleasure in keeping men like Charlie away from law abiding citizens, knowing the world would be a much better place without criminals like him. But Morgan knew he couldn't keep doing this job forever. He'd made quite a few enemies along the way and sooner or later he was bound to come across a young gunslinger who trying to make a name for himself and was just a little faster with a gun; or, more than likely, an enemy would probably shoot him in the back.

When it became too dark to follow the white man's tracks, Morgan decided to make camp for the night and start fresh in the morning . . . .

In the fading light Charlie Bates raced across the prairie toward the line shack at breakneck speed. He'd be safe at the old hideout, least for the time being. The only person who would think of looking for him there was Jess, and he wouldn't tell anybody about his whereabouts, because Jess was too afraid of him to be that stupid.

Meanwhile, he had some serious planning to do. The Martin girl had promised to keep her mouth shut. She would regret not keeping her word. And while he was at it, he would decide what to do about that knife-throwing-freak-of-a-friend of hers . . . .

Chapter Six

Rachel kept pacing the living room floor, occasionally glancing out the window across the field, praying that her husband and Chandler would find Samantha before she did something crazy, like try to physically attack Charlie Bates—or worse. Her daughter would do it too, Rachel knew, and she was afraid of what Charlie Bates might do to Samantha. She still could not believe that he was the man who'd done such an evil thing to poor Sarah. Charlie had been their ranch hand for nearly a year—though true, she hardly knew the man—but to think what he was capable of, and the fact that he'd been around their own daughter. Rachel shuddered to think what could have happened.

"Ma, you're beginning to wear a path in the floor."

Rachel turned to face her son. *If James only knew the truth*, she thought. *And thank God that he didn't.* When Sarah couldn't find Samantha, she had wisely confided in her and John about Charlie; obviously the girl knew her son well.

"Am I?" she said, forcing a reassuring smile.

"I'm sure Pa and Chandler will find Sam. I wonder why she would go into town when she knew that Pa would be furious," he muttered more to himself.

"Did you do your chores, James?"

"Why do I get the feeling that you're trying to get rid of me?"

"Whatever do you mean?"

"For one thing I already told you that I'd finished the chores when I came in."

"Did you?" Rachel said, frowning. She honestly couldn't remember.

"Okay, Ma—what is it you're not telling me?"

Rachel laughed nervously. "I guess I'm just getting a little forgetful in my older age."

"Now I really know something's wrong. You would never admit something like that."

"Like what?"

"That you're getting older."

From the top of the stairway, Sarah sat quietly listening to the conversation between James and his mother. Although she felt ashamed for eavesdropping, she couldn't help herself. She had to know if James knew about Charlie Bates. She didn't think she could face him if he ever found out what that horrible man had done to her. She was relieved to know that apparently John and Rachel hadn't told him.

Rising to her feet, as Sarah turned and started toward her room, a sudden sharp pain ripped through her belly, doubling her over in agony. She bit down on her lower lip to keep from crying out in pain as she slowly inched her way to her room. She managed to close the door behind her, before collapsing onto the floor . . . .

Hearing a horse's soft nicker outside, Rachel hurried to the door and flung it wide open. As she quickly descended the front porch steps, her brows knitted together into a worried frown, when she saw only Chandler and Samantha . . .

"Where's John?" she inquired.

"He should be home shortly." Chandler hoped that Rachel would accept that answer, because he didn't know what else he should tell her. He swung a long leg over his horse's head and dropped lightly to the ground; then he turned to help Samantha dismount.

Rachel hugged her daughter, thrilled to have her home safe and sound. She then stood her away, giving her a stern look. "Samantha Callahan, you should have told your father and I about Sarah. You gave us a real scare."

"I'm sorry, Ma. I guess I wasn't thinking. How is Sarah?"

"What about Sarah?" James asked as he hastened down the porch steps.

Rachel and Samantha exchanged worried glances.

James noticed the look that passed between his mother and sister. Their prolonged silence only added to his suspicions. "Is there something I should know?"

"Why don't we all go inside." Rachel didn't wait for a response, but lifted her skirt and turned to climb the porch steps.

When they were all seated around the kitchen table, James noted the way his sister kept nervously fidgeting in her chair, and his mother wouldn't even look at him. Chandler's expression was unreadable as always. "Will somebody please tell me what's going on? Samantha, why did you ask Ma about Sarah?"

"Why wouldn't I ask about Sarah?"

"You know what I mean."

When his sister remained silent, again James looked at his mother. When she wouldn't say anything either, he impatiently said, "Alright maybe you could answer me this—why didn't Pa come back with Chandler and Samantha?"

"John had some business in town," Chandler answered, before Rachel had a chance to reply. It was obvious the woman did not want to tell her son about Sarah, though personally he felt the young man should know the truth.

"What kind of business in town could my father possibly have?"

"I didn't ask . . . he didn't say."

Becoming even more frustrated, James eyed his sister and mother speculatively. He could tell by the expression on their faces that they were definitely keeping something from him, and he had a feeling it had something to do with Sarah. But as far as he knew Sarah was doing much better since he took her away from Jed's . . .

"Look, James, it's been a long day and I'm sure that Samantha and Chandler are probably hungry and tired," his mother firmly told him.

"Is that your way of saying this discussion is over?"

"Son, you are wise beyond your years."

James rolled his eyes.

Gladly wanting to put this entire day behind her, Samantha immediately stood out of her chair and wordlessly hurried from the room.

There's certainly something odd going on around here, James thought to himself, looking at Chandler and then back at his mother. But neither of them was going to tell him anything. With a sigh, he stood out of his chair and left the room.

Rachel watched her son disappear through the arched doorway, then she turned her eyes on Mr. Wade Chandler, who sat quietly across the table from her, gazing out the big bay window, a troubled expression on his handsome face.

"So—do you know where John went?" she asked.

"He didn't say where he was going, but I'm guessing he rode over to Jed's."

"Whatever for?"

Chandler finally looked at her. "Charlie works for Jed now."

"Oh no." Rachel couldn't believe the audacity Charlie Bates had to actually go to Jed, asking for a job. He must have felt confident that Sarah would never say a word to anyone. Her brows knitted together into a deep frown. She knew what her husband would do to Charlie if he found the man at Jed's. Rachel was seriously contemplating riding over to the Martins' place, when she heard the front door open and then close. She inwardly sighed with relief, recognizing the sound of her husband's boot heels echoing down the hallway toward the kitchen.

"John!" Rachel leaped out of her chair and threw her arms around his neck.

John hugged his wife back and kissed the top of her head. "I haven't been gone *that* long," he said, chuckling. He raised a questioning brow to Chandler, who shrugged and replied, "Your wife got it out of me . . . what can I say."

"I want to know everything that happened, John," Rachel said, backing away from him.

"I presume Samantha's okay?"

"She's in her room."

"If she's smart, she won't come out," he grumbled more to himself.

"You're avoiding the subject, John Callahan."

John sat heavily in a chair, pulling Rachel onto his lap. "There's really not much to tell. I rode over to Jed's, but Charlie wasn't there. I didn't say anything to Jed yet, because I'm afraid of what he might do—though who could blame the man. I think it's best to wait until Charlie's behind bars before we tell Jed. What do you think?"

"I think that's a wise decision," Rachel agreed.

"Do you have any idea where to start looking for this Charlie Bates?" asked Chandler.

John shook his head. "If I did, I wouldn't be sitting here."

"Samantha said she saw Jake playing cards with Charlie," Chandler informed him. "Maybe Jake might have an idea where to start looking."

"Now that you mentioned it—I did see Jake and Ralf on my way home—they were coming from the direction of town. Maybe I'll ride over to Jed's tomorrow and question Jake."

"I'll ride over with ya if you want?" Chandler offered.

John nodded. "Thanks."

"Well, it's getting late . . . guess I'd better get started on supper." When Rachel tried to slide off John's lap, he stopped her. "What are you doing?"

"We can all fend for ourselves tonight, Rachel. You look tired. Why don't you go on upstairs and get some rest."

"Are you sending me to my room?" Rachel asked in a teasing tone.

"As a matter-of-fact, I am." John stood out of his seat with his giggling wife in his arms. "And I won't take no for an answer, woman . . . one way or another, you're going to your room."

"Should I leave for a while?" Chandler's dark brow rose in amusement.

"Certainly not," Rachel nearly gasped from embarrassment. "John, put me down."

"If I'm not right back, then you have your answer," he said to Chandler. Then he turned and strode out of the kitchen with his precious burden in his arms.

When a loud blood-curdling scream rent the air, Rachel's eyes immediately flew open and she sat up straight in bed. Her mind clouded with confusion, she wondered what had awakened her? Had she had a bad dream? Rachel wondered. She looked out the window and saw that the sky along the horizon was just beginning to lighten . . .

it was morning already. John must be up, she thought, staring at the empty side of his bed.

Rachel lay back down on her pillow, closed her eyes. A few moments later an ear-splitting scream erupted outside her bedroom door and Rachel suddenly realized what must have awakened her. She threw back her covers and leaped out of bed and practically flew across the room and swung open the door. Rachel saw Samantha standing just outside Sarah's bedroom doorway, hysterically crying. Alarm bells were going off inside her head as she hurried across the hallway to look over her daughter's shoulder. Her hand flew to her mouth to stifle a scream when she saw Sarah lying on the floor in a pool of blood.

Knowing she needed to pull herself together if she was going to be any good for Sarah, Rachel fought the rising panic that was threatening to destroy all rational thought. "Run and get your father, Samantha!" she hollered at her daughter. When Samantha's feet seemed rooted to the spot, "Hurry!" she shouted at the top of her lungs.

Finally Samantha seemed to snap to her senses and dashed down the stairway.

Rachel knelt beside Sarah to feel for a pulse. Remarkably, the girl was still alive. Tiny as Sarah was, Rachel didn't have a whole lot of trouble lifting and carrying her over to the bed. She immediately checked to see if Sarah was still bleeding. And let out a sigh of relief, when she discovered the worst of the bleeding had stopped.

By then John and James came bursting inside the room. Rachel's worried eyes followed her son as he hurried over to the bed and knelt at Sarah's side. She blinked back tears, watching the way her son ever-so-gently took Sarah's small, pale hand in his and brushed it lovingly against the side of his face.

Rachel's amber-colored eyes met her husband's questioning blue one's. She knew there was a possibility that Sarah might not survive from the loss of blood, but she couldn't bring herself to voice it out loud. She had to believe that because Sarah was young and healthy she stood a good chance. It was just too early yet to tell.

"Jed and Ester should be here," she softly told him.

"I'll ride over there immediately."

After her husband quietly left the room, Rachel stepped over to her son, placed a comforting hand upon his shoulder. "You'll have to wait outside, while I change Sarah's clothes." When James hesitated, "It'll be all right, son," she assured him.

Obediently James rose to his feet. "I can't lose her, Ma," he said in a tremulous voice, before leaving the room.

If only someone had checked on Sarah last night, instead of assuming she'd gone to bed, Rachel thought. But there was nothing they could do about that now. *Or if only this town had a real doctor.* Unfortunately, the only doctor they had was actually a veterinarian. Then Rachel forced all negative thoughts from her mind as she began to unbutton Sarah's dress, her full concentration was on saving the girl's life.

Rachel glanced up momentarily when Samantha entered the room. "Why don't you take Daisy for a long ride today, dear," she suggested, trying to think of a way to get her daughter out of the house. "I'm sure under the circumstances your father won't mind." She finished fastening the last few buttons on Sarah's fresh nightgown, then straightened. "Go on, Samantha . . . there's nothing you can do here."

"Will Sarah live, Ma?" she sniffled.

Rachel looked at her daughter's grief-stricken face, wondering how she should answer. And decided that the truth would probably be wise. "I've done all I can, Samantha. Sarah's life is in God's hands now."

She watched Samantha leave the room looking completely defeated, wishing there had been something more she could say to help ease her daughter's pain.

Inside the barn, Samantha crooned to a jittery Daisy, as she tried again to pull the bridle over the uncooperative mare's head. Normally her horse looked forward to their rides, but, for some strange reason this morning, Daisy was fighting her. Maybe her horse sensed her depressing mood, Samantha thought.

"What's the matter with you, girl?"

"You're not going anywhere without me."

Samantha whirled around, startled by the sound of Chandler's voice. She frowned at him and snapped, "No wonder I was having a problem with my horse. Guess it's true what they say . . . animal's can sense trouble coming."

Chuckling, Chandler walked forward, leading Ranger behind him. "Did you forget that your father gave me strict orders not to let you out of my sight?"

"That was yesterday," Samantha said irritably.

"Sorry . . . until John says otherwise, looks like you're stuck with me." Chandler halted directly in front of her path.

Samantha gave an unladylike snort and sarcastically retorted, "Sending you to guard me . . . isn't that the same as sending a wolf to guard a lamb?"

"Not in your case."

Samantha glared at him.

"Look," he said, "I didn't come here to pick a fight."

"Personally I think fighting is your favorite pastime."

"Could we call a truce?"

"Why should we need to call a truce, if we're not fighting?"

Chandler grinned and winked. "Okay. You got me there."

Ignoring the infuriating man, Samantha turned to mount her horse, when a pair of strong hands grasped her firmly around the waist and then effortlessly lifted her on top of Daisy's saddleless back. She hissed at Chandler, "If I'd wanted your help I would have asked!"

He swung onto the back of his stallion. "You lead the way, Miss Callahan."

"If you don't mind, I'd rather be alone today."

"I'm sorry about Sarah," Chandler said sympathetically. "And I understand why you'd rather be alone, but I'm still coming with you. Look—you won't even notice me. I'll be as quiet as a little church mouse and only speak when spoken to. How's that sound?"

Samantha rolled her eyes as she nudged Daisy forward.

They rode side by side in silence across the grassy meadow, the only sound was the rhythmic clomping of the horses' hooves plodding over the ground. It was a beautiful morning, Samantha thought, though maybe a little on the warm side for mid July. At any rate, she was thoroughly enjoying herself, even in spite of the man riding alongside her, who seemed to have appointed himself as her personal bodyguard. Samantha smiled mischievously to herself. What she needed was a good run. Leaning over Daisy's neck, she clicked her tongue, and the little mare immediately shot forward, leaving Chandler and his stallion quickly behind . . . .

Samantha reached the pond first, sliding gracefully from Daisy's bare back. While she waited for Chandler, she began to walk her horse to cool her down. A short while later, she heard the sound of hoofbeats, looked over her shoulder, grinning. She knew how much it irritated Chandler, the way that Daisy could easily outrun his *muscular steed.*

Samantha tried not to laugh at Chandler's frustrated expression as he jumped to the ground, comical as it was. But when Ranger trotted away with Daisy like a docile puppy, Samantha could no longer hold back and dropped to her knees in peals of laughter.

"I just don't understand it," Chandler bellowed at nobody in particular. Which caused Samantha to laugh all the harder. "It's not *that* funny!"

"If you could only see your face." Samantha rose to her feet. She couldn't resist teasing him. "Look at it this way . . . Ranger could do a lot worse."

"I doubt that."

"You really are prejudice against my horse."

"That ugly mare's not a horse," he grumbled under his breath.

Samantha angrily scowled at Chandler. She wordlessly brushed past him and strode toward the pond, ignoring his shout of apology behind her. Reaching the edge of the pond, she hastily discarded her boots and stockings, rolled up her pant legs, then plopped down upon the flat rock and plunged her feet into the cool water. Already her anger had completely dissipated; who could stay angry surrounded by such beauty.

She turned and smiled at Chandler when he sat down beside her.

"Samantha, I'm sorry for what I said about Daisy."

"It's okay."

"So you forgive me?"

"As long as you promise to never call Daisy ugly again."

"I promise to try. I'm only joking," he said when anger appeared in her bright blue eyes. *She was awfully defensive of that ugly nag.* "This sure is a beautiful place."

"It's normally real quiet, too."

Chandler chuckled. "I can take a hint."

They sat in compatible silence for a while. Samantha stared out across the rippling water, absorbed in thought. Chandler closely studied the woman sitting beside him, noting the smooth, creamy complexion, the stubborn yet delicate chin, the long, slender neck. *And all that thick, gorgeous mane of hair.* How often had he thought about grabbing a huge handful of the silky locks and running it through his fingers.

When Samantha began to unbraid her long plait, Chandler noticed the small piece of leather strip she'd laid beside her. He picked it up and more closely inspected it. Suddenly his heart started to pound against his chest. *It couldn't be!*

"Where did you get this?" he demanded to know.

"What's the matter with you?" Samantha asked, wondering what had gotten into him.

"I need to know where you found this headband, Samantha?"

"Is that what it is?"

"Answer me!"

"I found it at the cabin."

Samantha noticed Chandler's handsome face suddenly paled. He rolled to his feet and began to pace back and forth, the headband clutched tightly in his hand. Her eyes intently upon him, Samantha, too, rose to her feet. She could hear him mumbling something under his breath. She was really becoming concerned, because she'd never seen him act so strangely before.

"Chandler, why is that headband so important?"

"It just can't be," she heard him say. "It's impossible."

"Would you please tell me what it is about that piece of hide that's got you acting like a deranged man who's been out in the desert sun too long?" Samantha snapped in frustration.

Chandler looked at her then with eyes filled with such pain, she wanted to throw her arms around him, but she didn't move. And what he said next could not have shocked her any more if he'd suddenly stripped naked and took off running across the field.

"This headband was my little brother's."

"I heard you didn't have any family?"

He never answered her. Samantha watched him walk over to a nearby tree and then he dropped to the ground as if his legs could no longer support him. Then, he just sat there, holding on to that piece of leather in his hand as if it were made of gold. Samantha had never seen a man look more miserable. Hoping she wasn't intruding on a very private moment, she walked over and knelt beside him, placing a gentle hand on his shoulder.

Chandler didn't even acknowledge her presence.

After a period of silence, Samantha softly asked, "What happened to your brother?" She watched his dark eyes take on a sad, faraway look.

For the longest time, Chandler didn't say anything, and Samantha was beginning to wonder if he might not answer her. Finally he began to speak, telling her about the day he'd taken his little brother hunting, how they'd been on their way back to the village when he sensed something was wrong, so he'd left Little Bear inside a hollow stump where the child would be safe and had gone on to the village alone.

Chandler stopped talking then, took a deep breath and let it out slowly, before continuing on with his story. "When I reached the village, nearly every tepee had been burned to the ground. I can still clearly see the smoldering remains of what had once been a peaceful village. I frantically searched for my father and uncle, but I never found them. I couldn't find anybody. It was as if the entire tribe had somehow disappeared. The only thing that makes any sense, it must have been an enemy tribe and they took my father and uncle and the others captive."

"Oh, Chandler, what a terrible thing . . . ?" Samantha couldn't even begin to imagine what it must've been like to live through such a horrifying experience. Now she knew the reason why Wade Chandler always seemed so sad, even when he smiled.

"What about your brother?" she asked after a period of silence.

"I rode back to the place where I'd left Little Bear inside the stump, but he wasn't there. I searched the entire area and there was no sign of a struggle, so—in answer to your question, I don't know what happened to him.

"Anyway, I've spent the last several years searching for my family and friends. I haven't seen hide nor hair of any of them since that day. And when I last saw Little Bear, he was wearing this headband."

"If you like, Chandler, on our way home, we could stop by the cabin . . . maybe we'll find some other clues there."

For the first time in years, Chandler felt there still might be hope of finding his family. He stared at his brother's headband a while longer, before handing it back to Samantha. "I think this belongs to you."

She shook her head. "No, you should keep it."

"But I want you to have it."

Knowing how much the headband must mean to Chandler, Samantha was deeply touched by the gesture. Gazing into his handsome face, she was thinking that no man had a right to look so beautiful. His eyes alone could take your breath away. And those eyes were now looking back at her, smoldering with some kind of emotion . . . she wasn't sure what . . . desire perhaps? She just didn't have enough experience with men to know.

He was certainly making her nervous, the way he was watching her. Samantha took the headband from his hand, and looked away. "I'll treasure this always."

She was trying to think of something else to say, and blurted out the first thing that came to mind. "Have you been with many women?"

Chandler burst out laughing.

Samantha inwardly groaned, mortified that she had asked him such a personal question, but it had slipped out of her mouth and she couldn't take it back, much as she wanted to. She could feel herself blushing to the roots of her hair. "I didn't mean to ask . . ." she stammered, "what I meant to say is . . . have you ever been married?" There, that sounded so much better.

"I was engaged once."

That piqued Samantha's curiosity enough for her to brave a look at him. He was grinning at her, but she ignored it. "What was her name?" She didn't notice his body stiffen.

"Morning Star."

"So—why didn't you get married?"

"Because she ran off with a white man!"

Samantha thought Chandler must be jealous—why else would he sound so angry? And why should it bother her if he was still in love with some Indian girl . . .

"She was gone when I came back from a long hunting trip," he went on to explain. "I heard she ran off with a white man who came upon our village by accident. I assume Morning Star married the man. It didn't really surprise me though—her running off with some white-eyes," he said bitterly. "Morning Star had always wanted to live in the white man's world . . . I guess she got her wish."

"I'm sorry, Chandler, I shouldn't have pried."

"You didn't." He rose to his feet. "We probably should be going."

Chandler and Samantha stopped by the cabin, but, after a thorough search of the place, they couldn't find anything that would prove Little Bear had been there, and Chandler was left pondering how his little brother's headband could have turned up at some white man's house so far away from the village. It certainly was a mystery. After all these years, could it be possible that Little Bear was still alive somewhere? Or was his headband proof that he was . . . *no,* he wouldn't even think that way.

As they headed toward the ranch, Chandler turned to look at the woman riding alongside him. Whether he liked it or not, Samantha was quickly becoming an important part of his life. Even though he hadn't known her very long, he knew that his life would never be the same without her. Things would definitely be a lot less complicated though if he were to leave the Callahan ranch and find employment elsewhere, Chandler rationalized with a bit of sarcasm, considering the fact that ever since he'd known Miss Callahan, he'd somehow been involved in one catastrophe after another. Yet, now, after discovering his brother's headband, he believed that God had led him to this town . . . .

Samantha watched Chandler surreptitiously. He certainly seemed to be deep in thought. And she couldn't help wondering if he was thinking about Morning Star. Was Chandler still in love with the Indian maiden? She tried not to feel jealous over some female she'd never even seen before, but she couldn't seem to help herself. She tried to picture Morning Star in her mind, and ultimately came to the conclusion that, by now, the woman was probably just an ugly toothless old hag. She laughed out loud at her mental drawing.

"What's so funny?" Chandler asked, raising a curious brow.

"Nothing," Samantha hastily replied. Then before he could question her further she asked, "Would you tell me more about your family?"

"What would you like to know?"

"Well—what were your parents like?"

"My father was the chief of our village," Chandler proudly informed her. "His name was Running Elk . . . he was a great chief . . . our people highly respected him. He was a big man like your father, Samantha. In fact, John reminds me of my father in many ways. My mother's name was Singing Wind. She died shortly after giving birth to my brother. It's sad that Little Bear never even knew her. My mother was a very beautiful woman . . . very soft-spoken . . . always smiling. And she always thought of others before herself. Even the men in our tribe respected my mother."

Looking at Chandler and knowing him the way she did, Samantha decided that Chief Running Elk and his wife Singing Wind must have been exceptional people to produce such a son. She happened to think . . .

"What's your Indian name?"

"Graywolf."

Samantha grinned. "The name definitely suits you—far better than Wade Chandler."

"Finally something we can agree on," Chandler said, chuckling. "When I decided to join the white world, I had to take a white man's name . . . and . . . well . . . Wade Chandler was the first name that popped into my head."

As they rode in compatible silence, Samantha could very easily picture Chandler as a young and fiercely painted warrior, galloping his stallion across the prairie, and wondered if he'd ever taken part in raiding a farm or a ranch. And that was something she would never ask him, afraid of what the answer might be.

"What are you thinking over there?" he asked.

"Nothing."

The strange way Chandler was looking at her, Samantha wondered if the man could actually read her mind. She certainly hoped not. She tried to hide her embarrassment by saying, "We're almost home . . . care to race the rest of the way?"

"Ranger nearly kills himself whenever he tries to keep up with that scraggly mare of yours."

"What if I gave you a head start?" she offered in a teasing tone.

"Against that bullet of yours, I doubt it would matter much. Besides, I could never win a race that way . . . Ranger has his pride."

"Then I'll see you at home." Samantha clicked her tongue and Daisy shot forward.

Chandler grumbled under his breath, when Ranger began to prance in place and shaking his head, wanting to run after his four-legged mate. Figuring why fight it, he let out a loud war whoop and leaned forward, giving his stallion his head. Suddenly Ranger reared up on his powerful hind legs and took off at a full gallop . . . .

Samantha skidded to a halt in front of the barn, slid gracefully to the ground. She looked back and grinned when she saw that Chandler was still quite a distance behind her. She led Daisy through the wide doorway and, after hastily removing the bridle, she grabbed the brush and began to run it over the mare's slightly lathered coat. She crooned, "There will never be a stallion that'll ever catch ya . . . isn't that right, Daisy girl?"

When Samantha heard Chandler enter the barn on his stallion, she couldn't help gloat. "What took you so long? Why that horse of yours looks plum tuckered out," she drawled. "Maybe you should consider putting him out to pasture."

"Ranger still gets me where I'm going," Chandler irritably replied, dropping to the ground.

"Eventually," Samantha added, giggling.

"Anybody ever tell you that it's not polite to insult a man's horse? Besides, that's no way to talk about the sire of Daisy's future foal."

"What are you talking about?" Samantha had stopped brushing her horse and was now looking directly at him.

Pushing his Stetson back, Chandler grinned at Samantha's shocked expression. He took sheer delight in announcing, "It appears, Miss Callahan, that your mare feels the same way about Ranger as he feels about her. Now—if my calculations are correct, I would say that we can expect the 'bundle of joy' early next spring."

At her stunned silence, he further crowed, "Your horse may be faster, but my stallion's much better looking, so let's just hope the colt takes after Ranger here."

"That's not funny!"

Chandler threw back his head and laughed.

Soon as the horses were cared for, Samantha hurried toward the house with Chandler. She could hardly wait to find out how Sarah was doing and had insisted Chandler come along with her, needing him for support. As they entered the house, Samantha immediately recognized Ester Martin's voice, talking with her mother. Anxious to inquire of her friend, she followed the muffled voices toward the kitchen, unaware of Chandler's sudden somber mood beside her.

When they stepped inside the spacious room, Samantha saw her mother was seated at the table with Ester, and the way she looked at her and smiled, assured Samantha that Sarah was okay. Then her mother's words confirmed what she already knew. "I'm glad you're home, Samantha . . . Sarah's doing much better. Oh, Chandler, I would like you to meet Sarah's mother, Ester Martin. Ester, this is Chandler, the new hired hand I was telling you about."

Twisting in her chair, Ester stifled a gasp of shocked disbelief, when she got a look at the man whom Rachel had spoken so highly of. She quickly turned back around and accidentally knocked over her empty coffee cup, sending it crashing to the floor. She instantly shot out of her chair and began to pick up the broken pieces with trembling fingers.

"Don't worry, Ester, it's only a cup," Rachel said.

"Forgive me for being so clumsy."

Samantha looked curiously at her mother, who only shrugged in reply.

Rachel, too, was wondering what was wrong with Ester. She watched the woman set the broken pieces of glass on top of the table, then she sat back in her seat, looking like she would spring out of her chair any moment.

"Are you all right, Ester?" Rachel asked. "Would you like another cup of coffee?"

"No!" She jumped to her feet. "I . . . I really should be getting home," she nervously stammered. "I . . . it's been a trying day . . . I'm sure you understand."

"Ester, isn't it?" Chandler held out his hand, peering into large, doe-like eyes that were as dark as his own. Reluctantly she placed her small, delicate hand in his and he squeezed it gently. Her hands looked like they had never seen a day of hard work.

"It was a pleasure to meet you, Mr. Chandler." Ester lowered her eyes, unable to meet his intense gaze. She pulled her hand back when he didn't let go. *How was it possible that Graywolf was here? Would he reveal her secret?*

Samantha watched Chandler leave the room through the back door without uttering a word to anyone else. Completely bewildered by Chandler's odd, almost rude behavior toward Ester, she looked at her mother and shrugged, not knowing what to say. Then she looked at Ester, frowning. The woman still seemed about as jumpity as a newborn colt. She found Ester's behavior about as odd as Chandler's.

"I'll walk you to the door," she heard her mother say.

"Please don't trouble yourself, I know my way out." As Ester crossed the room, she said over her shoulder, "Rachel, please tell Sarah I'll see her tomorrow."

After hearing the front door close, Rachel turned to Samantha, a quizzical expression on her face. "What do you suppose that was all about?"

"I have no idea."

"I've never seen Ester act so . . . like a frightened young filly around a man that way before. Not that I've been around Ester enough to know how she normally reacts around men," Rachel muttered more to herself. "But—normally she's quite friendly and rather talkative."

Chandler stood by the corral, watching John and the other men branding calves, only halfheartedly listening to the conversation. He still couldn't get over the fact that Ester Martin was Morning Star. And she was married to that Indian-hating white man Jed Martin. *How could she have allowed herself to get entangled with such a man?* he angrily wondered.

How long had it been since he'd last seen her? Chandler quickly calculated in his head: almost twenty years. Well—the years certainly had not marred her youthful beauty none. Obviously Morning Star must have led an easy life all these years. *The kind of life she always wanted*, Chandler thought bitterly. And it had been plainly evident in *Ester's* eyes that she didn't want her true identity known. She had managed to relay that much to him without uttering a word.

Suddenly another chilling thought occurred to Chandler: Jake and Sarah were Morning Star's children. He could see a lot of similarities where the boy was concerned—in both looks and actions—but who would ever guess that blond-haired and blue-eyed Sarah Martin was Morning Star's daughter; there was absolutely no resemblance between them. And Sarah was nothing like Morning Star. Unless the woman had changed, but Chandler had his doubts. He remembered the young Morning Star well; she had been selfish and conceited and a user of any man who would give her what she wanted. Her personality had been so different from the other Indian maidens; which was the reason why she'd never had many friends.

No wonder Jake was the way he was, Chandler mused. The kid was still wet enough behind the ears that you would have to lay him out in the sun all day to dry them off. With a father like Jed and a mother like Morning Star, poor Jake never stood a chance. Chandler could only assume that Sarah must have spent a lot of time around Rachel to turn out the way she did.

And to think he'd almost married the woman. Chandler then wondered why Jed had married Morning Star if he hated Indians so much. Even dressed as a white woman, Morning Star still looked full-blooded Indian. Which meant that their children were Indian, too; though Sarah looked like she didn't have a drop of Indian blood in her.

Chandler let out a frustrated sigh. Why should any of this matter to him now? That flame had gone out a long time ago—hadn't it? With his mind in absolute turmoil, Chandler wanted to get drunk . . . very drunk. Twirling on his moccasined heel, he headed for his horse.

Chapter Seven

Thick, black clouds finally gave way and released heavy drops of rain over the severely parched land, and the deprived ground greedily drank its fill. Soaked clear through her clothes from the unexpected rainstorm, Samantha rode steadily toward Bear Creek, becoming more and more angry with every passing mile. After Chandler's strange encounter with Ester, curiosity getting the best of her, she had gone to look for Chandler to question him, only to discover that he'd taken off on his horse. Having a pretty good idea where to start looking for the *big oaf,* Samantha spurred Daisy to a faster pace. *So help her if she found him at that hurdy-gurdy house*, she inwardly fumed. Though why should it bother her what Chandler did and with whom he did it. They hadn't even known each other very long . . . were hardly considered friends. She knew her jealousy was completely unwarranted.

But tell that to her heart.

Samantha kept telling herself that it was a huge mistake chasing after Chandler like some jealous wife, not counting the fact that she was already in trouble for disobeying her father again by leaving the ranch without his permission. She was seriously thinking about turning around and heading back home, but then her imagination began to plague her with images that involved Chandler with one of those scantily dressed females.

Samantha was so absorbed in thought that she didn't notice the lone man astride his horse upon the hill, watching her every move . . .

Jake was relieved that Samantha was alone, because it would save him an unwelcome visit to her father's ranch. Nudging his horse down the slight incline, he stayed a fair distance behind Samantha, marveling at the sight of her glorious hair cascading down her back. He'd always been so fascinated with her hair.

Figuring that Samantha had had plenty of time to come to her senses, Jake planned on asking her to be his wife. But even if she refused, it would not matter. Because, one way or another, he would have her . . . .

Morgan sat alone at a small corner table, nursing a bottle of whiskey, while he closely monitored the swinging doors. Since early that morning, he'd been tracking Charlie and had been rapidly gaining on the man, until the rainstorm washed away all his tracks. So he'd had no choice but to head back to town, figuring, sooner or later, either Charlie or the other man (he didn't know his name) would return to the brothel. Morgan was confident that if he could capture one man, then he would get the other; there were various ways of getting information from those who were not so willing to cooperate. And he had a gut feeling the two men were somewhere close by, he just needed to be more patient. He just wished they would hurry and show their faces, because he wanted to get this ordeal over with. He'd finally decided to go home and was anxious to see the old place.

Morgan's gaze began to wander around the room. Most of the men here this evening were already drunk, and some of them were casting hateful glances in his direction. Would these white men ever leave him alone? Casually folding his hands behind his head, Morgan leaned back in his chair, purposely exposing his gun. Usually that's all it took to change a man's mind about hassling him. And it appeared that these men were no different. They seemed to ignore him after that.

His eyes moved to the double doors. He wondered if the woman with the long, chestnut-colored hair (whose beautiful face he couldn't seem to get out of his mind) would venture in again tonight. He wanted to question her about the white man Charlie. The outlaw must have done something pretty awful to make the woman want to embed a knife in his heart.

When Morgan saw the next man who slipped through the batwing doors and headed toward the bar, he nearly fell out of his chair from shock. Except a little more lined with aged, the man's face was nearly identical to his own. *Graywolf! But this was impossible! His brother had been killed many years ago!*

Turbulent thoughts suddenly thundered through Morgan's brain like: *how?* and *why? Why did you leave me and never return, if you were still alive?* There was no doubt that the man standing at the bar had to be his older brother.

And he was now looking in Morgan's direction.

Casually pulling his hat lower to conceal his face, Morgan hoped Graywolf wouldn't notice him. He needed time to think, because he wasn't sure what he wanted to do. A terrible battle was raging inside him: while a part of Morgan wanted to run over and grab hold of his big brother and hug him with all his might, there was another part that felt like marching over there and knocking him to the floor.

Standing out of his chair, Morgan hastened toward the batwing doors, keeping his face hidden from view. This newest dilemma was definitely going to complicate matters . . . .

Samantha didn't hear the man approaching on his horse, until she heard a familiar voice say beside her, "Where are you headin'."

Her head twisted toward Jake. "None of your business!"

"Mind if I ride along with you?"

"Could I stop you," Samantha sarcastically replied.

Jake hadn't expected her to still be angry with him, but that wasn't about to stop him from doing what he came to do. "Would you slow down a bit, Samantha, there's something I wanna talk to you about."

"What is it, Jake?" She kept her horse at a fast trot.

"This is not the way I pictured our engagement," he grumbled under his breath.

Pulling back on the reins, Samantha now looked at Jake, confusion knitting her brow, certain she must have misunderstood. "What did you say?"

"I'm asking you to marry me?"

When Samantha finally found her tongue, she angrily snapped at him. "Have you lost your mind, Jake Martin?"

"Then your answer's no?"

"Have you lost your ears as well?"

"It's because of that Indian, isn't it?" Jake furiously spat.

"Chandler has nothing to do with my answer . . . it would still be the same . . . *no*," she firmly told him. "Now if you'll excuse me I . . ."

"Not so fast, Samantha." Jake's gun appeared in his hand. "I'm sorry, but you gave me no other choice. I didn't want it to be this way, but that Indian's confused your mind."

"I don't think it's *my mind* that's confused, Jake Martin."

"I'm not confused!" he hissed. "I know exactly what I'm doing!"

Samantha still didn't believe that Jake was actually serious. "Put that gun away and we'll forget this whole thing ever happened."

"It's too late for that now." Jake motioned with his gun. "I'm taking you to the cabin . . . maybe you'll change your mind, so get movin'."

"You would honestly shoot me if I refused to go with you?" Samantha said incredulously.

"Probably not." Jake then turned his weapon on her horse. "But I would have no problem shooting that nag of yours."

Peering into those dark brown eyes, a sudden cold chill ran down Samantha's spine. She'd known that Jake was troubled, but this? She felt so strange . . . it was hard to explain . . . like she was truly seeing the real Jake Martin for the first time. Because this stone-faced man now before her *was not* her childhood friend: this Jake even *looked* different. A rather handsome man—though not nearly as handsome as Chandler—Jake had always taken pride in his appearance. But today, he almost looked ill. His stubbly chin which had several days' growth of beard made him look haggard; his shaggy brown hair looked like he hadn't washed it in days. His clothes were dirty, too.

He motioned with his gun again, telling her to get moving, but Samantha refused to budge.

Unfortunately, in her haste to find Chandler, she'd forgotten to take her knife and wasn't wearing a gun either. But even if she had a weapon, Samantha didn't think she could actually use it on Jake. Ultimately she would have to go with him—unless she could maybe outsmart him. "It won't take long before somebody realizes I'm gone and my father will have every one of his hands out looking for me."

"But they won't know *where* to look," Jake confidently retorted. "You and I are the only ones who know about the cabin."

Samantha was just about to inform him that Chandler also knew about the cabin, but wisely kept her mouth shut, knowing that if she divulged that bit of information, there was a good chance that Jake would take her someplace else. Unless Jake came to his senses, her only hope was that Chandler would think of looking for her there. "I don't understand what you think you'll accomplish by holding me against my will?"

"If I get you away from that Indian, you might change your mind about marrying me."

"I already told you that Chandler had nothing to do with my answer."

"You promised to marry me, Samantha, and I have every intention of holding you to that promise! Now get movin'!"

Jake's eyes glittered with such fury, for the first time Samantha was afraid of him. Even so, she reminded him in a calm tone of voice, "We were only children then."

"You never should have lied to me, Samantha!"

"I never lied to you!"

Jake pulled back on the trigger. "If you don't get moving, I'm gonna put that nag of yours out of its misery. I mean it, Samantha!"

Tears flooded Samantha's eyes as she nudged Daisy forward. She thought about trying to outrun Jake; Daisy might be fast, but she couldn't outrun a bullet . . . .

Chandler frowned at the buxom, blond-haired woman, sitting across the table from him, who was batting her long lashes and moistening her bright red lips with her tongue. She was definitely attractive enough and he was certainly drunk enough, so what was stopping him from taking what she was so blatantly offering? And he instantly knew the answer: because this woman's hair wasn't a golden chestnut brown; nor were her eyes a brilliant shade of blue like a summer sky; and she didn't have that certain smile.

Chandler shook his head, grumbling under his breath, "She's ruined me."

"I beg your pardon?"

"Nothing."

Twila smiled seductively at the handsome Indian. He was finally losing the battle, she thought triumphantly. And it was about time, too. She'd been giving this man hints most of the evening; usually, it didn't take so long. She was beginning to think she might be losing her touch.

Chandler could tell by the way the woman was looking at him that she was getting the wrong signals. The sooner he got out of this place, the better. He quickly finished his beer, then scooted out of his chair. When she started to get to her feet, he placed a firm hand on her shoulder. "Sorry, honey . . . maybe next time."

Chandler could feel the woman's angry eyes on his back as he crossed the room. He pushed through the swinging doors and nearly collided with John. From the expression on the man's face, he immediately knew something was wrong.

"Have you seen Samantha?"

His heart began to pound with dread. "No, I haven't . . . why?"

"She's missing. I picked up her tracks just outside of town. I thought maybe she came here looking for you."

A thought suddenly occurred to Chandler. "Just out of mild curiosity . . . have you seen or heard from Jake today?"

"No . . . why?"

"It's just a hunch." Chandler was already mounting his horse. "Before it gets too dark, hurry and show me where you found Samantha's tracks."

Morgan found a secluded spot along the river to make camp for the night. He couldn't bring himself to go home to his parents' cabin just yet. He wasn't ready to face any more of his past ghosts; Graywolf was enough for one day.

After a quick supper of canned beans, Morgan lay upon his sleeping mat, gazing up into the starry night sky. Already he was having second thoughts about returning to the cabin; though he would at least pay his parents his respect. Then afterward, maybe he would leave town . . . permanently. No—he didn't really mean that. He was still probably suffering from the shock of seeing his brother.

Rolling over on his side, Morgan quietly stared into the flickering flames. He closed his eyes, trying to remember the last time he'd seen Graywolf.

It had been a warm sunny day . . . they had gone hunting and had been tracking a deer. He could see in his mind, himself and Graywolf, crouched behind some bushes and observing the animal, while it grazed in a nearby meadow. To a small boy like Morgan, it had seemed like hours that they'd been there, watching the deer. He was becoming more and more impatient, wanting to prove to his older brother that he was now big enough to participate in the hunt. He'd been practicing with the bow and arrows their father had given him.

"When can I shoot a deer, Graywolf?" he whispered.

"When your arms are strong enough to pull back the bow. Now be silent, Little Bear, before you scare away our evening meal."

Little Bear was frustrated that he wasn't going to get that chance to prove his skills today, but he didn't argue. He sat there, quietly, watching his older brother. He admired Graywolf and hoped to be just like him someday. He nearly held his breath in anticipation, as he watched his big brother carefully raise his bow in the air, pulling back the arrow. Then, several tense moments later, Graywolf released the arrow and accurately hit his mark.

Little Bear beamed with pride at how easily his older brother swung the heavy deer over his horse's withers. He vowed when he reached manhood that he would be strong and cunning like his big brother. Proudly he trudged behind Graywolf through the dense forest, carrying his long bow and quiver of arrows. He even tried to walk in Graywolf's footsteps, but his legs were still too short.

Suddenly Graywolf stopped and gave him the signal for silence.

"Something is wrong," Little Bear heard him whisper.

As he stood there beside his big brother, he was not afraid, because there wasn't another warrior in the entire tribe that was more cunning and powerful. When Graywolf started walking again, this time he had to practically run to keep up with his older brother's much longer and quicker strides as they hurried along the narrow path.

Little Bear did become a little frightened when Graywolf hid him inside a hollow tree stump and told him not to make a sound, but he did not utter a word of complaint, because he wanted Graywolf to be proud of him.

The last words his big brother had said to him were, "Do not move from this spot until I return," then he disappeared into the forest.

To a little boy it had been a terrifying experience waiting inside that hollow stump all alone. And it had seemed like an eternity before Little Bear finally heard footsteps coming. Naturally assuming that his brother had returned for him, he jumped out of his hiding place only to discover, too late, his huge mistake, for he was staring into the bearded face of the biggest mountain man he'd ever seen.

Little Bear turned and raced through the forest as fast as his chubby legs would carry him, but the big mountain man easily overtook him. He'd fought with all his strength as the man carried him away, screaming his brother's name.

But Graywolf never came . . .

Morgan had finally put that part of his life in the past. He'd accepted the fact long ago that Graywolf must have been killed and that was the reason he never came back for him. And now to discover that, after all these years, his older brother was very much alive, was an absolute shock to say the least. He honestly didn't know what to think . . . whether or not he should even bother to confront Graywolf. Besides, what did it really matter now? He wasn't that same frightened little boy anymore . . . .

Her hands and feet bound tightly to the chair, Samantha looked out the only window of the cabin. It was completely dark now. Her parents would be frantic with worry when she didn't come home tonight. She inwardly scolded herself—*you idiot—if only you hadn't gone looking for Chandler, you wouldn't be in this predicament.*

Samantha had finally given up trying to free herself. Her wrists now chafed and bleeding, hurt something awful. She was hungry, too, but she would starve before she'd ask Jake for a morsel of food; and she wasn't sure she would take any food even if he offered her some. Samantha turned her head, glaring at Jake. He hadn't moved from the little table in the far corner of the room since they'd arrived at the cabin. The way he just sat there in the chair, watching her, was beginning to give her the willies.

She'd taken just about all she could; her temper was close to exploding. "This has gone far enough, Jake . . . untie me this instant!"

He just kept staring at her; he didn't even blink.

"Did you hear what I said?"

No response.

"Jake Martin, I swear if you don't untie me . . ."

"Be quiet, Samantha, or I'll . . ."

"What? You'll gag me next?"

"Don't give me any ideas," he grumbled under his breath. "Now leave me alone . . . I'm trying to think."

"Is that what you're doing over there?" she sarcastically retorted.

"I mean it, Samantha. If you don't keep quiet . . ."

"So what are you thinking about?" Maybe if she could get Jake into a conversation, she could eventually talk some sense into him.

"I'm thinking about our future."

So much for trying to reason with him. "We don't have a future, you *blockhead.* Can't you get that through your thick skull?"

Suddenly lunging out of his chair, Jake pulled a bandanna from his pocket as he strode across the room. "Open that big mouth, Samantha!" he angrily snarled.

When she refused, he slapped her.

Ignoring the stinging pain in her jaw, Samantha furiously shouted, "Untie me and I'll gladly show you where you can stuff that rag!"

Jake's face turned red with rage. "So help me, Samantha, if you don't open your mouth, I'll hit it hard enough to swell it shut!"

"Very well," she calmly replied.

When Jake tried to thrust the hanky inside her open mouth, she suddenly clamped down hard on his fingers with her sharp teeth. "Let go of me!" he roared like a wounded lion.

With his fingers locked inside Samantha's mouth, Jake couldn't understand a word of her ramblings, but her glittering blue eyes spoke loud and clear. And as their struggle of willpowers wore on, his whole hand began to throb with pain. He warned her in a threatening tone, "Let go of my fingers, Samantha."

When she still refused to let go, Jake hauled off and punched her. She immediately released his fingers. "Why did you make me do that!" he thundered in fury.

Samantha did not reply.

Jake wrapped the bandanna around his bleeding fingers. Then he stood there, staring at Samantha. She was obviously out cold. Dang it! He hadn't meant to hit her so hard. Gently he touched the side of her face with the back of his fingers. Already her cheek was bruised and swollen where he'd just struck her. *Why did you force me to hurt you?* Jake inwardly shouted, now more angry at himself.

When his eyes caught sight of Samantha's honey-colored hair, Jake couldn't resist touching it. He'd always been enchanted by the unusually long mane. It spilled over the back of the chair in silky waves, touching the floor. Grabbing a fistful of the lustrous locks, he rubbed it against the side of his cheek, thinking it smelled like wildflowers.

With a wistful sigh, Jake bent over and tenderly kissed Samantha's bruised cheek, wishing she would love him the way that he'd always loved her . . . .

When Samantha did not come home all night, the entire Callahan ranch was up before the crack of dawn. John split his men into several small groups, wanting to cover as much of his spread as possible. After sending James into town to find out whatever he could, John decided he would personally ride over to Jed's and personally question Jake, while Chandler rode out to the pond. Rachel would stay home in case Samantha returned. And everybody agreed to meet back at the ranch later that afternoon . . .

Racing across the grassy prairie on his stallion, Chandler wished he would have followed his gut feelings and started searching for Samantha last night. After he and John had gone back to the area where John had spotted Daisy's tracks—only to discover that the rainstorm had washed them all away—his instincts had told him then that Samantha was in trouble—now there wasn't the slightest doubt in his mind, because he knew Samantha would never deliberately put her parents through a night like they had, unless something was seriously wrong.

Suddenly remembering the old abandoned shack, some inner voice told Chandler to look there. If Jake had Samantha like he suspected, the cabin seemed to be a logical place where he might take her. It was certainly worth a try.

Chandler changed direction and spurred Ranger faster. He started thinking, if Samantha was with Jake, could she have gone with him willingly? He didn't know her really well, but he felt he knew her well enough to know she wouldn't just run off with Jake that way. Besides, he sensed that Samantha's feelings for the Martin boy was only on a friendship basis. If Samantha was with Jake, Chandler was certain it was against her will. Anger began to build inside him as he thought about what he would do to Jake Martin if he harmed Samantha in any way.

A short distance from the cabin, Chandler slid to the ground. While tethering Ranger to a nearby tree, the stallion began to prance in place and shake his head. "What's the matter with you, boy?" No more had he said the words when Daisy suddenly appeared out of the forest. Now he knew that Samantha was here for sure.

After hastily securing both horses, Chandler moved stealthily through the thick brush, following a narrow path. When the little cabin came into view, he instantly recognized Jake's horse hobbled outside the door. Dropping to the ground, he crawled over to the window where he could look inside.

When Chandler saw Samantha bound to a chair, furious rage like he'd never felt before immediately surged through his veins. It was all he could do to stop himself from rushing through the door and grabbing Jake Martin and beating him to a pulp. He noticed something else: Samantha's head was hanging at an odd angle, and her eyes were closed. She was either sleeping or unconscious, Chandler couldn't tell for certain which. His eyes narrowed into smoldering slits when he found Jake. The kid was seated at a little table in the corner of the room, watching Samantha with the strangest expression on his face.

Staying close to the side of the building, Chandler skulked toward the front door. When he reached for his gun, he inwardly berated himself for being so careless as to go off and forget his weapon. He just couldn't seem to concentrate lately. And the reason for his absentmindedness was trapped inside a shack with some lunatic.

It appeared that Jake was more disturbed than Chandler had first thought, and he wondered if the kid was crazy enough to actually shoot him. Well—he was about to find out. But if Jake was going to shoot somebody, he would rather it be himself than Samantha.

As Chandler now stood in front of the door, he thought about knocking, but figured Jake couldn't be that stupid. The kid might be a little on the crazy side, but that didn't mean he was dumb. Though if it were only that simple, it would sure make his job a whole lot easier. Unfortunately, he couldn't take that kind of a risk. Taking a step back, Chandler lunged at the door. He hit it so hard that it broke completely off its frame and landed on the floor with a loud bang, bringing Chandler down with it.

Jake jumped to his feet and drew his gun, pointing it at the unexpected intruder. When he saw who it was, a sardonic sneer lifted the corners of his mouth. "Well, well, if it isn't the Indian. Don't even blink an eyelash."

After a long restless night, it was nearly noon before Morgan started to break camp, having taken all morning to finally reach a decision. He would go home for now, until he could figure out what to do about Graywolf. The two men he'd been tracking would just have to wait. He realized that those men had become an obsession. And where had it gotten him? He was only in his mid-twenties and already felt like an old man.

As Morgan mounted his horse and headed toward home, there were still so many thoughts swirling through his troubled mind. He knew that finding his brother was about to change his life dramatically, hopefully for the better . . .

But as Morgan approached the cabin, once again doubts about Graywolf began to surface in his mind. He was thinking about turning around and heading back to Bear Creek when he spotted the sorriest sight for a horse he'd ever seen. It was tethered to a tree alongside a rather nice-looking buckskin stallion. The grayish colored mare really looked more like a mule with a back so swayed it actually sloped in the middle.

"You have my sympathy, old man," he said with a chuckle to the buckskin.

Dismounting, Morgan tied his stallion to a low-hanging limb, wondering about the other horses' owners. Was it was possible somebody was now living in his cabin? After all, he hadn't been home in years. Meandering his way through the woods, he automatically took mental note of his surroundings, accustomed to living every day peering over his shoulder. He stopped near the grave sight where he'd buried his parents, which was now completely overgrown with shrubs. He noticed the saplings his father had planted years ago were now huge trees. Other than that, the place looked exactly the same.

Still, Morgan couldn't seem to shake this feeling that something was wrong. Cautiously, he circled around the small building, slowly making his way toward the front.

The first thing Morgan noticed was the door was missing. He could hear raised voices inside . . . though he couldn't understand what they were arguing about. He moved closer to the door, until he was able to clearly hear what they were saying . . .

"You pull that trigger, Martin, you'd better make the first shot count, because I guarantee you won't get another."

"There's no possible way I could miss from this distance."

"Then what are you waiting for . . . shoot."

Moving closer to the door, when Morgan peeked inside the cabin, his eyes widened in stunned disbelief. He saw his brother lying on the floor and there was some crazy kid waving a gun in his face. He also noticed the very woman who'd been haunting his dreams at night was bound to a chair. She appeared to be unconscious.

As alarm bells went off inside Morgan's head, he could feel the icy fingers of fear grip him around the heart. *He couldn't lose his brother now, not when he'd just found him!*

Drawing his weapon, he suddenly burst into the room. "Put down the gun, boy!"

Jake's face paled at the sight of the tall Indian who just barged inside the cabin. *He must be seeing double!* He was so shocked by the man's resemblance to the one lying on the floor that his gun slipped through his fingers.

Morgan pushed the kid aside and snatched his weapon off the floor, shoving it safely inside the waistband of his pants. Now that the crazy kid was unarmed, he looked at his brother, who was staring back at him, obviously just as stunned.

"Are you going to get off the floor?"

Chandler could not believe what he was seeing: *It was like looking at himself in a mirror. Little Bear had been but a small boy the last time he'd seen him. Now here he was a man full grown!*

The corner of Morgan's mouth lifted into a lopsided grin. "Well, well, big brother, it's been a while."

"Is it really you?" Chandler slowly got to his feet. He was having some difficulty accepting the fact that his little brother was now a grown man.

"You look like you've seen a ghost," Morgan said. "Are you all right?"

Chandler couldn't find the words to express what he was feeling. And there was such a hard lump in his throat that he didn't think he could speak if he tried. Moisture gathered behind his eyes as he continued to stare into the beloved face of his younger brother, noting the dramatic changes since he'd last seen Little Bear.

By now Samantha had regained consciousness. She kept blinking her eyes, thinking they must be playing tricks on her, that she was seeing two Chandlers. Then she remembered the man at the hurdy-gurdy house who'd grabbed the knife from her hand . . . he had looked enough like Chandler to be his twin brother . . . . so she hadn't been seeing things after all. This man must be the brother that Chandler had told her about.

Samantha was happy for Chandler—honestly she was—but the constant throbbing in her head was causing her to become a little impatient. She tried to keep the irritation out of the tone of her voice when she asked, "Could somebody please untie me?"

Chandler was instantly at her side, then his long fingers were fumbling with the rope behind her back. When he had Samantha freed of her restraints and saw how badly chafed her wrists were, he grabbed Jake by the front of the shirt, slamming him against the wall. "I oughtta beat you to a pulp for pulling such a stunt!" he snarled in a furious rage. "And if I did, it would be less than you deserve!"

"Chandler, no!" Samantha shouted. "My wrists look worse than they actually are . . . they don't even hurt!" That wasn't true, but she had to do something, because Chandler looked angry enough to carry out his threat and then some.

Chandler immediately let go of Jake. Then taking the same rope that was used on Samantha, he ordered Jake to turn around, and he lashed Jake's hands behind his back. "I wouldn't try anything if I were you . . . you've already worn out my patience!"

Samantha couldn't help but feel sympathy for Jake, though she doubted Chandler would understand. And her heart went out to Jake, because she was certain he felt guilty for what he'd done; he wouldn't even look at her.

Now that Jake was secured, Chandler turned to Samantha. "Do you want me to take a look at those wrists?"

She shook her head. "I'm fine."

"I guess I should introduce you to my brother." Chandler proudly announced, "Samantha, this is Little Bear . . . the brother I told you about."

"I sort of outgrew the name Little Bear," Morgan said with a wink.

Samantha grinned.

"You can call me Morgan," he told her. Then to his brother, he said, "I'll explain that later. We both have a lot to talk about."

Chandler grabbed hold of his younger brother, lifting him off his feet and giving him a huge bear hug, before setting him back down.

Jake chose that moment to make a run for his freedom.

"Let him go!" Samantha shouted at Chandler when he started to chase after him.

He stopped and whirled around so fast that Samantha collided with his chest. He reached out to steady her. "Don't tell me you're going to let Jake get away with what he did to you?"

"Please, Chandler, you don't understand . . ."

"No, I don't understand!"

"Jake's my friend," Samantha argued.

"Have you ever heard the saying, with friends like that you don't need enemies?"

"It's probably none of my business," Morgan calmly intervened, "but it's no use arguing about it now . . . the kid's already long gone."

"Jake was spoiling our little family reunion anyway," Chandler grumbled under his breath. He was not very pleased with Samantha at the moment. He was more angry at himself though, for not grabbing Jake when he had the chance, but he could always track the kid later.

"How 'bout I make us all some coffee," Morgan suggested.

Something suddenly occurred to Samantha. "This wouldn't happen to be your cabin, would it?"

"I guess you could say that." Morgan lit the wood inside the stove. "This place was actually my parents cabin . . . now it's mine."

"Your parents?" Chandler asked, confused.

"My adoptive parents."

Morgan grabbed the blue-speckled coffeepot from a shelf, filled it with water from the pump at the sink, threw in a handful of coffee beans, then set it on top of the stove to heat. He leaned against the counter to further explain. "This place belonged to an old couple named Samuel and Martha Johnston. That day we went hunting, Graywolf, it was a crazy old mountain man who found me inside that stump. Several days later, I managed to escape from him. Then Samuel and Martha Johnston found me wandering alone in the wilderness; they just happened to be on their way home from Miles City after purchasing supplies. They brought me here to this place. The Johnstons were an older couple and never had any children of their own."

Reading the question in his brother's eyes, "I couldn't have asked for more loving parents," Morgan assured him. "They treated me like their own son. It was Samuel who gave me the name Morgan—which, I'm sure you understand, I prefer to be called."

Chandler nodded. He knew that his brother was trying to tell him, in a roundabout way, that he was no longer that same child.

"And Martha taught me the white man's tongue . . . how to read and write," Morgan added.

"Where are they now?" Chandler wanted to know.

"They're both buried out back."

"What happened to them?" Samantha asked.

Anger flashed inside Morgan's dark eyes and his expression became thunderous. "When I was about fifteen, two white men came here and shot them both in cold blood. I spent the next several months learning how to use a gun . . . when I got good enough, I went after those two men and I've been looking for them ever since.

"The other night in town . . . when I grabbed that knife out of your hand . . . the man you were about to hurl it at . . . he's one of them."

"His name's Charlie Bates," Samantha said.

"He's the man who actually shot Samuel and Martha. There was another man with Bates that day he shot the Johnstons. I saw him at the brothel . . . playing poker at the same table . . . a skinny fella . . . wears a big black hat with a wide leather band."

Samantha looked at Chandler. "Sounds like Jess Merdock."

"You wouldn't happen to know where I could find these men?" Morgan inquired.

"They both work for a man called Jed Martin," Chandler informed his brother. He didn't mention that Charlie Bates might've hightailed it out of town, because he didn't want to have to explain the reason for the man's sudden departure, not in front of Samantha. It would only be a reminder of what Charlie had done to her best friend Sarah, not that she'd forgotten . . .

"How's this for irony, Morgan." It was going to take Chandler some time, getting used to calling his brother by a different name. "Jed Martin is Jake's pa."

"The crazy kid who was here?"

"That's the one."

"If Charlie Bates killed your folks, then why did you stop me that night?" Samantha angrily said to Morgan.

"Because I want him."

So do I, Samantha thought. Charlie Bates was an evil man and somebody should stop him before he had a chance to hurt another person. "I really should be getting home," she said to Chandler. "My parents are probably frantic by now."

"It would surprise me if John has the calvary out looking for you." Chandler rose to his feet. "You're coming with us, Morgan. And I won't take no for an answer . . . we have a lot of catching up to do. Besides, I want you to meet Samantha's folks."

Chapter Eight

Morgan stared at the mule-like horse in bewilderment, scratching his head. "You can actually ride that thing?" he said incredulously.

Samantha was becoming a little irate, always having to defend poor Daisy. "Mister Johnston, I would think that *you* of all people would understand how it feels to be looked upon with prejudice. You should be ashamed of yourself."

Chandler burst out laughing.

"And you're no better than he is!" Samantha hissed at him. "You've been belittling my horse ever since I met you!"

Morgan grinned at his brother and winked, then looked back at Samantha. The woman certainly had spunk and he liked that. "You're right, Miss Callahan. May I offer my humble apology for my rude manners."

Samantha rolled her eyes.

Morgan chuckled.

"How would you like to wager a bet, little brother?" Chandler patted Daisy on the rump. "This old mare here against that powerful steed of yours . . . what do you say?"

"You mean a race?" Morgan asked, almost sounding mortified.

Chandler nodded, fighting to keep a straight face.

"I think old age has completely taken over your senses, Graywolf. This must be some kind of joke . . . right? Surely you can't be serious?"

"I'm serious."

Morgan looked at Samantha. "You're okay with this?"

"Perfectly."

"So . . . what do I get when I win?" he wanted to know.

"You won't win," Samantha firmly replied. Too bad she would be way too far in the lead to see the shocked look on Morgan's face, she thought sarcastically.

"Come on, Graywolf, be serious. That old nag doesn't stand a chance against my stallion and you well know it."

"Just in case you *do* lose, Morgan, how much money can you afford?"

"The more I think about it, a race between that mare and my stallion just wouldn't be fair."

"Afraid Daisy might beat your precious steed?" Samantha taunted him.

"Daisy huh? Isn't a daisy suppose to be a beautiful flower?"

"Are we racing or not?" Samantha snapped.

"Don't you need a saddle on that plug?"

"She doesn't use a saddle," Chandler told him.

Morgan shook his head in disbelief. "Have it your way, little lady."

Chandler rode Ranger a short distance ahead of his brother and Samantha, then turned his stallion around to face them. He wanted a clear view of Morgan's shocked expression when Samantha's little mare flew ahead in the lead. He chuckled to himself in anticipation; he was really going to enjoy this.

"Get ready," he hollered out. "Go!"

Both horses started off evenly. Then, a few moments later, Daisy bolted ahead of Morgan's black stallion just like the little rocket Chandler knew she was, leaving his obviously stunned brother practically standing in place. He was doubled over with laughter when Morgan halted his horse alongside his. Already Samantha and Daisy were so far ahead, they appeared like a speck moving swiftly across the terrain.

"Well?" Chandler finally said when Morgan didn't say anything.

"So . . . I lost."

"That's all you've got to say?"

"What do you want me to say?"

"Maybe you're just in shock," Chandler muttered under his breath.

Actually that wasn't far from the truth. Morgan was wondering how it was possible that sway-backed mare could run like a bolt of lightning . . . .

"I didn't leave you that day," Chandler suddenly stated.

Morgan turned to look at him. "I never said you did."

"I think it's important that you know that I went back for you that day, but you were gone. I searched the entire area . . . there was no sign of a struggle . . . not a single footprint that might've explained what happened. Had I known . . ."

"There's no way you could've known, Graywolf. That mountain man covered his tracks so well, even the best tracker in our tribe could not have followed us."

"I've never stopped looking for you, Morgan."

"I believe you, Graywolf."

It had been Little Bear who'd last called him by his real name. Funny how his own name almost sounded foreign to his ears now. "If things had been different, you would have a warrior's name." Chandler sadly added, "But we can't dwell on the past."

"How'd you come up with a name like Chandler?" Morgan was curious to know.

"Actually Wade Chandler is my full name. That day we'd gone hunting—after I left you inside the stump, I raced home only to discover . . ." Chandler suddenly went silent at the horrible memory of seeing their village in complete ruins. "Nearly every tepee had been burned to the ground, our entire herd run off, and all our family and friends . . . a few had died that day, but the others . . . only thing I can think of . . . some enemy tribe destroyed our village and must have taken the others captive.

"Our father and uncle were not among the dead," Chandler answered his brother's unspoken question. "I've been to every reservation in Montana, looking for our Cheyenne brothers, and I had to pass myself off as a white man to do it. So I had no choice but to cut my hair and I changed my name to Wade Chandler."

"You'll always be Graywolf to me."

That brought a genuine smile to Chandler's lips. "I want you to know that underneath this white man's facade, I'm still a warrior."

Talking about the past dredged up unpleasant memories in Morgan's mind, events that he'd long ago put behind him. He didn't see any reason to tell his brother that the mountain man who had taken him that day was a white man filled with hatred for the Indians, and how he had starved and beaten him for days because of that hatred. It was then when Morgan realized that prejudice existed in the world. And what good would it do to tell his brother that the Johnstons had found him nearly at death's door . . . that he might have died if Martha hadn't nursed him back to health.

"I'm glad Samuel and Martha treated you well, Morgan," Chandler then said as if reading his thoughts. "I wish I could've met them."

"They didn't deserve to die the way they did," Morgan said bitterly. "That's the reason I became a bounty hunter."

"A little dangerous choice of profession, don't you think?"

Morgan shrugged.

"Samantha wouldn't have missed her target that night," Chandler informed him. "Maybe you shouldn't have stopped her." Though he was glad that his brother prevented her from doing something she would have later regretted.

"What *did* Charlie Bates do to Samantha?" Morgan asked.

"He ravished her friend. I think the girl will be okay . . . in time."

Morgan's jaw muscles tightened in fury and he said through clenched teeth, "Charlie Bates is worse than a serpent that crawls on the ground!"

Chandler couldn't argue with that.

Samantha arrived home way ahead of Chandler and Morgan. This gave her a chance to relate what happened to her much relieved parents. She did change the story though, making it sound like Jake had prevented her from leaving the cabin because it had grown dark and he was worried about her safety. Samantha did not want to be the cause of any more animosity between their families; there was enough already. She also told her parents how Chandler's brother had showed up out-of-the-blue, then proceeded to tell them everything she knew about this mysterious brother of Chandler's—which really wasn't very much.

After Samantha had finished speaking, she was hoping she'd convinced her father that Jake hadn't really done anything wrong and, considering that no actual harm was done, he might even be willing to forget the whole incident.

And it seemed to do the trick.

John had been completely taken by surprise, when he heard about the cabin on his property, a cabin that he'd never been aware of. Technically, the deceased old couple who'd supposedly raised this brother of Chandler's, had been squatters. That part of Samantha's story sounded almost too bizarre to be true . . . .

As Chandler and Morgan approached the Callahan ranch, Chandler noticed the entire family was gathered outside the house, apparently awaiting their arrival.

"You didn't tell me there would be a greeting party," Morgan commented.

Chandler chuckled. "Maybe I should've prepared you."

After they dismounted, Amos came over and took both horses' reins. He purposely lingered about, hoping to find out what was going on, until John dismissed him with a this-is-none-of-your-business look. He walked off toward the barn, grumbling under his breath, leading both horses behind him.

John eyed the tall Indian standing at Chandler's side. There wasn't the slightest doubt in his mind the man was Chandler's brother: the resemblance between the two was remarkable.

He firmly gripped Morgan's hand. "Mister Johnston, I'm John Callahan . . . . this is my wife Rachel . . . my son James . . . his fiancée Sarah. And you already know Samantha."

John wondered about the odd look that passed between Samantha and Chandler . . . like they shared some kind of secret, but he didn't say anything. "You know . . . the similarity between you boys is absolutely amazing."

"I'll take that as a compliment," Morgan replied with a wink toward his brother.

But Chandler wasn't paying any attention; he was wondering why John and Rachel appeared so calm when they had lunatic neighbor running loose. Jake Martin had held their daughter against her will and had nearly shot him when he tried to intervene, yet here they stood, acting as if nothing out of the ordinary had happened.

"You will be staying for supper, won't you, Mister Johnston?" Rachel asked.

Morgan could easily see where Samantha inherited her incredible beauty. He found Mrs. Callahan to be a very enchanting woman. Her daughter looked so much like her . . . except for the color of the eyes . . . Samantha's were a striking blue like her father's. Suddenly realizing that he was staring, he promptly removed his hat and politely replied, "Please call me Morgan. And I graciously accept your invitation, Mrs. Callahan."

Rachel smiled. "Good. Then if you gentlemen will excuse me."

John watched his wife's departing back for a moment, before turning to Chandler. "Why don't you take the rest of the day off . . . spend it with your brother. Besides, you've earned the extra time off . . . considering what you've been through since accepting this job," John added the latter with a stern look toward his troublesome daughter. "Need I even mention, young lady, you're not allowed off these premises."

"No, Sir."

"Morgan, it was a pleasure meeting you." John gave Samantha a last warning look, then he turned and walked away, calling over his shoulder, "You comin', James?"

James hastily pecked Sarah on the cheek, and hurried after his father. Sarah excused herself, then climbed the porch steps and disappeared inside the house. Samantha stood looking at Chandler, sensing there was something he wanted to say to her, but, for whatever reason, was holding back. Maybe he didn't want to say it in front of his brother . . .

"I really like your father," Morgan remarked. "He doesn't strike me as the kind of man who would approve of his daughter's . . . *questionable antics*."

Samantha scowled at him, folding her arms across her chest. "If you're referring to our *little race*, if you remember correctly, Mister Johnston, you were fairly warned."

"Nobody in their right mind would have guessed that swaybacked mare could run."

"Well . . . maybe you're not in your right mind," Samantha cleverly retorted.

Morgan's brow rose slightly. "Maybe I'm not." Deciding to teach her a little lesson, he moved deliberately toward the unsuspecting girl, while speaking in a husky tone of voice. "So—tell me, Miss Callahan—what does the *honorable lady* request then for payment? After all, you did win fair and square."

Chandler nearly burst out laughing, seeing the panic-stricken expression that transformed Samantha's lovely face. And her bright blue eyes were wide with fear. Surely she couldn't believe Morgan was actually serious . . .

"I . . . I really don't request any payment, Mister Johnston, because . . ." Samantha nervously laughed, "the whole thing was just a silly joke, so you really don't owe me anything." Morgan still kept walking toward her. She started to take a step backward, letting out a loud screech of surprise, when she tripped over her own foot and landed hard on her backside.

"Ouch!" Samantha got to her feet, pressing a hand to her smarting rear end, her temper finally exploding. "Why you . . . you overgrown *clumsy ox!* I oughtta . . ."

Morgan's mouth dropped in shock and disbelief, at the angry words that spewed from the young woman's mouth like a viper. Suddenly she spun around on her boot heel and stomped up the porch steps, slamming the door behind her.

"Did I hear her correctly?" Morgan asked.

"Every word, dear brother," Chandler replied, chuckling.

"I never knew such words existed."

"I'm sure you'll find Samantha's vocabulary quite educational. Since I've been here, I've learned a few new words myself."

Morgan could not remember the last time that he'd had such a delicious meal. After wolfing down a second helping—he would've had more but felt it would be considered bad manners—he leaned back in his chair, slowly sipping his coffee, casually scanning the other faces sitting around the table. He noticed the tender way James was looking at Sarah Martin; and the adoration that was shining in the girl's pale-blue eyes when she looked back at James. It was so obvious the young couple was in love. What that monster Charlie Bates had done to Sarah, it infuriated Morgan. He had yet another reason to want to see that man pay . . .

There seemed to be a heated discussion beginning to take place at the other end of the big oak table, Morgan noticed, between John Callahan and his independent daughter. He couldn't help but listen to the conversation.

"I thought you told me that Jake prevented you from leaving the cabin because he was worried about you riding home in the dark," John snapped at Samantha. "You didn't mention a word about Jake forcing you at gunpoint and then holding you there against your will. Did all those facts just *slip* your mind? Don't you dare say a word!" John shouted at his daughter in rising fury. "If Chandler hadn't told me the truth, I never would've found out what really happened! And you lied to me about how you got that bruise on your cheek!

"Well, what have you got to say for yourself?"

"You just told me not to say a word."

"Don't get smart with me, young lady!"

Samantha glared at Chandler for opening his big mouth, before turning back to her father and calmly replying, "You were already mad at Jake and . . ."

"*Mad* doesn't even come close to what I feel at the moment!" John furiously thundered. "Jake is a man now, Samantha! He's responsible for his own actions, so stop protecting him!" He stood out of his chair.

"John, where are you going?" Rachel said in rising panic.

"Where do you think I'm going?" he angrily bellowed.

Rachel leaped to her feet. "John, please don't go over to Jed's until you've had a chance to calm down."

"Please, Pa . . . Jake never actually hurt me," Samantha hastily added.

"God only knows what Jake would've done if Morgan hadn't gotten there when he did!"

"He never would have hurt me!"

"You don't know that for sure, Samantha!"

"John, you'll only make matters worse by going over there in your current state of mind," Rachel pleaded with her husband.

"Ma's right, Pa." James now rose to his feet, ready to physically stop his father from leaving if he had to, hoping it wouldn't come to that.

John raked a hand through his hair. He knew his wife was right. If he rode over to Jed's now, there was no telling what he would do to Jake if he got his hands on the boy. With a sigh, he sat back down at the table.

"If you decide to go after Jake, Pa, I'll ride over to the Martins with you," James eagerly offered as he seated himself in his chair.

Rachel frowned at her son. "Don't encourage him."

James shrugged.

"I doubt the Martin boy went home," Chandler said to John. "I would think that Jake's smart enough to figure there's a good chance the marshal will be looking for him. And that would be the first place he would look."

"I hadn't thought of that," John admitted.

"I'm so sorry for all the trouble my brother has caused."

"You have nothing to be sorry for, Sarah," Samantha told her friend.

"You have no control over Jake," James added, slipping an arm around her shoulder.

John suddenly felt guilty for rambling his big mouth without thinking of Sarah's feelings. It was just that sometimes it was easy to forget that Jake and Sarah were brother and sister, they were so different.

Chandler was wondering how John and Rachel would react if they knew the truth about Morning Star . . . alias Ester Martin . . . Jake and Sarah's mother. But maybe he shouldn't be so critical of *Ester* without just cause. After all, Morning Star was now a full grown woman, so maybe she had changed.

Chandler happened to look across the table at Samantha and caught her watching him with those icy blue orbs of hers. He knew she was angry at him for telling her father the truth about what Jake had done. He wouldn't be surprised if daggers suddenly shot out of her eye sockets, she looked furious enough. But how was he supposed to have known that she had fabricated some hairbrained story to her father. *He wasn't a mind reader.* Besides, she should've told her father the truth.

"May I please be excused?" Samantha asked her mother.

"Of course, dear."

"The look Samantha gave you before she left the room, I would sure hate to be in your moccasins," Morgan whispered in his brother's ear.

Chandler turned and scowled at him.

"We'll be herding the cattle to Cheyenne next month," John then said. "Morgan, how would you like to come along on the drive? We could sure use another hand."

"Mind if I sleep on it, sir?"

"Take longer to decide if you need . . . there's no hurry." John quickly drained the rest of his coffee, then stood out of his chair. "Come on, James, we'd best get back to work while there's still daylight."

After John and James left the room, Rachel and Sarah started to clear away the supper dishes, leaving Chandler and Morgan alone at the table.

"Come with us on the cattle drive, Morgan," Chandler urged his brother. "Just think . . . it would be like old times, camping out under the stars."

"I would like nothing better, but—I have another job to finish."

"You gonna waste the rest of your life hunting for those men?"

"You've wasted over half of yours looking for me. How old are you now, Graywolf, and you've never been married?"

"That's different!"

"Some men your age are already grandfathers."

"It's not like I'm ready for a rocking chair."

"Touchy, aren't we," Morgan chuckled. "Besides, I haven't declined John's offer yet." He wanted those two criminals more than anything, but he'd never in his wildest dreams ever expected to be reunited with his brother. And he was seriously considering going along on the drive; this just might be the chance he needed to start a new life.

"How 'bout we take a walk around the ranch," Chandler suggested.

Inside the barn where they could talk in private, "I wish you could have experienced the Indian way of life, Morgan, the way that I did," Chandler was saying to his brother. "Now the Indian way of life is gone forever. You'll never know what it's like to become a real warrior, count coup on our enemies, or go on a raid. You were so young the last time you saw our father, I bet you don't remember much about him."

You couldn't miss the pride in the tone of Morgan's voice as he spoke of their father. "I remember Running Bear clearly in my mind . . . like it was only yesterday when I last saw him. I remember Father was exceptionally tall, that he towered over most of the other men in our village. He had a natural leadership quality about him . . . always carried himself with confidence. And when Running Bear spoke . . . everybody would listen. I can even remember the sound of Father's voice."

Both men were temporarily lost in their own thoughts for a brief period, before Morgan asked hopefully, "Graywolf, do you think it's possible that our father and uncle could still be alive somewhere . . . maybe even some of our friends or other tribal members?"

"I've been to all the reservations," Chandler solemnly replied.

"It just doesn't seem possible that an enemy tribe could wipe out an entire village without any signs of a battle," Morgan rationalized more to himself. "Maybe they all ran for the cover of the forest and joined another tribe somewhere?"

"I suppose. Anything's possible. Except . . . if they did join another tribe, they would still be on a reservation somewhere."

Watching his brother's expression turn somber, Chandler figured that now was probably an appropriate time to inform him about Morning Star. "I have just recently learned the whereabouts of someone from our village . . . do you remember Morning Star?"

"She was the Indian maiden you were going to marry. If memory serves me correctly—she ran off with some white man. I do remember that she was very beautiful and you were devastated over her for many months."

"Wait until you hear the rest. It just so happens that Morning Star married that white man she ran off with—and she now goes by the name of *Ester Martin*."

Chandler knew the moment that Morgan understood what he was trying to tell him. "That's right . . . she's the crazy kid's ma . . . Sarah's, too."

Morgan shook his head in disbelief.

"Morning Star came here for a visit at the Callahan ranch the other day," Chandler explained. "I recognized her immediately . . . that's how I found out about her."

"You must have been shocked?"

"I guess you could say that."

"Sarah certainly doesn't look Indian," Morgan remarked. "But now that I recall Jake's face to mind, he does resemble Morning Star . . . least from what I can remember." As he tried to absorb this shocking information, a rather disturbing thought occurred to him. "Graywolf, you're not still in love with Morning Star, are you?"

Standing outside the barn door, listening to the conversation, Samantha covered her ears, not wanting to hear the answer. Suddenly she turned and fled toward the house. *She hadn't meant to eavesdrop.* Her mother had sent her to find Chandler and Morgan to invite them inside for some peach pie, so she'd just happened upon them by accident.

Samantha burst through the front door of the house, raced up the stairs to her room, and slammed the door shut. She leaned against the door for a moment to catch her breath, then she threw herself upon her bed, forcing back the tears. *Surely she must have misunderstood. Or maybe the whole thing was just some terrible mistake. How could Ester Martin possibly be this Morning Star . . . the very same woman whom Chandler had loved since his youth . . . the Indian maiden he'd almost married . . . it just couldn't be true!*

Then something else struck Samantha: if what Chandler said was true, that meant Sarah was Morning Star's daughter and Jake was her son. Her dearest friends since childhood was the daughter of the very woman who held the heart of the man, she what . . . *loved?*

Samantha inwardly groaned, wondering how she was ever going to face her best friend, now that she knew the truth about her mother. Then even a more horrifying thought crossed her troubled mind: *could Chandler be Jake's real father?* She'd never thought about it before, but Jake *did* look more Indian than white; where Sarah didn't look Indian at all. Was it possible that a brother and sister could look so completely different from each other?

Could Morning Star be the reason for Chandler coming to Bear Creek? Samantha then wondered. But, then, she remembered his shocked expression upon seeing Ester that day, thinking, no . . . Chandler had seemed genuinely surprised to see the woman. Samantha also remembered the way that Chandler had treated Ester . . . almost with a contempt. Those had not been the actions of a man in love, or, at least, that's the way it had appeared to her.

That didn't mean Chandler couldn't still be carrying a secret torch for . . . What-ever-her-name-was! Samantha inwardly cried. Her mind was now in such utter turmoil, she didn't know what to think or feel . . . .

Chandler stretched his long legs out in front of him, grinning to himself, as he answered his brother's question. "I met Miss Callahan at the hurdy-gurdy house in town. Apparently Jake's pa was on the rampage about something and Samantha had gone there to warn him. 'Course in the process, she got herself into a little trouble. And I . . . well . . . intervened."

"Samantha's like a magnet for trouble," Morgan chuckled.

Chandler couldn't agree more.

Both men turned at the sound of approaching footsteps. Morgan smiled at the sight of Mrs. Callahan. He really admired the lovely woman, thinking John was a lucky man.

"That peach pie's almost gone," Rachel said to them. "You boys had better hurry and come inside if you want your share, before James devours the whole thing."

"You're inviting us for dessert?" Morgan asked.

"Didn't Samantha tell you?"

"We haven't seen Samantha," Chandler informed Rachel.

"Oh. Maybe she just got sidetracked," Rachel said with a shrug. "I've made fresh coffee to go with that pie if you boys are interested." Then she turned and hurried out of the barn.

"If that lady weren't married . . ."

"She would still be old enough to be your mother," Chandler scolded his brother.

"Don't you know anything about older women, Graywolf?"

"I wonder what John would think if he heard you talk that way about his wife?"

"I didn't mean anything by it." Morgan went silent for a moment, then, "Besides, I'm not stupid . . . John Callahan is one man I would *not* want to tangle with."

Chapter Nine

Samantha stared out her bedroom window, watching her mother greet a glowing Ester Martin as she gracefully alighted from the buggy. She had the feeling that Jed's wife's obvious cheerful mood this morning had nothing to do with her daughter's swift recovery. The woman had probably gotten over the shock of seeing Chandler—or should she say *Graywolf*; now she was probably thrilled about having him in her life again. And as long as Sarah was here at the ranch, it gave Ester just the perfect excuse she needed to visit any time she wanted.

Her frown deepened as she watched her mother and Ester stroll toward the house. Samantha took this opportunity to more closely observe the Indian woman that Chandler had almost married. Although she had seen Sarah's mother many times before, she looked at the woman differently now. Ester Martin really was beautiful, Samantha thought depressingly. A far cry from the 'toothless old hag' she had envisioned Chandler's ex-fiancée to be. Ester's petite form was arrayed in a soft yellow linen gown this morning that accentuated her naturally dark skin. Her shiny coal-black hair was braided and wound around her head like a glorious crown. Long, sooty lashes framed huge doe-like eyes that were set in a heart-shaped face with absolutely flawless complexion.

No wonder Chandler's been pining away for the sultry beauty all these years.

With a sigh, Samantha turned away from the window and walked over to her dressing table, poured some water into the basin, then washed her face and sponge bathed her body. After dressing, she took her time brushing and braiding her long, thick mane, still trying to muster the courage to face her best friend. She couldn't keep eluding Sarah; it wouldn't take Sarah long to figure out that she was purposely trying to avoid her.

Samantha assumed that Ester was here this morning to help her mother start planning for James's and Sarah's wedding. Although she was truly happy for her brother and Sarah—honestly she was—she just couldn't share her mother's enthusiasm, because now Ester had yet another reason to *drop by* any time she wanted.

Samantha wanted so much to confide in her mother about Ester Martin. But she couldn't tell anybody, and especially her best friend whom she normally shared all her troubles. There was no way Sarah could ever find out about her mother's true identity.

Rising, she left her room.

As Samantha descended the wide staircase, she could hear her mother and Ester talking inside the kitchen. She stopped at the bottom of the steps, not really sure if she was ready to face the woman that Chandler had once been engaged to.

Her face flushed with anger when she heard Ester ask her mother about Chandler, saying that he looked familiar somehow . . .

Familiar indeed, Samantha furiously thought. Well, she wasn't about to stand here and listen while *Morning Star* connivingly pressured her mother for information about Chandler. Instead of going to the kitchen, she tiptoed across the foyer and then out the front door.

Once outside on the porch, a few unladylike words that were attached to Ester's name, slipped through Samantha's clenched teeth.

Then Ester Martin was suddenly forgotten when she noticed several riders approaching the corral where her father was branding calves. When she realized that it was Jed and his men, Samantha hoped that this was a friendly visit, but the nagging feeling in the pit of her stomach told her Jed was here for a more sinister purpose . . . .

When John noticed Jed and his men, he handed the branding iron over to Amos, then strode across the corral toward the gate to greet them. None of them dismounted, but remained seated on their horses, warning John that this was probably no social call. Whatever the man's problem was this time, he hoped it had nothing to do with James . . .

Morgan eyed the men astride their horses suspiciously, closely monitoring the situation. He could tell by John's mannerisms as he conversed with his *uninvited guests*, there could be trouble. Automatically reaching for his weapon, he grumbled under his breath. He never should have listened to his brother and left his gun belt inside the bunkhouse, but Graywolf had assured him that he was among friends here at the Callahan ranch and it wasn't necessary to carry a gun. *Apparently his brother hadn't been expecting angry visitors.* Besides, Graywolf claimed that he looked more like a gunslinger than a bounty hunter and thought it might be best to leave off his gun belt, until the men got to know him better, so Morgan had finally complied. Though there really wasn't much difference between a gunslinger and a bounty hunter—least as far as he was concerned, so he really didn't see the point.

Now Morgan wished he would've listened to his instincts. Not that he was bragging by any means, but he could have easily disarmed a few of Jed's men—if it came to that—before any of them got a chance to fire off one shot. He was simply that good. Now he could only hope that things wouldn't go that far . . .

"I've got work to do, so say whatever's on your mind," John firmly told Jed.

"Before I do, where's my wife?"

"She's inside the house with Rachel. Why?"

"Because I don't want Ester to hear this. I came here for that Injun," Jed bluntly informed him.

John looked over his shoulder at the sound of footsteps coming up behind him. He gave his son a warning look that clearly told him to keep silent, before turning back toward Jed and angrily replying, "We don't have any *Injuns* here."

"You know who I'm talking about, John. You might as well save yourself the hassle and turn the Injun over to me."

"If you think for one minute I would just hand you over one of my men, Jed . . . you're sadly mistaken!"

"Then I'll get him myself!"

"You'll have to go through me first!"

"That won't be necessary," Chandler hollered out as he walked over to stand at John's side.

"Stay out of this, Chandler," John warned him. "This is between me and Jed."

"Whatever the man's problem is, he can say it to my face." Although Chandler already had a pretty good idea what this was all about. He could plainly read jealousy in the white man's eyes, so he would guess that Morning Star must have told her husband who he was.

"You belong on a reservation with the other savages!" Jed furiously spat. "Well, well, if it ain't another one of 'em," he said with pure contempt.

Chandler hadn't noticed that his brother had walked over to stand beside him and John. "This isn't your fight, Morgan."

"Your enemies are my enemies, big brother."

"What are you tryin' to do, John . . . turn your ranch into an Indian refuge?" Jed snapped.

"What I do with my ranch, Jed, is none of your business," John angrily retorted. He could tell there would be no reasoning with Jed. It was time to change tactics. "I would advise you to get off my property, before somebody gets hurt."

"Are you threatening me, John?"

"Now you know me better than that, Jed . . . I never threaten." What John had not anticipated was just how far Jed's hatred for Indians would go.

Jed suddenly drew his gun. "Jess!" he shouted at the top of his lungs. Then he tossed Jess some rope and gruffly ordered him to tie the Indian's hands together and secure the other rope around his waist.

"What crime has Chandler committed, Jed?" John demanded to know.

"Just being an Indian is crime enough for me." Jed wasn't about to admit the real reason he'd come here this morning. He didn't want anyone to know that Ester had once been engaged to marry a heathen . . . then everybody would know of his wife's shame . . . that she, too, was Indian. He just couldn't take the humiliation. No, that wasn't exactly true. If he were really being honest, it was jealousy now driving him . . .

"You lay one finger on that man, Jed, you'll answer to me!"

"You're not in any position to be threatening me, John."

Dismounting, Jess reluctantly walked over and snatched the rope off the ground. He knew what his boss was planning to do and he didn't want any part of it. But he needed this job and felt that he had no choice but to do what Jed told him.

Morgan's smoldering dark eyes followed the man called Jess. He immediately recognized Charlie Bates's partner and itched to get his hands on the man . . .

When Jess made a move toward Chandler, John stepped in front of him to block his path. John could see the pleading look in Jess Merdock's eyes, asking him to get out of the way. But he didn't move; and his eyes remained fastened upon Jess. Then John heard Jed pull back on the trigger of his gun and hollered at him to step out of the way. Still, he refused to budge even an inch. John was thinking that Jed would have to literally shoot him, when suddenly an unexpected gunshot exploded through the air and the weapon flew out of Jed's hand.

"Tell your men to drop their weapons, Jed!"

John whirled around. "Rachel, go back inside the house!"

"Just as soon as Jed tells his men to drop their guns!"

"I mean it, Rachel!"

"So do I, John Callahan!" Rachel stood a short distance away with a very distraught looking Ester at her side. She kept her rifle tucked firmly under her arm, pointed directly at Jed. She could not believe this was happening again.

Ester had never felt so humiliated in her entire life. She never dreamed that Jed's jealousy would push him this far. Still, she should have known better than to tell him about Chandler's true identity, knowing how he felt about Indians. Sometimes she wondered why Jed ever married her. "Do as Rachel asks, Jed!" she angrily shouted at her husband.

Feeling he had no other choice, "Put down your guns, men," Jed ordered.

John walked over and picked Jed's gun off the ground, quickly emptied the chamber, tossing the bullets away, then he handed it back. "Don't ever come here again, Jed." Though it had been said in a near whisper, the warning was loud and clear. It was on the tip of his tongue to tell Jed to keep his boy away from his daughter, but figured that enough damage had been done four one day. Besides, he'd promised Samantha—albeit against his better judgement—that he wouldn't press charges against Jake. And he doubted if Jed and

Ester knew anything about the latest stunt their son had pulled, and what good would it really do to tell them.

Jed holstered his gun, watching Ester and Rachel approaching him. When he saw the accusing look in his wife's eyes, he suddenly felt ashamed for what he'd just done. But what disturbed him even more was the disappointed expression on Rachel's lovely face.

"Ester, I . . ."

"Don't even speak to me, Jed," Ester cut off her husband's words. She just couldn't bring herself to listen to his pathetic attempt to apologize; not that it would matter anyway . . . the damage had already been done. To Rachel she said, "I hope you don't mind if Sarah stays here until the wedding?"

"What wedding?" Jed asked.

"James and Sarah are getting married at the end of this month," Ester curtly informed her husband.

"That's only two weeks away and you never told me?"

"I didn't tell you because I knew you'd get angry." His thunderous expression proved her words true, but to Ester's relief, Jed at least had the decency to hold his tongue. She turned apologetic eyes to Rachel. "I'm so sorry for all the trouble."

"It's okay, Ester. And don't worry about Sarah . . . we'll take good care of her."

"I know you will. I guess I should be going then. I'll come back some other day and we'll get started on those wedding plans. I've probably worn out my welcome here for a while," Ester added with a scornful look toward Jed.

"Nonsense," Rachel told her. "You're welcome here any time."

"Thank you, Rachel," Ester said. She nodded to John, then hurried toward her buggy without a backward glance.

Wordlessly Jed and his men mounted their horses and followed after Ester.

"Do you think Jed will cause any trouble?" Rachel asked John.

His eyes still focussed on the departing men, "I don't know," he replied. "I'm more concerned about Jake. Which reminds me . . . tell Samantha not to leave the house for *any* reason."

Samantha stood quietly by the corral, her arms dangling over the top rail, watching the men branding calves—since she didn't have anything else better to do. Apparently, because of Jake, she was virtually a prisoner in her own yard, until her father stated otherwise. She had a half of mind to go after Jake herself—except her father would probably lock her in her room then—though in all fairness she knew he was only trying to protect her. Still, hadn't she proven many times over that she was quite capable of taking care of herself?

Samantha noticed that Chandler had hardly spoken a word to anyone since his run-in with Jed Martin this morning. She wondered if Jed was the cause of Chandler's withdrawn behavior, or was it because of Morning Star. She was awfully tempted to just bluntly ask the man if he was still pining over his lost love, but, of course, she wouldn't dare say such a thing. Whatever Chandler's true feelings for Ester were, it was none of her business.

Besides, did she really want to know?

Her brother seemed much more quieter than usual, too, Samantha noticed. The fact that his future father-in-law seemed to be on the rampage with everybody in his family, who could blame James for his somber mood.

Morgan appeared to be his old self, Samantha mused. She couldn't help comparing both brothers, noting there was very little differences between them. Morgan Johnston—the name suited him well—was only slightly shorter than his older brother. Though his hair was a lot longer than Chandler's shoulder-length locks—which he wore in a single plait down his back—he had the same copper-colored skin and muscular build. Even wearing white men's western-style clothing, Chandler's younger brother looked undeniably Indian.

Samantha smiled in appreciation. *And why shouldn't she.* After all, Morgan, who looked enough like Chandler to be his twin, was just as incredibly handsome . . .

Morgan smiled and waved at Samantha. He chuckled to himself, when she suddenly turned on her heel and walked away. He'd noticed the way she was intently scrutinizing his brother earlier; there was definitely something going on inside that mind of hers. If he thought it would do any good, he would give Miss Callahan some advice where his older brother was concerned, but she probably wouldn't listen . . .

"I wonder what's put a bee in her bonnet," Chandler grumbled to Morgan.

"So you've noticed."

"If you mean the way she's been avoiding me lately—"

"I could be wrong, but—I believe it's called jealousy."

Chandler straightened and frowned at his brother. "What are you talking about?"

"My guess is Samantha's jealous of your old flame."

"That's impossible. Samantha doesn't even know about . . ." Chandler suddenly went silent. Then, "Do you think she might've overheard when we were talking about Morning Star?"

Morgan rolled his eyes. "You're finally catching on, big brother. Remember the other night when Rachel found us in the barn and invited us to the house for peach pie, we were talking about Morning Star. And she'd seemed surprised that we hadn't seen Samantha.

"You know, Graywolf—you certainly don't know very much about women, especially for a man of your age."

"A man of my age . . . what's that supposed to mean?"

"You're what . . . in your mid-thirties now?"

"That's hardly an old man," Chandler angrily replied. "And in my defense, I happen to know plenty about women. I just can't seem to figure out *that* particular woman."

"You still don't get it, do you?" Morgan said, chuckling. "What's going on is so obvious that a blind man could see it. I'm surprised you haven't guessed it by now."

"Then I guess I'm blind!" Chandler hissed. "Exactly what are you getting at, Morgan?"

"Samantha's in love with you, Graywolf. I don't think she even realizes it." There was a slight pause, then, "And whether you want to admit it or not, I suspect that you're in love with her."

Chandler hastily ran a hand through his hair, muttering under his breath, "I must be completely out of my mind."

"You could do worse," Morgan chuckled.

"I've never met a more stubborn or determined woman in my entire life. Any man who falls for Samantha Callahan is just begging for trouble—and I've got enough already."

"You just haven't learned how to reason with her."

"Have you ever tried reasoning with a wildcat?" Chandler seriously retorted. When Morgan burst out laughing, he snapped in frustration, "You think I'm exaggerating?"

"Any woman can be handled, Graywolf—even the *wildcat*."

"And when did you become such an expert on women?"

Morgan shrugged, ignoring his brother's sarcasm.

Later that afternoon Chandler found Samantha inside the barn. As he stood there, watching her brush Daisy, he was thinking he must be crazy for ever allowing Morgan to talk him into confronting her about Morning Star . . . there was always the chance his brother could be wrong. But the more he thought about it, what Morgan had said made sense.

Chandler remained hidden within the shadows as he continued to watch Samantha brushing Daisy's mangy-looking coat. He wondered why she bothered; nothing short of a miracle would help that mare's appearance any.

Figuring he might as well get this over with, Chandler sauntered toward her. She looked over her shoulder and scowled at him. Her expression clearly said she didn't want him there, but that wasn't going to stop him. He halted beside her. "I wanna talk to you, Samantha."

She kept on brushing Daisy; she wouldn't even look at him.

"Are you going to tell me what's wrong?"

No response.

Chandler took her by the shoulders and swung her around to face him. "I wanna know why you're angry at me? And don't bother to deny it . . . you've been avoiding me like a sore subject the last few days."

"How dare you manhandle me!"

When she tried to brush past him, Chandler grabbed her by the arm. "You're not going anywhere, until you tell me what's wrong!"

"Let go of me you . . . you *barbarian!* What are you doing?"

"Something your father should've done a long time ago!"

"You wouldn't dare!"

Chandler easily scooped Samantha up in his arms and carried the kicking and screaming woman over to a bale of hay and plopped down. After pulling her across his lap—which wasn't an easy feat—his hand came down hard on her bottom. The names she called him would've made an outlaw blush. His hand came down even harder.

"My father will hear about this you . . . you slimy snake! You . . ." A loud screech erupted from Samantha's lips when another solid whack connected with her already sore posterior, instantly putting a halt to what she was about to say. Trying to protect her stinging bottom with her hand, she tried rolling off his lap, but he had such a strong hold on her she couldn't move.

"Let go of me!" she screamed at him.

"I can keep this up a lot longer than you can, Samantha!" Chandler shouted back at her. "Let me know when you're ready to listen to reason!"

"Okay . . . ! Okay . . . !"

Chandler's hand abruptly stopped in mid-air to drop at his side. When he let go of Samantha, she immediately shot off his lap, then stood there, glaring at him, while rubbing her smarting derriere. He could tell she wanted to call him every horrible name she could think of, but wisely held her tongue.

"So talk!" she furiously spat.

"Okay . . . I'll be blunt. Did you overhear a conversation between me and my brother about Morning Star?" Her guilty expression was answer enough. "Then you should know she means nothing to me."

"I don't care what she means to you!"

Now Chandler really *was* confused. "Then why are you so angry at me?"

"Isn't it obvious?"

"If you're referring to the spanking I just gave you, you were already mad at me before that."

"Why don't you mind your own business!"

"Why must you always be so stubborn?"

Samantha wasn't trying to be stubborn. *Honestly she wasn't.* She just didn't know how to explain something she didn't understand herself. There was no way she could ever admit to Chandler that it was plain and simple jealousy that was causing her anger, especially when she had no right to feel that way . . .

Gazing into eyes that were bluer than a summer sky, Chandler thought Samantha might act like she can't stand him, but her eyes were saying something quite different. Like a moth to a flame, he was drawn to her. Suddenly pulling her into his arms, his lips came down upon hers in a breath-stealing kiss. This had been something he'd wanting to do, since the very first time he had ever laid eyes on her.

Chandler was surprised when Samantha's arms slid around his neck and she was kissing him back. As the kiss deepened, a wave of desire shook Chandler to the heels of his boots. He knew if he didn't stop now, he wouldn't be able to. It was the hardest thing he ever did, gently removing those slender arms and setting her away from him.

"I'm sorry," Samantha murmured, lowering her eyes. She felt so ashamed, the way she had so eagerly responded to Chandler's kiss, and now he probably thought she was no better than the women at the hurdy-gurdy house.

"There's no need to apologize . . . you did nothing wrong. Look at me, Samantha."

There was such innocent trust in those bright blue eyes when she looked at him. And it struck Chandler then, quite unexpectedly, just how much he wanted this woman to be a permanent part of his life. He didn't know how or when it happened; he only knew that it had.

Neither of them were aware that they were no longer alone, until a deep voice said, "I hope I'm not disturbing anything."

Wondering how long Morgan had been standing there, Chandler irritably snapped at his brother, "And if you were?"

"Then I would say that I just spared you the wrath of a very overprotective father . . . John's looking for you."

When Samantha gasped and ran from the barn, Morgan stood grinning at his brother. "I hope I wasn't too late?"

"Nothing happened . . . if that's what you're insinuating?"

Morgan chuckled at Graywolf's angry scowl. "Guess I'd better get back to work."

Chandler's eyes followed his brother as he strode out of the barn, grateful that it had been Morgan who'd walked in on him and Samantha in such an intimate compromise. Knowing John's temper the way he did, the man probably would have started throwing punches and asked questions later . . . .

Seated at the kitchen table, Samantha was only halfheartedly listening, while her mother and Sarah talked excitedly about the upcoming wedding. She couldn't stop thinking about the way Chandler had kissed her inside the barn; her lips and body were still tingling. A dreamy smile lifted the corners of her mouth . . .

"What do you think, Samantha?"

"About what?"

Rachel looked curiously at her daughter. She was acting awfully strange, but shrugged it off. "About having the wedding outside on the veranda."

"I think it's a good idea. What do you think, Sarah?"

Sarah giggled. "Where have you been, Samantha . . . having the wedding outside on the veranda was my idea."

"Oh."

"Are you okay, dear?"

"Yes, Ma."

Samantha finally joined the conversation. Sarah's constant cheerful mood was becoming contagious. Soon, Samantha found herself laughing along with Sarah and her mother. She was enjoying herself so much—before she knew it, they had talked nearly the entire afternoon away. Samantha realized that her feelings for Sarah had not changed in the least. A lesson she learned was: never again would she ever allow anyone to come between her and her best friend. Besides, whatever happened between Chandler and Morning Star . . . er . . . Ester, all those years ago, had nothing to do with Sarah.

After Sarah excused herself and went upstairs to her room for a short nap, Samantha learned from her mother that Ester had not seen or heard from Jake for several days now, and nobody seemed to know of his whereabouts, either. Ester hadn't seemed real concerned over her son's absence, Rachel had told Samantha, because Jake had been known to stay out on the range from time to time. Rachel was certain that Ester didn't know anything about the cabin incident, and she hadn't had the heart to tell her. And for that, Samantha was grateful. Even though she knew what her father had said was true—that Jake was a man and responsible for his own actions—she still felt inclined to protect him.

Her mother had left the kitchen, and a short while later had returned carrying a white satiny gown neatly folded over her arm.

"What's that?" Samantha asked curiously.

With a wistful smile, Rachel held the gown out in front of her. "This is the dress I wore when I married your father. I made it myself . . . what do you think?"

"Oh, Ma, it's beautiful!"

"I've been saving this gown for your wedding day, Samantha," Rachel confessed through misty eyes. "Sarah told me she didn't have a wedding dress. I think this should fit her. Would you mind if she wore this, dear?"

"Of course not, Ma. I think it'll look beautiful on Sarah." Samantha moved her hand over the expertly-stitched gown, loving the feel of the silky material.

"When the day comes, this dress will look more beautiful on you," Rachel sniffled. She held it against her daughter's slender figure, adding more to herself, "I do believe this will fit you perfectly."

"Is that a hint?"

"Well, now that you ask, I hope I'm not too old to see you walk down the isle," Rachel said in a teasing tone.

"I'll try to hurry my wedding day along," Samantha muttered more to herself. Then, "Ma, do you think Jed will cause trouble if he comes to the wedding?"

Rachel carefully draped her gown over the back of a chair. "I honestly don't know what to expect from that man anymore." She sat at the table, reached for the coffeepot and added as she filled her cup. "But if Jed does come, I hope he controls that foul temper of his."

"I heard that Pa told Jed never to come back here."

"I'm sure your father would be willing to put their differences aside for one day."

Samantha wasn't so sure about that. "Well . . . we could always gag Jed and tie him to his horse during the ceremony."

A delicately arched brow rose slightly as Rachel seriously replied, "You know . . . that's not a bad idea."

"Ma, I was just joking."

"I'm not."

As Samantha lay in bed that night, she pondered how much her life had changed since meeting Wade Chandler at the hurdy-gurdy house. There had been a time when she used to fancy herself in love with Jake, but now she knew that whatever she had felt for him had been nothing more than a deep friendship.

The corners of her mouth lifted into a smile, remembering the way Chandler had kissed her inside the barn today, how it had made her feel. The man had awakened feelings inside her, feelings she had never experienced before. She had never felt anything even remotely comparable when Jake had kissed her those few times. To be honest—she hadn't really even enjoyed it.

But when Chandler had kissed her . . . her entire body had tingled . . . her knees had buckled . . . she'd even felt giddy. *Is this what it felt like to be in love?* Samantha wondered. *And was it possible to love a man you hardly knew?* Then she thought about Jake. She'd known him nearly her entire life and she *did* love him, but—like a sister loved a brother. While Jake had professed his love to her many times in the past, Samantha could not return that love. And she hoped she hadn't given Jake the wrong impression when she'd allowed him to kiss her; she'd only been curious what it was like. She then rationalized that it wasn't her fault if a simple kiss had meant more to Jake than it had to her.

Samantha closed her eyes and said a prayer to God, asking Him to help Jake, because he was definitely a troubled young man these days. She hoped that Jake would someday find a woman who could truly love him, the way he deserved.

Samantha then thought about her best friend Sarah. Hopefully Jed had enough respect for his daughter not to ruin what should be the most happiest day of her life. As Sarah's matron-of-honor, she was pleased that James had asked Chandler to be his best man, now that Jake would not be doing the honors for obvious reasons.

With all these thoughts going through her mind, it was late into the night, before Samantha finally drifted off to sleep . . . .

"Samantha . . . Samantha." Rachel gently shook her daughter by the shoulders. "Are you going to sleep the entire day away?"

"It can't be morning already," she moaned, pulling the covers over her head.

"We're all waiting downstairs, sleepy head, so don't be long."

"We?" Samantha managed to pry an eye open and was looking at her mother.

"Ester's here, so hurry up."

After the door closed behind her mother, Samantha flung her covers aside and laid there, staring up at the ceiling. The last thing she wanted to do was spend the day with Ester. She rolled over on her side, gazing out the window. Bright sunlight filtering through the lacy white curtains, told Samantha it was probably close to the noon hour.

She couldn't remember a time she'd ever slept so late. She swung her legs over the edge of the bed, grumbling under her breath, "Might as well get this day over with."

Rising, Samantha filled the basin with water from the pitcher, and washed her face. She donned a clean pair of blue jeans and a short-sleeved cotton shirt, then plopped down at her dressing table, looking in the mirror. She sighed, noticing the dark circles beneath her eyes, visible proof of yet another sleepless night. Picking up the hairbrush, she hastily ran it through her long mane of hair, then tied it back away from her face with a velvet ribbon.

When Samantha entered the kitchen, she saw Ester seated at the table with her mother and Sarah, appearing like she'd just stepped off the page of a fashion magazine. Suddenly feeling drab in comparison, she hurried across the room and dropped into the empty chair across from Sarah, who was quietly flipping through the pages of an old catalog.

"Glad you could finally join us," Rachel said with a warm smile. "There's a fresh pot of coffee on the stove, dear . . . help yourself."

Scooting out of her chair, Samantha walked over to the stove, and as poured herself a steaming cup of coffee, she could hear her mother and Ester talking softly, trying to estimate the approximate number of guests they could expect to be present for the wedding ceremony. She sat back down at the table with her cup, blew on it a bit, before taking a sip.

"Where is everybody?" she inquired of her mother.

"Chandler's helping your father with the branding today. James and Amos and some of the other men are rounding up more stray calves."

Samantha hadn't missed the gleam that flashed in Ester's eyes at the mention of Chandler's name. She had to fight to keep the jealous anger out of her voice when she asked her mother, "And where's Morgan?"

"He said he had something important to take care of this morning."

When Samantha heard Ester ask her mother if Morgan and Chandler were brothers, she could barely contain her fury. *As if the woman didn't already know, wasn't it plain as day that the two men were brothers.* "Isn't it obvious?" she snapped.

Rachel frowned at her daughter, curious about Samantha's rude behavior toward Ester . . . it just wasn't like her. But this was not the time nor the place to question her. "So ladies . . . where should we start? Any suggestions?"

"Sarah and I can do all the alterations on the dress," Samantha quickly volunteered, hoping that would keep her and Sarah busy up in her room most of the afternoon. Then she wouldn't have to watch Ester *drool* whenever Chandler's name happened to be mentioned.

Sarah couldn't believe it was her reflection staring back at her in the full-length mirror. The satin gown made her look like a beautiful princess out of some fairy tale. She ran her fingers over the row of tiny pearl buttons that were perfectly stitched around the bodice, knowing this dress must have taken Rachel many painstaking hours to complete. She twisted in different directions, trying to get a better view of the back.

"If you don't hold still, Sarah, you'll wind up with a crooked hem," Samantha gently scolded her friend.

"Samantha, are you sure you don't mind if I wear this dress?" she asked. "I know your mother was saving it for you on your wedding day."

"I don't mind at all, Sarah. I want you to wear the dress." Samantha then muttered more to herself, "Besides, it's not like I'll be needing a wedding dress in the near future."

Sarah giggled.

Leaning back on her heels, Samantha admired her handiwork. "Not bad," she complimented herself. Then, "James won't be able to take his eyes off you, Sarah."

Confused by the sad expression that suddenly clouded her friend's face, Samantha rose to her feet. "Sarah, what's wrong?"

She lowered her eyes and replied in a voice that was barely audible, "I don't want James to be disappointed in me."

"Disappointed in you . . . how?"

"I'm afraid, Samantha."

"Could you be a little bit more specific?"

Sarah's cheeks flushed crimson and she turned away, unable to look even her best friend in the eyes. "I'm afraid . . . afraid to . . . to . . . because of what happened."

Samantha could feel herself blushing, knowing what Sarah was trying to say, but she was determined to help her friend. She thought about the way she'd felt when Chandler kissed her inside the barn. "I think you're worrying over nothing."

"But what if I can't . . ."

"Then James will understand . . . he loves you, Sarah."

"Maybe you're right," she reluctantly agreed with a sigh. But deep down in her heart, Sarah wondered if James loved her enough.

Chapter Ten

James and Sarah's wedding day dawned warm and clear. Since bright and early that morning, Rachel had been filled with nervous energy, busy issuing orders to everybody around her. She'd even managed to chase John completely out of the house with her unintentional henpecking. But she wanted everything to be perfect and there was still so much that needed to be done before their guests started to arrive.

John had given his men the entire day off. Those who would not be attending the ceremony had gone into town to spend the day. John had placed Amos (a renounced fiddle player) in charge of the music preparations. After helping Amos round up the other wanna-be-players and listening to them play, John felt that a badly needed rehearsal was in desperate order. It was obvious that none of them had played in years . . . .

In the privacy of her room, Samantha was trying to help a very anxious Sarah get ready for her big day. With the ceremony soon to begin, Sarah was so jittery that she could barely sit still in front of the mirror, long enough to allow Samantha to finish her hair.

"Hold still, Sarah. You're more jumpy than a kangaroo."

"I can't help it, Samantha . . . I've never been so scared in my life." She groaned. "Even my stomach is tied in knots."

"Relax, Sarah, everything's going to be fine," Samantha tried to calm her friend. She wondered if her brother was as restless as his bride . . . .

Inside the bunkhouse, crowded around a small table with Chandler, Morgan, Amos, Ernie, and a couple of new cowpunchers that his father had hired, James was having trouble keeping his mind on the cards in his hand. Finally in frustration, he folded his cards and set them in front of him. Hard as he tried, he just couldn't seem to concentrate on the poker game; all this waiting was driving him crazy. He wondered if it was normal for a groom to feel this nervous just before the wedding, but who was he going to ask . . . none of the men sitting around this table had ever been married, so how would any of them know how a young groom felt.

James heaved a sigh, nervously fidgeting in his seat.

"Could ya keep quiet and quit squirmin' around in your chair, boy," Ernie complained. "You're more antsy than a June bride."

"Sorry."

"You know, James, it's not too late to change your mind," Morgan said seriously as he began to shuffle the cards.

Chandler frowned at his brother. "You make it sound like his very life is threatened."

"Then if marriage is so wonderful, big brother, why aren't you hitched yet?"

"Yeah, Chandler," Ernie threw in, "why is that?"

"I just haven't found a woman worth marrying is all."

"Are any of 'em worth marryin'?" Ernie retorted. "A woman will try to change a man from the moment she says *I do.* Personally, I like my bachelor life."

"And I'm sure the women of Bear Creek prefer you as a bachelor," Amos quipped.

Morgan and Chandler burst out laughing.

Suddenly standing out of his chair, James began to pace around the room. He grumbled at nobody in particular, "I'll remember this day when one of you decide to get married."

"Bears will grow wings and fly before that ever happens," mumbled Will.

They all burst out laughing, except for James, who snapped back at them. "That's probably true, because I doubt there's a woman in the entire state of Montana who'd be dumb enough to marry any of your ugly hides!"

There was more hoots of laughter.

Ernie held out his bottle of whiskey toward James. "Here, boy . . . this oughta help calm them nerves some."

Angrily snatching the bottle from Ernie's hand, James took a long swig. Immediately he could feel the warm liquid travel down his throat and then it seemed to ignite inside his stomach, causing him to cough and sputter. "Are you . . . trying to kill me?"

As the men were howling with laughter, John appeared inside the doorway, frowning his disapproval. He could tell that poor James had already taken a pretty good ribbing. Folding his arms across his chest, he looked sternly at each man seated around the table.

"Fun's over, boys. You mind giving my son and I a little privacy?"

Several men rose in unison and quickly scrambled out of the bunkhouse. Now John looked sympathetically at his son. He remembered his own wedding day and knew exactly how the boy felt. He just wanted to make sure that James was marrying Sarah for the right reasons.

"The ceremony's about to begin," he announced. "But I'm not so sure the groom's ready."

James looked at his father, confused. "What do you mean?"

"Are you absolutely certain, son, that you wanna go through with this wedding?" At James's frown, he hastened to explain, "Don't get me wrong—it's perfectly normal to feel a little . . . apprehensive, so long as that's what's really bothering you. Bluntly put—I hope you're not marrying Sarah out of pity—because of what happened to her."

"I love Sarah, if that's what you're asking, Pa." James shoved his hands inside his pockets and began to pace around the room. "Were you this nervous when you married Ma?"

"You bet I was," John admitted. "Most men about now begin to have doubts in some form or another . . . that's perfectly understandable. Getting married is a big step, son . . . comes with a lot of responsibility. But there was one thing that I never doubted, even for an instant—and that was the way I felt about your mother. And, James, if you feel even half for Sarah what I felt for your mother, you and Sarah will do just fine."

"I really do love her, Pa. And—thank you."

"Then you'd better hurry, son . . . go get your suit on, before that bride of yours changes *her* mind . . . looking the way you do."

James laughed nervously. "I guess it shows I didn't get much sleep last night."

"And I doubt you'll be getting much sleep tonight, either." John burst out laughing at his son's shocked expression.

The Reverend had been kind enough to lend Rachel the dozens of chairs she would need for the special occasion. And with Ester's help, she had transformed the veranda into a mini-outdoor church, by arranging the chairs in several neat rows. Then, at the beginning of each row, Rachel had carefully placed a large vase of flowers to form a makeshift isle. Smaller vases filled with white and yellow daffodils decorated the heavy tables of food. All the flowers had just been freshly picked that morning from Rachel's own flower garden.

Finally everything seemed to be ready.

Taking one last quick sweep of the backyard, Rachel let out a weary sigh. She hadn't realized just how much hard work went in to planning a wedding, but it had been well worth it. She couldn't wait to see the expression on her soon-to-be-daughter-in-law's lovely face.

By the time Reverend Peters arrived, all the guests who were coming for sure were already present. As Rachel had feared, Jed refused to come to his own daughter's wedding, so John had gladly volunteered to give away the blushing bride.

Rachel was so proud of her men; she had never seen her husband and son look more handsome than they did today. But it was Samantha who'd captured every male's attention. Standing beside Sarah, she was easily as beautiful as the bride, dressed in an elegant blue floor-length gown. The silky material hugged her every curve and fluttered at her blue slipper-clad feet in the gentle breeze. The short sleeves showed off her long, slender arms; the modest bodice was trimmed in a darker blue velvet ribbon which tied in back to form a perfect bow, accentuated her small waist. Tiny blue flowers had been carefully weaved throughout her massively long hair that had been left unbound and hung nearly to her knees in reddish, golden-brown waves.

Even Morgan seemed mesmerized with Samantha, Rachel noticed. And Chandler hadn't been able to take his eyes off her since she'd first stepped outside the door onto the veranda.

After Reverend Zachariah Peters spoke the words that made James and Sarah husband and wife, the reception was now officially underway. Grouped together in front of the large wood-platform dance floor that John had constructed in the back yard, Amos, along with three other 'fellow musicians', were attempting to play a song that Rachel didn't recognize. She laughed out loud, watching James and Sarah, as they struggled to keep in step with the off-key tune. In spite of the trouble the newlyweds were having, Rachel thought her son and new daughter-in-law looked good dancing together. She couldn't have been more pleased with James's choice for a wife if she had handpicked the girl herself.

"May I have this dance?"

Rachel turned and smiled at her husband. As she slipped her arm through his, "It would be an honor," she playfully replied.

Chandler's dark eyes filled with jealous anger, while several young cowboys—the same men who'd escorted Morning Star to the wedding—all took turns twirling Samantha around the makeshift dance floor. Standing there, watching the other couples having fun, already he was beginning to feel about as much out of place as a fish out of water.

Chandler happened to catch sight of Morgan. He, too, seemed to be watching Samantha, and he was wearing that familiar irritating smirk upon his face. Chandler scowled, wondering if his brother found humor in everything. His eyes followed Morgan as he turned and casually meandered his way through the dancing crowd, over to a table where Ernie was passing out glasses of beer to the men.

Turning his attention back to Samantha, Chandler's eyes darkened even more and narrowed into slits of anger, when he noticed the way her newest dance partner had his muscular arm curled around her waist.

"Why aren't you dancing, Graywolf?"

"Must you sneak upon a person?" Chandler hissed at Morgan. "You just took ten years off my life, which I cannot afford."

"Are you just going to stand there watching, while every cowboy on the place takes turns dancing with Samantha—who doesn't look very pleased at the moment, I might add."

Chandler's head swung toward his brother. "The only dance I know how to do would require the beat of a drum." He grumbled to himself, "Come to think of it, a war dance would suit my mood about now."

Morgan threw back his head and laughed. "Wait here."

"Where are you going?" Chandler hollered at Morgan's departing back. But he might as well have been talking to the wind, because his brother completely ignored him.

Samantha swore if another one of these 'big oafs' stepped on her feet, she would not be responsible for her actions. She forced herself to smile at her new 'dance partner' which actually looked more like a sneer. She had to bite down on her bottom lip to keep from crying out in pain when the *big galoot* she was dancing with tripped and landed on her already sore foot. He quickly apologized, then continued to thrust her about the dance floor like nothing ever happened. She wanted to scream her outrage, but kept on smiling instead.

As the cowboy swept her past Chandler again, Samantha looked at him with pleading eyes, and frowned, when Chandler only glared at her.

When the music finally ended, Samantha, in so many unladylike words, told the *clumsy ox* to get lost, then she spun around on her heel and marched toward Chandler, ready to give the inconsiderate man a piece of her mind. *The least he could have done was attempted to rescue her.* But she hadn't gotten very far when a strong arm slid around her waist and then she was being twirled once again onto the dance floor.

Assuming the man who'd grabbed her was the same cowboy she'd just got through dancing with, Samantha hissed, "Let go of me!" and then her mouth suddenly snapped shut when she found herself staring into the handsome face of Morgan.

"You were saying?" he chuckled.

"I'm so mad I could spit!"

Morgan burst out laughing. "You do have a way with words, Miss Callahan." He continued to move her around the dance floor, peering down into a beautiful but angry face. "My brother sure does have his hands full where you're concerned."

"Don't even mention your brother to me!"

"Now what's got your feathers all ruffled?"

"My feathers are more than ruffled!"

"How can a woman with a face of an angel have such a foul temper?"

Samantha honestly didn't know how to respond: Morgan had just complimented and insulted her, all in the same sentence. So she didn't say anything. Besides, she was finally starting to enjoy herself, because Morgan was turning out to be quite a superb dancer . . . .

Chandler observed his younger brother as he whisked Samantha about the other twirling couples with the graceful ease of a ballet dancer. He wondered where Morgan had learned to waltz like a fancy Eastern gentleman. He couldn't help but feel a little envious.

"Care to dance?"

Chandler's body stiffened at the sound of Morning Star's voice. He really didn't want anything to do with Jed Martin's *wife*. Why couldn't the woman just leave him alone. He refused to even look at her as he snapped in reply, "Why don't you ask your husband!"

"My husband's not here." Ester could not take her eyes off Graywolf. He had once asked her father for her hand in marriage; now she almost wished she'd never left the village. Graywolf had turned out to be an extremely handsome and virile man. Dressed in a dark blue snug-fitting suit, with his coal-black shoulder-length hair pulled back into a neat queue, what woman could resist him? And she certainly was not immuned. Ester couldn't help wondering, now that her marriage to Jed was a complete failure and there seemed to be no hope, was it possible she still stood a chance with this man . . .

"Graywolf?"

Chandler whirled to face her. "What do you want from me, *Ester?*"

"Aren't you even a little happy to see me?"

It appalled Chandler what he read in Morning Star's dark smoldering eyes, as she stood there, gazing up at him. Desire. Hunger. If he wasn't careful, the woman would probably try to devour him. He adamantly replied, "No!"

Ester tried to hide the hurt she felt. Surely Graywolf couldn't have forgotten what they had once shared in their youth. Slowly, seductively, she slid her hand over the hard muscle of his upper arm, then smiled prettily, batting her long, sooty lashes.

He jerked his arm from her grasp as if her touch had just burned him. "Don't you have a husband to go home to?"

Ester's bottom lip began to quiver.

"Save your tears, Morning Star . . . they don't work on me anymore."

"I made a terrible mistake marrying Jed," she sniffled.

"Why are you telling me this?"

"Because I . . . I've never stopped loving you."

"If that's true, I don't know what to say." Though Chandler didn't believe it, not for a minute. And even if what Morning Star said *was* true, it would not matter, because she was now another man's wife. Besides, what he'd once felt for her was no longer there—and wondered what he ever saw in the woman . . .

"Am I disturbing something?"

Hearing his brother's voice, Chandler inwardly sighed with relief. When he turned and saw Samantha standing at Morgan's side, immediately he went to Samantha and wrapped a possessive arm around her waist, hoping Morning Star would take the hint.

But Ester's stunned gaze was still locked on the tall, handsome man she remembered as Graywolf's pesky little brother . . . only . . . he wasn't so *little* anymore. She couldn't remember his name, but he had grown into an extremely handsome man . . . like his older brother.

"It's absolutely amazing," she finally remarked to him, after a while, "the resemblance you share with Graywolf."

Morgan had been watching the heated discussion between his brother and Morning Star, which was the reason he was standing here now. He remembered how vain the Indian maiden was, always having to be the center of every man's attention, and figured out a clever way that would probably get rid of the irksome woman. He slid an arm around Samantha's shoulder and said in a suggestive tone of voice, "That's not all we share."

Samantha gasped.

Chandler grinned.

Her face turning red with jealous rage, Ester wordlessly stormed away.

"That wasn't funny!" Samantha snapped at Morgan, pushing away from him. "I bet she goes straight to my mother! Was that really necessary?"

"The woman deserved it," Chander said in defense of his brother.

"So you use me to . . . to . . . whatever!"

"It did the trick . . . it got rid of her."

"But, Chandler, that's no way to treat your lost love," Samantha tauntingly retorted.

"I already told you . . . Morning Star means nothing to me."

"Yet the instant my back is turned, who do I find you with?"

"*She* came over to *me*!"

"And you couldn't just walk away?" Samantha angrily threw back at him.

Morgan was beginning to wonder if these two getting together was such a good idea. They seemed to bring out the worst in each other. But, then again, if his brother did marry Miss Callahan, he certainly would never lead a boring life, Morgan thought, chuckling. Nor would the poor man hardly ever have a moment's peace.

"Cover for us, Morgan," Chandler suddenly said. Then he grabbed Samantha, tossing the infuriating woman over his shoulder as he walked away.

"Put me down this instant, you . . . you thick-headed buffoon!" Samantha shouted at the top of her lungs. When he refused to listen, she began to pummel his back with her fists.

Never once breaking stride Chandler brought his free hand down hard upon her bottom. Just as he expected, a string of unladylike words shot out of her mouth. Again his hand came down upon her rear end, harder this time.

Samantha didn't utter a sound.

When Chandler figured they were far enough away from the wedding party where nobody would hear them, he abruptly dumped her on the ground. She instantly rolled to her feet and actually took a swing at him.

"Are you crazy?" he shouted.

Again Samantha came at him with both fists flailing. Chandler nearly laughed, she looked so ridiculous, coming at him like some prized fighter, dressed in an elegant gown. But he didn't dare laugh, knowing it would only make her madder than she already was. He easily caught both her tiny wrists in his large hand and held on to them. Then Samantha did the very last thing he would have expected: she burst into tears. He immediately let go of her.

Now watching Samantha stand there, her hands covering her face, her shoulders shaking, while she cried her eyes out, Chandler felt like the worse kind of heel. With a sigh, he walked over and, gathering her in his arms, he stood holding her against his chest, crooning to her like he would a hurt child.

Feeling Chandler's strong arms embrace her, Samantha's tears flowed even harder. She wasn't really sure why she was crying, she only knew that she couldn't seem to stop. As his calloused fingers moved slowly up and down her spine, gently kneading the tension away, her sobs were soon reduced to mere sniffles.

"I'm sorry, Samantha," he murmured against her ear.

She leaned back looking at him with those brilliant blue eyes so trusting, the tears glistening on the ends of her long, sooty lashes. Chandler felt like somebody had just punched him hard in the gut, and he had this sudden overwhelming urge to protect her from all harm. Without realizing what he was doing, his head moved toward her . . .

He's going to kiss me, Samantha thought as her eyelids fluttered closed. The instant his warm lips touched hers, hundreds of butterflies began to dance around in the pit of her stomach; and that wonderful tingling feeling was spreading through her entire body. She wrapped her arms around his neck; then his strong arms encircled her. And as the kiss became more urgent, if Chandler had not been supporting most of her weight, Samantha would have crumpled at his feet. His lips began a slow trek across her flushed cheek; then he began to plant searing kisses along the sensitive curve of her neck, moving down her collarbone . . .

Samantha's eyes flew open.

When Chandler felt her body stiffen, it was like tossing cold water on a fire. His hands dropped at his sides and he quickly stepped away from her. As he fought to get his emotions more under control, he suggested, "I think that we probably should be getting back to the party—before we're missed."

Samantha, who wanted to fling herself back into his arms, could only nod in reply.

"Wait a second—" Chandler smoothed the tangles in her knee-length hair with his fingers, noticing some of the tiny blue flowers that had been so carefully weaved into her beautiful mane had fallen out, but there was nothing he could do about that. Then he brushed several smudges of dirt off her silky dress. "That should do it . . . at least you look presentable now."

He grinned when she blushed and shyly lowered her eyes. He playfully tapped the tip of her nose. "You'd better go on. I'll follow behind in a little while."

Chandler stood there, watching Samantha Callahan hurry across the field toward the house, her knee-length hair swishing behind her like reddish gold silk. He'd never seen her look more beautiful than she did today. During the wedding ceremony, he'd noticed there had been more eyes on Samantha than there had been on the bride and groom, and how badly he'd wanted to punch every male who'd been staring at her.

Suddenly the tiny hairs on the back of Chandler's neck began to tingle, and he had the uneasy feeling that somebody was watching him. His keen eyes scanned the surrounding area, but he didn't notice anything out of the ordinary.

Figuring it was probably just his imagination, Chandler headed back to the party . . . .

Jake Martin emerged from the trees, his furious gaze narrowing upon Wade Chandler's departing broad back, his hatred for the Indian growing even stronger. As he had stood watching the tender love scene between Samantha and Chandler, he'd seriously considered shooting the Indian right then and there just for putting his hands on his woman. And he might've shot him, too, if he thought he could've gotten away with it. Jake wished he'd never asked the Indian to escort Samantha home that night. *What could he have been thinking.* Wade Chandler probably would've been long gone by now; the man would have just passed through town like so many other drifters. But there was no time to dwell upon what he wished he would've done. He had to think of a way to get Samantha alone. And with such a large crowd of people hanging around her place—not counting her personal watchdog—it was going to be a rather difficult task. But Jake wasn't about to leave town without at least telling the woman he loved good-bye . . . .

When Samantha returned to the party, she noticed that quite a few of the guests had already gone home. She was relieved that nobody seemed to have noticed her brief absence. Standing on the edge of the dance platform, Samantha giggled, while several couples struggled to keep in step with a slightly out-of-tune waltz. She thought the so called 'fiddle players' sounded like they were getting a little better. Slow dancing to a song that only James and Sarah seemed to hear, the new bride and groom had eyes only for each other. Her parents were the same way, Samantha noted with a smile. Her mother's face seemed to glow with happiness as she gazed adoringly into her husband's eyes. Ever since she could remember, this is the way it had always been between her mother and father. It was obvious that John and Rachel Callahan were completely devoted to each other. She could only hope that someday she, too, would find that same kind of special love . . .

A hand on her shoulder startled Samantha out of her thoughts. Then a familiar voice whispered next to her ear, "I don't think I told you how beautiful you look."

She looked over her shoulder, smiling at Chandler. And the huge smile he bestowed upon her, nearly took her breath away. Again Samantha was struck by Chandler's incredible handsomeness, with those inky-black eyes and their extremely long lashes.

"Would you care to dance?" she asked him.

"I would if I could."

"You mean you can't dance?"

"Sorry to disappoint you, but—no, I can't."

"It doesn't disappoint me." It had never once occurred to Samantha that Chandler didn't know how to dance, especially when his brother could dance so beautifully. That might explain why Chandler had glared at her, while she had danced with practically every male there, Samantha now realized, feeling a little guilty.

They stood there, in compatible silence, watching the couples twirl by. Samantha was just about to offer Chandler a dance lesson, when she spotted Ester striding toward them. She elbowed him beside her. "Don't look now, but your *lost love* approaches."

Chandler followed Samantha's line of vision, and frowned. Suddenly grabbing Samantha by the hand, he walked swiftly in the opposite direction, pulling her along the outer edge of the dance floor behind him. When Chandler spotted Morgan, he quickened his steps, hoping his brother's presence might discourage Ester's pursuit.

It seemed to do the trick.

Ester stopped in her tracks. She'd almost made a spectacle of herself in front of Graywolf's brother. *How dare Graywolf avoid her.* Well, he wouldn't get away with it. A smug, satisfied grin twisted Ester's lips. She had a better way to get even. Twirling on her boot heel, she stormed off in a hurry . . . .

Morgan noticed his brother approaching with Samantha in tow. Behind them stood a furious looking Morning Star. It took him only a moment to surmise the situation. He chuckled under his breath, finding the whole thing amusing. As Graywolf halted beside him, he couldn't resist a teasing remark. "Having a little problem?" He winked at Samantha who stood on the other side of Graywolf. Her face was flushed either from the brisk walk she'd just taken or from embarrassment, Morgan couldn't tell.

"Oh, oh," he said. "Don't look now but Morning Star returns with reinforcements."

Samantha turned her head and inwardly groaned when she saw both her parents walking with a very smug-faced Ester. It didn't take a genius to figure out that Ester must have told her parents a real doozy. "Your old girlfriend certainly doesn't waste any time!" she snapped at Chandler. Although she knew she wasn't being fair.

"Would you please quit referring to that woman as my old girlfriend!"

"What's the matter, dear brother . . . having female troubles?" Morgan chuckled.

Chandler scowled at him. "Is everything funny to you?"

"This definitely is."

"Oh . . . Samantha, there you are," Ester called out. Her voice sounded genuinely concerned as she added, "I got worried when you and Chandler disappeared."

Samantha glared at the older woman, but held her tongue.

Ester ignored Graywolf's furious expression. She'd gotten her point across without actually accusing him of any wrongdoing. Pleased with her performance, she turned apologetic eyes toward John and Rachel. "Evidently there's been a little misunderstanding on my part. I can see that your daughter wasn't—harmed in any way."

Reading Ester Martin like a book, John wasn't one to beat around the bush. "Just exactly what are you implying?"

Wishing she could slap the smirk off Graywolf's handsome face, Ester tried to smooth over John's obvious anger toward her. "I only meant that . . . well . . . that it's not proper for a young lady to be alone in the company of a single gentleman. Honest, John, I was only thinking of your daughter's reputation."

John didn't believe that explanation for an instant. Though he couldn't understand why it should bother Ester whether Samantha was in the company of Chandler or any other single gentleman—as she had so kindly put it. He didn't bother trying to curb the angry tone of his voice when he answered her, because he wanted Ester to know just how much her suggestive remark about Chandler and Samantha infuriated him. "For your information, not that it's any of your business, I gave Chandler orders not to let Samantha out of his sight. Because of that fruitcake son of yours, my daughter isn't safe even on her own property . . ."

"John . . ."

"Stay out of this, Rachel!"

"Are you suggesting my son . . ."

" . . . isn't quite right in the head, you bet I am!" John wanted to say more, but the pleading look on his wife's face stopped him.

Anger flared in Ester's eyes, before she wordlessly did an about-face and headed toward her buggy. Several of Jed's men saw their boss's wife leaving the party, and immediately walked off the dance floor to follow after her.

During the commotion the music had stopped. John gave Amos a signal, and the men resumed playing. He turned to his wife. "I'm sorry, Rachel. I know Ester's your friend, but I wasn't about to let her insinuate that Samantha and Chandler . . ."

"Ester had that coming, John."

"Then you're not mad at me?"

"Of course not." Rachel doubted her husband had noticed, but there had been something odd about Ester's behavior tonight. In her opinion, Ester had been acting more like a jealous female. But why on earth would she be jealous over Chandler?

"Let's not give any more thought to what happened here," John said. "And I suggest we don't waste good music."

"Good music—are you going deaf, Pa?" Samantha teased.

"They do still sound a bit rusty," Rachel said, laughing.

"Mrs. Callahan." Morgan bowed politely at the waist. "I would be honored if I could have the next dance . . . that is . . ." he arched a dark brow toward John and added, "if your husband wouldn't mind?"

"Just don't step on my wife's delicate feet."

"I'll do my best." Morgan took Rachel by the hand, then he gracefully twirled her onto the dance floor.

While John observed his wife and Morgan, he slid a surreptitious glance at the somber man standing at his daughter's side. There had been something peculiar about Ester's actions tonight. He wondered if Rachel had noticed the possessive way Ester had looked at Chandler. But why would Jed's wife be jealous over a man she hardly knew?

It was well past midnight before the wedding reception finally came to an end. After all the guests had departed, an exhausted Rachel dropped wearily onto one of the bales of hay that John had scattered around the yard to use as temporary benches. Her once neatly bound chestnut hair had come undone, and now hung down her back in thick waves. She had removed her shoes and stockings, and sat massaging her aching feet, wondering if she looked as old as she felt.

Hearing footsteps behind her, Rachel looked over her shoulder and smiled at her husband. In the bright moonlight, she could clearly see the handsome face that still turned many a woman's head. For a man in his late forties, her husband was in excellent physical condition, Rachel thought with admiration. He had long ago done away with his tie, and now had unbuttoned his shirt, exposing his broad, muscular chest to her appreciative view.

"You look as tired as I feel," he remarked. "Turn around."

"Mmmm . . . that feels wonderful," Rachel sighed with pleasure as John gently massaged the tension for her neck and shoulders.

"Everything went smoothly today, I think . . . even in spite of Ester."

"I think so too," Rachel agreed. "She was sure mad though when she left here. John, do you think we'll hear from Jed?"

"Naw. But even if we do, don't you worry about Jed." He yawned and said, "I don't know about you, but I'm glad this wedding business is all over with. Now I just got Samantha to go and we'll finally have the house to ourselves."

"John, what a mean thing to say," Rachel gently admonished her husband, but there was a smile on her face when she'd said it. "Besides, James and Sarah will be staying here with us, until they can build a home of their own."

"Yeah . . . but I know they'll be eventually moving out. Samantha, on the other hand, unless she can find a husband who'll allow her to wear the pants in the family, she'll be with us until we're old and gray."

"John," Rachel giggled, "I know you don't mean that."

"You 'bout ready for bed, Rach?"

"Couldn't we just sit out here a while and enjoy the quiet?"

In answer John straddled the bale of hay and slid his arms around his wife, pulling her snugly against his chest, and kissed the top of her head. He smiled when she nuzzled her cheek against his shoulder. Their arms wrapped around each other like a young couple in love, they sat there in compatible silence. Rachel was thoroughly enjoying the tranquility of the moment when John suddenly burst out laughing. Frowning, she sat up straight and twisted to look at him.

"What's so funny?"

"I was just remembering when James tried to carry his bride over the threshold and stumbled over Sarah's dress . . . the way they both landed sprawled out on the floor." John started to hoot with laughter. "I bet Sarah's face is still beet red from the incident."

"Shame on you, John Callahan . . . the poor child was totally embarrassed." Then, Rachel began to giggle. "It was rather funny though, wasn't it."

"That's what I'll always remember most about James and Sarah's wedding day . . . how my son ever-so-gallantly tried to carry his beautiful, blushing bride over the threshold . . . then dropped her at his feet."

John and Rachel howled with laughter.

Samantha could hear her parents talking and laughing as she sneaked past them, hurrying toward the barn. She inwardly upbraided herself for so thoughtlessly forgetting to feed poor Daisy. The instant she opened the barn door, the little mare poked her head over the side of the stall and nickered softly.

"Sorry, girl," she spoke to her horse. "I bet you're hungry."

Feeling along the wall for the lantern in the darkness, Samantha grumbled under her breath, when she discovered it wasn't hanging in its proper place. With a muttered oath, she moved slowly across the hay-strewn floor to her horse's stall, then lifted the latch. Daisy nearly knocked her off her feet as she bounded through the gate, trotted away a few feet and then suddenly turned with a loud nicker, pounding her hoof nervously over the ground. It was a peculiar way for her horse to act. If Samantha didn't know any better, Daisy wanted her to follow her out of the barn.

"What's the matter with you, girl?"

Hidden in the far corner of Daisy's stall, Jake didn't move a muscle, trying to decide whether he should call out to Samantha or wait until she got close enough to grab her. He hadn't expected that crazy horse of hers to create such a fuss over his presence; the stupid mare should be used to him by now. He was afraid that Samantha would bolt out the door before giving him a chance to explain his reason for being here.

Jake could hear Samantha trying to calm the skittish mare, and nearly panicked when he heard her call out, "Is somebody there?" He held his breath when he heard the stall gate creak open wider and then there was the sound of footsteps.

"I said is somebody there?"

He had no choice now but to answer. "It's me, Samantha."

"Jake!" Samantha gasped. "What are you doing here?"

He could hear the fear in her voice, and let out a sigh. It made him feel bad that she was afraid of him; though he could understand why she feared him and really couldn't blame her. "Would you please just listen to what I have to say?"

"Say whatever then leave!"

"I wanted to tell you good-bye and that I'm sorry for what I did."

"You'd better go, Jake, before my pa finds you here."

"Do you forgive me, Samantha?"

When Daisy nickered, Jake snapped, "Could you possibly keep that nag quiet before she wakes the entire bunkhouse?"

"Daisy has more right to be here than you," Samantha angrily replied.

"Okay, I deserved that."

"You deserve a lot more than that, Jake Martin."

"Wait a second." A moment later, Jake struck a match and lit the lantern he'd taken from the hanger. "Now I can see your face while we're talking."

"We're through talking . . . this conversation's over."

"I'm leaving town, Samantha," Jake hastened to inform her. "I doubt very likely I'll be coming back any time soon, so this might be the last time we'll see each other."

When Jake saw Samantha's shoulders slump in defeat, he knew he'd won. He quickly went on to say, "You should know I would never hurt you. I was just jealous over the Indian and temporarily lost my head," he admitted. "Can't you understand?"

Peering into eyes that were nearly as dark as Chandler's, *how could she let Jake leave without forgiving him?* Samantha asked herself. And the answer was immediate: she couldn't. Even after everything he'd done to her, she still considered Jake her dear friend. Smiling faintly, she jokingly said, "You certainly do have a mean right hook."

Jake visibly winced. "I'm especially sorry about that."

"Now that you're forgiven . . . would you please leave, Jake?" Just in case he was tempted to try anything stupid, she thought to add, "I've been gone quite a while already . . . Pa could be looking for me as we speak."

"I love you, Sam." Jake pecked her on the cheek, then slipped quietly out of the stall.

Samantha stood there, watching the gate swinging back and forth, where Jake had just disappeared. Her heart went out to Jake, even after everything he'd done. She also felt depressed, knowing there was nothing she could do to help her childhood friend. Because there was already enough animosity between her father and Jed Martin, she decided not to mention Jake's visit tonight . . . .

Chapter Eleven

John peered down at his sleeping wife, wondering how was it possible that Rachel was more beautiful now than she was the day he'd married her. In her youth Rachel had been a real beauty, but she'd been a skinny girl then, with hardly any shape; the mature woman she'd become was a whole lot curvier and had filled out nicely in all the right places. John smiled down at her. The way her delicate hands were folded beneath her cheek, he thought it made Rachel appear so much more vulnerable somehow.

Which made him start thinking . . . tomorrow morning he would be leaving on the cattle drive and would be gone for at least two months, possibly longer. Every year it was becoming more difficult to leave his wife behind; only this time, for some unexplainable reason, he could not seem to shake this uneasy feeling he'd been having lately. It could just be the simple fact that he wasn't getting any younger and what if something happened to him? What would become of his lovely wife?

Rachel's amber-colored eyes fluttered open. She smiled when she saw her husband's handsome face looming over her, wondering how long he'd been awake. She reached up with her hand to brush away some hair that had fallen across his brow . . . that's when she noticed the faint worry lines crinkling the corners of his eyes.

"John, what's wrong?"

John had forgotten how this woman seemed to have the uncanny ability of practically reading his thoughts. Maybe that should be a warning he was getting senile; already he was forgetting things. "I'm just a little concerned about leaving you alone tomorrow—that's all."

"But I won't be alone . . . James and Sarah will be here with me. Besides, I've stayed by myself hundreds of times . . . care to try again?"

Letting out a frustrated sigh, John figured he might as well tell her the truth or he'd never hear the end of it. "What if something happened to me . . . what would you do?"

"You're not ill, are you?" Rachel turned over on her side.

"No—it's nothing like that. Please answer the question."

Rachel was thoughtful for a moment. "Well . . . the old farmer who lives on the other side of town is always available," she said in a teasing tone.

"I'm serious, Rachel."

"I'm sorry, John . . . I'm not sure what's really bothering you."

"I'm not getting any younger."

"So that's what this is about," she muttered to herself, before reminding her husband, "You're a man in your prime, John."

"Yeah . . . and everything goes downhill from here."

"I suppose it's possible you could be confined to a rocking chair in a couple of years," Rachel said, trying not to laugh.

"Could you stop with the jokes?"

"So what do you want me to say, John? You're in better shape than most men that is Chandler's age."

"I'm not so sure that's a compliment . . . we don't even know how old the man is."

"Now who's not being serious." Rachel tossed the covers aside and swung her legs over the edge of the bed. She looked over her shoulder at her frowning husband and, trying to keep a straight face, she said in a serious tone, "Would you prefer I bring you breakfast in bed this morning, dear, or do you think you can find the strength to come downstairs?"

"That isn't funny, woman."

When John tried to grab her, Rachel jumped to her feet, so he only grabbed air. "Maybe you are getting older, John . . . your reflexes *are* a bit slower these days." She burst out laughing at his scowling expression.

She walked over to her dressing table and sat in the chair, looking in the mirror. Behind her she could see her husband was still watching her with a frown upon his handsome face. Biting back a grin, she picked up her hairbrush and began to run it through her long tresses. "I hope you didn't take me seriously, John . . . what I said about your reflexes."

"Come back to bed, woman, and I'll show you just how good my reflexes still are."

Rachel laughed.

"I take that as a no then." John sighed and laid back on his pillow, quietly observing his wife as she quickly and expertly (from years of practice) braided her lustrous hair which was nearly as long as Samantha's. He remembered Rachel's mother and sister had extraordinary hair like his wife and daughter; and Rachel's great grandmother's hair had actually touched the floor in her stocking feet, or so he'd heard.

"Have I ever told you how beautiful you look in the morning?"

Rachel smiled at her husband in the big oval mirror. "I do remember you mentioning it a time or two."

John got out of bed and walked over to his wife where he planted an affectionate kiss on the back of her long, slender neck. He stood watching her finish winding and pinning her plaited hair on top of her head. Afterward, he snatched his pants off the floor and pulled them on, then went to his dresser and grabbed a clean shirt . . .

Twisting slightly in her chair, Rachel marveled over her husband's still youthful physique as she watched him dress. John was tall and powerfully built. Rachel thought he was much more handsome now in his prime than he'd been as a younger man. She couldn't understand why he would be so worried about getting older.

John pecked her on the cheek. "Call me when breakfast is ready."

Rachel's eyes followed him out the door. John turned and winked at her before closing it behind him. A smile of contentment played upon her lips as she rose from her chair and hurriedly dressed.

Standing at the kitchen sink, as Rachel began to peel the small mound of potatoes for breakfast, she was thinking about the newly married couple upstairs, how important it was for James and Sarah to spend some time alone together. She smiled, remembering what the first several months of marriage had been like for her and John. Her husband had been such a romantic back then, and he still was sometimes when the mood suited him.

Rachel's thoughts turned back to her son and his new bride; the newlyweds certainly didn't need a meddlesome mother hanging around them. But what could she do that would allow them the privacy they needed? And then an idea suddenly struck Rachel. Though she'd never been on a cattle drive before, it would be the perfect solution. Besides, being a rancher's wife, maybe it was about time she went along with her husband on a drive. And wouldn't the men appreciate a woman's touch with the meals instead of having to consume Amos's gut-wrenching beans day after day.

Excited about her decision, Rachel couldn't wait to tell her husband . . . .

"There's no way you're going with me, Rachel," John emphatically argued.

"And why not?" she demanded to know.

"Because women don't belong on cattle drives."

"That's ridiculous . . . Samantha goes with you every year."

"She's different."

"You're going to have to give me a better reason than that, John Callahan."

"Okay. I'm your husband and I said no—that's reason enough."

"Not for me, it isn't."

"Woman, you're being unreasonable."

Rachel scowled at John as she watched him shovel several bites of food in his mouth. He was trying to ignore her now and she knew why. Because as far as her husband was concerned, the subject was closed, and he didn't want to discuss it any further. *Well, he wasn't getting off so easy.* "As I remember, John Callahan, just a little while ago, you were worried about getting old and what if something happened to you while you were away . . ."

"I've come to my senses since then."

"You have to *have* sense to begin with to be able to lose it," Rachel angrily retorted, tossing her napkin on top of the table.

Outside on the back veranda were Morgan and Chandler, along with several other ranch hands, who were all waiting for John, when they happened to hear John and Rachel's raised voices from inside the kitchen. None of the men had ever heard their boss and his wife argue before, so naturally they were just a little curious what all the hollering was about. They gathered around the back door to listen, pressing their ears against the wood.

And that's how Amos found them. When he realized what the men were doing, the disgust was evident in the tone of his voice. "You should all be ashamed of yourselves . . . eavesdropping on a private conversation."

But by now the shouting match had grown loud enough to pique even Amos's curiosity. He stepped closer toward the door to listen with the other men . . .

"Forget it, Rachel! I won't change my mind!"

"But I'm no longer *asking* your permission, John!"

"And don't bother asking me because you don't have it!"

"But I don't *need* your permission!"

"You don't know what you're saying!"

"I know *exactly* what I'm saying, John Callahan . . . you're just not used to hearing me say it!"

"You have no idea about the dangers on a drive!"

"It couldn't be any more dangerous for me than it is for Samantha!"

"Samantha knows what she's doing . . . I don't have to worry about her!" John took a deep breath and let it out slowly, then more calmly added, "You, on the other hand, have no idea of the dangers you'd be facing—I would have to look out for you, Rachel, every minute of the day."

"But Samantha had to learn, didn't she?"

"Woman, when did you become so blasted stubborn?"

"This is something I really want to do, John."

John wasn't sure how to handle this side of his normally soft-spoken wife. She'd never defied him on anything or questioned his authority before. Couldn't she understand that he didn't want her along on this drive for her own safety? Maybe if she'd come to him sooner . . .

"Look, Rachel . . . I don't want to argue with you anymore but . . ."

"Good, because I'm coming with you."

"You're staying home . . . where you belong!" John angrily shouted as he slammed his coffee cup down on the table.

"John Callahan, don't you dare take that tone of voice with me!"

"Ma, Pa, what's all the yelling about?"

John and Rachel both turned at the sound of James's voice. He stood inside the doorway, his expression a mask of worry.

"Maybe *you* can talk some sense into your mother," John hollered at his son. "She wants to come along with us tomorrow, so would you mind explaining to her about the dangers of a cattle drive . . . hopefully she'll listen to you!"

"Your father seems to think he can order me around like one of his hired hands!" Rachel furiously retorted.

The room suddenly went still. The tension between his parents was obvious. After a brief period of silence, James finally spoke, but tried to choose his words carefully, not wanting to make a bad situation even worse. "I don't want to take sides . . . but . . . well . . . if Ma wants to come with us, Pa, I really don't see any reason why she . . ."

"Who asked you?" John snapped.

James calmly replied, "You just asked me to explain to Ma about the dangers of a cattle drive, but I see no reason . . ."

John pointed toward the back door. "Leave us . . . I wanna talk to your mother alone."

"But . . ."

"Do as your father says, son."

Though James was a little reluctant to leave his parents alone, he obediently crossed the room, then, with his hand resting on the doorknob, he sent his mother a sympathetic look, before stepping out the door and closing it behind him.

Amos had practically fallen at James's feet in his haste to get out of the boy's way. He could only imagine what James must be thinking, seeing them all standing around the door and now trying to look as inconspicuous as possible, which only made them look more guilty.

"What's going on here?" When it suddenly dawned on James what the men had been doing, he said accusingly, "You were listening!"

"So . . . is your ma going with us or not?" Ernie had the audacity to ask. Which earned him a slap in the back of the head from Amos.

John noted the stubborn tilt of his wife's delicate chin as she stood leaning against the counter, glaring at him. This wasn't getting either of them anywhere, so he decided to try a different approach. "Rach, please try to understand . . . cattle drives are not only dangerous, but are also strenuous. We're in the saddle before dawn and ride till dusk. And sometimes the dust is so bad, you can barely see your own hand in front of your face."

"Do you think running this ranch while you're away isn't hard work?" Rachel argued.

"Okay . . . just answer me this, Rachel. Why is coming along on this cattle drive so important to you?"

"Without me here, James and Sarah would have the whole house to themselves. Surely, John, even *you* can understand that." Rachel could tell her husband was weakening, so she hastily added, "You won't regret having me along, and I promise I'll do whatever you say."

"I just don't want you to get hurt."

"But, John, I can get hurt just as easily running a ranch as I could driving cattle," Rachel logically pointed out.

John let out a sigh and ran a hand through his shaggy hair. "Tell you what . . . I'll think about it. Now come here." He stood and Rachel went willingly into his outstretched arms. He held her close, kissed the top of her head. She nestled her cheek against his chest.

"And you say Samantha gets her stubborn side from me," he teased her.

Rachel leaned back smiling at him. "Maybe she gets her stubbornness from both of us."

"If Samantha ever marries, her husband has my sympathy."

"John, what a mean thing to say," but Rachel was grinning.

Though John would have liked nothing better than to stand there holding his lovely wife in his arms, there was a lot of work he needed to get done today. Reluctantly, he set her away from him, kissed her on the cheek. "I've gotta get back to work. I'll see you at supper."

As John headed toward the corral, he was wondering when his wife had become so darn headstrong. He'd never seen Rachel so determined to have her own way. Then, again, had there ever been a time when she hadn't got what she wanted? considering he never could deny her anything. John chuckled to himself. Rachel would be getting her way this time, too, because he'd already decided to take her along with him.

He would wait a while though before he told her the good news. After all, he couldn't let her think he'd given in so easily.

Besides, having his wife along just might prove to be beneficial, John mused. It would be a welcome change for the men to be able to enjoy his wife's home cooking, instead enduring Amos's beans just about every day. Those beans of his could make a man miserable . . . .

A loud cheer went up from the men when they heard their boss's wife would be accompanying them on the cattle drive. Every man there knew Rachel could prepare a meal that would melt in your mouth. Amos wasn't quite as enthused as the others; he felt a little insulted because the men preferred Rachel's cooking to his own.

That evening the entire family gathered inside the formal dining room for a sort of celebration supper. Rachel had spent hours in the kitchen, preparing her family's favorite dishes. Chandler and Morgan had both been invited to join them, but Morgan had respectfully declined the offer and had stayed behind in the bunkhouse to play a little poker with Amos, Ernie and Will.

Chandler wouldn't have missed this feast for anything. After John gave the blessing, he eagerly heaped his plate (which was more the size of a platter) with mounds of delicious foods. He looked across the table at Samantha and winked, then he picked up his fork and began to eat, only halfheartedly listening to the conversation between John and James . . .

"Don't look for us till the end of September at the earliest . . . that's if nothing goes wrong. And, James, don't forget Suzie's due to foal any day now . . . best to keep her inside the barn from here on out until she does."

"I already know that, Pa."

Leaning back in his chair, John quietly observed his son for a moment. "Guess I keep forgetting you're a man now."

"Then if we can agree that I'm a man . . . can't you trust me to handle things around here while you're away."

"I'll say no more on the subject." John winked at his wife, then shoveled another huge bite of food into his mouth.

"I'm glad you're coming with us, Ma. For once I won't be the only female surrounded by a bunch of men." Samantha looked at her brother to add, "Sometimes they seem to think that just because you're a woman that it automatically makes you their servant."

James pretended to look shocked. "You mean it isn't true?"

When Chandler burst out laughing, Samantha kicked him under the table. She then said to Sarah, "If you're not careful my brother will have you waiting on him hand and foot and expect his breakfast in bed."

"Sarah wouldn't mind doting on her man once in a while," James said confidently. He turned to his wife to sweetly say, "Isn't that true, my-beautiful-blushing-bride?" But all he got was a scowl. "Well, maybe I was wrong," he muttered under his breath.

Howls of laughter around the table caused James to blush.

"Apparently your 'blushing bride' has a different opinion," Samantha teased her brother. "You certainly have a lot to learn about the female gender."

James frowned at his sister.

"Mrs. Callahan," Chandler said, "I'm glad to hear that you're coming with us in the morning. I'm looking forward to some of your home cooked meals."

"There—you see what I mean, Sarah?" Samantha told her friend. "Chandler's a perfect example of the way a man's mind works. He only thinks of his stomach and whether there's a woman around to slave over the stove."

Sarah giggled.

"All this talk about food reminds me . . . did the men tell you about the grizzly story?" John asked Chandler. At the negative shake of his head, John went on to say, "I'm sure you heard about Amos's famous beans . . . believe it or not, those beans actually saved our lives once. It was on one of our cattle drives a few years back, while we were all sleeping this—huge grizzly wandered into our camp. Amos had served us beans for supper that evening—as usual. Anyway, some of us happened to wake up that night in time to see this huge grizzly running away from our camp as if it couldn't get out of there fast enough." John started to laugh. "Even the bear couldn't stand the smell around that campfire . . . if you get my meaning. And the next day, the odor was so bad, even our own horses shied away from us. Remember that, son?"

James added, "Pa claimed that's what kept the cattle moving ahead of us at such a fast pace, that even the cows couldn't stand to be near us."

Rachel was holding her stomach from laughing so hard, even though she'd already heard this story many times before. "Please, John, stop."

Noting the skeptical look on Chandler's face, Samantha informed him, "It really did happen . . . I was there . . . honest." She shrugged when he didn't seem to believe her.

Rachel was still laughing when she stood out of her chair and began to clear away the dirty dishes. "Guess these dishes aren't going to do themselves."

Sarah helped her.

"How 'bout us men head on out to the bunkhouse and join Morgan and the others for a quick hand of poker," John suggested.

"I'll be out later maybe," Chandler replied. He watched John and James leave the dining room, glad to have a moment alone with the beautiful woman still seated across from him at the table.

"My father must really like you."

He arched a questioning brow at her, so Samantha clarified, "If my father didn't like you, he never would've left us alone together."

"Why—I almost feel privileged."

Samantha laughed. "Now don't let that go to your head, Mr. Chandler."

"Miss Callahan, how would you like to step outside for a breath of fresh air?"

"I guess I could use some fresh air."

Rising, Chandler held out his hand to Samantha. She was smiling as she placed her small hand in his much larger one, then he pulled her to her feet.

Seated beside Chandler on the front porch steps, Samantha wished she knew more about this intriguing man who had so quickly become a significant part of her life, again asking herself the question: *was it possible to fall in love with a man you hardly knew?* And reminding herself—again—that she didn't even know the man. Chandler could easily have some horrible flaw in his character, like Jake. Until now, she'd always believed she was a pretty good judge of people; but not anymore. After all, hadn't she known Jake practically her entire life and look what happened? Obviously she hadn't known him at all. Now she was having these strong feelings she couldn't explain for a man who was nearly a stranger to her. Sometimes all Chandler had to do was look at her a certain way with those dreamy ebony eyes and her legs would turn to mush. It wasn't like her to be so fanciful either, so what made Wade Chandler so different? Maybe what she felt for the man was simple infatuation; she was so confused.

"Samantha?"

Both Chandler and Samantha twisted around and saw Sarah standing inside the doorway. Samantha immediately scooted closer to Chandler and then patted the empty spot on the other side of her, inviting her dear friend and new sister-in-law to join them. But Chandler sensed Sarah's need to speak to Samantha in private, so he excused himself and walked off in the direction of the bunkhouse.

Sarah closed the door, then she plopped down on the front porch step beside Samantha. "I'm so sorry for disturbing you and Chandler, but—I just had to tell somebody before I burst with happiness." In a more hushed tone of voice, Sarah said, "You were right, Samantha . . . about James, I mean. He *does* love me. Not that I really doubted it . . . well . . . guess I sorta did."

"Sarah, what are you talking about?"

"I told James about Charlie, Samantha," Sarah rushed to explain. "Don't worry . . . it's okay," she quickly added at her friend's sudden fearful expression. "I told James it would only make matters worse for me if he tried to do anything about it now, and he promised me he wouldn't."

Samantha hoped Sarah was right, but knowing her brother's temper, she had her doubts.

"Anyway . . . James was so patient and understanding, I could hardly believe it. I used to think that all men were selfish and demanding creatures like my father and brother. But after last night, I know it's not true . . ."

It felt strange to Samantha, talking about her brother in such an intimate way, but she and Sarah had always shared everything.

"Oh, Samantha, I can't even begin to tell you how wonderful it feels to be in love. I hope someday you find a man as kind and gentle as James."

"Are you sure we're talking about my brother?" Samantha teased her friend.

Sarah giggled. "Oh you."

"I'm really happy for ya, Sarah."

"You're in love with Chandler, aren't you?" she suddenly asked.

The question really caught Samantha off guard, but she managed to conceal her surprise. Besides, how could Sarah possibly know what she felt for Chandler when she wasn't even sure herself? "Don't be silly, Sarah . . . Chandler and I are just friends."

"Remember who you're talking to, Samantha. We've been friends way too long . . . you can't hide anything from me. I've seen the way you look at Chandler when you think nobody's watching. And if you ask me . . . the man's crazy about you."

Samantha gave an unladylike snort. "The man can barely tolerate me."

Sarah tried not to grin. "That's not true."

"Well . . . whether it is or isn't, it doesn't matter."

Their conversation was brought to an abrupt end at the sound of approaching footsteps. Shading her eyes against the glare of the setting sun, Samantha thought that Chandler had returned, and sighed, when she realized that it was her father walking toward them. Her disappointment did not go unnoticed by Sarah.

"Better get to bed early tonight, Samantha," John said as he halted at the bottom step. "We'll be leaving first thing in the morning."

Samantha rolled her eyes. "Yes, sir."

"Marriage really suits you well, Sarah." John chuckled when his daughter-in-law's face turned beet red. "Don't forget what I said, Samantha." He walked away toward the bunkhouse.

"Go to bed early like a good little girl," Samantha mumbled under her breath.

Sarah looked at her, then both girls burst out laughing.

Chapter Twelve

Beneath a vast clear blue sky, the wide column of cattle spread over the grass-covered prairie as far as the eye could see. John carefully guided his big bay gelding toward the front of the herd, leading a lone steer behind him. Mounted on a gentle chestnut mare, Rachel rode alongside him, her face flushed with excitement. Having never been on a cattle drive before, she observed everything around her with large, curious eyes.

"John, why are you leading that bull to the front of the herd?"

"So the cows will follow him," he patiently explained. "Old Burt has walked this trail so many times, I bet the old boy could just about find his way to Cheyenne on his own."

"Where's Morgan going?" she asked curiously, when she saw him canter past them on his big black stallion on the outskirts of the herd.

"Morgan's going to scout for us," John told his wife. "His job is to find the best places to make camp at night where the cattle will have plenty of water and good grazing, and to make sure the area we pass through is safe."

"Why wouldn't it be safe?"

John looked seriously at his wife. Although he didn't want to alarm Rachel, he answered her question honestly. "On occasion we have had some trouble with cattle rustlers. I've never bothered to tell you before

. . . it's never really been a big problem . . . only some minor incidents. The other possible difficulties we could face is Indians."

Rachel tried to hide her fear as she calmly said, "I thought they were all on reservations?"

"Most of them are these days. And the majority of the Indians we encounter are usually friendly enough, but there are still a few renegades roaming around the area and they don't appreciate us herding our cattle over their lands. I won't lie to you, Rachel . . . it's very possible we could encounter one or two Indians . . . possibly more. They'll probably demand a few cows and then let us on our way . . . sometimes others might be a little more greedy. But most Indians we've come upon in the past just watch us from a distance and don't bother us at all."

"What about Samantha? John, what if . . ."

"Samantha's perfectly safe with Chandler," he quickly assured his wife. "She's been coming with me on these cattle drives practically since she could straddle a horse. She knows exactly what to do. Besides, we're more likely to get harassed by a few cattle rustlers than attacked by Indians."

That didn't make Rachel feel any better. She was beginning to think that coming along on this trek may not have been such a good idea.

"I wonder how Chandler and Samantha are doing," John remarked more to himself. "They're riding drag today."

"What's that?"

"It means they're riding at the end of the herd . . . it's their job to make sure that no strays get left behind." He chuckled and added, "Nobody likes *that* particular job."

"Why not?"

"You'll eventually find out for yourself," John replied. "Riding drag, especially with a herd this size is the worst job of all, because the dust is almost unbearable at times. That's why we all take turns."

Rachel noticed that John didn't seem the least bit worried, which made her feel a lot more at ease. She knew John well enough to know that, if Samantha were in any real danger, he would not have allowed her out of his sight.

"So what are my duties, boss?" she asked in a teasing tone.

"Easy. Just make sure we get a decent meal once in a while."

"Amos's beans are really that bad?" Rachel said, giggling.

"You'll get the chance to judge for yourself tonight."

Rachel was thinking that maybe she would skip supper . . . with all the stories she'd heard so far about Amos's beans. "John, how do the cows know to follow Old Burt?"

"They just do." He winked at her and added, "I guess it's just instinct . . . how most females seem to automatically know that the man's their boss and leader." He burst out laughing at his wife's *'you-got-to-be-kidding'* expression. "Did you know, Rachel, if there was a stampede and Old Burt ran off the edge of a cliff, his ladies would follow him—even then?"

"You can't be serious?"

"It's true. Next to a sheep, a cow is probably about the dumbest animal God ever created."

"Well, then, let's just hope that *Old Burt* can still see where he's going."

John chuckled.

Samantha's eyes scanned the long column of cattle that stretched out before her. They had traveled several miles already and, so far, only a few cows had tried to stray. This was sure making her job a whole lot easier.

She turned to look at her handsome companion, who rode tall and straight in the saddle beside her, smiling in feminine appreciation. Chandler was clad in a pair of snug-fitting buckskins that showed off his long, muscular legs. Without a shirt and wearing a leather headband, he looked every bit the savage today.

"I think I've already spit out enough dirt to fill a ditch," she heard him grumble.

Samantha's smile widened. "You'll get used to it."

"Considering that I prefer the fresh air, I doubt it."

"I thought you told my father you had lots of ranch experience," Samantha said suspiciously. "You sound like you've never been on a cattle drive."

"I—might have exaggerated the truth slightly," Chandler confessed.

"You might have mentioned it."

"I needed this job . . . what was I suppose to say? That most of my life I've been a part time gunslinger and a drifter. And I was a warrior before that," he sarcastically muttered under his breath. "A man has got to start somewhere and—I figured with all of my outdoors experience that ranching just seemed the most logical choice of work. So . . . when your father offered me a job, I accepted." He shrugged, adding, "Besides, how hard can it be to chase a bunch of cattle across the prairie?"

"You'll eventually discover that driving cattle is not as easy as you think, Mr. Chandler. Have you ever been through a stampede?"

"Do buffalo count?"

Samantha rolled her eyes. "Trust me, the dust is the least of your worries."

"So . . . why don't you give me a quick lesson?"

"You can't simply be told how to stop a stampede . . . you learn from experience. If we ever find ourselves in the middle of a stampede, I think it would be best if you just stayed out of everybody's way. You know the old saying—watch and learn."

They rode in compatible silence then. Samantha glanced up at the cloudless blue sky. If her calculations were correct, they should be stopping soon for the mid-day break.

"That mare has the worst protruding backbone I've ever seen," Chandler remarked.

"So you've already told me."

"How you can sit astride that thing without a saddle is beyond me."

Samantha scowled at him. "Must you always degrade my horse?"

"I wasn't trying to degrade your horse, I was just simply stating a fact."

"How would you like it if you were always having to defend Ranger?"

"Guess I never thought of it that way."

"Well, maybe you should, then you'd know how I feel."

"Tell me something, Miss Callahan . . ."

"Don't call me that . . . it sounds too . . . *spinsterish*."

"Would you prefer I call you, *Sam*?"

"Only my family and closest friends call me that."

"So we're not even friends?"

"I never said that."

"Not in so many words, but . . ."

"To be quite blunt, I'm not sure what we are."

She looked straight ahead then, obviously wanting to end the conversation. Chandler wasn't sure what she'd meant by that last remark. He shook his head at the way she sat astride her horse, her delicate chin tilted at that stubborn angle he was beginning to recognize only too well, her back stiff as a board.

And it didn't come as a surprise to Chandler when Samantha gave him the silent treatment the rest of the afternoon . . . .

When they stopped to make camp that evening, Chandler was chosen to stand guard over Samantha, while she bathed in the nearby river. Seated on a hollow stump, with the rifle tucked under his arm, he could hear her splashing in the water behind him. He wished she would hurry a little faster, because he could definitely use a bath himself before supper.

"You can turn around now," he heard her holler out.

Chandler inwardly groaned as he watched Samantha move slowly toward him with cat-like grace. She had left all that gorgeous hair undone and it hung around her slender form like a protective barrier. The setting sun caused the long, flowing, light-brown mane to sparkle with reddish-gold highlights. The lovely vision Samantha Callahan made would haunt his dreams for many nights to come.

She stopped directly in front of Chandler. When she smiled, it nearly took his breath away, she looked so beautiful. His dark brows furrowed into a deep frown. *Didn't she realize what she was doing to him? For crying out loud, he wasn't made of stone.*

"Is something wrong?" she asked.

"Go back to camp, Samantha."

"What's the matter?"

"I said go back to camp!" Chandler hadn't meant to snap at her that way. He watched the different emotions play across Samantha's lovely features and, true to her nature, it took only a few moments for anger to win the battle.

"No problem." She angrily spun around and marched back toward camp.

Chandler observed her rapidly departing back. Well, at least she didn't swear at him, so her temper was improving. With a regretful sigh, he turned and stood there, quietly gazing out over the slow-moving river, the wavering surface nearly hypnotizing him. His lips twisted into a self-satisfied grin when he thought about what he might have done with the *spitfire* in the old day. One thing was for sure, he would have tamed Samantha's lashing tongue by now . . . 'course he would have had a heck of a fight on his hands. But, unfortunately, this was no longer the old days, and he certainly was not a young warrior anymore.

Something he had to come to terms with: what he felt for Samantha was much more than just mere friendship. The problem was, he wasn't quite ready to settle down just yet. And even if he was ready, did he really want to settle himself with that tongue-lashing tigress?

Chandler looked over his shoulder when he heard footsteps coming up behind him. He was a little disappointed when he saw his brother striding toward him. He didn't know why—lest he was a glutton for punishment, but he'd been hoping it was Samantha returning.

"There was a time you would have heard me coming long before now, Graywolf." Morgan halted beside him and added, "I was just curious—are your skills just a bit rusty or are you getting old?"

"If you came here to insult me, little brother, I should warn you, I'm in no mood for . . ."

"I'm asking for a reason."

Chandler didn't like what he read in Morgan's somber expression. "What's wrong?"

"I haven't even told John about this yet . . . I wanted to discuss it with you first. I found some unshod pony tracks a ways back."

Morgan didn't have to say any more; Chandler knew what those tracks meant. "Have any idea what kind of Indians?"

"My guess is Comanche."

"Comanche don't usually come this far north."

"They will if they're hungry enough."

"Yeah . . . I suppose you're right." The bitterness had been clearly evident in the sound of Chandler's voice. It infuriated him that the Indians who refused to live on reservations were automatically labeled as *hostile* and were considered renegades. But their only crime was having to hunt farther into what was considered white man's territory, because they had to feed their hungry families. And the white man just kept on taking more and more of the Indians' land.

"Do you have any idea how many Indians we're talking about?" he asked Morgan.

"Maybe twenty or more."

"Could be a raiding party," Chandler said more to himself. Then, "We'd better tell John—and I don't think we should mention this in front of Rachel or Samantha . . . there's no need to scare the women . . . least not yet."

Both men headed back toward camp.

Upon hearing the news about the Indians, even though they'd never had a serious problem with them in the past, John wasn't taking any chances, especially with his wife and daughter. He posted extra guards that night. And at the first hint of daylight, John roused Amos. After a quick breakfast of bacon and leftover biscuits, they were on their way. Rachel noticed the men were rather solemn this morning, and they rode more cautiously with guns in their hands, while their eyes constantly scanned the horizon, but, never having been on a cattle drive before, she just assumed it was nothing out of the ordinary.

Riding at the back of the herd with Chandler, Samantha knew something was wrong, and she said as much to her somber companion. "You wanna tell me what's going on?"

"What do you mean?"

"I've been on dozens of cattle drives with my father . . . I know when something's wrong, so you might as well tell me."

Chandler should have known they couldn't fool Samantha. Maybe it had been the wrong decision not to tell the women. He knew that John was only trying to protect them, but didn't they have a right to know . . .

"Well?"

He let out a sigh. "Morgan found some Indian tracks yesterday . . . probably Comanche. We suspect they might be following us. It could be just a hunting party—or they could be renegades . . . we're just not sure."

"And you didn't think it was important enough to mention?" Samantha's eyes narrowed upon him and she said in an accusing tone, "Just when were you planning on telling me—after one of 'em scalped off all my hair?"

"Are you trying to be funny?"

"Does it look like I'm laughing?"

"Sometimes it's hard to tell," Chandler grumbled under his breath.

"Does my mother know?"

Chandler shook his head. "Your father didn't want to worry you or your mother . . . that's why we didn't say anything."

"If it's a raiding party, maybe if we offer them a few head of cattle, they'll leave us alone."

"Maybe." But Chandler wasn't so sure.

After several miles and her husband hadn't uttered a single word, Rachel was finally becoming suspicious. As John rode silently alongside her, she eyed him curiously, noting the rigid expression, how he would sometimes peer over his shoulder, then he would touch his gun in its holster, like he was making sure that it was still there.

"John, what's wrong?"

At first he said nothing, and Rachel thought that maybe he hadn't heard her. Then he looked at her with such concern in his eyes, that frightened her much more than what he said.

"For once I shouldn't have given in to you, Rachel. I never should have allowed you to come along on this drive."

"Would you please be a little more specific?"

"Okay. I didn't want to say anything, but—Morgan found some Indian tracks yesterday."

"Indians!" Rachel gasped.

"No . . . ! Don't look around!" John warned her. "We all need to remain calm and act like nothing's out of the ordinary. Listen to me, Rachel . . . just keep walking your horse like we're taking a Sunday ride."

When John saw tears rolling down his wife's pale, frightened face, it angered him that if the Indians did attack, he was nearly powerless to protect her. They wouldn't stand much of a chance, because there were just too many of them. Even so, he would fight to his death to save his wife and daughter.

Suddenly a thought occurred to John. *Samantha might stand a good chance of escaping the Indians by outrunning them on Daisy.* Then he would only have Rachel to worry about. He could only hope and pray that Chandler would think of it . . . .

On the top of the ridge, Chandler noticed there were several Indians astride their ponies, watching them. His only thought was of Samantha's safety—but how was he going to get her out of there if the need arose? And then the answer came to him as swiftly as that swaybacked, four-legged creature could run . . . *Daisy.* Samantha could very easily outrun these Indians, but the problem would be getting her to agree . . .

"Do you see them?" he asked.

"I see 'em."

Chandler was surprised by Samantha's outward calmness. If she was afraid, it certainly didn't show, where most women would already be reduced to hysterics. "If those Indians even look like they might attack, I want you to run like the wind."

"I'm not going to run . . ."

"This is not the time to . . ."

"Forget it! I won't run like some coward!"

"Do you have any idea what those savages will do to you?" Chandler angrily asked. When Samantha didn't say anything, he bluntly added, "Remember what Charlie Bates did to Sarah?"

How could she forget. "I won't leave those I love behind," Samantha argued. Funny, how it took a life-threatening crisis to make her realize just how much this man meant to her. "What I'm trying to say, Wade Chandler—I love you."

Chandler thought his ears must be deceiving him, but there was no mistaking the love he saw shining within the depths of those incredibly blue eyes, looking back at him. And he couldn't deny the truth any longer: he felt the same way about Samantha. How and when it had happened, he had no idea. Maybe it was the first moment he ever saw her, standing inside that hurdy-gurdy house; never had he seen a more beautiful woman. But it wasn't Samantha's beauty that drew him to her; he loved her inner strength, her determination, and yes, even her head-butting stubbornness. He wouldn't want her any other way.

His expression softened. "I love you, too, Samantha Callahan. And I know this might be the worst timing, but—will you marry me?"

"Are you only asking me to marry you because you think we may not come out of this alive?"

That wasn't exactly the answer Chandler had been expecting. And why couldn't she at least pretend to be a little bit enthused? "Is that a yes or a no?"

"I don't know what to say."

"Yes would be nice."

"But are you absolutely certain you want to marry me, Chandler? You know how stubborn and argumentative I can be—most of the time."

Chandler couldn't help grin. "Trust me, I know. And now that we can agree that I am *officially* your future husband, I insist that you do as I say and . . ."

"Not so fast . . . I haven't agreed to marry you yet." Samantha looked down her nose at him to firmly add, "And even if I did say yes, that wouldn't give you the right to order me around. I know what you were going to say and I already told you that I'm not going anywhere, so you can get that thought out of your head."

"Haven't you heard a word I've been saying?"

"You know it's not too late to take back your proposal," Samantha angrily replied.

"Is that what you want me to do?"

"It is, if you think you can boss me around."

Chandler shook his head in disbelief . . . .

The Indians followed them on their ponies for several miles, then they suddenly disappeared behind the ridge. Chandler breathed a sigh of relief. At least for now, they were safe. He could only hope the Indians had come to the conclusion that they were no threat and would leave them alone. John wanted to get out of the area as quickly as possible, so they drove the cattle until well after dusk before they finally stopped to make camp.

Morgan, Ernie, and Will, took the first watch, leaving the rest of the men to tend with the horses and cattle. Samantha started a campfire, while Rachel helped Amos prepare a quick supper, which consisted of canned beans, biscuits, and coffee. Some of the men were so exhausted, after hurriedly wolfing down their food, they immediately crawled into their bedrolls and were fast asleep before their head hit the pillow.

Propped against a log in front of the campfire, silently staring into the low-burning flames, John's mind was troubled. His wife slept peacefully on the ground beside him, and he was glad she didn't understand the kind of danger they were in. He hoped Chandler and Morgan were right, if the Indians were going to attack, they probably would have done so by now, though they were not completely out of the woods just yet.

John looked over at Chandler who seemed to be in deep thought. Samantha sat beside him with her arms wrapped around her legs and her knees drawn up against her chest. She, too, seemed to be lost in thought. When a sudden cool breeze chilled the evening air, he watched Chandler remove his shirt and then slip it around Samantha's shoulders. John couldn't help smile at the tender gesture.

"Pa, do you think the Indians are still following us?"

Samantha had spoken so softly, John had barely heard her. Not wanting to disturb his wife, he answered in the same low tone of voice. "I don't know. Chandler or Morgan could better speculate what the Indians might do better than I could. But while we're on the subject, I want your solemn word, Samantha, if the Indians do attack, I want you to hightail it for home on Daisy and tell Sheriff Sanders. He can round up some men. And, Chandler, you go with her."

"Pa, by the time that slow-as-snails sheriff rounds up enough men, I could ride all the way to Bear Creek and back. Besides, I've already been through all this with Chandler. I'll give you the same answer I gave him—I'm not going anywhere."

"Now you listen to me, young lady, you'll do as I say and I won't hear another word about it." Although John had whispered the order, the sternness of his words were very clear.

"You keep forgetting I'm a grown woman and old enough to make my own decisions."

"Don't force my hand in this, Samantha." John looked seriously at Chandler. "If you have to hog-tie my daughter, you have my permission."

When Chandler grinned at her, Samantha glared back at him. She knew it would do no good to argue with either man, so she remained silent. It didn't matter what her father or Chandler had to say, she would do what she wanted anyway.

"I might as well go relieve somebody . . . I'll never get any sleep tonight." John got to his feet as he added, "You two had better get some shuteye . . . morning comes awfully early."

"Good night, Pa."

Chandler watched John disappear into the shadows, before turning his attention to Samantha, who was now looking at him with that certain stubborn tilt to her chin that he'd already come to know too well. "Your pa's right . . . we should try and get some sleep."

"I just wanna sit here a little longer."

"I know you're angry at me, so you might as well say what's on your mind."

"Please, Chandler, I don't want to argue with you."

"That would be a first," he muttered under his breath.

Samantha pretended she didn't hear that. Frankly, she was just too tired to argue with the man, but she was too frightened and worried to try to sleep. She kept expecting to see a bunch of painted savages to suddenly materialize out of the shadows and strike them with their tomahawks. But, after only a short while, complete exhaustion forced Samantha to stretch out on her bedroll. She fought to stay awake, as she quietly stared into the flickering campfire. Before too long, her weary eyes began to flutter. And, soon, she was fast asleep.

Chandler smiled at Samantha. She looked like an angel with her features relaxed in slumber, and that razor-sharp tongue of hers finally quieted. He marveled at the way her glorious mane of hair spilled over her body like a thick blanket. Unable to resist, he reached over and took a handful of her long hair and brought it to his face, rubbing the silky strands against his cheek, noticing it smelled like wild flowers . . .

"She asleep?"

His brother's voice broke the spell. Chandler had been so preoccupied with Samantha, he hadn't heard Morgan's approach. Lucky for him that Morgan wasn't an enemy trying to sneak upon him. "Yeah . . . why?"

Morgan squatted beside the fire and helped himself to a cup of coffee, before informing his brother, "Our friends are still out there watching us. I saw one of them. You know the Indians better than I do, Graywolf, what do you think they want?"

He shrugged. "I wish I knew for certain."

"Well—whatever they want—I think we're about to find out."

"What makes you say that?"

Very calmly, Morgan replied, "The Indian standing behind you with a rifle."

The tiny hairs on the back of Chandler's neck warned him that Morgan wasn't joking. Very slowly, he twisted around to see the Indian—whom he guessed was Comanche. Most Comanches were on the short side though, but this man was tall. He gestured with his rifle. It was obvious what the Indian was telling them to do. Chandler looked at Morgan, then both brothers simultaneously rose to their feet.

Hearing a woman's sharp gasp, Chandler turned his head to warn Samantha with his eyes not to try anything foolish, and prayed she would listen. Miraculously, Rachel was still sleeping, completely oblivious to what was happening around her.

The Indian let out a bird-like call. Then about a dozen more Indians emerged from the dark shadows and stepped into the campsite, each holding a rifle, their gruesome features appearing almost ghoulish in the flickering firelight. These Indians were all Comanche, too, Chandler noted. They were all dressed the same, wearing only a thin breechcloth and knee high moccasins.

"What now, chief?" Morgan said sarcastically.

Chandler wondered if the tall Indian could understand English when he noticed the man's eyes hardened even more . . .

Ernie was the first to leap out of his bedroll. "What the . . . ?" He was quickly met by one of the savages who hit him in the back of the head with the butt of his rifle, and he instantly crumpled to the ground.

Now, as the entire camp became fully awake, one by one, the men were all quickly apprehended by the Indians. When Rachel let out a blood-curdling scream, Samantha ran over to her mother's side, wrapping her arms protectively around her.

Chandler could see the poor woman was visibly shaking, while Samantha tried to console her, wishing there was something he could to help ease her fears, but he dared not move. He turned back to the tall Indian who appeared to be the leader, wondering why the man was now looking at him with an odd expression.

"Do you speak English?" he finally inquired.

"I speak the white man's tongue," the Indian bitterly replied.

"What do you want?" Morgan bluntly asked.

Big Bear glared at the tall Cheyenne. "The buffalo once covered these prairies like a thick, brown blanket, until the white man came along and stole our land and chased away all the buffalo. It is only fair since the greedy white man drove away our only means of survival . . . we will take some of your cattle."

"I think that can be arranged," Morgan replied in a more friendlier tone. He inwardly sighed with relief. Apparently all they wanted was a few head of cattle.

Chandler watched as John was being escorted into camp by several more armed Comanches. He wondered if there were more Indians. So far, he counted close to twenty—as Morgan had predicted. With the amount of men John had, they were greatly outnumbered.

John was almost to them now. The Indian behind John gave him a last hard shove forward, causing him to nearly collide with Chandler.

"What do they want?" John asked.

"They want some of your cattle," Morgan informed him.

"They can have the whole herd if they promise not to hurt anyone."

A tall Indian stepped directly in front of John and angrily hissed, "We do not want all of your cattle, white man . . . only what we need!"

"Then take what you *need!*"

Chandler didn't like the way one of the Comanches was leering at Samantha. When he tried to take a step in her direction, his last memory was Samantha screaming his name, before darkness overtook him . . . .

Everything happened quickly after that. Morgan went into a rage and charged at the Comanche who'd hit his brother over the head with a rifle, punching the man with such brutal force that it knocked him clean off his moccasined feet. It had taken four or five Indians to finally subdue Morgan. Then their leader said something to them in a guttural language, and they suddenly released him.

"Speak English!" Morgan furiously demanded.

Big Bear stepped directly in front of the tall Cheyenne. Even in the pale moonlight, at this close proximity, he could more clearly get a look at his face—noting the square jaw and finely chiseled features—to realize this man was no half-breed as he'd first thought, but was full-blooded Cheyenne. But what piqued his curiosity the most, was how much this Indian resembled Running Elk.

"Why are you with these white men when you are obviously one of us?"

"I'm no renegade!" Morgan spat.

Anger flickered inside Big Bear's ebony eyes and then was quickly gone. He spoke in perfect English, wanting this man to understand every word. "You turned your back on your own people to live like a white man. You are worse than a renegade."

"Whatever you say, chief."

Remembering the way this man had looked upon the beautiful white woman, Big Bear smiled malevolently. *The big Cheyenne would soon regret his words.* He spoke to his companions in his own tongue, then five warriors stepped forward to seize Morgan. They had quite a battle on their hands, because Morgan fought like a seasoned warrior. When John tried to help, he was met with the same fate as Ernie and Chandler.

Rachel screamed when one of the Indians hit John in the back of the head, using the butt of his rifle like a club. He went down like a felled tree, and did not move. She raced to her unconscious husband's side, dropping to her knees. Tears blurred her vision when she saw the huge, bloody bump on his head. Rachel couldn't believe this was happening . . .

John's men stood by, helplessly, watching the horrifying scene that was taking place before their eyes, knowing there was nothing they could do. But Samantha refused to just stand there and do nothing, while these savages wreaked havoc on her family and the man she loved. In a sudden cry of rage, she leaped upon the nearest Indian's back, grabbing fistfuls of the man's long hair. She locked her strong legs around his waist and hung on with all her might, as he twisted from side to side, trying to throw her off his back.

Big Bear and the other Indians all laughed as they watched their friend struggling with the white woman who clung to his back like a flea on a dog. And Big Bear's admiration for the white woman with the unusual hair grew, because not only was she beautiful, but brave, too. He was seriously thinking about keeping her for himself . . .

Lying upon the ground trussed up like a Thanksgiving turkey, Morgan pulled with every bit of strength he possessed against the ropes that bound him hand and foot. But it was no use. He couldn't even budge. These savages were about to take Samantha and there was nothing he could do about it. Ignoring the blood already oozing from his wrists, he strained even harder, struggling to break free. He swore an oath that these Comanches would rue the day they ever set foot in this camp when he saw one of the Indians slap Rachel as she tried to stop them.

Morgan would never forget that Indian's face . . . .

Chapter Thirteen

After Chandler regained consciousness and Rachel had finished bandaging his head wound, it had taken a lot of arguing on Morgan's part to finally convince his crazed brother that it would be wise to at least wait until morning to go after Samantha. Though it probably wouldn't help ease Graywolf's mind much, Morgan knew the Indian leader who'd taken Samantha had wanted her for himself, so she was in no immediate danger—and right now there was even a more life-threatening decision they had to make where John was concerned.

"Rachel, staying here will do John no good." Morgan had been trying to reason with the distraught woman, but he couldn't seem to convince her to herd the cattle to the next town where a doctor could take a look at John. He hadn't regained consciousness yet.

"I won't go!" Rachel cried, vigorously shaking her head. "I won't do it! I won't leave here without my daughter!"

"Morgan's right, Mrs. Callahan," Ernie then tried. "John needs a doctor."

"I realize John needs a doctor," Rachel snapped. "I'm sorry, Ernie," she immediately apologized. She then turned pleading eyes toward the older man who knew her husband nearly as well as she. "Amos, what do you think I should do?"

Only partially listening to the heated conversation, Chandler didn't hear Amos's response as he paced back and forth like a caged mountain lion, ignoring the constant throbbing pain in his head as he tried to come up with a plan of his own. Though he agreed with Morgan, that the Indians would not harm Samantha, that for now she was safe, he was still finding it impossible to just sit here and do nothing, while he waited until it was light enough to track them. It was a few hours away till morning. He would go crazy by then.

Suddenly coming to a decision, Chandler walked over to his horse, grabbed his saddlebags, then headed into a stand of trees that grew alongside the river. When he was certain that nobody could see him, he dropped his saddlebags on the ground. Carefully, he removed a small bundle of clothing: these were the same garments he'd worn as a young warrior. He had packed them away after changing his name and hadn't touched them since.

After hastily shedding the clothes he was wearing, save for his knee high moccasins, Chandler pulled on his breechcloth and sleeveless deerskin shirt, surprised they still fit. Then he tied the blue-beaded leather band around his head.

At last, Chandler picked up the necklace his father had given him when he was just a boy. Holding the precious gift in his hand, he stared at the small, circular emblem, glistening in the bright moonlight, remembering the day his father had given it to him . . .

"That was a brave thing you did, my son," his father had said in a voice filled with pride.

Graywolf puffed out his little chest, basking in his father's praise. He watched Running Elk walk over to the lifeless cougar lying upon the ground with a long arrow protruding out of its head and kick at the large animal with a moccasined foot. His father had been skinning a deer when the cougar skulked into their camp. When Graywolf had spotted the danger, instead of panicking like most boys his age might have done, he immediately raced for his father's bow and arrows. He'd shot the animal just as it had been ready to pounce upon his father's back.

Running Elk walked back to where Graywolf stood, looking down upon his son, with an expression that beamed with love and admiration. He removed his necklace and then secured it around Graywolf's neck.

Running Elk had told him, "My father gave me this necklace, Graywolf, when I was just a boy about your age . . . now it is yours."

"Thank you, Father." Graywolf fingered the emblem lovingly, knowing how much this necklace had meant to his father . . .

From that day forth until he was forced to live as a white man, Chandler had worn that necklace with pride. Moisture gathered behind his eyes as he once again tied it around his neck, noticing the metal emblem felt cool against his chest. Raising his arms in the air toward heaven, he began to pray for the woman he loved . . . .

The sun was just beginning its ascend above the horizon, turning the sky into a dazzling shade of crimson, when 'Graywolf the warrior' emerged from the trees.

Rachel was climbing out of the back of the chuckwagon when a tall Indian suddenly appeared before her. She turned to flee and then stopped in her tracks when she heard a familiar voice call out her name.

She whirled around, staring in complete shock and disbelief. "Chandler?"

"Sorry, Rachel, I didn't mean to scare you."

"What did you do to yourself?"

He shrugged and the faintest hint of a smile lifted the corners of his lips. "How's John?"

Rachel lowered her head so Chandler couldn't see the tears filling her eyes. "He still hasn't regained consciousness."

"I'm really sorry . . . you know how I feel about John." Chandler was silent for a moment, then thoughtfully added, "John is a strong man, Rachel, and I'm sure he'll pull through. So try not to worry." He touched her on the sympathetically shoulder, then walked away.

As Rachel watched Chandler's departing back, "Oh, John, what should I do?" she sniffled, then covered her face and burst into tears.

After breakfast several of John's men rode out of camp to round up any stragglers that might have wandered off the previous night. Rachel sat vigilantly at her husband's side, her pale face a mask of worry, while Morgan and Chandler tried to make her see the logic in driving the herd on to Cheyenne. Even Amos hadn't been able to get through to her.

"I'm not changing my mind," Rachel more firmly repeated.

Morgan peered into the woman's amber-colored eyes which still looked red and puffy from crying so much. "Rachel, I understand how you feel, but you must listen . . ."

She vigorously shook her head. "I'm not going to listen to anybody but John! He'll tell me what to do!"

Chandler's worried eyes met those of his brother's, before reminding Rachel in a gentle tone of voice, "But John can't tell you what to do." He let out a frustrated sigh when she pretended not to hear.

"I know John would not leave this place without Samantha," she finally stated.

"Even if it meant losing you?" When Rachel looked at him with eyes that were filled with such pain, Chandler felt like an insensitive heel. "I'm sorry, Rachel, I shouldn't have said that."

"It's okay, I know you're only trying to help."

Chandler rose to his feet. There was nothing more he could do here and those Indians were getting farther away. "You try talking some sense into her, Morgan . . . I can't wait around any longer . . . I've wasted too much time already."

"Wait, Graywolf." Morgan also got to his feet. "You can't go after Samantha alone."

"I really don't have another choice . . . John can't spare any men."

"Then I'm coming with you."

"No, Morgan . . . you stay here with Rachel."

"You can't go riding into an Indian camp alone," Morgan more persistently argued.

"I want my daughter back more than my own life," Rachel then cried, "but not at the risk of yours, Chandler."

"Look . . . you'll both just have to trust me on this. I think I have a plan that just might work." Actually Chandler hadn't the slightest idea what he was going to do just yet, but Rachel already had enough to worry about.

"You love my daughter," she said matter-of-factly.

It shocked Chandler that Rachel could possibly know how he felt about Samantha when he'd been having trouble figuring out his own feelings. Only his mother had ever been able to read him so well. Now that he thought about it, Rachel Callahan was very much like Singing Wind; not in looks, of course, but in mannerisms. For Rachel was not just beautiful on the outside, but was beautiful on the inside—just like his mother had been.

"You got me there," he replied.

"Then I trust your instincts. Just please be careful, Chandler."

"You just worry about John . . . let me worry about Samantha." She smiled at him reassuringly, which he could tell was a forced effort, then she turned her attention back to John.

Chandler motioned to his brother, then they walked together a short distance away, so Rachel couldn't hear them talking.

"I'm worried about her, Morgan."

"Yeah . . . I know what you mean."

Morgan's expression became even more serious. "Take care of yourself, Graywolf, and don't forget to watch your back." What he didn't bother to mention, he was going to help drive the herd to the nearest town, then he was coming after his brother.

"Don't worry . . . I plan on getting both me and Samantha back safe and sound." There was a slight pause, before he said, "I asked Samantha to marry me."

Morgan didn't seem overly surprised. "You sure you wanna marry that tongue lasher?"

Chandler chuckled. "I'm sure."

"You're a braver man than I am." Morgan was thoughtful for a moment. "You know, Graywolf, maybe we're underestimating your—*betrothed.*"

"What do you mean?"

"If I know Samantha well enough—and I think I do, I'd say about now that them Comanches are real sorry they ever took the *spitfire.*"

Samantha sat rigidly behind the Indian on his pony as they traveled across the grass-covered prairie, her hands secured around his waist, wishing she could give the man a piece of her mind. Unfortunately, the gag stuffed inside her mouth prevented her from doing so. Okay . . . maybe sometimes she had to learn the hard way when to keep her big mouth shut. But how was she supposed to have known the Indian could speak English so well? Though she did get some satisfaction, knowing the man had understood everything she'd said to him.

They had traveled hard all through the night and didn't stop until this morning to finally rest and water the horses. That's when Samantha and Big Bear (she had learned the Indian's name) had had their little disagreement. When he gave her some food, she took the hunk of meat and threw it back at him, and had told the man in so many words where he could put it; then Big Bear had forced this dirty rag in her mouth, while his friends cheered him on.

Samantha knew that she was now the topic of the Indians' conversation, because occasionally one of them would point to her and laugh. She wished she knew what they were talking about, and where they were taking her . . . probably to their village, she assumed. But Big Bear refused to tell her anything. She was grateful for all the bareback riding she'd done over the years, otherwise, she would not be able to take the grueling pace the Indians were keeping. She smiled smugly to herself. *Little did any of these savages know that she could outride the best of them on her worst day.*

What Samantha did not realize, she was quickly gaining the Indians' utmost respect. They were all intrigued by the unusual white woman and her luxuriant head of hair; for none of them had ever seen hair like hers before. Several had already tried to bargain with Big Bear for this special female, offering him whatever price he asked. But Big Bear had politely refused them all; no way could he part with such a prize.

They were getting close to the village, and Big Bear wanted to make one last stop for the white woman's sake. They halted beside the river to water and rest the horses. When Big Bear twisted around to look at his captive, he was met by that same pair of piercing blue eyes. He knew removing that gag from her luscious mouth would be a huge mistake, but he did it anyway.

"I demand you take me back this instant!" she immediately spewed at him.

"I cannot."

"My fiancé is Indian . . . he'll track you down and . . . !"

"Enough!" Big Bear hissed. "You will learn obedience and your proper place!"

"Are you deranged?" she screamed at him.

"I do not know this word . . . de-ranged."

"It means . . . oh never mind what it means!" Samantha pressed her lips tightly together to keep from saying what she really wanted to say. After all, she might be stubborn but she wasn't stupid. But when the Indian gave her that smug look before turning back around, she came awfully close to changing her mind. She had to remind herself, i*t won't do you any good to lose your temper.*

Big Bear allowed Samantha a few moments of privacy. She stepped behind some nearby bushes and squatted, then, using her teeth, she tried to loosen the knot on the thin strip of leather binding her wrists. But the knot was tied too tightly. She finally gave up. Now frantically searching the ground around her, she looked for a sharp rock or a stick, anything she could use to possibly cut through the tough hide . . . but there was nothing. If she was going to try to escape, she'd better hurry and think of something quick, because Big Bear would soon be wondering what was keeping her. She then thought about making a run for it, but knew she wouldn't get very far . . . .

Chandler had been pushing Ranger hard most of the day. A glimpse of the cloudless blue sky told him it was getting close to the evening hour and, knowing it would not do him or Samantha any good if he rode his poor horse into the ground, he halted under a shady tree beside the slow-moving stream, and dismounted.

"Where's that ugly nag of yours," he grumbled under his breath.

Chandler had brought Daisy with him. He thought it was comical, the way the little mare followed so docilely alongside the stallion. Ranger nickered; then, a moment later, there was an answering call from Daisy. Chandler shook his head, laughing, when the ugly grayish-colored mare suddenly appeared over the rise and was now trotting toward him.

"Hurry up, *Daisy*."

After caring for both horses, Chandler walked over and knelt beside the edge of the stream, then splashed some cool water over his face and chest. Rising, he began to search the ground for any sign that would confirm the Indians had traveled this way. If they did pass through here, they had covered their tracks well. So far, he could only guess he was headed in the right direction. Spying something what looked like a piece of cloth lying on the ground, Chandler hurried over to pick it up. It was a piece of Samantha's clothing! His lips curled into a smile, knowing she had left him a clue. It also meant that she was okay. Now he had to only figure out which direction they might have taken.

After a while, Chandler let out a frustrated sigh. Apparently his tracking skills just weren't quite as good as they used to be. Maybe part of his problem was that he needed to quit thinking like a white man and start thinking like a full-blooded Cheyenne warrior—*and listen to his instincts.*

Vaulting onto Ranger's back, Chandler headed in a westerly direction with Daisy trotting alongside him . . . .

Big Bear bounded onto the back of his pony, then reached over to grab Samantha's arm and swung her on behind him. At least this time she wasn't forced to ride with her arms around the man's waist, and for that she was grateful. Although these Indians hadn't actually harmed her in any way, Samantha couldn't help but feel leery of them. All the horrible stories she'd ever heard about the Indians flashed through her mind and she wondered if they were true, especially what she'd heard about the Comanches.

Samantha sensed that Big Bear could easily become violent if provoked. She thought the name Big Bear suited the arrogant man perfectly. She supposed that, under different circumstances, she would consider the Indian handsome. He was quite a bit taller than all of his friends; and his features were more chiseled. She didn't think he was full-blooded Comanche.

They hadn't ridden very far when Big Bear suddenly halted and gruffly ordered Samantha off his horse. This time, she stubbornly refused to obey. She might be afraid of the Indian, but she still had her pride. And she was tired of him constantly ordering her around.

"Can't you ask me nicely?" she snapped back.

Although Big Bear had to admire the white woman's courage, he could not allow her to get away with treating him with such disrespect. Staring into those icy-blue eyes glaring down at him, he let out a sigh. When he reached for the woman she kicked him hard in the chest with her booted foot, something he hadn't been expecting.

Ignoring the laughter from his fellow companions, Big Bear viciously yanked the woman off his horse by her hair, forcing her to stand directly in front of him. Amazingly she did not even flick an eyelash, but continued to glare at him with those piercing blue eyes of hers. Big Bear was beginning to wonder if there might be something wrong with the white woman's mind. Tempted as he was, he did not strike her. Instead, he wound more of her long hair around his hand, tightening his grip. He knew this had to be causing her a considerable amount of pain, yet she stubbornly just stood there, still glaring at him. Any other woman by now would have cried for mercy. Big Bear knew it was going to take a lot of patience on his part to break such a defiant spirit. And this white woman was about to get her first lesson in obedience.

Big Bear applied even more pressure on her hair.

Samantha refused to cry out in pain when the Indian tried to force her to her knees. It felt like he was pulling her hair out by its roots, but she didn't care. *There was no way she would ever grovel at this man's feet.* As their struggle of will powers wore on, she could hear the other Indians laughing and shouting words she wished she could understand.

Suddenly the Indian let go of her hair. He said something to his friends in that same guttural language. Immediately they all mounted their horses, then looked in her direction with what Samantha could have sworn was compassion she saw in their eyes, before they rode away.

Samantha's eyes narrowed suspiciously on Big Bear, wondering why he'd sent the other Indians away. He just stood there, staring back at her with that irritating smirk upon his full lips, his muscular arms folded across his broad chest. *Oh how much she wanted to slap that arrogant grin off his handsome face.*

Big Bear saw absolutely no fear inside the beautiful white woman's sky-blue eyes. Teaching this stubborn female obedience was going to be much harder than he thought. Pulling the gag from the waistband of his breechcloth, he stalked toward her.

When Samantha noticed the rag dangling from the Indian's hand and realized what he was planning to do, she shouted in a furious rage, "Don't you dare come near me, you heathen!"

In the blink of an eye Big Bear had her on the ground, then, applying just enough pressure to her chest with his knee to hold her in place, he tried to pry open her mouth. Samantha fought him with all her strength, but he finally managed to get the rag inside her mouth. Then he secured her hands behind her back.

Slightly out of breath from the exertion, Big Bear leaned back on his haunches, ignoring her angry muffled words. He was beginning to think he'd made a terrible mistake taking this white woman captive. But, whether he decided to keep her or not, he could not bring her to his village acting the way she was. Didn't the woman realize she could be severely punished for striking a chief's son? Which was the reason he had ordered the others to leave when she'd kicked him, although he trusted his close friends, knowing they would never say a word.

Big Bear continued to watch the white woman with keen interest. He'd never seen a more glorious mane of hair on any female before. She jerked away from him when he reached out to touch the thick, wavy mass. Grabbing a handful of her hair, he watched it slip through his fingers. It was sort of the color of bee's honey, and he noticed how it seemed to glow beneath the setting sun like the white man's golden nuggets.

His eyes raised to meet hers. The way she was looking at him, Big Bear could easily read her thoughts. He was glad that hostile mouth of hers was peacefully gagged. Crazy or not, she was a rare beauty indeed. If he decided to keep her, she would give him strong sons. And that particular thought lifted the corners of Big Bear's mouth . . . .

It was well after dark before Chandler finally stopped to make camp for the night. He found a secluded spot beside the river, and wearily dismounted. Using a long length of rope, he tethered both horses so they could graze upon the luscious grass and easily reach the river to drink. Then he started a small fire and, while he waited for his supper to cook, needing to rid himself of the long day's dirt and grime, he removed his clothes and went for a swim . . . .

After supper, Chandler lay upon his bedroll, quietly gazing into the flickering flames. Again he thought about his plan, hoping it would work. He didn't think the Indians had gotten a very good look at his face, because it had been awfully dark—plus he was now dressed completely in Indian garb—so there was a good chance the Comanches would not recognize him. He didn't even want to think about the possible consequences if the Indians discovered his ruse. If he was fortunate enough to catch up with them before they reached their village, he had no doubt that Samantha was intelligent enough not to give him away. Then all he had to do was wait for the Indians to bed down for the night, so he and Samantha could slip away.

Chandler heaved a long, weary sigh. Unless he got a decent night's sleep, he would be no good to Samantha. Forcing all distressing thoughts from his mind, he closed his eyes. Exhausted as he was, within a matter of minutes Chandler was fast asleep . . . .

Big Bear knelt silently beside the sleeping woman and, careful not to wake her, he ran his fingers through her knee-length hair, liking the feel the soft texture. He was absolutely mesmerized by the white woman's unusual hair. In the early morning sunlight, the honey-colored mane sparkled like golden silk. Now gazing down upon the sleeping beauty, it was hard to believe that a mouth so lovely could possess such a viperous tongue.

As Big Bear watched the gentle rise and fall of her chest in peaceful slumber, he smiled to himself. But that smile instantly faded when he noticed the woman had awakened and was glaring at him with those same pair of defiant blue eyes.

She scrambled to her feet, turning her back to him, holding out her bound hands. She wanted him to remove her restraints. Big Bear let out a regretful sigh, knowing it would be a huge mistake, but he did it anyway. Just as he'd expected, the moment her hands were freed, she jerked the gag out of her mouth and immediately that sharp tongue of hers became a viper ready to strike its prey.

"I demand you take me back to my family!" Samantha spat furiously, her fists on her hips.

"I cannot do that."

"And why not?" she demanded to know.

Big Bear shot to his feet. "Woman, never question my authority! You must obey me!"

"For your information, I obey no man but my father!"

"Your father must be quite a warrior," he mumbled in Comanche.

"Speak English!"

With a feral growl Big Bear grabbed hold of the woman and threw her over his shoulder as he angrily strode toward his pony. She kicked her legs and pummeled his back so hard that it nearly knocked him off balance. He was thinking that maybe Little Doe Eyes wasn't as beautiful as the white woman, but the shy Indian maiden at least knew her proper place.

Tossing the still raging female over his horse's withers, Big Bear jumped on behind her and, grasping the gag firmly in his hand, he slapped the woman hard on the backside and then stuffed the rag inside her mouth when she let out a scream. As Big Bear nudged his pony into a slow canter toward the village, he'd finally come to a decision about his white captive: he would take the girl to his father.

In front of a large, decorated tepee, Samantha was abruptly dropped to the ground; then Big Bear was off his horse, roughly jerking her to her feet. The Indian shoved her ahead of him, forcing her through the small opening. Once inside, Samantha's wary eyes remained fastened on Big Bear, who angrily brushed past her and walked directly to the back of the tepee where there was an older man sitting on top of several buffalo robes. She couldn't clearly see the man's face, but he wore only a breechcloth and his gray hair was braided in two long plaits that hung past his waist.

While both men began to converse in that strange-sounding guttural language, Samantha watched them through her thick veil of lashes. Big Bear sat cross-legged in front of the older man, whom she guessed was the young brave's father. She could tell by the tone of Big Bear's voice that he was angry about something—no doubt that *something* was her. She wished she could understand what they were saying . . .

"But you cannot leave the woman here, my son. You never should have taken her from her people . . . that was a foolish thing to do."

"But, Father, I thought you could use a slave to do all your menial tasks." Big Bear added in a huff, "A chief should not be doing womens' work!"

"Since the death of your mother, I have lived alone. I do not need nor do I want another woman to take her place."

"But she would not have to take my mother's place upon your sleeping mats."

Chief Running Elk observed his young son with suspicion. Why did he get the feeling there was something Big Bear was not telling him . . . ?

"Tell me, my son, why is it that *you* do not take the woman to your own tepee?"

Big Bear looked over at the chestnut-haired beauty. Even now, she stood glaring at him with those bright sky-blue eyes. After a short period of moody silence, he answered his father honestly. "I cannot control her."

Running Elk chuckled. "So you choose to give her to an old man?"

"But you are chief!"

"But your captive does not understand the Indian way."

"She can learn."

Chief Running Elk let out a heavy sigh and said with regret, "We have lived in this valley for many years in peace. There is a good chance the white man will come looking for the woman. You are a grown man now, Big Bear, I cannot tell you what to do, but this I will say. As your chief, I want you to think about the safety of the tribe and seriously consider taking the woman back to her own people."

"You are wise as always, Father."

"That is why I am chief," Running Elk said, chuckling.

Chandler had been trailing these Comanches for several hours. He was certain they were the same Indians that attacked their camp . . . where else would these Indians have gotten the cattle they were herding along with them. But there was no sign of Samantha. The only thing he could figure was they must have split up their band somewhere along the way, and the others had gone in a different direction. The Indians must be getting close to their village, he figured, because they were taking extra precautions to eliminate all their tracks . . .

Chandler halted Ranger at the edge of the hillside, then sat there staring, awestruck, at the breathtaking view before him. The snow-capped mountain peaking through the billowy clouds, looked close enough you could reach your hand out and touch it. A waterfall cascaded over the edge of a high cliff to splash into the river below. Meandering its way through the valley floor, the river sparkled like jewels in the late afternoon sun.

Smoke curled from the tops of the numerous cone-shaped tepees that dotted the grassy meadow. The wonderful aroma of venison stew mingled with the flower-scented air, causing Chandler's stomach to rumble with hunger, reminding him that he hadn't eaten since early this morning. The sight of the peaceful little village took him back to a time when he had lived a carefree life among his own people.

Hearing the sound of approaching hoofbeats behind him, Chandler stiffened. Knowing it would do no good to run, he turned his stallion around to face his enemies.

He immediately noted the two young braves astride their ponies were not full-blooded Comanche, but they spoke the same guttural tongue. They appeared to be in a disagreement about something. Now they were looking at him with the oddest expression on their faces.

The Indians nudged their ponies forward, giving Chandler the signal to follow them as they passed by him. Although he felt a little apprehensive about riding into an Indian village, what choice did he have? He obediently followed the two men down the hillside. Ranger nickered softly, and Daisy suddenly came crashing out of the trees . . . .

Morgan slowed his mount to a walk long enough to study the ground. Satisfied he was headed in the right direction, he kneed his horse to a canter. His brother was leaving tracks that were easy enough for a child to follow, and he could only pray that none of the Comanches had backtracked. The best he could tell, Graywolf was about a day's ride ahead of him . . . maybe if he hurried, he would find his brother before some enemy did.

His concern for Graywolf and Samantha was growing stronger with each passing mile. Again Morgan berated himself for wasting so much time trying to talk Mrs. Callahan into herding the cattle to the next town, or he probably would have caught up with Graywolf by now. He could only hope that Amos would be able to talk some sense into the woman.

Morgan wondered if his brother had managed to catch up with the Indians yet. For all he knew, those Comanches could be holding Graywolf prisoner even now. With that frightening thought, he urged his stallion to a faster pace . . . .

As they rode through the small village, Chandler noticed that most of the Indians looked at him with mild curiosity. Some of the men pointed and laughed at Daisy. And he was surprised by the anger that rose within him, but he ignored it. He smiled and winked at a couple of young maidens, standing outside a tepee; they giggled and shyly turned away. About half way through the village, the two Indians halted in front of a large tepee which had a huge elk and a bear painted on the hides. Chandler instinctively knew that this was the chief's lodge. The Indians dismounted, giving him a signal that clearly told him to wait.

Chandler remained seated upon his stallion, while Daisy grazed nearby on some grass. As he watched the two men disappear inside the tepee, for some unexplainable reason, he had this uncanny feeling that something was about to happen.

A short time later, the same Indians emerged through the small opening, followed by a tall and mostly gray-haired man, Chandler guessed was probably the chief. When they pointed in his direction, the older man whirled around.

Chandler gasped out loud as he stared at the face of his father . . . .

Chapter Fourteen

Chief Running Elk could not believe his aging eyes as he stood staring into the face of his eldest son. Graywolf was now what? . . . he quickly calculated in his mind . . . almost thirty-five summers. Blinking back tears of joy, he noted the slight changes that had taken place since he'd last seen his oldest son. Graywolf was more muscled now and more matured in the face, otherwise, he looked much the same way he remembered.

After the two men embraced, Running Elk spoke to his son in Cheyenne. It saddened him when Graywolf answered in the white man's tongue. "Guess I've lived as a white man so long, it appears I've forgotten some of my own language."

"Come . . . let us go inside where we can talk in private," the chief suggested in English.

In all the excitement Chandler hadn't noticed the curious spectators that had gathered outside his father's lodge. He smiled and nodded his head in greeting, before following Running Elk through the small opening.

Once inside and his eyes had had a chance to become accustomed to the dimmer light, Chandler was in for yet another surprise . . .

"Samantha!"

She was instantly on her feet and running straight into his outstretched arms. "Oh, Chandler, I knew you'd come!" When he set her back on her feet, she stood staring at him. "I didn't recognize you at first."

"You're certainly a sight for sore eyes."

Chandler chuckled when she blushed. He gently brushed her silky-soft cheek with the backs of his fingers. Now knowing Samantha was safe, he could feel the tension leave his body.

From where he sat on the buffalo robes, Big Bear eyed the tall Indian who ducked inside the tepee behind his father. Whoever this man was, he seemed well acquainted with his white captive. He also seemed to know his father. Never having had a whole lot of patience, Big Bear didn't wait for proper introductions.

He rose to his feet and spoke in Comanche. "Who is this man, Father?"

Running Elk turned to his youngest son, his face beaming with pride, as he answered in the Comanche tongue. "This is your brother, Graywolf."

Big Bear's ebony eyes widened in stunned disbelief. He'd heard all about the sons that had been lost to Running Elk years ago. In Big Bear's childhood days, Graywolf had been like an imaginary hero to him. Now seeing his oldest brother's face more clearly, the resemblance to his father was amazing. And there was something else familiar about this man . . .

Big Bear inwardly groaned when he remembered where he'd seen this man.

Chandler immediately recognized the young Comanche and informed his father, "This man was one of many who rode into our camp two days ago. They stole several head of cattle from the man I work for—and took this woman here," he swung a thumb in Samantha's direction.

Big Bear told his father, "I had no idea who this man was." Then he turned to his older brother and said, "I am sorry if I caused you any trouble," in the same perfect English.

Running Elk frowned at his youngest son. "I'm afraid, Graywolf, sometimes your brother Big Bear acts before he thinks . . ."

"My brother?" Chandler repeated. Completely taken by surprise with this unexpected turn of events, he took a closer look at the young brave standing before him. The similarities to Running Elk were definitely there. Why hadn't he noticed it before?

"Tell them about Morgan," Samantha whispered beside Chandler.

In all the excitement, Chandler had forgotten about his brother. "Father, there's something I need to tell you. Little Bear . . ."

"Is your brother with you?" Running Elk asked, his aging eyes brightening even more at the prospect of seeing his other son.

"Little Bear is—well," Chandler chuckled nervously and added, "he's not little anymore, Father. Unfortunately, he didn't come with me. I probably should mention . . . he goes by the name of Morgan now."

"Mor . . . gan," Running Elk repeated the name.

"Father, is Morgan the son I remind you most of?" Big Bear inquired.

Running Elk nodded.

Chandler was curious if the reason Big Bear was named after Morgan, if the young brave also possessed a strong, inquisitive character. As a boy, sometimes Morgan's curiosity had gotten him into a lot of trouble—like the time he'd found a bear cub and had brought it home. The mother had nearly destroyed their tepee, trying to get at her cub . . .

"You said your brother had taken some cattle and had stolen the white woman," Running Elk said to Graywolf.

While Samantha stood quietly in the background, only halfheartedly listening to the mens' conversation, she was taking this opportunity to study Chandler's father. She guessed that Running Elk was somewhere in his late fifties—or maybe even possibly in his early sixties. Whatever the man's age, he was still in good physical condition. There didn't appear to be an ounce of fat anywhere on his lean body. His waist-length hair—which had once been pitch-black like Chandler's—was mostly gray now and had dulled somewhat with age. She definitely knew where Chandler and Morgan had inherited their good looks—for even at this age, Running Elk was still a very handsome man. Samantha smiled appreciatively. *So this is what Chandler will look like when he's older.*

Samantha grinned when she realized that Big Bear was getting a thorough chastising for what he'd done from Chief Running Elk. *Good*, she thought. The young man deserved a severe tongue-lashing at the very least, for all the trouble he'd caused. 'Course on the other hand, if Big Bear had not abducted her, Chandler never would have found his father.

It sounded odd hearing Chandler's Indian name . . . no . . . actually Graywolf was his *real* name. For some reason, until now, Samantha hadn't really thought of Chandler as being Indian; not that him being Indian bothered her in any way . . .

"What happened to you and your brother after the Comanches attacked our village?" she heard Chief Running Elk say.

"Comanches attacked our village?" Chandler hadn't known that. He tried to hide the contempt he was now feeling, knowing his father must have married a Comanche woman and had a son.

Running Elk knew what Graywolf was thinking, and hoped his eldest son would eventually accept the fact that he'd married a woman who should have been his enemy. But most important, he did not want there to be any animosity between any of his sons. When he and Graywolf were alone, he would tell him all about Big Bear's mother . . .

After Chandler had gotten over the initial shock of learning that his father had married a woman of the very people who had destroyed their entire village, he briefly explained to Running Elk what happened to him and his brother after the attack. He told his father how he and Little Bear had become separated . . . how he'd taken the English name of Wade Chandler . . . then had spent the last several years, drifting from town to town, searching all the reservations for his family and friends.

Chandler then informed his father everything he knew about Little Bear—now known as Morgan Johnston. He told him about Samuel and Martha Johnston, the childless couple who had raised Little Bear, the tragic way his brother's adoptive parents had died; and afterwards, how Morgan had become a bounty hunter and had gone in search of the two men responsible.

Samantha had listened, fascinated, hearing all about Chandler's life-experiences as a drifter/gunslinger, before she knew him. She found it rather ironic how both brothers had chosen the same profession. She discovered a lot of other interesting things she hadn't known about this intriguing man.

When Chandler talked about the Callahan ranch, there was no mistaking the great admiration in the sound of his voice when he spoke about John Callahan. He didn't mention to Samantha that when he'd left camp, John still hadn't regained consciousness. He felt there was no need to unduly alarm her, because he felt certain that John would eventually make a full recovery, so, for now, he didn't say anything.

At this point Chandler thought this might be a good time to announce his plans to marry Samantha. He told his father, "The white woman Big Bear captured . . . her name's Samantha Callahan . . . she's John Callahan's daughter. I've asked her to be my wife. After what Big Bear has done, I hope she hasn't changed her mind."

Running Elk frowned at his youngest son. If Big Bear was going to take his place as chief someday, he had to learn to be a wise leader and put the safety of the tribe first, instead of acting and then thinking about the consequences later.

Big Bear pointed out defensively, "Father, if I had not taken the white woman, we may never have known what had become of my brothers."

"Maybe for once my youngest son's thoughtless deeds have proven wise." Running Elk then said to the white woman who would soon be his daughter-in-law. "I am very pleased with my son's choice for a wife. I'm sure you will give him many strong sons." He chuckled when she blushed. He turned to Graywolf. "I would like to meet this—John Call . . . a . . ."

"Callahan," Chandler repeated the name. Then, "Father, I was thinking that—maybe after the cattle drive—Morgan and I could come back here and visit for a while."

"This old man's prayers have finally been answered."

"It's settled then."

"What is a—cattle drive?" Running Elk inquired curiously.

"It's what the white men call it when they take their cattle to a big town, then they sell the herd for money."

"White men do strange things," the old chief muttered under his breath, wondering why men would waste such good meat.

Samantha giggled about what Running Elk said. She thought white men did strange things herself at times. While Chandler and his father continued to talk about the old days, she mosied over to look out the small opening. She noticed that several women stood outside their tepees, stirring what smelled like venison stew in large iron pots. These Indian women were doing what most white women were doing about this time of evening. At least in that way, they were much the same. It was hard to believe that Chandler was raised in an Indian village and lived in a lodge that probably looked a lot like this one.

"You haven't told me what happened to our uncle," she heard Chandler say to his father.

"I'm afraid your uncle did not survive, Graywolf."

Chandler forced back tears gathering behind his eyes. "And the others?"

Running Elk went silent for a brief period, while he collected his thoughts. "As you already know—most of our warriors had gone hunting that day. Had you and your brother not headed off in the opposite direction . . ." he could not even finish the sentence.

"The Comanches had purposely waited until all of our warriors were far from the village, then they attacked us with a vengeance. With only a few old men and the women to defend ourselves against so many, it did not take long for the Comanches to overpower us. You should know your uncle killed several enemies that day, protecting the women and children.

"Those of us who had survived the attack were taken hostage. I prayed with my whole heart, Graywolf, that you and your brother would be spared—that you would stay away from the village long enough for the Comanches to do what they will . . . I was grateful that your mother was not alive . . . they would have used her the same way they used many of our women."

"Under the circumstances, Father, how could you marry a Comanche woman?" Chandler fought to control his anger, reminding himself that it was Big Bear's mother he spoke of.

"I was getting to that. Later I learned the Comanches attacked our village because I chose to live in peace with the white man. They hated me for that, and purposely kept me alive to witness the horrible treatment of my people. That was the worst kind of torture possible!" he furiously added. "Big Bear's mother . . . she was a beautiful Comanche woman who was gentle and kind and—what is the white man's word? appalled by the treatment of our people. It was Bright Leaf who helped me escape, and what was left of our people."

"You mean others are here?" Chandler asked hopefully.

Running Elk sadly shook his head. "I am all that is left now—and Old Deer Woman. The other Comanches who'd escaped with us that day . . . they are what remains of Bright Leaf's people, here in the village."

Big Bear had not known the grisly details about the attack on his father's village many years ago. He was as shocked as Graywolf to learn that his own mother's people had been responsible for that attack. The only thing his father had ever told him about his first wife, Singing Wind, was that she had died giving birth to Little Bear, the same way his own mother had died. He'd always assumed that Graywolf and Little Bear—or Morgan—had been killed during the attack. He was pleased that he now had two older brothers . . . .

"I cannot wait to meet Morgan," he remarked to Graywolf.

"You already *have* met him, Big Bear." At the camp you raided," he answered the young brave's questioning look. He grinned and added, "From what I was told, it took four or five of your warriors to hold him down."

Big Bear inwardly groaned. He remembered the tall Indian well. *No wonder the man had reminded him so much of Running Elk.* He should have learned more about the odd occurrence, before he'd acted so foolishly. So—the fearless Cheyenne was his own brother . . .

"What is this?" Running Elk asked.

"There was no real harm done, Father, so there's nothing to worry about." Chandler then winked at Big Bear, who smiled back at him.

Samantha had been listening to the conversation and was curious . . . "Chief Running Elk, how did Bright Leaf help you escape from the Comanches?"

It pleased Running Elk that the young maiden had been intrigued by his story. His lips curled into a smile. "Big Bear's mother was as intelligent as she was beautiful," he proudly answered her. "Bright Leaf purposely waited for a fierce rainstorm, then she gave all the warriors an herb that put them to sleep for several hours. Not only did we walk right out of that Comanche camp with no trouble at all—the rain washed away all our tracks. And when the Comanches finally came to, they could not follow us."

"You never told me that my mother had earned such a big coup," Big Bear remarked to his father in Comanche.

Running Elk shrugged. "I was a prisoner in the Comanche camp at the time. It was a part of our past we did not like to talk about," he said in the same tongue.

"What happened to Bright Leaf?" Samantha wanted to know.

"She died shortly after Big Bear was born," the chief replied in a voice barely audible.

It saddened Samantha, knowing the kind of troubled life that Chandler had endured over the years; and apparently so had Morgan. She turned to look out the small opening, viewing the villagers somehow in a different light. She saw several children chasing each other in a game of tag, while their mothers prepared the evening meal. Some of the men sat quietly outside their lodges, either repairing their weapons or fashioning new bridles for their horses. These people worked hard for what little they had, especially the women; and all they wanted was to live in peace. These Indians were nothing like the heartless savages they were portrayed to be, Samantha thought. And she now believed that most of the stories she'd ever heard about the Indians had probably been greatly exaggerated.

Her face suddenly split into a huge smile when she noticed Daisy tethered beside Chandler's stallion a short distance away. "Daisy!" she shrieked as she dashed out of the tepee.

"Who is Daisy?" Big Bear asked curiously.

"Samantha's horse," Chandler grumbled in reply. "I'd better go after her before she gets into trouble." He was already headed toward the opening with Big Bear on his heels.

Outside the tepee Chandler immediately noticed the small group of Indian men who had gathered by the tree where Daisy was hobbled, and were all pointing and laughing at the swaybacked mare. He could very easily understand why it infuriated Samantha so, the way most people responded to Daisy; he wasn't exactly pleased himself, knowing these braves were making jokes about the mare. *And*, knowing Samantha's temper the way he did when it came to her horse, Chandler quickened his steps . . .

"Stop laughing at my horse!" Samantha shouted at the top of her lungs. "I don't believe this—even *Indians* are prejudice!"

"Have you ever seen such a back on a horse," Spotted Eagle said in Comanche to his friends. "I have seen better looking mules," another remarked.

They all burst out with laughter.

"I insist you speak English!" Samantha demanded.

"The white woman . . . she defends the ugly mare."

"I think it is her horse," Spotted Eagle suggested. He understood the white man's tongue enough to make out some of her words.

"I would race my mare against your precious stallion any day!" she furiously spat.

"Samantha!"

She whirled around at the sound of Chandler's voice.

He stepped in between her and the Comanche brave she was rudely upbraiding. "I suggest you calm down, woman, before you start a war!"

"How would you like it, if everywhere you went people always laughed at Ranger?"

"I understand, but you can't . . ."

"You should put that poor mare . . . how does the white man say? . . . out to field," Big Bear said, then burst into peals of laughter.

Chandler frowned at the young brave whom he'd just discovered was his brother. Feeling compelled to protect poor Daisy's dignity, he winked at Samantha, then turned back to Big Bear and said, "I bet this old mare here," he slapped Daisy on the bony hindquarters adding, "could outrun your swiftest steed."

Big Bear suddenly stopped laughing. "You are joking."

A broad grin spread across Chandler's face. "Who has the swiftest horse here?"

"That would be me," Big Bear smugly replied.

From on top of the hillside, perched upon his stallion, Morgan had been surveying the small village below for quite some time. His gut feeling told him that Graywolf and Samantha were down there somewhere, and his gut feelings were usually never wrong. There appeared to be some sort of gathering taking place, he noticed . . . a horse race perhaps? He was thinking about riding into the Indian camp when he suddenly sensed he was no longer alone.

Slowly, Morgan twisted around in the saddle. His dark gaze narrowed on the two Comanche braves astride their ponies. He inwardly berated himself, because he should have heard them coming. He wondered if these Indians could have taken part in the raid . . . why else would they be looking at him with recognition in their eyes?

Soars-like-a-Hawk looked over at his companion and stated in Comanche, "This man must be the brother of Graywolf, the chief's other son."

"Chief Running Elk will be pleased."

One of the Indians signaled Morgan to follow them. He nudged his stallion forward, hoping he wasn't making a huge mistake.

As Big Bear proudly rode his great black stallion toward the starting point, he frowned, when he saw it was the white woman perched upon the ugly mare. His brother Graywolf stood beside her, grinning from ear to ear.

He halted beside the mare. "I do not race against women."

"You can't expect me to ride this horse . . . my legs would drag on the ground." Chandler thought it was about time the arrogant young man learned an important lesson on humility.

"Then I will not race!"

"What's the matter, Big Bear . . . afraid I might beat you?" Samantha baited him.

"Have it your way, white woman, but you will not beat me."

"Why you conceited, egotistical, pompous . . . !"

"Samantha," Chandler loudly interrupted. He stepped closer to her and whispered near her ear, "As long as you're here, you have to control that temper of yours. Besides, there are other ways to handle a man with an oversized ego. You know as well as I do that Big Bear will soon be eating his own words."

"Very well," Samantha said through gritted teeth.

By now a fairly large crowd had congregated around the two horses that were about to race. Even the women—their curiosity getting the best of them—had left their cook pots to watch with their husbands. Chandler wasn't surprised the majority of the people pointed and laughed at the swaybacked mare. He couldn't understand a word of Comanche, but it wasn't hard to understand what they must be talking about. He could almost hear them saying—*the silly white woman must be crazy to race that sorry mare against Big Bear's stallion.* His lips twitched with amusement. Samantha soon would be the talk of the entire village.

"Graywolf, what is happening?" Running Elk suddenly said beside him.

"Father, you're just in time. Big Bear and Samantha are about to race."

"That horse my future daughter-in-law rides . . . I have seen better looking buffalo."

Chandler threw back his head and laughed. "There's no doubt about that. But watch carefully, Father . . . you're about to see something remarkable."

Having trouble keeping Raven under control, Big Bear looked over at the white woman who was calmly seated upon her sickly-looking horse. He could not believe she was foolish enough to race that sorry mare against his powerful steed. He snickered to himself. He wondered if the poor old nag would keel over before they even had a chance to race.

"Ready when you are, white woman."

"My name's Samantha, so you can stop calling me white woman."

"My brother would be wise to dull that sharp tongue of yours!"

"*You* would be wise not to think so highly of yourself!"

"And *you* would be wise to keep silent!"

"Are we going to race or not?" Samantha snapped.

"Don't you need a head start?" Big Bear taunted her.

Samantha ignored him, peering straight ahead.

Suddenly Big Bear's stallion reared up on his hind legs then took off at a run. Grinning mischievously, Samantha purposely held Daisy back, allowing the conceited young brave quite a fair lead, then, leaning over her horse's neck, she made the familiar clicking sound with her tongue and the little mare shot forward . . .

The smirking grin that was upon Big Bear's face disappeared as the white woman flew past him on her horse like a speeding arrow, leaving him and his stallion quickly behind. He could not believe his eyes! Already her horse had circled the oak tree and was about to fly past him again, headed in the opposite direction toward the finish line . . . .

Chandler smiled to himself, when Big Bear reached the oak tree and kept right on going. *No doubt the young man went off somewhere to lick his wounds*, he thought, chuckling under his breath. The moment Samantha reached him, she slid off her horse and threw her arms around his neck. While some of the villagers congratulated Samantha on her victory, Running Elk ran his hand over the mare's swayed back, shaking his head in complete bewilderment.

"I do not understand . . . it is impossible," he finally said after a while.

"I don't understand it myself," Chandler agreed with his father.

Morgan spotted the Indian racing his magnificent black stallion with the flowing mane and tail across the meadow. He remembered the Indians who raided their camp—the leader had ridden a horse just like this one. This only confirmed what he'd already suspected: these had to be the same Indians who'd taken Samantha and tied him up like some piece of meat!

Anger churned within Morgan as the Comanche braves escorting him rode their ponies on ahead to greet their friend. They talked very briefly, then the two braves galloped off toward the village, while the remaining Indian now trotted his black stallion toward him. Morgan's dark eyes became dangerous slits as the Comanche drew a little closer. It was the same Indian all right; he would never forget the man's face.

Without a word of warning Morgan leaped from his horse and flew through the air, knocking the Comanche off his stallion and sending them both crashing to the ground. Morgan was on his feet in an instant, dragging the other man up with him; then he drew back his arm and let his fist fly. The punch was so powerful, it literally lifted the Indian off his feet.

At the sound of approaching hoofbeats, Morgan whirled around. At first he thought that one of the Comanche's friends had returned. Straightening his spine, he was ready to confront this enemy as well. His eyes widened in surprise when he recognized the big buckskin stallion galloping toward him.

"Graywolf!"

Chandler skidded to a halt. "I hope you didn't kill him," he said, dropping lightly to the ground. He muttered to himself, "I was afraid something like this might happen," as he walked over to where Big Bear lay motionless on the ground.

Morgan eyed his brother in anger and confusion, wondering why Graywolf would even lift a finger to help the Indian. And he put his disturbing thoughts into words. "Why are you fussing over that Comanche like a mother hen when he and his friends were the ones who raided our camp?"

After helping Big Bear to his feet, Chandler touched the horrible bruise already forming on the young man's left cheek—at least nothing appeared to be broken. "I guess there was no real damage done."

Big Bear grinned, rubbing his smarting jaw.

Now Chandler turned to Morgan to try and explain, not knowing where to even begin. "It's a long story." He heaved a sigh, running a hand through his shoulder-length hair. "This man you nearly beat to a pulp . . . his name is Big Bear. He's the chief's son and . . ."

"I don't care if he's the general's nephew!"

"Would you just listen, Morgan!" Chandler snapped in frustration. He turned to Big Bear. "I would like to speak with my brother in private."

Big Bear nodded his understanding. "Good luck," he said to Graywolf. Then he vaulted onto the back of his stallion and rode away.

Chandler stood there, quietly looking at Morgan, while he gathered his thoughts, trying to decide the best way to break the news about their father. Knowing his brother the way he did, he decided that maybe a direct approach would be best . . .

"That brave's jaw you nearly broke—was Chief Running Elk's son."

"I don't give a hoot who he was!"

"Didn't you hear what I said, Morgan? *Chief . . . Running . . . Elk*," Chandler slowly and carefully repeated the name. When Morgan's eyes widened in stunned recognition, he added sympathetically, "I know this comes as a complete shock . . . trust me . . . it's exactly the way I felt when I first learned the truth."

"But—how's that possible?"

"I'm sure by now Father knows you're here, Morgan, and is anxiously waiting to see you. So let's head back to the village and I'll explain everything on the way."

A short while later, Morgan was staring into the aged face of his father in total shock and disbelief. His hair, once shiny and black as a raven's wing, was a duller gray now; it was a lot longer, too. And there were more wrinkles around the eyes, though they were still sharp and alert—other than that—Running Elk looked much the same way he remembered. When his father stepped forward and put his arms around him, Morgan fought back the tears gathering behind his eyes, still unable to utter a word.

Silently observing the now full-grown man standing before him, Running Elk's own eyes misted with tears. His son Little Bear had been only a small boy when he'd last seen him, and here he was suddenly a grown man. This meeting was such a shock to the aging chief, it had taken him some time, before he trusted his voice enough to speak.

"It is so good to see you, my son."

"It's good to see you too, Father."

Running Elk touched Little Bear's beloved face; he could hardly believe the man standing before him was real. "You are the near image of your older brother, Graywolf."

Morgan's mouth lifted into a lopsided grin. "So I've been told."

"I heard you already met Big Bear," the chief said in a teasing tone.

Now that he knew the truth about the young Comanche brave, Morgan could see some resemblance to Running Elk. "I hope your jaw's okay?"

Big Bear's teeth flashed pearly white in contrast to his dark complexion when he smiled. "You have a fist like a rock, but I think I will live."

Morgan and Chandler burst out laughing.

Suddenly clapping his hands together, Running Elk happily announced, "There will be a big feast this night in honor of my two eldest sons, for they have finally come home."

The ominous sound of the drums seemed to keep beat with Samantha's pounding heart as she watched the couples swaying back and forth in time to the music. The way the men and women moved gracefully around the huge campfire, it reminded Samantha of the white man's waltz. The celebration feast (as Chandler had called it) was very similar to the potluck gatherings back home. The Indian women had prepared huge amounts and various dishes of food that looked equally as appetizing. She had come to the conclusion that the Indian's way of life was not so much different from that of her own people.

Although Samantha was trying to enjoy herself, she couldn't stop worrying about her family. She'd overheard Chandler and Morgan talking, and had learned that her father hadn't regained consciousness . . . that the Indian had hit him pretty hard in the head. She knew her mother must be a basket case, and she prayed that God would help them. Samantha wondered if Amos had talked her mother into continuing on with the cattle drive, or were they still camped in the same place, waiting for her and Chandler to return. The more she thought about everybody, the more she wanted to leave the village as soon as possible.

Samantha's wandering gaze happened to settle upon Chandler, who was seated around a small campfire a short distance away, talking with his father and brothers. She had never seen Chandler so relaxed and this carefree, for he smiled and laughed often. And somehow it made him appear vulnerable—which seemed so ridiculous, because Chandler was just about the strongest man she knew.

Hearing Running Elk's burst of laughter, drew Samantha's attention to the chief. She quietly observed Chandler's father, while he conversed with his sons. Running Elk was an intelligent individual with an enormous sense of humor. It was so easy to understand where Morgan had inherited his endless teasing nature . . . .

As dusk gave way to cloak the landscape in darkness, Samantha noticed how the shadows cast by the flickering firelight seemed to give Chandler an even more incredible, sensual appeal. Unable to take her eyes off him, a warmth seemed to spread throughout her entire body. And it was suddenly difficult to breath . . .

Feeling eyes were watching him, Chandler looked up and caught Samantha staring at him so intently, it caused his heart to thud against his chest. Never taking his eyes off her enchanting face, he politely excused himself, then rose to his feet and walked toward her.

Wordlessly Chandler stretched out his hand to Samantha. When she placed her small, trembling hand in his, he pulled her to her feet; then he led her into a nearby stand of trees for some privacy. After walking only a short distance, he stopped and turned to face Samantha. In the dappled moonlight, they stood silently gazing into each others' eyes. Chandler reached out and took her heavy plait of hair in his hand, unbraided it, then arranged the thick, knee-length mane around her slender form.

"Hair this beautiful should never be confined," he said in a voice that was suspiciously shaky.

She lowered her eyes, blushing.

"Look at me, Samantha."

Her long lashes raised and Chandler found himself staring into eyes shining with so much love, it caused his chest to tighten. "I love you, Samantha Callahan." Then he kissed her with all the love he felt in his heart.

Afterward, Chandler stood there, resting his chin on top of her head, holding her tightly in his arms, as he fought to control his passion-raged body. It was amazing how this woman could stir his blood like no other, but—no matter how much he wanted her, he vowed not to touch her until they were properly wed.

Samantha clung to Chandler's narrow waist as she nuzzled her cheek against his bare chest. She felt so protected with his strong arms wrapped around her this way, she wished they could stay like this forever. But, of course, they could not.

With a sigh, she moved away from him. "I should be getting back to my parents."

"Yeah . . . I know."

"I just don't want them to worry."

"Samantha?"

She turned around to face him. "I can tell by the tone of your voice, I'm not going to like whatever it is you're about to say."

Chandler didn't really like the fact that she was able to read him so well. "Then I might as well just come out and say what it is I want to say instead of beating around the bush. I want you to stay here at the village with my father until after the cattle drive. I know you'll be safe here just in case we run into anymore Indian trouble."

"Forget it, Chandler, I'm coming with you." Samantha stubbornly folded her arms across her chest and added, "For your information, I've been going on these cattle drives with my father since I could sit on a horse. Besides, I could probably get into more trouble if I stay here."

She had a point there, Chandler thought. Still, he felt she might get into *less* trouble if she remained with his father. "Why must you always fight me?"

"Why must you always try to order me around?" Samantha firmly retorted.

"That wasn't an order, it was a simple request."

"It was more of an order made to *sound* like a request."

"Okay . . . I'm *asking* you to stay here with my father until I get back."

"And I already gave you my answer . . . *no*."

"Well at least you didn't spew a bunch of *vile words* at me like some trail hand," Chandler angrily muttered to himself. "Imagine *my* surprise."

"Why you arrogant, domineering and overbearing . . ."

"Careful."

" . . . jughead!"

Chandler burst out laughing.

Chapter Fifteen

Samantha strolled along the well-worn path that led to the river, unaware that somebody was following her. She had waited until the Indian women returned to the village before taking her own bath this morning. She supposed she could have gone with the other women, but she felt a little uncomfortable bathing in the company of strangers—even if they were all female.

When Samantha reached the edge of the river, she dropped the clean change of clothes that Chandler had thoughtfully provided for her, on the grassy bank. Looking around her, making sure she was alone, she hastily undressed, then, grabbing the cake of soap that Chandler had given her, she waded waist-deep into the river.

Samantha had just finished washing and rinsing her hair when she suddenly sensed that someone was watching her. She whirled around, and gasped, when she saw Chandler standing there on the shore. She immediately crossed her arms over her chest to cover herself.

"Turn around!" she angrily snapped.

Feeling a little embarrassed, Chandler did a quick about-face. But, before he'd turned his back on Samantha, he'd caught a glimpse of her standing in the river beneath the golden glow of the morning sun. She was even more beautiful than he'd ever imagined . . .

"I'm decent now."

Chandler turned back around to face her. She had wrapped a blanket around her shoulders, and he couldn't help grinning at the tiny bare feet peeking out from underneath. "Sorry. I thought you were just going for a walk."

Samantha scowled at him. "When I asked you for a bar of soap and if you happened to bring along a clean change of clothes—don't you think that might have been a pretty good hint that I was coming here to bathe?"

"Okay . . . you got me there. Look—before I forget what I was going to say, I wanted to tell you, we'll be leaving first thing in the morning, and Morgan's coming with us."

"Fine. And now that you've told me . . . do you mind if I finish bathing?"

"Not at all."

Grumbling under his breath, Chandler walked a short distance away and plopped down upon a hollow log, making sure his back was to Samantha. Behind him, he could hear her splashing around in the river. He inwardly groaned, remembering how beautiful she had looked, clothed in nothing more than her long, flowing mane of hair. Needing something to occupy his amorous thoughts, Chandler removed the knife he carried inside his knee high moccasin, picked up a nearby piece of wood and began to whittle away at it.

His brows creased into a frown. Samantha must still be angry at him this morning over their little disagreement last night. Surely she couldn't be angry at him just because he'd seen her bathing? And he really hadn't seen that much anyway. Honestly, he wasn't really sure what her problem was, but—dag-gonnit, he'd let her have her way, didn't he? She was leaving with him tomorrow morning like she wanted . . . wasn't that enough? His frown deepened. Maybe the frigid water would help cool that temper of hers. *Women*, Chandler thought in mounting frustration. *Who could figure them* . . .

"You can turn around now," he heard her call out.

Tossing the hunk of wood he'd been whittling on to the ground, Chandler carefully slipped the knife back inside his knee high moccasin. Rising, he turned and started walking toward Samantha, figuring he was probably about to get another dose of that venomous tongue of hers, but wait—was that a smile upon her lovely face? And—did he just hear her apologize for the way she'd treated him? This was completely out of Samantha's character. But what stunned Chandler speechless, was when she rose upon her tiptoes to kiss him on the cheek like nothing ever happened. Shaking his head in utter bewilderment, he followed behind Samantha, trudging up the slight-inclining path that led toward the village, wondering if he'd ever understand this complicated woman.

When Chandler and Samantha arrived back at Running Elk's lodge, Morgan was standing outside, watching their approach. Chandler noticed his brother was grinning from ear to ear and, still mulling over conflicting thoughts about his so called—*fiancée,* he was in no mood for Morgan's sometimes irritating sense of humor.

"Would you wipe that silly smirk off your face," he snapped at his brother.

"My . . . aren't we touchy."

"And one would think you'd take the hint."

"There's no need to take your bad mood out on Morgan," Samantha snapped at Chandler.

"*My* bad mood," he angrily retorted. "Wasn't that *you* who bit my head off just a while ago, or was that somebody else?"

"That's because you sneaked upon me while I was bathing!"

Morgan's brow rose questioningly toward his brother.

"It's not what it sounds like! And why am I telling you this!"

"I didn't say a word." Morgan was having trouble keeping a straight face. Apparently the two lovebirds must've had some kind of spat—but what else was new.

Samantha glared at the small group of giggling Indian maidens standing nearby. There was one particular sultry beauty who kept batting her long lashes at Chandler. She instantly became enraged with jealousy. *How dare that woman openly flirt with my fiancé*, she furiously thought. She felt like marching over there and giving the woman a piece of her mind, and she might have, too, if the Indian maiden could understand English.

Knowing what that look in Samantha's piercing blue eyes meant, Chandler grabbed her by the arm and started to usher her away. But she managed to jerk her arm free and then she shoved Chandler so hard that he tripped over his own foot and landed sprawled out on the ground.

"Woman, have you lost your mind?" he growled as he rolled to his feet. His eyes narrowed angrily on his brother who was doubled over with laughter.

"You should marry one of them!" Samantha screeched in a fit of fury, shoving a thumb in the Indian maidens' direction. "I'm sure they would be much more docile!" Then she twirled on her boot heel and stormed off.

"Where does she think she's going?" Chandler hollered at nobody in particular. He took a deep breath, and exhaled slowly. Then, in a voice that sounded completely defeated, he said, "What am I going to do about Samantha's temper, Morgan?"

"Well—I've been giving that some thought."

"And?"

"I have absolutely no idea."

"I thought you were such an expert when it came to the opposite sex?" Chandler said sarcastically.

"Not where your *betrothed* is concerned."

His eyes narrowing in the direction Samantha had taken only moments before, Chandler grumbled under his breath, "Speaking of the *spitfire*, I'd better go after her, before she gets herself in trouble."

Chandler's long strides carried him quickly through the small village. It didn't take him long to discover Samantha's whereabouts: all he had to do was follow the sound of her voice—which seemed to be raised in anger—probably at some poor Comanche brave for insulting her horse. He found her by the tree where Daisy was kept tethered and, just as he'd feared, beside her stood an Indian brave who was receiving the sharp edge of her tongue. Chandler was awfully tempted to turn and walk away and let *Sam* fend for herself, but—if the Indian's expression was any indication of his inner fury—he'd better get his *beloved* out of there.

Knowing there would be no reasoning with the ranting woman, Chandler walked directly up behind Samantha and, without a word of warning, picked her up and tossed her none-too-gently over his shoulder, then headed toward the river.

Samantha screamed and kicked and called him a few choice names, which Chandler was grateful the villagers who were watching could not understand. She punched him in the back; his hand came down hard on her well-positioned derriere.

"Ouch! How dare you strike . . . you . . . you . . . I can't even think of a word despicable enough to call you!"

"I'm sure if you think hard enough a word will come to mind!"

Now a man on a mission, Chandler marched along the path that led to the river, turning abruptly down a steep slope (deciding to take a shortcut) and nearly lost his footing as he fought to hang on to the kicking bundle in his arms. A look of triumph spread across his determined features as he approached the slow-moving river. He waded out a short distance and then dropped his burden into the icy cold water.

Samantha let out a high-pitched scream and when she tried to stand, Chandler held her firmly in place with one hand, while grabbing her swinging fist with the other. She had no choice but to remain seated, while the frigid water lapped around her quivering chin.

"Stop fighting me, Samantha!"

"Let me up this instant!" she furiously hissed.

"Just as soon as that temper of yours cools!" Chandler yelped in pain when she managed to free an arm and her fist caught him in the groin.

"My father will hear about this!"

"Your father should have done this a long time ago and saved me the trouble!"

"Well you won't have to worry about any more trouble in the future because the wedding's off!"

"You don't mean that!"

"Yes . . . yes I do mean it!" Samantha screamed at the top of her lungs.

Chandler let go of her at once. "And I refuse to marry a spoiled-rotten brat!" He then did an abrupt about-face and angrily waded toward the shore.

Samantha sat there shivering in the river, until Chandler disappeared into the trees. Only then did she get to her feet and wade to the shore, where she collapsed upon the ground and burst into tears, now realizing what she had done. *She hadn't meant to say all those terrible things. She had spoke out of anger. Oh would she never learn to control her temper.*

But there was something deeply troubling Samantha that was causing her to act this way; since coming to this village, she'd been noticing changes in Chandler that bothered her. *Or maybe she should start calling him Graywolf,* she thought sarcastically. No—that wasn't fair. And she berated herself for even thinking such a thing. She should be happy that Chandler seemed to thrive in this place; she'd never seen the man this happy before. Unfortunately, what bothered Samantha, she feared that when she and Chandler left this place, things would never quite be the same between them again. She was thrilled for Chandler, that he'd found his family, yet, at the same time, there was an overwhelming sadness engulfing her, because of an inner voice that kept telling her she should let him go.

Samantha started thinking, now that Chandler and Morgan were finally home where they belonged, there was no reason for either man to leave this beautiful place; nor was there any reason for her to stick around. She was perfectly capable of finding her own way back. She wouldn't even bother telling Chandler good-bye, because he would only insist on accompanying her to her parents. Besides, it would be less painful this way . . .

Finally coming to a decision, Samantha got to her feet, swiping at the tears rolling steadily down her cheeks as she hurried to get Daisy . . . .

Inside Running Elk's tepee, Chandler was only partially listening to the conversation between his father and Morgan. His mind was on a certain stubborn blue-eyed beauty with long, flowing hair. He would wait a while longer, allowing Samantha a sufficient amount of time to cool off, then he'd go look for her. They'd both said some pretty awful things in anger. He hoped she hadn't meant what she said about not wanting to marry him . . .

"Didn't you hear me, Graywolf?" Morgan interrupted his disturbing thoughts.

"Oh . . . sorry . . . guess my mind's preoccupied."

"I said it's still early enough . . . we could leave today if you like."

"We'll leave first thing in the morning as planned."

After the cattle drive Morgan would return to the village and stay with their father—at least through the winter. Running Elk had wanted both his sons to remain, but Chandler knew Samantha would not be happy here, and even though he wasn't exactly pleased with her at the moment, he knew he'd be miserable without her. A secret smile curved his lips. Come to think of it, he would be happy anywhere so long as that quick-tempered female was at his side . . .

An Indian's excited voice at the tepee entrance snapped Chandler to attention. He watched the man called Soars-like-a-Hawk duck inside through the small opening. As Chandler listened to his father and the young brave converse in the Comanche tongue, he wished he could understand what they were saying, especially when he noticed his father's worried expression.

Big Bear finally translated. "Soars-like-a-Hawk says Spotted Eagle saw Samantha leave the valley on her horse."

Chandler was on his feet in a flash. "Why didn't Spotted Eagle stop her?"

Big Bear shrugged. "I do not know."

Chief Running Elk immediately began to issue orders in Comanche. "Soars-like-a-Hawk, bring both my sons' horses . . . they will be leaving right away. Tell Spotted Eagle's wife to prepare them some food."

Soars-like-a-Hawk nodded, then silently disappeared the same way he'd come.

"Do not worry, Graywolf . . . my future daughter-in-law could not have gone very far," Running Elk tried to assure his eldest son.

"You don't know Samantha," Chandler muttered under his breath. There were so many things that could happen to a woman in the wilderness, especially a woman as daring as Samantha.

A short while later, Chandler and Morgan were saying farewell to their father and younger brother, then they mounted their horses and headed out of the village. Spotted Eagle's wife had graciously provided them with enough pemmican to last several days. Running Elk had offered to send along several of his best warriors with them for protection, but Chandler and Morgan had refused, figuring they were needed at the village to ensure the safety of the tribe; though it was very doubtful there were any real enemies lurking about, the valley was so well hidden.

Chandler and Morgan easily found Daisy's hoofprints and—from what they could tell—Samantha was only a few short hours ahead of them.

"At least she's headed in the right direction," Chandler remarked.

"I bet we find her by nightfall," Morgan stated with confidence.

"And if we don't?"

"We'll find her." After a slight pause, Morgan seriously added, "I hope you won't try and stop me, Graywolf, because I plan on giving that hardheaded woman of yours a spanking she will never forget."

"You'll have to wait your turn."

Samantha scolded herself for not thinking of her stomach before venturing on this confounded journey. She hadn't eaten anything since yesterday. Now her belly rumbled with hunger loud enough to frighten away any game that might happen along. As usual, she had acted without thinking of the consequences.

Glancing toward the horizon at the setting sun, Samantha figured she had better locate a spot to make camp for the evening. Besides, she had already pushed poor Daisy beyond her endurance, and it was most important that the little mare get plenty of rest and a proper meal. After all, she was now eating for two . . .

Finding a well-secluded spot beside the river, Samantha slid to the ground; then, picking handfuls of grass, she used it to rub Daisy's lathered coat thoroughly dry. Only then, did she allow her horse a drink from the river. Afterward, she allowed Daisy to roam free to graze; there was never any need to tether the little mare, she always stayed close by.

Now that her horse was cared for, Samantha plopped down upon the grassy bank at the edge of the river, removed her boots and stockings, then plunged her tired feet into the cool water. She was thinking about her empty belly again when a sudden movement caught the corner of her eye, and she turned her head and saw the rabbit taking advantage of the thick clover that grew alongside the edge of the river, a short distance away.

Carefully, Samantha reached for her boot to retrieve her knife; then, ever so slowly, she got to her feet, and crept toward the little critter.

She let out a sigh when the rabbit suddenly scampered away. She then began to search around, trying to find something else for supper that might fill her hungry belly. When she couldn't find even a single berry, she was beginning to think she had foolishly allowed her only promising meal to hop away. Though she probably couldn't have harmed the little fella anyway.

Samantha decided to try her hand at fishing . . .

Lying flat on her stomach on a big boulder that set on the very edge of the river, grasping her knife firmly in her hand, Samantha patiently waited for a plump morsel to swim by. With the remainder of daylight quickly fading, making it nearly impossible to see, if she didn't catch something soon, she would have to wait until morning.

Samantha had just about given up when she noticed the large trout swimming directly toward her. Drawing back her arm, she held her weapon steady . . .

"Just a little closer," she whispered under her breath.

Suddenly her knife went sailing through the air . . .

Holding her supper on a stick over the campfire, famished by now, Samantha eagerly tore off a sizable chunk, not caring if the fish wasn't quite thoroughly cooked. To her utter delight, the juicy meat practically melted in her mouth. She didn't mean to brag, but it was the tastiest fish she ever had. As Samantha quietly sat there, consuming her bountiful meal, she thought about her family, wondering how her brother James and her new sister-in-law were getting along. She sure missed talking with her best friend Sarah Martin . . . oops . . . it was Sarah Callahan now; she would have to try to remember that.

Samantha hoped her parents weren't too worried about her, after all, they should know by now that she was more than capable of taking care of herself. How she missed them all something fierce. She even missed Ernie, and he sometimes got on her nerves.

Her wandering thoughts ultimately drifted to Chandler. If he were only here with her right now, she would gladly take back all those horrible things she'd said in anger. She wanted to tell him how sorry she was. She prayed if anything happened to her that—in spite of the cruel things she'd said—he would know in his heart just how much he'd meant to her.

Samantha felt a painful stab of jealousy when she pictured Chandler in the arms of one of those giggling Indian maidens. It was bound to happen, too, sooner or later. She couldn't expect Chandler to live celibate for the rest of his life.

A sudden cool breeze caused Samantha to shiver, reminding her of yet another problem: trying to keep warm through the night. Even though the days were hot and muggy in this mountainous region, the nights in comparison could sometimes get downright cold, even in mid-August. If only she'd thought to grab the long-sleeved shirt that Chandler had given her to wear, she wouldn't be sitting here shivering right now. It was her own stupid fault, for not thinking things through—as usual.

Scooting a little closer to the cozy fire, Samantha began to notice how the flickering flames seemed to cast eerie-looking shadows on the nearby forest; and the same harmless noises that she'd heard during the day, now sounded like warning bells going off in her ears, now that darkness had set in.

Samantha wrapped her arms around her legs and pulled them tightly against her chest, then began to rock back and forth, trying to stop her teeth from chattering—more from fright than from the cold. She tried not to allow fear to override her logical thinking, and tried concentrating on the soothing noises: Daisy munching on the grass several feet away; the constant rushing sound of the nearby river; the musical chirping of the crickets; the croaking frogs.

After a while, Samantha could feel herself start to relax, but she fought to stay awake just in case some unwanted intruder happened upon her little campsite. Finally, exhaustion won out in the end. Soon, her eyelids fluttered closed, and her chin drooped to her chest . . . .

A coyote's lonely howl in the distance jerked Samantha wide-awake. She wondered how long she'd been asleep? From the looks of the campfire, probably not long. She instantly became more alert when Daisy started acting fidgety about something.

"What is it, girl?" she whispered, getting to her feet.

Samantha strained her ears, listening for any sound that might be out of the ordinary. There wasn't enough moonlight that enabled her to see very far in front of her. Then she thought she heard something . . . a low growling sound.

Suddenly Samantha remembered: *the fish!* She'd forgot to dispose of her leftover supper. *Oh how could she have been so careless!*

Immediately trembling with fear and dread, her frightened eyes scanning the darkened perimeter around the campsite, Samantha reached down to remove the knife she always kept inside her boot, wondering what kind of predator was out there . . . *a wolf . . . coyote . . . possibly a bear?* Daisy nickered and began to paw nervously at the ground. *If only she could get to her horse*, Samantha thought. But already it was too late to try and make a run for it. She could see what looked like a bear—*an enormous grizzly*—coming through the trees.

Samantha had never known such gut-wrenching fear in her entire life, and it took her several panic-stricken moments to react. She turned and raced to the nearest tree, praying the bear wouldn't notice her. Carefully slipping the handle of the knife between her teeth, she hoisted herself onto the lowest hanging branch. As she began to climb higher in the tree, she looked over her shoulder just in time to see Daisy bolt into the forest. She was relieved, knowing at least her horse had made it to safety.

Samantha continued to climb higher . . . and higher. When she heard the grizzly's angry roar, she risked a quick glance downward and saw the enormous animal was pacing at the bottom of the tree. Parking herself on a sturdy limb and removing the knife from her mouth, Samantha let out a high-pitched scream, hoping it would frighten the bear away. Or maybe by some miracle of God, somebody would hear her cries and race to her rescue. Over and over again, Samantha screamed at the top of her lungs, until she was nearly hoarse. But all her efforts only seemed to anger the huge beast even more.

Below her, Samantha could now hear thick branches snapping like twigs and knew that the monster was coming after her. Placing the handle of the knife between her teeth, she tried to climb higher up the tree. But, by now, Samantha was shaking so badly from fright, she nearly lost her grip several times. She wondered how much farther she would have to go before the bear gave up or she reached the top of the tree.

When her boot slipped on a branch, Samantha felt the grizzly's razor-sharp claws rip through the bottom part of her leg. The pain was absolutely excruciating and only the knife in her mouth prevented her from screaming in agony. She swallowed back a wave of nausea as she forced herself to climb faster, ignoring the throbbing pain in her leg.

Now that she was nearing the top of the tree, Samantha had no other choice but to prepare for mortal combat. Perching herself upon a stout enough limb, she clung to it with wobbly legs, while grasping the knife in her shaky hand. Tears of fright streamed down her cheeks and she swiped them away. She had to remain calm. Taking a deep breath, and letting it out slowly, she drew back her arm, waiting for her chance to strike.

The grizzly was now so close to Samantha she could actually see the animal's huge, snapping teeth gleaming in the silvery moonlight, and she could feel the trunk of the tree swaying under the grizzly's massive weight. Trying to muster every ounce of courage she possessed . . . *ready* . . . *aim* . . . she mentally told herself.

When the bear was a little closer, Samantha released her knife.

The monster let out an angry roar that was loud enough to shake the tree. She could hear the sound of branches breaking as the grizzly plummeted toward the ground . . . .

The sudden silence seemed almost eerie to Samantha as she clung desperately to the branch, while resting her head against the cool trunk of the tree. Now that the danger was over, the constant pain in her lower leg reminded Samantha of the wound she'd received, and she was almost afraid to examine the extent of her injury. At least she could move her leg without much difficulty, so hopefully that meant there was no permanent damage done.

But Samantha needed to rest for a while, before she attempted to climb down from the tree. She squeezed her eyes shut, trying to block the horrifying experience she'd just endured from her mind. She forced herself to think of something pleasant; so what could be more pleasant than her wedding day . . .

Samantha imagined herself and Chandler both standing before Reverend Peters. Chandler's handsome face beamed with pleasure as he gazed into Samantha's eyes. But instead of the customary suit and tie, she pictured Chandler dressed in a pair of creamy white doeskin pants, and a shirt that was made of the same velvety soft material with long fringe that reached to his knees. A pair of intricately beaded knee high moccasins hugged his feet. And a single white feather adorned his shoulder-length coal-black hair.

As the reverend pronounced them husband and wife, Samantha stared into Chandler's ebony eyes, eyes that were framed with the longest sooty lashes she'd ever seen. A dreamy smile lifted the corners of Samantha's lips. She'd always thought that Wade Chandler's eyes were too beautiful for a man . . . .

"Samantha . . . Samantha . . ."

Her eyelids suddenly fluttered open. She blinked several times, trying to focus on the blurry face before her eyes. When she saw that it was Chandler, she wondered if she was still dreaming? Then Morgan's face appeared beside Chandler's, and Samantha realized this wasn't a dream. Then she remembered . . .

"*The bear!*" Samantha tried to sit up but a firm hand held her in place.

"The bear can't hurt you now, Samantha," she heard Chandler say. She knew he wouldn't sound so calm if it wasn't true . . .

"I don't know how you did it, woman, but you planted the blade of your knife right between that grizzly's eyes."

"I've never seen anything like it," Morgan added.

"Daisy!" This time Chandler didn't stop her when she tried to sit up.

"Daisy's with her man," Chandler informed her, firmly adding, "Where she belongs." There was no misinterpreting the meaning of his words.

Samantha scowled at him.

"I think she's feeling better," Morgan said, chuckling. Figuring they could use a little privacy, he rose to his feet. "I'll go see to the horses." Then he walked away.

"How did I get down from the tree?" Samantha wanted to know.

"You don't remember?"

She shook her head.

"I carried you. It was Morgan who saw you in the tree . . . I climbed it to get you down. When I reached you, your arms were clutched so tightly around the trunk, I had to pry them apart. You were lucky you didn't fall out of the tree." Chandler was about to scold her for leaving the village the way she did, when she suddenly burst into tears.

"Oh, Chandler, it was awful!" Samantha cried and covered her face with her hands.

Pulling Samantha into his lap, Chandler wrapped his arms protectively around her, then sat there, rocking her like a child, while she related what happened. He nearly froze with fear when he realized just how close he'd come to losing her.

"Shhh . . . it's over now," he crooned against her ear. "Do you think you can ride?"

"I don't know . . . my leg."

With Samantha still in his arms, Chandler stood and gently set her on her bare feet. "Morgan and I cleaned your wounds the best we could and wrapped your leg. You have several nasty gashes on your lower calf."

Morgan returned then and seriously added, "You're gonna have some scars."

"Where are my boots?"

Samantha frowned when Chandler handed her something that looked like a piece of shredded leather. "What's this?"

"Your boot."

"That boot probably saved your leg," Morgan said.

Samantha stared in wide-eyed fascination at what was left of her boot. "I want to see the bear," she suddenly announced.

"I don't think that's such a good idea," Chandler replied.

"Why not?"

Chandler and Morgan exchanged concerned glances. "The grizzly that attacked you it . . . well . . . it's one of the biggest darn grizzlies I've ever seen," Chandler informed her. "Morgan and I think it would be best if you didn't look at it."

"I still wanna see it."

It was against Chandler's better judgement, but if Samantha wanted to see the bear . . . He let out a sigh, then wordlessly scooped Samantha up in his arms and carried her over to the huge, fury mound lying on the ground, and set her on her feet.

Samantha's eyes were round as saucers. Chandler had not been exaggerating. *The grizzly was gigantic.* She'd heard enough stories about grizzly bears to know that she had to be looking at one of the biggest. It was lucky for her that last night it had been too dark to clearly see this enormous monster chasing her up the tree, otherwise, she might not have had the courage to do what she'd done.

"Why is it missing a front claw?" Samantha asked.

Chandler reached inside his pocket and pulled out the big claw, holding it out to her. "I found it embedded in the tree trunk. I was going to keep it, but it's yours, if you want it?"

Samantha visibly shivered. "You keep it." After getting a good look at the size of that claw, she was almost afraid to look at her leg, which was beginning to throb again.

"My leg . . . it's pretty bad, isn't it?"

"I'm no doctor, Samantha, but—your leg looks pretty bad to me. You have a really deep gash that needs some stitching and I'm no seamstress and neither is Morgan. We bound the wound the best we could, but you need a doctor." Chandler was also worried that infection might set in, but he didn't say anything. He didn't have to be a doctor to know her leg was bad. In fact, he couldn't believe she was able to stand on it. His biggest concern at the moment, was to get Samantha to the nearest town as quickly as possible.

Chapter Sixteen

Home . . . Samantha wanted to go home. She hadn't had a decent bath in days. All she wanted to do was take a long, hot bath and sleep in her own bed. She had ripped her shirt and pants, trying to flee from the bear and, without her boots, she must look like a street urchin. Squinting her eyes against the bright afternoon sun, it seemed like they had been riding in circles for hours, Samantha thought, or maybe the landscape just looked the same. Her leg was throbbing constantly now, but she didn't want to complain. Besides, the less they stopped, the sooner she would be reunited with her family. Maybe her father had sent the men on ahead to Cheyenne with the herd, and they could all go home.

Samantha thought it felt much hotter today than usual. Again she swiped at the perspiration that constantly dripped from her sweaty brow. She shifted restlessly upon Daisy's bony back, trying to find a more comfortable position.

"Are you all right, Samantha?" she heard Chandler ask.

Samantha turned and smiled at him, but didn't say anything. She just didn't seem to have the strength to reply.

"Samantha?" Chandler frowned when she just kept looking at him.

Guiding Ranger closer to Daisy, he reached over and touched her forehead. At that moment Samantha suddenly slumped forward. He slipped an arm around her waist, pulling her from her horse onto his lap. With Samantha now cradled in his arms, he could actually feel the heat radiating from her feverish body. He hollered at his brother to stop.

"What's wrong?" Morgan asked, halting beside him.

"Samantha's burning up with fever!" Chandler yanked the bandanna from around his neck, quickly saturated the cloth with water from his canteen, then began to wipe Samantha's flushed face. "She's not responding!"

Morgan had feared something like this might happen. "Her leg must be infected."

"What are we going to do?"

"Just sponging off her face won't lower a fever like that. I think I remember where there's a stream . . . follow me." Morgan spurred his mount into a run.

Holding Samantha securely against his chest, Chandler kneed his stallion into a full gallop and raced after his brother across the grass-covered prairie . . . .

Chandler halted his horse beside the tree-lined stream, and dropped to the ground with Samantha in his arms. He held her close, while Morgan grabbed his bedroll and hastily spread it over the grassy bank alongside the stream where a small pool had formed.

Ever so gently Chandler lay the still unconscious Samantha upon the ground, then began to unbutton her shirt. When Morgan handed him a silky, lace-trimmed blanket to cover her with, he quirked a dark brow at his brother.

"Don't ask," was all Morgan would say.

Chandler shrugged, thinking he would have to try and remember to question his brother about the frilly blanket later. He then explained to Morgan where to look for some special herbs that would help bring Samantha's fever down as he fumbled with the remainder of her buttons. After Morgan had gone to look for the herbs he needed, Chandler finished removing Samantha's clothing, leaving on her chemise; then he covered her lovely form with the blanket Morgan had given him, trying not to pay any attention to the long, well-shaped legs just begging for his touch.

Chandler dipped his handkerchief into the swirling water, then began to sponge bathe Samantha's flushed face and chest. Even the late afternoon heat did not prevent the tremors that caused her body to twitch and shake, or stop her teeth from chattering. When she started to speak incoherently, Chandler knew that was a bad sign. He gently turned Samantha over onto her stomach, lifted the blanket just enough to expose the bandage, then carefully removed the long strip of cloth that covered her entire lower leg. He gasped when he saw the ugly red slashes. But the wound that concerned him was the angry, pussy-looking gash that started under her knee and zig-zagged nearly to her ankle; part of this deep gash on her calf went clear to the bone, and this was the area that was obviously infected.

Never having a weak moment in his entire life, Chandler had to look away and take several deep breaths to settle the queasiness in his stomach; then he scooted closer to the edge of the stream and quickly splashed some cold water over his head and chest. He sat back on his haunches and closed his eyes, allowing the cool droplets of moisture to absorb the heat from his body. After a while, he lifted his face toward the cloudless blue sky and began to pray for the woman he loved, begging God to spare her life . . . .

At the sound of footsteps, Chandler looked over his shoulder and saw Morgan walking toward him . . . there was something in his hand. Apparently his brother had found the herbs he would need to help fight the infection. Good. He would need all the help he could get. When Morgan saw Samantha's leg, his face visibly paled. Chandler knew what had to be done. Wordlessly, he got to his feet and walked over to his horse, then began to rummage through his saddlebags, looking for some matches.

Knowing what his brother was about to do, Morgan gathered some nearby twigs in a hurry and put them in a pile . . .

Now holding the blade of his knife over the low-burning flames, Chandler periodically looked over at Samantha, not sure anymore if he could do this.

"Graywolf, you know she could die if we don't lance the wound, but if you can't . . ."

"Hold her down, Morgan, so she doesn't move."

"Are you sure?"

Chandler nodded, then immediately went to work. While he tended Samantha's leg, he was grateful that she remained unconscious—for the pain would have been excruciating. When he was satisfied that all of the poison had been removed from the infected gash, he thoroughly cleansed the wound, then applied a moss poultice, using the herbs that Morgan had found, and carefully rewrapped the leg with a clean strip of cloth.

"I guess all we can do now is wait," Chandler announced, leaning back on his haunches and wiping the sweat from his brow.

"Samantha's strong, Graywolf. I think she'll pull through." Though Morgan didn't really believe his own words. He wasn't a doctor, but it didn't take a well-trained eye to tell the infection in her leg was serious.

All through the night Chandler remained ever vigilant at Samantha's side, constantly bathing her feverish body and forcing plenty of water down her throat. When a really bad spasm ripped through her, his eyes welled with tears, because there was nothing he could do but watch her writhe in pain. Afterward, he raised the canteen to her parched lips, and, as usual, she batted it away. This time, when a string of unladylike words followed, the faintest hint of a smile played upon his lips.

"You should rest for a while, Graywolf . . . you've been at this all night." Morgan knelt beside his brother, placing a comforting hand on his shoulder. "I'll take care of her."

"I'm not tired."

"What good will it do Samantha, if you collapse from exhaustion?"

"She needs a doctor, Morgan," Chandler said, wearily running a hand through his hair.

"Samantha can't be moved right now . . . she's too weak. Look—I feel every bit as frustrated and helpless as you do, big brother, but—I don't need two patients on my hands. So please try and get some rest."

"I can't, Morgan. I'm afraid if I close my eyes, even for a moment . . ." Chandler couldn't even finish the sentence.

Morgan finally gave up arguing with Graywolf, and offered to help in any way he could. When Samantha began to relive the nightmare of the grizzly attack, both men took turns holding her down. All the thrashing around was only making her fever worse. This went on for most of the day, and Chandler and Morgan were beginning to wonder if the nightmares would ever end. And when they finally did cease, there was nothing but deathly silence.

For the next two days whenever Samantha's fever would rage out of control and the nightmares would come, either Morgan or Chandler would hold her down, while the other would force lifesaving liquid between her parched lips. Her slender body was growing weaker before their very eyes, and by the morning of the third day, they were both at their wits-end.

Kneeling beside the stream, Chandler splashed his face with cold water, then sat back on his heels, gazing at the distant mountain, a worried frown creasing his brow. Rising, he began to pace restlessly, back and forth, like a caged panther. He stopped abruptly in mid-stride and turned to Morgan.

"We have to do something."

"What do you suggest we do?"

"I don't know, but we can't just sit by and . . . What's the matter?"

"I think someone's coming." Morgan drew his gun.

Chandler and Morgan were completely taken by surprise when they saw Chief Running Elk, along with Big Bear, his friend Soars-like-a-Hawk, and an old man they didn't recognize, emerge out of the trees on horseback.

Morgan looked at Graywolf and shrugged, then holstered his gun. The men were almost to them now. "Father, what are you doing here?"

"We came to help," Running Elk said matter-of-factly, nodding in Samantha's direction. They all dismounted, and Morgan led the horses away. Big Bear went with him.

"I brought Wise Owl," Running Elk announced. "He is knowledgeable in all healing herbs, Graywolf. He will help your woman. Because my eyes are getting too old to clearly see, your brother and Soars-like-a-Hawk tracked you here."

Chandler nodded to Wise Owl and Soars-like-a-Hawk. "How did you know, Father . . . about Samantha, I mean?"

Running Elk smiled at his eldest son. "Our Father in heaven has ways of telling His children things He wants them to know." He then said something to Wise Owl in Comanche. The old man nodded his head, then walked toward the still form, lying upon the bedroll.

Nobody interfered as Wise Owl knelt beside Samantha and lifted the blanket just enough to reveal her injured leg. Chandler was amazed at how the old man moved with the agile grace of a much younger man. And even though his hands were gnarled from old age, his fingers moved nimbly as he skillfully worked on Samantha's lower leg. When Wise Owl seemed satisfied that all the pus had been removed from the infected wound, he applied a thick salve and replaced the moss, then rewrapped her leg, using a long strip of soft leather. Then he mixed some kind of powder in some water and forced it down Samantha's throat.

Chandler was grateful that Wise Owl did not speak English when several colorful words slipped past her parched lips. He inwardly groaned when he noticed his father's shocked expression. Apparently the chief knew the white man's tongue better than he thought. He scowled at Morgan who burst out laughing.

Knowing Samantha was now in capable hands, the anxiety of the past several days suddenly seemed to catch up with Chandler. He felt so utterly exhausted and drained, he could barely remain standing on his feet. He headed to his own bedroll and nearly collapsed upon it . . . .

Seated at a table in a crowded saloon, Chandler noticed the man standing at the bar, watching him. His thin lips were twisted into an evil grin; he had the eyes of a madman. Chandler had barely recognized Charlie Bates—the man who attacked Sarah Martin. He watched Charlie push away from the bar and was now walking toward him. Suddenly everything around Chandler seemed to be moving in slow motion. He sat frozen in his seat as he watched Charlie reach for his gun and raise the weapon, pointing it directly at his chest. Soundlessly a ball of fire escaped from the end of the barrel . . .

Chandler's eyes suddenly flew open and he sat up straight, gasping for breath. His heart was pounding in his ears, and he took a deep breath, letting it out slowly, trying to calm his racing heart. He told himself that it had only been a bad dream.

Although it had seemed so real . . .

Then Chandler remembered, "Samantha." After the horrible dream he'd just had, he was almost afraid to look, afraid of what he might find. When he turned his head to look at Samantha, he could not believe his eyes. She was wide-awake, lying on her side, facing him. And in the early morning light he could clearly see there was a smile upon those lips. Although she was still quite pale and there were dark smudges under her sky-blue eyes, she was the most beautiful sight he'd ever seen.

Rising, Chandler walked over and knelt beside her. He took her small, pale hand in his and brought it to his lips, tenderly kissing each fingertip.

"Care to go bear huntin'?" he teased.

"Maybe some other day." Samantha's voice sounded a little raspy from the high fever. "You look tired, Chandler."

"And you look beautiful." He reached out and touched her silky cheek with the back of his hand. "Better get some rest now."

"So should you." Then she closed her eyes.

Chandler smiled when he realized that Samantha was already asleep . . . .

Later that afternoon, Soars-like-a-Hawk and Wise Owl headed back to the village, leaving behind Chief Running Elk and Big Bear, allowing the newly reunited family this opportunity to spend some extra time together. Big Bear had gone hunting for some fresh meat and had not yet returned. Chandler was grinding some special herbs for Samantha's tea like Wise Owl had showed him. Morgan sat quietly beside his father, gazing into the crackling flames of the campfire, each man engulfed in his own thoughts.

Running Elk turned to study the handsome profile of his second son. The white couple who had raised Morgan had done a good job. Though he was very proud of the grown man seated beside him, he wished he could have been there to see Little Bear grow to manhood. After silently observing Morgan for quite some time, he could not stand the pain he read in his son's face any longer.

He bluntly stated, "You love the beautiful maiden . . . is this not so, my son?"

Morgan's head swung toward his father. *How could he have known?* Surely, it couldn't be *that* obvious? Not when he'd fought so hard to hide what was in his heart—the love he felt for Samantha Callahan. And he loathed himself for it.

Although Morgan hated to admit it, he couldn't lie to his father. "Yes—it is so," he reluctantly confessed. Then he hung his head in shame, adding, "I didn't mean for it to happen."

Running Elk chose his words very carefully. "Sometimes we have no control over such things," he said, remembering his own personal experience with Graywolf's and Morgan's mother. Singing Wind had already been promised to another warrior when he fell in love with her, and she with him. But at least that warrior had not been his own brother. "You must put the white maiden from your heart, my son."

"Samantha will soon be Graywolf's wife . . . I would *never*, for any reason, *ever* interfere with that, Father. For I also love my brother."

"I know this," Running Elk sadly replied.

Morgan looked straight ahead. Watching the tender way his brother cared for Samantha, it nearly brought tears to his eyes. "I will help Graywolf take Samantha back to her family, and then I will leave."

"Will you return to your people?"

"At least for a while."

"You must pray to our heavenly Father for guidance, my son . . . that is the only way you will ever find inner peace. I believe there is more that troubles you, but we will talk later . . . your brother returns from his hunt."

As Big Bear dropped the small deer on the ground beside the fire, Morgan sarcastically remarked, "You expect to feed four grown men on that itty-bitty doe?"

"I did not hear you volunteer to go hunting," Big Bear snapped.

"Had I known we might starve, I would have gladly volunteered."

Big Bear scowled. "I provided the meat," he said, thumping himself on the chest. "Now . . . which one of my brothers will prepare it?"

Grumbling under his breath, Morgan rose to his feet. He effortlessly picked up the deer and slung it over his broad shoulder, then headed toward the river . . . .

The men were all seated around the small campfire, talking and laughing. Samantha lay on her bedroll beside Chandler, quietly listening to the mens' conversation, while they ate their meal. Licking the juice from the tips of his fingers, Big Bear spoke with his mouth full of food. "This is the best venison I ever tasted. I believe Morgan will make somebody a good wife one day."

They all burst out with laughter; even Samantha couldn't help laugh.

"If you're making me an offer, you're not my type," Morgan retorted.

"You have severely wounded my young heart," Big Bear said, placing a hand over his chest pretending to be hurt.

Morgan rolled his eyes.

"My sons have much humor," Running Elk chuckled.

"Except for Graywolf. He's too serious to be funny."

Chandler frowned at Morgan. "And you're not serious enough."

"Tell us again, Graywolf, about Samantha's brush with the mighty grizzly, so I can tell the other warriors at the next lodge meeting." Big Bear had already heard the story several times, but he would never grow tired of hearing it. From the first moment he ever laid eyes on Samantha, he'd known she was an unusual woman. And he'd developed a strong respect for his oldest brother, because he seemed to be the only one who could handle the headstrong beauty.

As Running Elk listened to Graywolf speak, it still amazed him how such a mere wisp of a woman could have killed a giant grizzly with nothing more than a white man's pocket knife. He felt a tremendous sense of pride and admiration for his future daughter-in-law. When Graywolf displayed the huge grizzly claw, Running Elk proudly boasted, "My new daughter will be the talk of the village for many moons."

Samantha had closed her ears when Chandler started talking about the grizzly attack. Just the mention of a bear, caused her to relive that horrifying night all over again . . .

"We should be heading back to the village," Running Elk suddenly announced.

"Father, Samantha and I will probably come for a visit next spring," Chandler said.

"You and Samantha will be joined by then?"

Chandler nodded.

Running Elk was pleased. He couldn't wait to be a grandfather. Though, at the same time, it saddened him that Singing Wind was not here to share his joy.

Samantha pulled the coverlet over her head, trying to block out the morning sunlight. Beneath her private cocoon, she could hear the sound of muffled voices. She tried to roll over on her side, and groaned, when a stabbing pain shot through her lower leg, reminding her of her injury. And for some reason the wrinkled face of an old man hovering above her flashed in her mind.

Now Samantha could smell the aroma of a rabbit roasting, which caused her belly to rumble with hunger. With a defeated sigh, she tossed the cover aside. Standing directly in front of her line of vision was a pair of knee high moccasins. She followed the long, muscular legs encased in a pair of snug-fitting buckskins, then past a broad chest, until they came to rest upon a familiar, handsome face, smiling down at her.

"I heard you stirring," Chandler said, squatting beside her. "Are you hungry?"

"Famished."

"I'll be right back."

"Chandler, wait."

He turned around.

"I could really use a bath," Samantha whispered.

"You'll have to be careful of your leg."

"I'll be careful."

"After breakfast then."

Just the thought of a bath made Samantha feel better. When she tried to sit up, a sudden wave of dizziness washed over her. She grabbed hold of her head, trying to keep it from spinning, while fighting the queasy feeling in her stomach. When the dizziness had passed, this time, much more slowly, she sat up straight.

Chandler returned with a plate of food and a steaming cup of coffee. Samantha was grateful for the coffee, but she wrinkled her nose at the large chunk of meat. "If I eat all this, I won't be able to move." She then took a small bite of the tender rabbit, chewing it real slow, hoping it would stay down.

"Where's your father and Big Bear?" she asked, when she noticed they were no where in camp.

"They left bright and early this morning."

"I didn't even get to say good-bye."

"You were still sleeping and I didn't want to disturb you. Besides, you'll be seeing them soon enough. Don't forget, I promised my father we'd come for a visit next spring."

"I didn't forget."

"After your bath—if you think you can ride, Samantha, we should be leaving. I'm sure by now your parents must be panic-stricken."

Chapter Seventeen

Rachel stood quietly at the window, peering down at the busy street below. Through teary eyes, she watched the people strolling along the boardwalk, wishing she could spend the entire day shopping—it was such a lovely Saturday afternoon. She looked over her shoulder at her husband who was just about finished packing his saddlebags, wondering how she could convince the stubborn man that he was being foolish—that he should still be in bed—that he was in no shape to be gallivanting around the countryside.

Swiping away her tears, Rachel turned to face her husband. "John, I know in my heart Samantha's okay . . . please give Morgan and Chandler . . ."

"We've already been over this, Rachel."

"But you can't go after Samantha alone," she stubbornly argued. "If you hadn't sent the men on to Cheyenne . . ."

"If I hadn't, we might have lost the entire herd . . . I didn't have much of a choice." John carefully sat on the edge of the bed, holding his throbbing head in his hands.

"John, are you okay?" Rachel cried, rushing to his side.

"No, I'm not!"

When John saw his wife flinch from the hostility in his voice, he felt ashamed of himself. God in heaven help him; he just wasn't himself these days. In a much more calmer tone, he said, "I couldn't bare it, Rachel, if anything happened to you. You'll be safe here at the hotel."

Rising, he wrapped his arms around his distraught wife, gently kneading the tension from her back. "I didn't mean to holler at you."

Rachel looked up at him, her misty amber-colored eyes begging him to stay. John was tempted to give in, but this was something he had to do. "You'll just have to trust me, Rachel."

She turned a stiff back on him.

With a sigh John grabbed his saddlebags off the bed and slung them over his shoulder, then he walked out the door, closing it behind him. He headed down the long corridor, descended the stairs, which led directly into the lobby. He stopped at the front desk, like he'd done the past several days. The owner, a middle-aged fellow who was always impeccably dressed and hardly ever said a word, glanced up from his book work and shook his head. So there was still no word from James, and he wondered what could be taking so long.

Once outside the hotel, John hurried down the boardwalk toward the livery to fetch his horse. He hadn't gone very far when he could have sworn he heard Samantha calling him. He halted in his tracks and turned around.

But there was no sign of her.

Thinking that bump on his head must be causing him to hear things, John started walking along the boardwalk again.

"*Paaaa!*"

Whirling around, John wondered if his eyes were now playing tricks on him—because, unless he was mistaken, that was Samantha racing Daisy down the middle of the dusty street. She waved at him, and his entire face split into a huge smile.

Dropping his saddlebags on the ground, John caught his daughter in his outstretched arms when she leaped from Daisy's back. Tears gathered behind his eyes as he crushed Samantha against his chest in a tight bear hug.

"Your mother and I have been worried out of our minds!"

"I'm sorry, Pa . . . we tried to get back as fast as we could."

"We?" John stood Samantha on her feet, and frowned, when he noticed her disheveled appearance. Her long, beautiful hair hung around her body in a mass of tangles. Her clothes were torn and dirty.

And her boots were missing. Through her tattered pants he saw a bandage that covered her lower leg.

"What happened to you?" John demanded to know.

"It's a long story, Pa," Samantha replied. "Here comes Chandler and Morgan!" she announced excitedly, waving an arm high over her head, trying to get their attention.

Both Chandler and Morgan noticed father and daughter immediately. John towered over just about everybody in town, so you couldn't miss him. And Samantha, with her clothes hanging off her slender body in shreds, looking like she'd just been in a fight with a bobcat, stood out like a sore thumb.

As the brothers drew closer, it was Chandler who first noticed the smoldering glint in John's piercing blue eyes, and those angry eyes were focussed on him. It didn't take a mind reader to figure out what must be running through John's head. He remarked to his brother, "I have a feeling that John's not going to give us a chance to explain."

By now, Morgan was also well aware of the wrath they were about to face. He seriously suggested, "You know, Graywolf, it's not too late to turn our horses around and hightail it out of town while we still can."

"Yeah . . . I know what you mean," Chandler muttered more to himself, thinking Samantha's father looked mad enough to bite the head off a rattlesnake.

Both men halted their horses.

"Hello, boys," John calmly said.

Chandler looked over at Morgan, not really sure what to do. He remained seated on his horse, trying to decide the best way to handle his 'father-in-law-to-be'. Then, without a word of warning, John lunged forward and grabbed him out of the saddle and, before Chandler knew what was happening, he suddenly found himself sprawled out in the middle of the dusty street, gazing up at the cloudless blue sky. He shook his head, trying to clear it, hoping his throbbing jaw wasn't broken . . .

Perched upon his stallion, grinning from ear to ear, Morgan watched John easily haul his brother to his feet by the front of his shirt. He winced when the big man's fist connected with Graywolf's jaw *again.* "Ouch—I bet that smarted," he chuckled to himself.

But Morgan's smile suddenly disappeared when John swung around to face him, and those bright-blue orbs of his narrowed into angry slits. "Oh, oh." His eyes widened in alarm as John quickly began to close the distance between them.

Morgan figured that he might as well get down from his horse . . . which he did in a hurry. He hastily tried to reason with the man. "I don't blame you for being angry, John, but—you know how headstrong that daughter of yours . . ."

"Pa, wait!"

Samantha left Chandler's side and raced toward her father and Morgan, jumping in between the two men. "What happened to me wasn't their fault! I was attacked by a grizzly!"

John immediately calmed down, dropping his fist at his side. He then noticed the small crowd that had gathered in the street to watch and angrily snarled at them, "Haven't you people got something better to do!"

Whispering amongst themselves, they all dispersed in different directions.

Chandler walked over to join his brother, John, and Samantha. He saw the apologetic look in John's eyes and tried to make a joke. "Anybody ever tell ya, you got a fist like a rock?"

"I've had a few complaints," John admitted with the hint of a smile. "Look, Chandler, I don't really know what to say, except that . . . well . . . when I saw Samantha I thought . . . I'm not exactly sure what I thought."

"Forget about it . . . just next time, remind me to duck."

John led Samantha, Chandler, and Morgan along the boardwalk—ignoring the curious stares—to the hotel where he and Rachel were staying. Inside the lobby he gave the errand boy some money to take their horses to the livery. After adding another room to his bill for Chandler and Morgan, John told both men to wait for him inside the adjoining saloon, then he took Samantha by the arm and escorted her up the stairs.

Chandler's eyes followed John and Samantha, before turning and heading toward the batwing doors with Morgan. As they entered the saloon, "Maybe a stiff drink will help dull the pain in my jaw," he grumbled more to himself.

Morgan chuckled. "Why don't you grab us a table back there in the corner," he told his brother, "while I get us a bottle of whiskey."

With a sigh Chandler retreated to the back of the room, where he dropped wearily into an empty chair at a small table, his back toward the wall, as was his habit. This way, he could keep an eye on the swinging doors; one never knew what kind of riff-riffraff might enter the place, so it paid to be a little cautious. It was a bit early in the day for the saloon to be this busy, Chandler thought, noting the room was filled mostly with down-on-your-luck cowboys, probably hoping to win enough money to last them between jobs. He noticed the two disreputable-looking men—or more accurately—*heard them.* They were seated near the piano, loudly whistling at the scantily dressed blond who was singing—or trying to.

Morgan returned with a bottle of whiskey and a couple of glasses, which he placed on top of the table. He straddled the only other chair and spoke in a whisper, as he poured them each a drink. "Over there . . . at the large table, there's a man who keeps looking this way . . . think they want us to join them for a friendly game of cards?"

Chandler peered over Morgan's shoulder. "Not likely. They probably aren't used to seeing Indians here in town—especially an Indian wearing a gun. Why don't you hide that thing, Morgan . . . put these white men at ease."

"I don't hide what I am."

"Then why don't you just wear a sign on your back that says 'beware-of-big-bad-bounty-hunter', Chandler sarcastically said.

"They probably can't read anyway."

Standing at the bar, grasping an empty drink in his hand, Charlie Bates had recognized the Indian the moment he'd stepped inside the saloon. He was the same Indian who had stopped John Callahan's crazy daughter from using him as a human target that night in Bear Creek. The other Indian with him looked enough like the man to be his twin brother. These must be the same Indians John Callahan had hired—his old boss Jed Martin had been furious over it for weeks. So apparently they must've found the girl and brought her back. It appeared that the Indians were going to stick around, now getting to that *female misfit* was going to be much more difficult, because he'd heard that one of the Indians was sweet on the girl. Looks like getting to this town before John Callahan and his precious cattle had been the easy part.

His eyes glazed over with hatred. Indians shouldn't be allowed to be in the same room with decent white folks. The longer Charlie sat there drinking, the more furious he became . . . .

Rachel had burst into tears of joy at the sight of Samantha. When she questioned her daughter's ragged appearance and was told about the grizzly attack, she nearly swooned when she saw the deep gashes that covered the back of her leg.

"Oh, Samantha!" Rachel cried. "You're going to be scared for life!"

"Ma, my leg looks a lot worse than it actually is," she tried to assure her mother, though it was starting to throb again. "And a little scar isn't going to matter."

"Where were Chandler and Morgan?" John angrily wanted to know. He hadn't realized, until now, just how bad his daughter's injuries were.

"If you'll both calm down, I'll explain what happened."

"I'm listening!" John snapped.

Before her father exploded into another fit of rage, Samantha hastily informed her parents that the Indian who'd abducted her had turned out to be the son of Chief Running Elk, who just happened to be Chandler and Morgan's father. Both of her parents had been just as astounded by this news as she had been. Then she proceeded to tell them everything leading up to the grizzly attack, including how she had foolishly left the village on her own.

Samantha had to pause a moment, trying to calm her fears, before finishing her story. Part way through, when she noticed her mother's terror-stricken face, she abruptly changed the subject, and began to talk more about the Indians, telling her father how Chandler's people were being forced to steal cattle to replace the thousands of buffalo that were being driven away from their hunting grounds, because of the white settlers' constant invasion of their lands.

"Maybe we could deliver a small herd of cattle to Chandler's father's people every year on our way to Cheyenne," John said.

"Oh, Pa, that would be wonderful!"

John started toward the door. "I'll send somebody up with a bath," he said to Samantha. With his hand resting on the knob, he looked at Rachel over his shoulder. "I'll be waiting inside the saloon with Chandler and Morgan."

"Now just hold on, John Callahan . . . the saloon is no place for a married man!"

"You have nothing to worry about, Rachel . . . I only have eyes for you." John winked at his angry wife, before closing the door behind him.

"Indeed!" Rachel hissed.

As John's eyes scanned the crowded room for Chandler and Morgan, he suddenly became enraged, when he noticed Charlie Bates standing at the bar. While he was seriously contemplating whether to confront his daughter-in-law's attacker, or let the sheriff handle it, Charlie slammed his glass on top of the bar, then started across the room.

A sudden sense of foreboding came over John for some reason. Evidently others seemed to sense that something was about to happen, for men were scrambling out of their chairs, trying to get out of the way . . .

Only half listening to his brother, the hairs on the back of Chandler's neck kept warning him that something was wrong. His gaze shifted around the room. At first, Chandler thought that he must be seeing things, or maybe he'd consumed too much whiskey. Because that was Charlie Bates—coming toward him . . . just like in his dream.

Chandler sat frozen in his seat, unable to move. He noticed Charlie's eyes—they were the same hateful eyes that had been in his dream, glowing with insanity. And—just like in his dream—everything seemed to be moving in slow motion. Was that John he heard shouting at him to watch out? Morgan must've heard it too, because he turned his head. Now Morgan was standing out of his chair and then Chandler felt the breath leave his body when his brother's strong arm struck him across the chest just as the end of Charlie's gun exploded . . . .

Chandler lay on the floor, ignoring the burning pain in his side, watching, mesmerized, as Morgan swung back around to face Charlie while simultaneously drawing his gun. Then he saw his brother's horrified expression as he dropped to his knees beside him. Suddenly Chandler felt so tired, and he was having trouble keeping his eyes open . . .

Morgan became alarmed when Graywolf appeared to lose consciousness. But after examining the bullet wound and discovering that miraculously the bullet had cleanly exited out the back, he let out a sigh of relief. Morgan had seen enough bullet wounds over the years that he could tell by the amount of blood flowing from the small hole, that no vital organs had been hit. He quickly tore off a long strip of material from his shirt and wound it snugly around Graywolf's waist to help stanch the flow of blood.

When Chandler opened his eyes, Morgan and John were leaning over him, a worried expression masking their faces. He tried to sit up, and let a low groan, when an excruciating pain tore through his left side.

"You were lucky, Graywolf," Morgan told him. "The bullet went clean through . . . there was no real damage done. But I don't think you should try and move just yet," he said, holding him firmly to the floor.

Chandler slapped his brother's hand away and snapped, "Would you help me to my feet?"

Morgan chuckled and winked at John. "I think he's going to be okay."

"Trust me," Chandler grumbled, "I'm not ready to join my grandfathers in the happy hunting grounds just yet."

After Morgan helped him to his feet, Chandler noticed Charlie Bates's still form lying on the floor only a few short feet away. "Looks like justice has finally been served," he said to his brother.

Morgan couldn't agree more. For the first time in years, he felt a terrible burden had been lifted off his shoulders, now that the man responsible for the death of his adoptive parents could never harm another innocent person. He could even forgive the other man who'd been with Charlie that day, for he now understood that Jess Merdock had been too afraid of Charlie Bates to try and stop him. His job was finally done . . . .

Inside the little restaurant across the street from the hotel, John, and Rachel, along with a fidgety Samantha, waited for Chandler and Morgan to join them for breakfast. Both men were still over at the sheriff's office. As it turned out, there had been quite a hefty reward on Charlie Bates; apparently the evil man had committed several other crimes over the years. So Morgan was collecting the reward money, and Chandler had gone with him.

Ever since Samantha had found out that Charlie Bates shot Chandler, she'd hardly let the man out of her sight. Even now she was worried because he'd been gone so long. In her opinion, Chandler should still be in bed, though he kept insisting he was fine. She wasn't the only one who wished that Chandler and Morgan would hurry; she could tell her father was becoming impatient, the way he kept drumming his fingers over the top of the table. She knew he was anxious to get started for home. Samantha couldn't wait to get home, either; she missed her brother and Sarah. And she couldn't wait to see old Suzie's foal, since James had sent them a telegram announcing the newest member of their family.

So maybe it was nervous energy that caused Samantha to suddenly blurt out, "Did I tell you that Chandler and I are getting married?"

John's head swung toward his daughter. "No, you didn't."

"Oh . . . well . . . I guess I must've forgot to mention it in all the excitement."

"How could you forget something as important as that?" John asked.

Samantha shrugged.

"We've all been through quite an ordeal, John," Rachel reminded her husband. "I'm sure it just slipped Samantha's mind."

"Just out of curiosity . . . were you and Chandler engaged before the Indian attack?" John inquired of his daughter.

Samantha shook her head, wondering what the Indian attack would have anything to do with her engagement? "I thought you would be pleased by the news."

"Ignore your father, dear . . . he just can't stand the fact that he's getting old." Rachel, too, would have thought her husband would be pleased. "Personally, I'm thrilled by the news. Maybe I'm a little surprised it's so soon," she added more to herself. "So—when's the big day?"

"Yes . . . when *is* the big day?" John wanted to know.

Samantha noticed her father had the oddest expression on his face, but shrugged it off. "We haven't exactly set a date yet, but it should be in the near future."

"What's your hurry?"

It suddenly dawned on Samantha what her father was thinking. Her brow knitted together in an angry scowl. How could he even think such a thing! But what angered Samantha the most, she was a full-grown woman and was tired of being treated like a child. She felt like letting her father think the worst, but poor Chandler was already a wounded man. She was about to set her father straight on his twisted assumption when her mother intervened.

"Samantha, wait in the lobby while I speak with your father."

She didn't have to be told again. Casting a disappointed look at her father, Samantha scooted away from the table and headed toward the lobby.

Rachel had also figured out why John was behaving so oddly. She waited until her daughter was out of earshot, before turning her angry eyes upon her husband. "John Callahan, how could you imply such a thing?"

"If it's true, Chandler's a dead man."

"You can't be serious!" Rachel noticed that several people in the restaurant were beginning to stare, so she lowered her voice before adding, "Has it been so long that you can't remember what *we* did before we were married?"

"Chandler's old enough to know he should've kept his pants on!"

"But we don't even know if he took them off yet!"

Hearing loud gasps and whispers, Rachel suddenly stood out of her chair, her angry eyes scanning the shocked faces around the room—which by now had gone completely silent. "Where I come from, it is impolite to eavesdrop on a private conversation!" Then she gracefully sat back down in her chair.

John threw back his head and laughed. He couldn't believe what his 'prim and proper' wife had just done. If he lived to be an old man, he would never forget the expressions on the other diners' faces. He laughed all the harder . . .

Her husband's laughter became contagious, and now Rachel was laughing. When several people rose from their tables to leave, she said in a hushed whisper, "I bet their tongues will be busy wagging about what they overheard for many weeks to come."

"I have no doubt about that," John chuckled.

Abruptly John stopped laughing, and Rachel followed his line of vision across the room. She inwardly groaned, when she spotted a very stone-faced Chandler walking toward their table. As John started to get out of his chair, she reached over and grabbed his arm. "John, please don't say anything you might regret . . . remember he's going to be our son-in-law."

"Stay out of this, Rachel."

Chandler's smoldering eyes held John's piercing blue ones as he crossed the room. Samantha had stopped him inside the lobby to warn him about her father. The hot-tempered man could think what he wanted, but he was going to have his say. His anger did soften somewhat when he caught the pleading look in Rachel's worried eyes. But she had to understand he couldn't back down from her husband, although he didn't want to fight with the man, either.

"Can we talk here or should we step outside?" Chandler bluntly asked John. He inwardly sighed with relief, when John motioned for him to take a seat, which he promptly did just in case the man changed his mind.

John eyed Chandler for several long moments, before he finally spoke. "I'll say this only once . . . if you ever hurt Samantha in any way, you'll answer to me . . . simple as that."

"Then you have nothing to worry about, John, because I would never do anything to hurt Samantha." Then Chandler leaned forward to seriously add, "Neither will I allow you to interfere with my wife."

"I would never interfere—unless you gave me reason."

Rachel hurriedly translated what her husband was trying to say in his roundabout way. "In other words, Chandler, you have our blessing."

"Well why didn't he just say so." Chandler leaned back in his chair, a sheer look of utter relief on his face.

Rachel happened to look toward the lobby and noticed Samantha's head peeking around the corner of the doorway. Then Morgan's face suddenly appeared above her daughter's. The two of them looked so comical, she couldn't keep from laughing as she waved them over.

When Chandler saw Samantha striding toward them, he immediately got out of his chair to help her into her seat. He winked at his brother and teasingly offered, "Would you like me to hold your chair, too?"

"I think we've given these good people enough to talk about for one day," John said with a wink toward his wife. "Maybe Morgan better seat himself."

"Did we miss something?" Samantha asked her father.

"Never mind," Rachel said, giving her husband a stern look.

John took the hint and quickly changed the subject. "I guess a toast is in order." He raised his coffee cup, then matter-of-factly stated, "Chandler, Samantha's your problem now."

Everybody sitting around the table burst out laughing, except for Samantha, who didn't find any humor at all in her father's so called 'toast'. She wasn't *that* much trouble.

"Your father was only joking, dear," Rachel told her daughter, noticing her frown. "Weren't you, John?"

"I was *mostly* joking."

Samantha's frown deepened.

John threw back his head and laughed.

Just then a short, bald-headed man appeared beside their table. "Excuse me, but I'm going to have to ask you folks to either quiet down or leave the restaurant. Your . . . loud behavior is disturbing the other customers."

It bothered John that he would be snubbed by this little man just because he wasn't dressed as fancy as some of the other diners. "Well—we certainly wouldn't want to disturb the other customers," he sarcastically replied.

"Please, mister, I don't want any trouble."

Rachel easily recognized that particular look on her husband's face. "Please, John, let's just finish our breakfast and be on our way."

She was mortified when John suddenly stood out of his chair and actually growled at the little man. The poor fellow toppled over the table behind him in his haste to leave the room, drawing hoots of laughter from the other customers.

"John Callahan, was that really necessary?"

He only shrugged, then dropped back into his seat.

"Now what," Rachel muttered under her breath when she noticed the hotel manager was heading in their direction. The always well-dressed man wordlessly handed her husband a telegram, then turned and walked away.

"What does it say, Pa?"

"I can't read, if you keep talking," John grumbled.

There was complete silence at the table, while John finished reading the telegram. Suddenly his eyes widened and he let out a low whistle.

"John, what is it?" asked Rachel.

"According to James . . . Ester left Jed and she's moving back East to live with her sister. Jed's thinking about selling the ranch . . . well I'll be."

"What?" Rachel and Samantha said in unison.

John stared at his wife with a baffled expression. "How long have we been gone?"

"I'm not sure . . . maybe a few weeks . . . John, what is it?"

It was so quiet at the table now, you could have heard a pin drop, as everybody anxiously awaited John's answer. His face suddenly split into a huge grin. "How does Grandpa and Grandma sound to you, Rach?"

Samantha let out a squeal of delight and clapped her hands. "I'm going to be an aunt! Did you hear that, Chandler?"

"I heard," he chuckled.

"John, Rachel, looks like congratulations are in order," this from Morgan.

"We haven't been gone *that* long, have we?" Rachel said when she finally found her tongue. It's not that she wasn't happy about the news . . . she *was* happy . . . really she was . . . it's just that . . . being a grandmother sounded so old.

Reading his wife's thoughts, John leaned over to whisper in her ear, "Mrs. Callahan, you have nothing to worry about . . . you're just as beautiful today as you were the day I married you . . . being a grandmother won't change anything."

Rachel's amber-colored eyes welled with tears. "Oh, John, what a lovely thing to say."

"What did he say?" Samantha wanted to know.

"That's none of your business, young lady." John gulped down the rest of his coffee, then stood out of his chair. "I don't know about the rest of you, but I'm ready to go home."

"You coming with us, Morgan?" Chandler asked, also getting to his feet.

"Thought I'd tag along to make sure that you and this fair maiden here get properly hitched, that you don't back out."

"I have no intentions of backing out," Chandler assured his brother. He winked at Samantha, and laughed when she blushed.

Morgan *did not* want to admit it to himself, but there was a small part of him that was hoping Graywolf *would* back out and that he might stand a chance of winning Samantha for his own; at the same time, he truly wished them all the happiness in the world. Torn between his loyalty to Graywolf and his love for Samantha, Morgan was thinking it would be a whole lot less painful, the less time he spent around the happy bride and groom. Maybe it would be for the best if he returned to his father's village . . . .

John stayed behind to pay the bill, while the others clamored outside the restaurant. He eyed the little man behind the desk with the better-than-thou attitude. "Look, mister . . . ?"

"The name's Harold Smyth."

"Figures," John muttered under his breath. When he pulled out a wad of money from his vest pocket, he thought that ole Harold's eyes would pop out of his head. "So what do I owe ya?" he snapped at the irritating little man.

"And you are . . . ?"

Harold suddenly sounded so much more friendlier, which irked John even more. "The name is John Callahan. And you, Harold, may call me, *Mister* Callahan."

"You couldn't possibly be *the* John Callahan from Bear Creek—the same man who owns one of the largest ranches in the state?"

John thought the little man might actually faint, he looked so pale. His voice was filled with sarcasm as he replied, "I happen to be from Bear Creek and—yes, I suppose I do own one of the largest ranches in the state—though why should that matter. Something wrong, Harold? You look a little under the weather."

Harold could not believe his luck. Whoever would have guessed that this man was just about the richest man in the state? Why—he was dressed just like any other cowboy in town. "I beg your pardon, Mr. Callahan, I never meant to be so rude."

"Tell you what—you take this hundred dollar bill here," John said, stuffing the money inside the stunned man's fancy shirt pocket, "and keep the change." When he just stood there with his mouth wide-open, John couldn't resist, "By the way, Harold, I could buy this entire town with just my pocket change." Without another word, he turned and strode out the door.

Outside the restaurant John noticed the owner from the livery was leading their horses up the street with their gear packed and ready to go. After the man looped the horses' reins around the hitching post, John thanked him and handed him some money.

"John, what took you so long to pay the bill?" Rachel asked, a suspicious gleam in her amber-colored eyes.

John effortlessly lifted his wife into the saddle, handed her the reins, before casually replying, "Why—whatever do you mean?"

"Don't give me that innocent act, John Callahan, I know you better than that."

"Okay, you got me there," he said, chuckling. "Don't worry, I didn't touch the little runt."

"I hope you didn't lose your temper?"

"I came awfully close, but then . . ." he winked at her and added, "I thought of your words of wisdom, my love."

Rachel rolled her eyes and let out an unladylike snort.

John was laughing as he swung into the saddle. He looked over his shoulder at Samantha, Chandler, and Morgan, already mounted on their horses, and waiting.

"Are ya all ready?" he hollered out.

"We're ready," Samantha eagerly replied.

As they all headed out of town, Morgan was thinking that Graywolf would always have his hands full where Samantha Callahan was concerned. But there would never be a dull moment in their marriage—nor any peace for that matter, he thought, chuckling.

Suddenly there was a vision forming inside Morgan's mind: he saw his brother Graywolf chasing a small daughter through a grassy meadow; and the little girl had long, honey-colored hair—just like her mother's . . . .

Chapter Eighteen

The journey home to Bear Creek was uneventful. With Amos and the other men not due back from Cheyenne until the end of September, Chandler and Samantha planned on having their wedding then, which was only a few short weeks away. Morgan had returned to his father's people, but had promised to be there as Chandler's best man. Samantha could only hope and pray that nothing would go wrong to interfere with her wedding plans.

Her Aunt Ruth and Cousin Rebecca were due to arrive in town tomorrow on the stage, and Samantha was looking forward to seeing her relatives. She'd been just a little girl the last time she saw her aunt, and she'd only seen a picture of Rebecca.

Filled with nervous energy this morning, Samantha decided to ride into town. She still needed to find a wedding gift for Chandler and she wanted it to be something special. Inside the kitchen, she hastily scribbled a note to her mother, telling her where she'd gone so she wouldn't worry, then, grabbing her floppy hat and slamming it on her head, she headed to the barn.

Her father had warned her against riding Daisy until the little mare had had a sufficient amount of time to regain her strength, after all, she was due to foal in spring. So she chose a dainty chestnut mare named Gilda. She decided to use a saddle today, because she was going to do some shopping and didn't want to get her clothes dirty. It had been so long since she'd ridden with a saddle, she had a little difficulty getting the darn contraption on the horse.

Samantha was almost to town when a man she'd never seen before stopped her to ask directions to Bear Creek. With a handsome and clean-shaven face that was almost boyishly innocent-looking, she thought he seemed harmless enough, but something still told her to ride away. She should have listened to her instincts.

Before Samantha even realized what was happening, the man had produced a small length of rope and had hastily tied her hands to the saddle horn. Now straining against the bonds that held her hands, Samantha glared at the man's broad back leading her horse, again wondering who he was and what did he want with her. They'd been riding in a southerly direction for several miles now and he hadn't uttered a single word; he refused to tell her anything. Whenever she asked him a question, he would simply grunt in response.

Samantha now wished she would have taken the time to eat a bigger breakfast this morning. She was awfully hungry, and thirsty, too. The big brute had a canteen, but she loathed the thought of asking the man for a drink. On the other hand, her stubbornness would not quench her thirst.

As much as she hated to ask . . . "Hey, mister?" she hollered at his rigid back. "Could I please have a drink of water?"

When he didn't even flinch a muscle, Samantha thought maybe he hadn't heard her, then he suddenly halted his horse and climbed down from the saddle. With wary eyes she watched him grab his canteen and walk toward her.

"Tilt your head back," he snapped at her.

Surprised the man had actually spoke, Samantha bit back what she so desperately wanted to say to him. She knew it would do no good to ask him to untie her hands, so she obediently tilted her head back as he lifted the canteen to her lips.

After a moment, Samantha began to cough and sputter. "Are you trying to drown me?" she furiously spat at him.

Wordlessly he popped the cork back inside the canteen, snatched up the reins to her horse, climbed back in his saddle, then they were once again on their way.

Samantha wiped the beads of perspiration trickling down the side of her face on her shoulder, then, bending her head forward, she tried to adjust her floppy-suede hat to shade her eyes from the glaring sun, but her fingers were too numb. She was about to holler at the wretched man for help, but snapped her mouth shut.

They rode at the same steady pace for what seemed like hours to Samantha. It wasn't until the sun had sunk below the horizon when he abruptly halted his horse beside the river and gruffly announced, "We'll camp here for the night."

Samantha gritted her teeth to keep from saying something that might get her in trouble, while he untied her hands, then helped her down from her horse. She walked around a bit to stretch her legs, rubbing the circulation back into her numb hands.

"Take off your boots."

Samantha whirled around. "I beg your pardon?"

"I said take off your boots."

"I heard what you said, but . . ."

"Then why'd you ask?"

"Why do you want me to take off my boots?"

"So you won't try to escape."

It occurred to Samantha to inform the *dolt* that if she really wanted to escape she would do so with or without her boots . . . 'course she wasn't stupid enough to say so. She was worried he would find the knife she had hidden in the side of her boot. With him watching her so closely, there was no way she could possibly retrieve her knife before she gave him her boots. And it was the only weapon she had to defend herself against this man, considering there was no way she could physically fight him. Not counting that he towered over her by more than a foot, he easily outweighed her by a good hundred pounds. Plus, the snug-fitting shirt he was wearing did nothing to hide those powerful biceps, and his shoulders were about as wide as a barn.

With no other choice, Samantha yanked off her boots and handed them to the infuriating man. She watched him carelessly toss them over beside his saddlebags, then he proceeded to build a fire. As he worked, he made a gesture with his hand, telling Samantha where to sit, so she angrily walked over and plopped down upon the hollow log where he'd indicated. She was seriously thinking about making a run for it, but, unfortunately, there was no way she could get to her horse before her captor would easily overtake her. She considered her only other options then: behind her was the river which flowed more swiftly in this area, and she wasn't that good of a swimmer; and in front of her lay the wide-open prairie. She let out a defeated sigh. At least for now, there wasn't much she could do about her dire situation.

Well—wherever this man was taking her, Samantha was confident that Chandler would find them, and when he did, she would not want to be in this man's boots. Whoever he was, you could sure tell he was used to living outdoors. Already there was a fresh pot of coffee simmering over the coals, and he was stirring—what smelled like beans and bacon—in a large iron skillet. Again she wondered who this man was and what did he want with her . . . ?

Samantha reluctantly accepted the plate of food he wordlessly held out to her, figuring it wouldn't do her any good to starve herself just because of foolish pride. Balancing the plate on her lap, she removed her floppy hat and set it on the ground beside her, then, flipping her long, thick plait over her shoulder, she began to eat her meal, unaware of the curious glances from the man who sat across from her on the other side of the cozy fire . . .

Dressed in a pair of faded blue jeans and a blue-and-white-checked flannel shirt, Clayton could not remember ever seeing a more beautiful woman. He wondered how she'd managed to hide all that hair underneath her hat. He bet if she stood that long braid would hang to her knees! Her hair was a most unusual color . . . sort of the color of honey with red and gold highlights. He remembered that her eyes were the purest blue . . .

When the woman looked up at him with those sky-blue eyes, Clayton had to look away, suddenly ashamed of himself for ever agreeing to Billy's latest scheme. But he needed the money and Billy had offered him quite a large sum for the capture of Samantha Callahan. Billy was hoping the woman's fiancé would come after her, and that this Wade Chandler would ultimately lead him to the man he really wanted . . . his brother Morgan. He was the bounty hunter responsible for Billy having to spend time in prison. Clayton might have had serious doubts about Billy's plan, but no more. Wade Chandler would come for the woman; what man in his right mind wouldn't.

"Would you at least tell me your name?"

The woman's voice snapped Clayton out of his disturbing thoughts. What would it matter now if he told her his name. He quickly shoveled more beans into his mouth, before replying, "My name's Clayton Bradford."

"Would you please tell me why I'm here?" When he didn't answer her, Samantha softly muttered under her breath, "No, I don't suppose you would."

She decided it was probably best not to pressure him with any more questions—for now. At least she'd finally persuaded the man to tell her his name: *Clayton Bradford.* Though the name didn't sound familiar to her, she had the feeling that Clayton Bradford knew who *she* was.

When it was time to turn in for the night, Samantha grimaced, while Clayton tied her sore wrists together; then he proceeded to tie her feet. "Is this really necessary?"

"So you don't go anywhere," he replied matter-of-factly.

"I thought that was the reason you took my boots," she snapped in frustration.

"Go to sleep . . . we have a long way to travel tomorrow."

How was she supposed to sleep like this? Samantha angrily wondered. Though in all honesty she wasn't real uncomfortable since Clayton had kindly given her his own bedroll. She rolled over on her side—which took a little maneuvering. She watched Clayton lay down upon a thin blanket that he spread over the hard ground just a few short feet away, then he leaned back against his saddle, laid his hat beside him, and closed his eyes.

In the flickering firelight, Samantha was struck again by how handsome Clayton Bradford really was, especially without an angry scowl upon his face. He had thick, wavy, light brown hair which had blond streaks from the sun; and big brown eyes. He had a well-shaped nose, and a full, sensual mouth. Mister Bradford certainly didn't look like your usual outlaw.

"Oh, Chandler . . . please hurry," she whispered.

The next morning Samantha awoke with a start. It took her a few moments to remember where she was. Turning her head, she found Clayton seated beside the cozy fire, sipping a cup of coffee. His back was toward her. She quietly laid there, watching him, her mind racing, trying to think of a way to escape . . .

"Better eat some breakfast," he suddenly said.

Samantha wondered how he knew she was awake. "I'm not hungry."

"Suit yourself. But it'll be late afternoon before we stop for lunch."

"Could you please hurry and untie me?" she asked, struggling to a sitting position. "I need to . . . to . . ." Her cheeks flushed scarlet from embarrassment.

Hearing him chuckle, Samantha's embarrassment quickly turned to anger. If it wasn't for this man, she would be home in her own comfortable bed! "I'm glad you're so amused!"

With a sigh, Clayton rose and walked over to kneel beside the woman, then began to untie her hands. "Don't try to run away," he firmly warned her.

"May I have my boots?" Samantha had hissed the question at him, while rubbing the circulation back into her hands and feet. "Even if I tried to run away, I wouldn't get very far." To prove her point, she tried to stand, but her legs were too weak to hold her up.

Clayton didn't think the woman was as helpless as she was trying to make him believe, but what harm could she really do? He walked over and snatched her boots off the ground and then tossed them to her. "Remember—don't try nothin'."

Glaring at the man, Samantha pulled on her boots. She let out an inward sigh of relief, when she felt the knife still safely tucked inside its sheath. On tingling legs from lack of circulation, she wobbled over to some nearby bushes and ducked behind them. She soon discovered that her arms weren't working any better than her legs. Even if she could get a clear enough shot at Clayton, her arm was still too weak to throw her knife. Besides, she didn't think she could actually stab him anyway. But at least she did feel somewhat better just knowing that her knife was within easy reach if she needed it.

"Hurry up, lady," she heard him holler out.

Knowing she had no way of escaping the man for now, Samantha stepped away from the bushes, then limped over to where Clayton stood waiting with their horses. When she tried to put her foot into the stirrup and missed, suddenly strong hands circled her waist and lifted her into the saddle.

While Clayton once again secured her hands to the saddle horn, "I want to know where you're taking me!" Samantha angrily demanded. "Ouch! Do you have to tie that so tight?"

"Sorry, but Billy would shoot me on sight if you got away."

"Who's Billy?"

Clayton hadn't meant to let the name slip out, but he rationalized the woman would be finding out soon enough who Billy was, so what harm could it do to tell her now. "Billy Baxter's the man who sent me to find you."

"What does this Billy Baxter want with me?"

It was obvious to Clayton the woman didn't recognize the name of one of the most notorious gunfighters. "You're just the bait, lady."

"I don't understand."

"Billy's really after Morgan."

"What does this man want with Morgan?"

"Look . . . I've told you too much already." Clayton hastily gathered the woman's reins and mounted his horse.

"Wait! I still don't understand why Billy sent you to find me?"

Noting the stubborn angle of the woman's chin, Clayton had the feeling he wouldn't get another moment's peace until he gave her the answer she wanted. "Billy's confident that Wade Chandler will come after you. You are his woman, are you not?" Her blush was answer enough for Clayton. "The rest is simple. Billy figures this Wade Chandler fella will do anything to save his woman, including leading him to Morgan."

"In other words . . . you're using me, to get to Chandler, to get to Morgan," Samantha spat with contempt.

"That's the plan."

"There's something about your *little plan* that your stupid boss didn't think of."

"Oh? What's that?"

"Nobody knows where Morgan is, not even Chandler." That wasn't true. Morgan was probably with his father's people—least that's where he said he was going—but nobody knew that's where he went for an absolute fact. She wanted to laugh at the sudden panic-stricken look on Clayton's handsome face. Apparently *Brilliant Billy* hadn't thought of that.

"You're lying."

"And what if I'm not?" Samantha countered. "Before you get into a lot of trouble for nothing, Mister Bradford, I would advise you to take me back home."

"Billy can decide what to do." Clayton then nudged his horse forward, putting an end to the conversation.

Samantha glared at Clayton Bradford's back. She was furious they were using her as some kind of bait to capture Morgan. But what could she do to stop them? There was one thing about their plan that *would* work: Chandler would do whatever it took to rescue her, even at the cost of his own life. And she just couldn't let that happen . . . .

Samantha kept shifting in her seat, wishing she would've used a more comfortable saddle, thinking, if only she had ridden Daisy to town, she could have easily outrun Clayton—but what good was wishful thinking—it certainly wouldn't get her out of the predicament she was in. They were leaving Bear Creek farther and farther behind, and she wasn't familiar with this part of the country. Flat grasslands stretched out before her as far as the eye could see; overhead the cloudless blue sky seemed to go on forever. There was hardly a tree or a bush she could use as a landmark that would help her find her way back home if she managed to get away. And, although Samantha still felt confident that Chandler would find her, under these new circumstances, she now hoped he wouldn't.

Clayton pushed them hard all that day, taking only short breaks just long enough to water and rest the horses. It was well after dark when he finally stopped to make camp for the night. And the next morning, when Samantha got her first glimpse at the totally unfamiliar terrain that now surrounded them, she became even more alarmed. *She had absolutely no idea where they were.* And Clayton was back to his old mute-self again, refusing to speak to her.

It was nearing the evening hour when Samantha spotted what appeared to be a small cabin in the distance up ahead. This was probably where Clayton was taking her, she presumed, considering this was the only form of shelter she had seen since they began this journey.

A short while later, Samantha's suspicions were confirmed, when Clayton halted his horse in front of the worst looking run-down shack she'd ever seen. As if reading her thoughts, she heard him say, "I know this is nothing compared to that mansion you live in, but you'll get used to it."

I won't be here that long! she wanted to scream at the man.

After Clayton hastily untied her hands, Samantha jerked away from him, when he tried to help her down from her horse. He backed away from her, and she slid wearily to the ground. She balanced on wobbly legs, while rubbing her smarting wrists.

Clayton pushed her toward the door. "I'll ask Billy not to tie your hands, if you promise not to try nothin'," he whispered just before they entered the cabin.

When Samantha's eyes had a chance to adjust to the dimmer light, she discovered that the inside of the shack was in worse condition than the outside. There was an old potbellied stove that sat in one corner of the room; the only other furnishings was a small table and two rickety chairs, and a dirty cot that sat against a wall.

Samantha assumed the man lying on the cot with his back toward her—who appeared to be sleeping—must be Billy Baxter. She gasped, when he suddenly rolled over and she was staring into the pair of coldest blue eyes she had ever seen.

Samantha watched him slowly get to his feet and move toward her. She thought he had the walk and look of a gunslinger. He wasn't very tall, she noticed, and was rather on the slender side. For some reason, she'd been expecting a much bigger man; this man wasn't much taller than she. It was hard to tell his age under all that facial hair, but she guessed he was probably somewhere in his late twenties.

Samantha silently stood there, inwardly seething, while those frigid blue eyes observed her like a steer on an auction block. She never flinched when he removed her hat with a surprisingly quick hand, and heard his intake of breath when her long plait fell down her back.

"I just might keep her for myself," he casually remarked.

"You won't be keeping me at all!" she angrily spat, finally losing her temper.

The unexpected backhand that followed knocked Samantha to the floor. Ignoring the throbbing pain in the side of her face, she got to her feet, then, standing directly in front of the outlaw, she tauntingly said, "Shall I turn the other cheek?"

When he drew back his hand again, a loud voice stopped him. "She won't be any good to us, Billy, if you knock her senseless!"

His raised hand immediately dropped at his side. "Tie her up, Clayton. I wouldn't want such a *prize* to get away."

"Her wrists are practically raw, Billy. With both of us here, I see no reason to . . ." Suddenly Clayton went flying across the room when Billy viciously punched him.

"You just do what you're told, Clayton!" he hissed.

Samantha was stunned by what she'd just witnessed. Billy Baxter might not be a very big man, but he was obviously as strong as an ox! And it was easy to tell that Clayton was leery of the much smaller man; evidently with good reason. She was surprised by the compassion she saw inside Clayton's brown eyes when he looked at her. So, to make it easier for him, she willingly held her wrists out in front of her, while he tied them together.

The door opened then, and Samantha saw a pretty, blond-headed girl enter the cabin, struggling with a large bucket of water. She wore a ragged-looking brown dress that was way too big for her slender frame.

"What took you so long, Doreen?" Billy snapped.

"I'm sorry, Billy, but . . ."

"Never mind! Me and Clayton have some business ta tend to . . . I expect my supper on the table when I get back." He hesitated by the door. "I won't be far, Miss Callahan . . . don't try anything stupid." Then, "Doreen, watch her!"

Samantha threw invisible daggers at Billy Baxter's departing back as he strode out the door with Clayton. Then her eyes settled upon the blond-haired girl who was clumsily shoving wood inside the stove.

"Doreen?"

"Billy will hurt you, miss, if ya don't do what he says," she said in a shaky voice, without looking away from her task.

"I'm not afraid of Billy."

"You should be."

"What are you doing with a man like that?" Samantha bluntly asked.

Doreen had gotten the fire going and had set the blue-speckled tin coffeepot on top of the stove to heat. "Billy's my fiancé."

Samantha couldn't hide her shock.

"I have to get supper ready before Billy gets back." Doreen emptied a couple of tin cans into a large iron kettle. "I hope ya don't mind beans."

"Doreen, if you untie my hands . . ."

She whirled around. "I can't! Billy would . . ."

Doreen's mouth snapped shut when Billy entered the cabin. Samantha wondered why Clayton wasn't with him, and hoped the gunslinger didn't do something to the other man. She watched Doreen nervously spoon some beans onto a tin plate and hand it to Billy.

"Canned beans again," he angrily complained. "What good is a woman if she can't even cook? These beans are still cold!"

When Billy took a step toward Doreen, Samantha stepped in the gunslinger's path. "Why don't you pick on somebody more your own size!"

"Woman, I'm beginning to think you're just plain crazy!" In a fit of fury Billy hurled his plate across the room, splattering his beans all over the wall, then slammed out the door so hard that the force nearly knocked it off its hinges.

Samantha turned to Doreen. "You surely can't be serious about marrying that . . . *preening peacock.*"

She lowered her eyes, clasping her hands tightly together in front of her. "Billy says it's a sin to keep livin' together."

"An outlaw with morals . . . how noble," Samantha spouted more to herself. "Listen to me, Doreen, if you help me escape, I promise I'll take you with me."

Her pale-blue eyes grew round as saucers. "Billy would hunt me down!"

"My father will protect you!"

"No one can protect me from Billy!" Doreen cried. "Clayton tried once and Billy nearly beat him to death!" She then burst into tears.

Samantha sighed in frustration. Doreen was obviously terrified of the outlaw and who could blame the poor girl. She now realized that Doreen was maybe only a couple of years younger than herself . . . not nearly as young as she'd first thought . . . yet there was such an innocence about her. With that creamy complexion and those large, pale-blue eyes, and that perfectly shaped rosebud mouth, Doreen reminded her of a porcelain doll.

Samantha wanted to gain this young woman's trust and try to get them both out of a dangerous situation. She confided, "I'm supposed to get married at the end of this month. Listen to me, Doreen. I guarantee my fiancé will find me, and he'll protect both of us from Billy."

"I hope your man does find you, Samantha."

"How did you know my name?" When Doreen shamefully hung her head, Samantha easily guessed, "You knew Billy was coming for me?"

She nodded in reply.

"It's okay, Doreen . . . you couldn't have stopped him anyway."

"What's your fiancé's name?"

"His real name's Graywolf . . . he's full-blooded Cheyenne . . . his father's a chief." When Doreen's eyes widened in alarm, Samantha assured her, "Don't worry, Chandler is—that's the name he goes by now—actually his full name is Wade Chandler but everybody calls him Chandler. Anyway, he's really quite civilized . . . definitely more civilized than that bullying buffoon of a gunslinger."

Both women jumped when the door suddenly burst open and Billy strode into the room, and this time Clayton was with him.

"What's goin' on here, Doreen?"

"Nothin', Billy, we were just talkin'."

"What were you talking about?"

When Doreen didn't immediately answer, Billy tried to grab hold of her arm, but she jerked away from him. "Don't touch me!" Standing up to Billy not only surprised herself, but obviously Clayton as well, and especially Billy. Somehow she'd finally found the courage to defy him. Her chin went up a notch. "If you ever strike me again, I'll leave."

"What did you say, Doreen?" Billy said incredulously.

"Leave her alone, Billy."

He whirled on Clayton. "Doreen's *my* fiancé, and I would advise you to never forget it!" Then he took his gun from its holster, checked the barrel, while calmly saying, "I'm going out to rustle up somethin' decent for supper. I'm tired of canned beans." He holstered his gun and started toward the door. "You comin' with me, Clayton?"

"Yeah, sure."

Samantha sighed with relief when the door closed behind Clayton. For a moment there, she thought Billy was going to start shooting. They might be safe for now, but she sensed the man was a walking volcano just waiting to explode.

Chapter Nineteen

Silently pacing the confines of her bedroom, Rachel padded over to look out the window. The sun was just rising, turning the slate-blue sky into a brilliant shade of crimson, just along the eastern horizon, and filling the room with early morning light. She rubbed at her sleep-deprived eyes, again wondering who would have taken Samantha and why? That question had haunted her troubled mind all night. But there was no time to dwell upon such disturbing thoughts. With her sister and niece due to arrive at the ranch this morning, she had to be strong. Ruth and Rebecca were coming all the way from Boston just to attend Samantha's wedding at the end of the month . . . only . . . now there might not be a wedding . . .

No! She refused to think that way.

Hearing her husband stir, Rachel looked over her shoulder to find him awake and propped upon his elbow, watching her with a concern expression on his face.

"You haven't slept yet, have you?" John asked.

"You haven't slept much either."

Rachel turned to look out the window again. Behind her she could hear the slight rustle of bed covers, then the sound of her husband's bare feet pattering across the hardwood floor. A moment later, she felt strong arms slip around her waist.

"We'll find Samantha, Rachel . . . never doubt that."

There was a knock on the door. Figuring it must be Chandler, John hastily slipped on his pants and shirt, then hurried to answer the door.

"Sorry to disturb you, John, but I'm ready to leave whenever you are."

"I'll be right down, Chandler."

After closing the door, John turned to his wife. "Please go back to bed, Rachel. It'll be several hours yet before Amos gets back from town with Ruth and Rebecca."

"How can I rest when Samantha's missing?" she shrieked at him. "Oh, John, I'm sorry!" she cried, and covered her face with her hands.

Chandler stood at the kitchen window, watching the new day begin, quietly gazing out across the field, while he waited for John. His thoughts were on Samantha. He felt he would know in his heart if something drastic had happened to her. They would soon be husband and wife . . . finally. From the very first moment he'd ever laid eyes on Samantha Callahan, he had wanted her—it had just taken him some time to realize just how much he needed her. His hands clenched into tight fists, until his knuckles turned white. He couldn't wait to get his hands on the man who'd taken her!

"You ready, Chandler?"

He'd been in such deep thought, he hadn't heard John enter the room. He turned around. "The horses are already saddled and waiting."

Upon awakening it had taken Samantha a moment to remember where she was. Raising her head slightly off the floor, she glanced around the pre-dawn lit room. After making sure that everybody was still asleep, she tried to loosen the rope on her wrists, but her hands had gone completely numb . . . she couldn't even move them. Billy had insisted on tying her feet together last night, so her legs were numb this morning as well. Even if she could somehow manage to free herself, she doubted if she'd have the strength to make a run for it.

Her head turned at the sound of footsteps.

Doreen put a finger to her lips as she slowly tiptoed across the room toward Samantha. Her body was still stiff and sore this morning from the beating that Billy had given her several days ago, the day Clayton had gone into town for supplies. She stopped suddenly in her tracks when Billy asked her what she was doing.

"I . . . I'm getting Samantha a drink of water." Doreen now headed for the water bucket.

"You can untie her, Doreen, so she can stretch her legs a bit." From his cot Billy warned the woman, "If you try anything, you'll regret it."

Samantha glared at him, but held her tongue.

Doreen's hands were trembling as she struggled to get the rope off Samantha's wrists. When she finally did get the rope off and saw how badly chafed her wrists were, tears gathered in her eyes. She gently touched the angry-looking wounds and whispered, "I'm so sorry."

"It's not your fault, Doreen. My hands are numb . . . could you help me get the rope off my ankles?" Samantha asked.

"Of course."

Afterward, Doreen was having some difficulty trying to help Samantha stand, when suddenly a pair of strong arms lifted her to her feet. Samantha turned and smiled at Clayton, who still had his arm around her shoulders for support. She'd already come to the conclusion that Clayton Bradford had some decency in him, and couldn't help wonder how the man had ever gotten himself tangled up with a monster like Billy Baxter.

"You goin' soft on me, Clayton?" Billy taunted him from across the room.

"I don't agree with your treatment of women."

"You're the one that brought her here, remember?"

"Which was a huge mistake on my part!" he snarled back, more angry at himself.

Billy rose off the cot, now holding a gun in his hand. "You should know better than to talk to me that way."

Clayton turned to face him. "You gonna shoot me, Billy?"

"If you give me no other choice," he matter-of-factly replied.

"I'm not wearing my gun."

"Not that it would do ya any good."

"Please, Billy . . . Clayton's your friend!" Doreen shouted.

"I don't have any friends!" he furiously spat. Then, in a sudden calm tone of voice, "But don't worry, Dory, I won't shoot him—so long as he keeps doin' as he's told."

Chandler halted his horse and climbed down from the saddle to more thoroughly study the tracks on the ground. "This is where Samantha was taken," he informed John.

Leading his horse behind him, Chandler searched the surrounding area, until he found what he was looking for. He squatted, pointed at some horse's tracks on the hard-packed, grassy ground, and told John what happened. "There was only one man. A big buck I'd say by the depth of those hoofprints. They're headed south."

Chandler mounted his horse, and they were on their way. He began to question his future father-in-law. "Do you have any idea what's out that way?"

"Just miles and miles of prairie."

"Are you absolutely sure?"

After several thoughtful moments, John replied, "This entire area is cattle grazing land . . . clear to the next state and probably then some." Then his eyes widened when something else occurred to him. "Line shacks."

"I beg your pardon?"

"There's probably line shacks between here and the next state," John informed him.

"And we'll check them all, if we have to."

John and Chandler kneed their horses into a canter.

Samantha walked single-file, along the well-worn path, between Clayton and Doreen. She didn't know about her companions, but she was suspicious why Billy had asked Clayton to take her and Doreen to the river to bathe—had even said it with a smile—actually a sneer would be a more appropriate description—she didn't think the man was capable of smiling. At any rate, she'd noticed that Billy had been acting rather strange since his run-in with Clayton that morning—or maybe that was the way Billy normally acted.

Maybe the outlaw was waiting to ambush them somewhere along this very trail, Samantha began to wonder as she nervously glanced around her, grateful for the knife still concealed inside her boot. She noted there really wasn't very many places where a man could hide: only a few scattered bushes and some small scraggly-looking trees dotted the landscape in this area.

The trail now widened enough to where Samantha could easily walk beside Doreen. She started to notice the way the young woman's face seemed to glow as she watched the tall man leading their way to the river.

"You'd better not let Billy catch you looking at Clayton that way," Samantha said just loud enough so only Doreen would hear.

"I . . . don't know what you mean?"

"I think you do. Look, Doreen, I was just warning you for your own good."

Her slight shoulders slumped in defeat as she softly confessed, "No man has ever treated me the way Clayton does. He's so kind and gentle . . . always lookin' out for me. If Billy ever suspected that I have feelings for Clayton . . ."

"I wouldn't worry about it. Billy's too arrogant not to believe that you worship the ground he walks on," Samantha said with contempt.

Doreen giggled.

The path came to an abrupt end near the edge of a slow-moving stream. After Clayton told Samantha and Doreen that he'd only be a stone's throw away and to holler if they needed him for anything, he walked away. Samantha's eyes followed him as he went downriver a ways to disappear inside a stand of trees.

Samantha turned her attention back to Doreen, watching the younger woman wade out into the shallow water with her dress hiked up to her knees. Now that Doreen was away from Billy, she seemed perfectly at ease, Samantha thought. What a drastic change from the frightened girl back at the shack. She couldn't help but smile, watching Doreen splash around in the stream like a playful child.

Seeing Doreen having so much fun, Samantha hastily removed her boots and stockings, rolled up her pant legs, then waded into the stream. The swirling water felt wonderful against the skin on her bare calves; and the warm sunshine soothed the aching muscles in her back. Samantha was enjoying herself so much, that soon, all her troubles were entirely forgotten . . . .

Leading Ranger behind him, Chandler searched the deserted campsite, trying to find some kind of proof that Samantha and the man with her, had passed through this way. Spotting something lying on the ground, he hurried over to pick it up. It was a hair ribbon, and he would bet his last dollar that it belonged to Samantha. He felt in his gut that Samantha had purposely left the hair ribbon here for him to find . . .

"What's that in your hand?"

Chandler held up the hair ribbon so John could see.

"That's Samantha's," he said with relief. "Then we're headed in the right direction. Can you tell how far ahead they are?"

"I would say a half of days' ride—maybe a little more," Chandler estimated. "If we hurry, we might even catch up with them tomorrow morning."

Doreen spread the blanket she'd brought along with her over the ground, plopped down upon it, then began to remove the tangles from her wet hair, using her fingers. There was a rare smile upon her lips. She was so happy and relieved to be away from Billy. She couldn't remember the last time she'd felt this carefree. Unfortunately, they would have to return to the shack soon, before Billy came looking for them. They'd been gone too long already, and Doreen knew that Clayton would take the brunt of Billy's anger, as he always did.

Samantha dropped down on the blanket beside Doreen. She hated to spoil all the fun, figuring it was probably on rare occasions when the poor girl ever got any time alone away from 'Billy the abuser', but she hadn't seen any sign of Clayton since he'd left them by the river. She didn't want to frighten the younger woman, but she was starting to sense that something might be wrong. "Have you seen Clayton?"

"I'm sure he's around here somewhere."

Since Doreen didn't seem overly concerned about Clayton's whereabouts, Samantha did relax somewhat. After all, Doreen knew Clayton better than she did. Before they had to head back to the cabin, where she would be under Billy's constant surveillance, Samantha thought that now would be a good time to learn whatever she could about the outlaw Billy Baxter, because the more one could learn about one's enemy, the better.

"Why does Billy want Morgan so bad?" she bluntly asked Doreen, curious if her story would correspond with Clayton's.

"Billy feels Morgan's responsible for him having to spend time in prison."

"Did it ever occur to the man that he spent time in prison because of his *own* actions?"

Doreen shrugged. "I guess he sees it differently. When Billy got out of prison and found out that Morgan and his brother were working on a ranch near Bear Creek—that this brother was engaged to the rancher's daughter—that's when Billy got this hairbrained idea. He figured that by capturing you, Samantha, he could use you to lure

Chandler into leading him to Morgan. 'Course Billy paid Clayton to do his dirty work, as usual," she muttered more to herself.

"Billy didn't twist Clayton's arm," Samantha angrily pointed out.

"Billy uses him, the way he uses me." Doreen felt the need to defend Clayton. "The man's like an evil shadow that follows you wherever you go—there's no escaping him, Samantha. I know, because . . . because I thought I was free of Billy once. But I was wrong! I will never be free of the man . . . never!" She covered her face and burst into tears.

"I'm sorry, Doreen." Samantha slipped an arm around the distraught young woman, vowing she would try and find a way to get Doreen away from Billy.

When a man's shadow suddenly appeared across the blanket, Samantha stiffened. She turned her head and when she saw that it was Clayton, let out an inward sigh of relief.

"What's wrong with Dory?" he wanted to know.

"What do you think?" Samantha angrily replied. "How much longer are you going to allow that . . . that . . . *lunatic* to intimidate everyone?"

"Please, Samantha, it's not Clayton's fault," Doreen sniffled, swiping away her tears.

Rising to her feet, Samantha planted both fists on her hips. "You got me into this mess, Clayton Bradford, now you're going to get me out of it!" At least he had the decency to look ashamed, Samantha noticed. She more calmly added, "And I'll help you."

"How?" Clayton snapped. He was more angry at himself for not standing up to Billy than he was at the woman standing before him, who had the guts to point it out.

Samantha had no choice but to trust Clayton, because she couldn't defeat Billy on her own. Her wrists were still sore from where the rope had rubbed her skin raw, but she would just have to do the best she could. Hoping she wasn't making a terrible mistake, she reached over and grabbed one of her boots, then pulled out her knife.

"How long have you had that thing?" Clayton demanded. His brown eyes were accusing, and there was a deep scowl on his face.

"You didn't really expect me to tell you that I had a weapon," Samantha replied defensively, then said in a teasing tone, "Look—if it's any consolation, I'm glad I didn't use it on you." She then pointed to a tree several yards away. "Do you see that knot on the trunk?"

Clayton nodded. "What about it?"

Figuring a demonstration would speak much louder than words, Samantha drew back her arm and sent her knife sailing threw the air, hitting her mark precisely where she wanted.

Clayton let out a whistle.

"That was amazing!" Doreen shrieked.

"Okay . . . so you know how to use a knife," Clayton admitted. "But last I knew, a bullet's a lot faster and I've never seen a faster gun than Billy."

"Well pardon me, but I thought I was speaking to a man!" Samantha angrily hissed.

For a minute there, she thought Clayton might actually strike her, the man looked furious enough. Although she did feel bad for what she'd said but—*dang it!* she couldn't fight Billy alone! It frustrated her that Clayton refused to stand up to the outlaw, so maybe the only way she could get through to the man was getting him fighting mad.

Chapter Twenty

Rachel stepped outside the front door as Amos halted the wagon in front of the house. She saw her sister Ruth climb down from the seat—followed by a lovely young woman—whom she assumed must be her niece Rebecca. Her eyes welled with tears. Becca had been a little girl the last time she'd seen her sister . . . had it been that long ago . . . ?

As they walked toward her, Rachel hastened down the porch steps, noting the minor changes that had taken place in her older sister: Ruth still wore her long, chestnut hair the same way—a braided plait wound around her head—but was now sprinkled with several strands of gray. Her creamy skin was nearly free of wrinkles. And those were the same light-brown eyes she remembered. Apparently these past several years had treated her sister well.

Ruth now stood before her and, seeing the tears glistening in her sister's eyes, caused Rachel's own to fill with tears. Suddenly her arms went around her older sister in a crushing hug and she cried out, "I'm afraid, Ruthie, you might've come all this way for nothing!"

Ruth gently patted her sister's head. "I know. Amos told us what happened. You listen to me, Rachel. I have no doubt that John will find Samantha—you'll see. And I'm in no hurry to get back home. In fact, if you and John have no objections, Becca and I were planning on visiting for at least the next couple of months. So I'll be here for as long as you need me."

"Oh, Ruthie, that would be wonderful," Rachel sniffled, wiping away her tears with the backs of her hands.

"Excuse me?" came a soft-spoken voice.

"My goodness . . . I almost forgot . . . Rachel, this is Becca."

Rachel smiled at the beautiful young woman standing before her, once again fighting back tears. Her niece reminded her so much of her daughter. Rebecca was only a little younger than Samantha—and about the same height and build. She also had inherited what was the Thomas womens' trait: pulled away from her face with a blue ribbon that matched her dress, her chestnut tresses (maybe a shade or two darker than Samantha's) hung down her back past her hips in bountiful waves. Their great-grandmother Thomas's hair (which had never been cut) had touched the floor. But Rebecca's eyes were light-brown, like her mother's.

"You were just a little girl when I last saw you," Rachel sniffled. She hugged her niece tightly and kissed her on the cheek.

"Hello, Aunt Rachel." Rebecca didn't remember her aunt much. She found it a little uncanny just how much the woman resembled her mother.

"So where's that strapping nephew of mine?" Ruth inquired.

"James and Sarah will be here tomorrow," Rachel informed her sister. "James bought his father-in-law's ranch . . . he couldn't get away today." She softly added, "They don't even know about Samantha yet."

"It's going to be okay, Rach."

Rachel smiled faintly. Other than John, her sister was the only other person who ever called her Rach. She felt so much better just knowing Ruth was going to be staying with them. "Come on inside the house . . . I'll show you to your room."

Grabbing both suitcases, Rebecca followed behind her mother and her Aunt Rachel . . .

As they climbed the wide staircase to the second floor, Ruth ran her hand along the banister, admiring the beautiful, hand-carved cherry wood. She was completely impressed to learn that John had built this lovely home with his own two hands. She had no idea that her brother-in-law was gifted with this kind of talent, though it didn't surprise her. She'd always known that John was an extraordinary man. When they reached the top of the stairs, Ruth stopped to stare at the huge crystal chandelier that sparkled like jewels, which hung from the ceiling over the foyer. Somehow she hadn't noticed it when they'd first entered the house.

Rachel led them into a beautifully decorated and spacious guest room. There was a large, four-poster bed with matching end tables. Her sister being the seamstress that she was, Ruth presumed that Rachel must have made the lovely quilted bedspread. Against one wall stood a mahogany chest of drawers. Beside that was a rosewood commode which held a hand-painted rose-flowered pitcher and matching basin; there was a stack of fresh towels on the bottom shelf. There was also a dressing table with a huge, round mirror; a tall bookcase filled with a variety of books. Plush carpet covered most of the hardwood floor. White-lace curtains fluttered at the open window. And french doors led outside onto a balcony that overlooked the flower garden.

"Aunt Rachel, the room is absolutely breathtaking," Rebecca gushed, setting the suitcases on the floor.

"The room *is* lovely, Rach," Ruth agreed.

"I hope you and Becca will be comfortable here, Ruthie."

"I know *I* will." Their house in Boston was considered a mansion—and felt like a dungeon, Rebecca thought—it definitely lacked the cheery atmosphere that this house had.

Rachel smiled at her niece. "While you two are getting settled, I'll make us some tea." She then quietly left the room.

A short time later, the two sisters were seated at the kitchen table. Rebecca had claimed exhaustion and had remained inside the room. Ruth knew that her daughter had only used exhaustion as an excuse to give her some private time alone with Rachel. After so many years, there was so much to catch up on . . .

"I'm so glad you're here, Ruthie."

Ruth snapped out of her thoughts, took another sip of her tea. "If John's even half the man he was twenty years ago—and from what little you've told me about this Chandler—you have nothing to worry about, Rach."

"I believe it's a mother's job to worry."

"Isn't that the truth," Ruth agreed with a knowing grin.

Trying to concentrate on more positive thoughts, Rachel asked, "How's Bernard? I wish he could have come with you . . . Ruthie, what's wrong?"

Ruth let out a long sigh, leaning back in her chair. "I don't know how to put this—other than to just come out and say it. The truth is, I was planning on asking you and John if Becca and I could stay here at the ranch for a while, because . . . you see . . . I . . . I've left Bernard." She bluntly added, "He's having an affair."

Rachel gasped. *How could Bernard do such a thing!* She could easily picture her cold, business-like and sometimes over-domineering brother-in-law in her mind, thinking, Bernard definitely had his faults, but she never would have dreamed that *philanderer* would've been one of them. "What are you going to do?"

"I'm not sure yet—I've been married too many years just to throw it all away. I'm hoping when Bernard realizes that I'm not coming back, he'll come here." Ruth shrugged. "I guess I'll confront him then."

"Then Bernard doesn't know that you know . . . ?"

" . . . about his indiscretions?" Ruth shook her head.

"Does Becca know?"

"I haven't told her yet."

Rachel spoke as she poured them both some more tea. "Of course you and Becca are more than welcome to stay with us for as long as you want . . . permanently if need be. I don't know how you can be so calm about this, Ruthie. If John ever did anything like that . . ."

"John is too much of a man to allow some . . . some chesty, painted-faced call girl to influence him." Ruth noticed her sister blush. "I could've said much worse."

Rachel had forgotten how outspoken her usually mild-mannered older sister could sometimes be if she was pushed too far.

John and Chandler had pushed the horses through the night, taking only brief stops to water their weary mounts. Chandler had hoped to catch up with Samantha by late morning, but he'd lost the tracks once, so they'd had to double back, which had cost them precious time. It was morning already. Now Chandler was hoping to catch Samantha by this evening—that is—if nothing else went wrong. He took another drink from his canteen. It was abnormally hot today—even for late August.

Looking over at John, Chandler noticed the front of his flannel shirt was already drenched with perspiration and it wasn't even near the hottest part of the day yet. Though John was in excellent shape, especially for a man his age, he wasn't used to this kind of exertion in this kind of heat.

Chandler suddenly halted his horse. "This is where you turn back."

John pulled back on the reins. "What are you talking about?"

"You're in no condition to go on . . . neither is your horse. In case you haven't noticed, John, that stallion of yours is about ready to collapse. Ranger might be use to strenuous exercise, even in this kind of heat, but he can't carry us both. Under the circumstances, you'll only slow me down . . . I can travel much faster by myself. Trust me on this, John," Chandler persisted when it looked like he might protest. "I know what I'm doing."

Much as John hated to admit it, he knew that Chandler was right. He hadn't said anything, but for the last several miles, he'd been getting a little light-headed and was even having some trouble staying upright in the saddle.

"Take a look at your horse, John, he's done for the day," Chandler added.

"You're right," he reluctantly agreed. "But if you're not back by the end of the week . . ."

"I give you my solemn word, I will find Samantha and bring her home. I won't come back until I do. You just tell Rachel she has a wedding to plan."

John's lips twitched in amusement. "I'll do that."

After the two men clasped hands, John turned his horse around and rode off in the opposite direction. Chandler watched him for a short time, then he nudged Ranger into a slow canter, his every thought was consumed with finding Samantha. He was no longer Wade Chandler: he was a full-blooded Cheyenne warrior named Graywolf . . . .

As Samantha strolled behind Doreen along the narrow path that led back to the tiny cabin, she noticed a sudden, unusual stillness that seemed to penetrate the air. She looked over her shoulder, and frowned, when she saw Clayton was nowhere in sight. She tried to convince herself that the man probably just needed a moment of privacy, but she couldn't seem to get rid of this sinking feeling in the pit of her stomach and, in spite of the late afternoon heat, a cold chill ran down her spine as the little shack came into view . . .

Samantha stopped in her tracks. "Doreen, wait."

She turned around. "Is something wrong?"

"I'm not sure."

Without any kind of warning dozens of ferociously painted Indians on horses suddenly materialized out of nowhere and swarmed the tiny shack. Their loud war-whoops sounded terrifying to Samantha's ears as they circled the little cabin, their numerous arrows flying swiftly through the air. When Samantha heard several retaliating gunshots, she knew that, no matter how good Billy Baxter was with a gun, the outlaw didn't stand a lick of chance against the Indians. *There were just too many of them.*

"Where's Clayton?" Doreen suddenly screamed in panic-stricken terror.

Samantha grabbed the hysterical girl and pulled her back up the trail. "Dang it, Doreen! Stop fighting me! There's nothing we can do for Clayton or Billy now! If we don't hide, we'll suffer a worse fate than the men if those Indians catch us!"

Two menacing-looking Indians appeared in front of Samantha, blocking her path. Painted the way they were, she thought even their horses seemed frightening. Doreen let out a sudden, blood-curdling scream and then took off at a run toward the cabin, but Samantha stood her ground, knowing it would do no good to run.

One of the savages raced past Samantha on his horse to go after Doreen, while the other Indian tried to grab hold of her. She fought him like a wild woman, but he easily overpowered her. When he tossed her roughly across his horse's withers, she bit him in the thigh. The Indian let out a howl of pain and then his hand came down hard upon her backside. Samantha bit her lower lip to keep from crying out. Now she was being bounced up and down on her stomach as the ground moved before her eyes in a rapid blur. Behind her, she could hear Doreen screaming, and when she tried to lift her head, the Indian seized her by the hair and jerked her to a sitting position in front of him; then his arm went around her like a vise. She turned and glared at him, and was met by a pair of smoldering black eyes.

"Do not defy me, white woman!" the Indian snarled at her in perfect English.

Samantha wanted to say something, but the malevolent expression on the Indian's face, changed her mind. She looked straight ahead.

Chandler fought the rising panic when he saw the charred remains of what had once been a small building. He didn't have to search hard for clues to understand what had taken place here. It was obvious that Indians had attacked this cabin. He swung out of the saddle, then, leading Ranger behind him, began to look for any sign to prove Samantha had been here.

Several feet away from where the front door had once stood, Chandler found some faint boot tracks. Squatting closer to the ground, he soon discovered the smaller tracks belonged to Samantha alright; he would recognize her tiny boot prints anywhere. Even as he frantically searched for any clue that would tell him of Samantha's whereabouts, his gut feeling told him the Indians had taken her. And now getting her back had just become more complicated.

In the back of the cabin, Chandler discovered a well-worn dirt path, and *here* is where he finally found what he was looking for. He could easily tell where Samantha had fought with an Indian . . . probably Kiowa—he guessed—from the shape of the moccasin prints; and there had been another female with her.

Chandler was about to mount his horse when he thought he heard somebody call out for help. He listened more carefully . . . *there* . . . he heard it again! Leading Ranger, he hurried back toward the cabin.

Chandler found an injured man, concealed behind some bushes. There was soot all over his face; and his clothes were dirty and torn. Looking for any serious injuries, he wondered if this could be the man who'd abducted Samantha . . . the tracks had led him to this place. He couldn't find any serious wounds or broken bones, but he was no doctor.

When the man suddenly opened his eyes, Chandler didn't miss the look of surprised recognition—yet he was certain he'd never seen this man before . . .

"Wade Chandler?" he croaked in a raspy voice.

"Who are you?"

"Name's Clayton," he replied, struggling to sit up.

"Maybe you shouldn't move, mister."

"The Indians . . . they took them . . . all my . . . fault." Then Clayton lay back on the ground and closed his eyes.

Chandler frowned. "Maybe you should start from the beginning, mister, and you can start by telling me how you know my name."

But the man had lost consciousness . . .

Samantha tirelessly placed one foot in front of the other. It seemed like she'd been walking, and sometimes jogging, behind the Indian's horse for hours. Every so often he would tug on the rope that was secured around her waist, to hurry her along. This time she wasn't ready and lost her balance, dropping to her knees, but instantly rolled to her feet. Now she had to practically run to keep up with the faster pace.

Samantha glared at the Indian's broad bare back. *The heathen would have to drag her before she would ever cry out for mercy!* When he turned around and sneered at her, Samantha could tell by the smug expression on his face, he was just waiting for her to break . . . wanted her to break. *You'll be waiting indefinitely!* she inwardly fumed, while her piercing blue eyes shot daggers through his body.

But after a few miles Samantha was becoming close to exhaustion. She didn't know how much longer she could keep up this pace. Without thinking about the consequences of her actions, in a complete fit of rage, she suddenly stopped in her tracks and yanked on the rope with all her might, jerking the Indian off his pony. She was too furious to notice the howls of laughter from the other Indians. Her capture shot to his feet and stomped toward her. Their eyes collided in a battle of wills as he halted directly in front of her.

"You will learn your place, white woman!" The Indian snatched the rope off the ground, then he leaped upon the back of his pony, and rode away at even a faster pace.

It didn't take long for Samantha's legs to start cramping so badly that she wanted to scream in agony. Still, she kept on running. Already her knee-length hair hung down her back in thick, sweaty strands; her flannel shirt was drenched with perspiration and clung to her body. Still, she kept on running . . . and running . . . until . . . finally . . . she could not go another step . . .

Doreen cried out when she saw Samantha collapse to the ground.

A pair of dark, angry eyes were secretly watching the deplorable treatment of the beautiful white woman by the Kiowa who forced her to run behind his horse when it was obvious she was close to dropping from exhaustion. Yet, he could not help feeling great admiration for the woman's courage. It hadn't been so long ago since he'd last seen Samantha Callahan, and wondered how the woman had managed to get herself in such a dangerous situation. The stubborn beauty seemed to have a special talent for getting herself into trouble.

Black Hawk became furious when he saw Samantha crumble to the ground and didn't get up. If she was hurt in any way, the Kiowa who had mistreated her would pay with his life.

He gave a signal to his companions, then they slowly descended the hillside . . . .

When Samantha opened her eyes and saw the handsome face that was so much like Chandler's, looming above her, she wondered if she was dreaming? She squeezed her eyes tightly shut and then opened them again. The handsome face was still there . . .

"Morgan?"

"How do you feel?"

When Samantha tried to sit up, a strong hand held her firmly to the ground. She suddenly remembered . . . "Doreen!" Again she tried to sit up.

"Relax, Samantha . . . the Indians are all gone," Morgan assured her. "And your friend is safe." She ceased struggling then, so he removed his hand. "Big Bear is looking after Doreen."

Samantha remembered Chandler and Morgan's younger brother well. In her opinion, the egotistical warrior was an Indian version of the white man's *Casanova*. "You left that fox to look after an innocent lamb," she sarcastically snapped.

Morgan burst out laughing.

"Hearing you say that wounds my young heart."

Samantha immediately recognized Big Bear's voice. She turned her head, and her eyes followed the muscular legs up, until they came to rest upon another familiarly handsome face. Big Bear was smiling at her. "Yeah—I just bet it does."

"I would never take advantage of a woman in distress," he stated in perfect English.

"You would take advantage of a woman if she was unconscious."

"Samantha remembers you well, Big Bear," Morgan said, chuckling.

"But, Black Hawk, can I help it if women are drawn to me like bees to honey," the young warrior innocently said.

Samantha rolled her eyes. "Don't flatter yourself, Big Bear."

"You still have a viper's tongue, I see."

"And still quite capable of striking, if you give me good reason."

Big Bear frowned at his brother when he burst out laughing. He grumbled something in Cheyenne, then walked away.

"What did he say?" Samantha asked.

"I'm not sure."

"Well, whatever it was, I'm sure it was something insulting," Samantha muttered under her breath. "By the way, why did Big Bear call you Black Hawk?"

"It's my new Indian name."

"Maybe living with your father's people isn't such a good idea."

Morgan threw back his head and laughed. That was something else he loved about Samantha Callahan: her sense of humor.

Later that evening, seated beside a cheery fire, Samantha more closely observed Chandler's brother Morgan, while he conversed with several other warriors. It had only been a couple of weeks ago since she'd last seen him. Nearly Chandler's mirror image, Morgan had completely discarded his western-style clothes for Indian garb; and he now wore his long hair in two braids. But there was something else different about him—it wasn't the obvious—there was a subtle change—something she couldn't quite put her finger on—but it was there, nevertheless.

And it suddenly dawned on Samantha what was different about him: Morgan was normally always teasing somebody, it was just in the man's nature . . . and now . . . he seemed much more serious. She noticed that Morgan never once laughed—the whole time he was talking. Occasionally he would smile, but the smile didn't reach his eyes.

Just then a couple of dozen Indians rode into their camp. Samantha knew these were the warriors returning from battling the Kiowas who had attacked the cabin and taken her and Doreen. She didn't pay them anymore attention after that. Now Samantha concentrated on what she was going to do about Doreen, who, at the moment, was sleeping peacefully near the crackling fire. She didn't think the poor girl had any family . . .

"Mind if I have a seat?"

Samantha looked up to find Morgan standing there. She immediately scooted over on her bedroll, patting the empty spot beside her.

He seated himself Indian-style, then silently stared into the flickering firelight for a few moment's, before he finally spoke. "You wanna explain to me how you wound up in the company of a bunch of Kiowas? And who's your friend?"

Samantha took a deep breath, then proceeded to tell Morgan about Clayton Bradford, the man who'd abducted her on her way to town. She told him all about Billy Baxter and how the gunslinger had planned on setting a trap for him. Morgan felt that justice had been served when he learned that Billy Baxter was more-than-likely killed in the Indian attack on the cabin.

Samantha ended her story with, "My friend's name is Doreen. She was Billy's fiancée."

"But she's hardly more than a girl."

"Actually Doreen's only a couple of years younger than me . . . she's almost nineteen."

Samantha looked seriously at Morgan. "Now I have a question of my own. Why are you riding with that band of renegades?"

"That band of *renegades* just saved your neck and your friend's from the Kiowas," Morgan angrily reminded her.

"You know what I mean."

"They asked me to lead them."

"And Chief Running Elk . . . does he agree with what you're doing?"

"Whether my father agrees or not, Samantha, I am a man. Running Elk would never tell me what to do. He knows I must make my own decisions."

Samantha changed the subject. "How is your father, Morgan?"

"As a matter-of-fact, Father has asked me to take his place as chief. He doesn't think Big Bear's mature enough, but—I haven't decided yet. If I did become the next chief, my band of *renegades* would have to find themselves a new leader and things could get worse. So far, I've managed to keep the hotheads under control—though they have every right to be angry."

Suddenly Samantha recalled Morgan's Indian name . . . *why hadn't it clicked before?* "You couldn't possibly be *the* Chief Black Hawk the army's been looking for?"

"Technically I am a war chief, so—yes, I suppose that I am."

"Just in case you haven't heard, the army arrived in Bear Creek during our absence and they're now camped outside of town."

"I heard."

"If the army were to capture you, Morgan, you could be shot on sight . . . or worse!"

"What could be worse than being shot?"

"This isn't the time to be funny!"

"You're right. Because it isn't funny that the only other alternative an Indian has is to spend the rest of his life on some stinkin' reservation where the land is so worthless that even the white man doesn't want it," Morgan bitterly retorted. "That so called 'band of renegades' that I ride with, Samantha, only want what every man wants . . . to be able to live on their own land in peace like a free man and take care of their families."

"I'm sorry, Morgan."

"Did you know that Graywolf is considered a hostile, because he's disobeying the army's orders, too?"

Samantha's face paled. Although she knew what Morgan said was true—she just didn't think of Chandler as an Indian—she thought of him as just an ordinary man. Why Wade Chandler or Graywolf or whatever you wanted to call him, was more civilized than most white men in town.

"Chandler now works for my father and we're about to become husband and wife—that should count for something."

"It should, but it doesn't. Graywolf is still full-blooded Cheyenne . . . same as I am."

Morgan watched Samantha's beautiful face pale even more. He hated to be the cause of her distress, but she had to know the truth of the situation, when all it would take is some prejudice citizen in Bear Creek to sound an alarm and the army would be knocking on John Callahan's front door. Morgan wished he could take the woman in his arms and comfort her, but knew it would be a terrible mistake if he touched her. He realized his feelings for Samantha had not diminished in the least these past couple of weeks, and he hated himself for his weakness. Although he would never act upon his feelings, neither could he help the way he felt.

But Morgan had kept those feelings well hidden, even from his brother—which had been the reason why he'd hightailed it to his father's people the first chance he'd gotten, hoping that if he could just get away from Samantha for a little while, maybe it would help. Now—as he feasted his eyes upon her enchanting face—he realized his feelings for her hadn't changed in the least—if anything—they were stronger than ever.

Before he said or did something he might regret, Morgan needed to get away from her. He suddenly rose to his feet, and walked away.

"Where are you going?"

"Go to sleep, Samantha," he gruffly ordered over his shoulder.

"Now what's the matter with him?" Samantha wondered out loud.

It was nearly dusk by the time Chandler had finished tending to Clayton's many cuts and scrapes. Though the man didn't have any life-threatening injuries, what did concern him was a deep, puncture wound in his right shoulder, which had been caused by an arrow and was already showing signs of infection.

Chandler decided that he might as well make camp here tonight, thinking it would be better to start fresh in the morning, since he wouldn't be able to follow the Indians' trail in the dark anyway. He knew the Kiowas would not kill the women, but his jaw muscles tightened and his hands clenched into fists, when he thought about what they might do.

After hearing Clayton Bradford's story, Chandler felt he should be furious with the man for taking Samantha, but he wasn't. As he watched Clayton lying beside the campfire, tossing and turning in his sleep, it was obvious the man had suffered enough already.

At least Morgan would no longer have to worry about Billy Baxter, and for that Chandler was grateful to the Indians. Now all he had to do was figure out a way to get Samantha back . . . hopefully Doreen, too. What he needed was a detailed plan. After all, he was only one man against many. Even though Clayton would probably survive his injuries, the man was still much too weak to be of any real help . . .

Chandler added some more wood to the fire, then he collapsed wearily upon his bedroll. Folding his hands behind his head, he quietly lay there, gazing up into the starry night sky, wondering how Samantha was faring—if she was all right. There was nothing he could do about anything at the moment, so, forcing all thoughts from his mind, he closed his eyes . . . .

A hawk kept circling over Chandler's head, then suddenly the bird soared higher into the vast blue sky and then it swooped back down toward the earth, landing on the ground just mere feet in front of him. Then he saw Morgan walking toward him. His brother stopped to wave at Chandler, beckoning for him to follow, then he turned and walked away . . .

When Chandler woke the next morning, the first thing he saw was a hawk flying overhead in the cloudless blue sky, and suddenly he knew that he must go to his father's village.

He rolled over on his side and was surprised to find Clayton already awake and even had a pot of coffee heating on a flat rock near the campfire. Yawning, he sat up straight, pulled on his boots. Then he rolled to is feet, stretching the kinks out of his aching muscles.

"That coffee ready yet?" he asked Clayton.

"Yeah."

Squatting beside the fire, Chandler grabbed the only empty cup and poured himself some coffee. "How do you feel this morning?"

"Like I was attacked by a bunch of Indians."

"A man with a sense of humor."

"No . . . I really feel that way."

Chandler grinned. "Do you think you can ride?"

"I'll manage."

"I think I know where to find the women."

"Where?"

"My father's village." At Clayton's confused expression, Chandler added, "You're just going to have to trust me on this."

Chapter Twenty-one

John sat across the breakfast table from his still very attractive sister-in-law. Nothing had changed about Ruth Thomas Smith, except—she now had a few strands of gray hair. He'd always liked Rachel's older sister and was glad she was here . . .

"It's really good to see you, Ruth," John commented between bites of food. "Boston certainly must agree with you . . . you haven't aged much."

"And you, John, you're even more handsome than I remember." Ruth laughed when she noticed her brother-in-law blush.

John went on to say, "Rebecca, why—when I last saw you, you were just a child—now look at you, you're a grown woman already. I doubt you remember me."

Becca really liked her Uncle John. She found it awfully hard to believe that her father and uncle were close to the same age; her father was bald-headed already and looked several years older than her uncle. She thought it was Uncle John's beautiful, sky-blue eyes that first captured a person's attention. "I'm afraid I don't remember you or Aunt Rachel very much."

"Well, don't feel bad . . . the Rebecca I remember barely stood taller than my knees."

"Oh, Uncle John," Becca said, laughing.

Again Rachel was thinking how much her young niece reminded her of Samantha. *They even had the same laugh.* Rachel prayed that Chandler had already found Samantha and they were on their way home this very minute . . .

Sensing his wife's sudden change of mood, John tried to reassure her. "I wouldn't be here, Rachel, if I didn't have complete confidence in Chandler. He was right insisting I come home when I did. He will find Samantha."

"I know."

Rising, John walked around the table to place a gentle kiss upon his wife's forehead, and whispered, "You know where to find me, if you need me."

"I'll be fine, dear." Rachel didn't want John to worry about her.

"Ruth, Rebecca, I'll see you ladies at supper." John then disappeared out the back door.

"I wish that husband of mine would take the day off," Rachel remarked to her sister. "He just got home late last night. He must be exhausted."

"That's about the only thing John and Bernard have in common . . . they both work from dawn till dusk. But I'm not sure if that's a compliment," Ruth added more to herself.

Rachel nearly jumped out of her seat when the back door suddenly opened and James entered the kitchen, immediately followed by his wife Sarah. While James walked directly over to his Aunt Ruth to properly greet her with a huge, bear hug, Sarah plopped into the empty chair beside Rachel, then began to fill an extra plate with food. Rachel smiled at her daughter-in-law. Sarah was expecting their first grandchild, though you couldn't tell . . . yet. It seemed like the poor girl was constantly eating these days.

James set his aunt back on her feet. Even though he didn't remember his Aunt Ruth, he would've known her anywhere, she looked so much like his mother. It was rather uncanny how much his cousin Rebecca reminded him of his sister . . .

"I'm looking at John twenty years ago," Ruth said, her eyes filling with tears. She lovingly touched her nephew's precious face. James was barely walking on chubby little legs, the last time she'd seen him. She brushed a thick strand of wavy black hair from his brow. "I always knew you would grow into a handsome man just like your father."

James could feel his cheeks grow warm from embarrassment. He helped his aunt back into her chair, then he turned his attention to his mother, now noticing the dark smudges under her amber-colored eyes. "Pa told me and Sarah about Samantha." There was a slight pause, then, "Ma, why didn't anyone come get me? I would've gladly gone with Chandler."

"There was nothing you could have done, son. Besides, you have your own ranch to run and a wife to think about now."

"I know Chandler will find Samantha, Ma."

"I'm sure he will, dear."

Sensing his mother's reluctance to talk about the subject, James seated himself on the other side of his wife, and inquired of his aunt. "Didn't Uncle Bernard come with you?"

"I'm afraid your uncle couldn't get away." Ruth saw no reason to say anymore about her philandering husband, not yet anyway. "Your wife is lovely, James."

He grinned at Sarah who was busy shoveling leftover fried potatoes into her mouth; she'd already finished off several link sausages.

"I heard I'm going to be a great aunt?"

"I think you're great already, Aunt Ruth."

Ruth laughed. "You really are your father's son."

"That's about the best compliment you could ever give me."

"And I meant it as a compliment."

Rachel really wasn't listening to the conversation. She was thinking about when she and John had first moved to Bear Creek—Samantha had been just a baby then—not long after that James had been born. Those first few years they had lived in this old rickety shack that was already here, until John had finished building the big house they now lived in. Cramped as they were inside that tiny one-room cabin, those had been the happiest years of Rachel's life. Her eyes began to fill with tears, but she blinked them away. It seemed like only yesterday—James and Samantha had been small children—now they were grown.

Rachel turned to look at her daughter-in-law. Soon James would be a father; it was hard to believe. She was thrilled that James and Sarah didn't move away like so many newly married couples did, but had bought the very house that Sarah grew up in. When Sarah's father decided to sell their ranch (after his wife left him and moved back East to live with her sister) Sarah couldn't stand the thought of some stranger living in their old place, so James insisted on buying the ranch—though Sarah felt it should have gone to her older brother, but nobody knew where to find Jake, so that only left her to keep the ranch in the family. In spite of the fact that Sarah had come from a rather dysfunctional family, Rachel couldn't be more pleased with her son's choice for a wife if she had hand picked the girl herself. Sarah Martin had turned out to be a wonderful, caring young woman . . .

Rebecca wasn't sure what to think of her cousin James. She couldn't understand how he could make jokes at a time like this, but—maybe it had been for his mother's benefit—maybe he was trying to pretend like nothing was wrong. James was definitely a younger version of her Uncle John. In fact, she'd never seen a father and son look more alike.

She smiled at James's wife Sarah. The young woman hadn't stopped eating since she'd sat down at the table. Her gaze settled on her mother. She was laughing at something James had said. She hadn't seen her mother this happy or talkative in years. Meals around their own table back home were always quiet, almost gloomy. There always seemed to be constant tension in the air between her parents these days . . .

"Becca, you've hardly said a word."

"I'm sorry, Mama . . . guess I don't feel much like talking."

John watched the man approaching the house on horseback, wondering what possible business an army lieutenant could have here. He dropped his hammer and walked over to the porch to await the unexpected guest. His eyes settled, suspiciously, upon the young and impeccably dressed lieutenant as he halted his horse just a few feet away from him. The man remained seated in the saddle like a king about to issue an order, which irritated John immensely. In his opinion, it was plain bad manners.

Wordlessly the lieutenant reached inside his shirt pocket, pulled out a folded piece of paper, then held it out toward John. His piercing blue eyes collided with cold, metallic-gray ones. It was on the tip of John's tongue to tell the rude man what he could do with that paper, but curiosity got the best of him.

John hastened down the steps and snatched the paper out of the lieutenant's hand. He forced his expression to remain calm as he stared at the sketching on the paper: the drawing was an excellent portrait of

Morgan; his own wedding picture didn't look this good. He refolded the paper and wordlessly handed it back to the lieutenant.

"Have you seen that Indian?" the man impatiently demanded.

"Who is he?"

"A Cheyenne war chief . . . Black Hawk."

John wondered how Morgan had managed to get his face plastered on an army Wanted poster so quickly? The man had only been gone what? maybe a couple of weeks.

"So what's the Indian done?"

"It doesn't matter what the Indian's done . . . he's wanted by the army." In an accusing tone of voice, the lieutenant added, "Anyone caught harboring the Indian will be severely punished. I heard in town that this Indian is a friend of yours, Mr. Callahan . . . that he might've worked here. Is that true?"

"You know my name . . . it's only fair that I know yours."

"Lieutenant Jason Brown."

"Well, Lieutenant Brown, I don't think who my friends are, is any business of yours *or* the army's," John sarcastically replied.

"I could arrest you on the spot, Callahan!"

"You could try," he calmly retorted.

Following John Callahan's line of vision, Jason turned his head and saw several men had stopped working and were now watching them, listening. He looked back at the rancher. "I hope they're not stupid enough to interfere."

John's eyes narrowed on the arrogant lieutenant. Put some men in a uniform and it turned them into tyrants. "Mister, I would advise you to get off my property before I lose my temper."

"I was hoping we could do this the easy way. I'll be back, Callahan." Without another word he swung his horse around and rode away.

John glared at Lieutenant Brown's stiff, departing back. He'd heard a rumor around town about this newest war chief of the Cheyenne; apparently it was true. He never would've dreamed that it was Morgan. It was said that this Black Hawk was causing a lot of trouble by attacking the white settlers that were coming to the area. At least, so far, nobody had been seriously hurt; but if the settlers kept coming at the rate they were, that was bound to change. John considered Morgan a good friend and would never reveal his whereabouts. Besides, he couldn't blame the Indians for causing trouble. They were only fighting over land that was rightfully theirs. And he couldn't blame them for refusing to live on the reservations; he wouldn't live on any of them either. The land the army assigned the Indians wasn't fit for animals, let alone man.

A lot had changed in the short time they'd been away on the cattle drive. The army had arrived in Bear Creek and had established quite an impressive campsite on the outskirts of town. John hadn't been surprised by the move; he'd been expecting the army to come down hard on the Indians. And it appeared that they were going to be sticking around for a while, looking for the so called 'renegades'. John knew this meant Chandler wouldn't be safe now. And if Samantha were to get caught with him, it could put her in danger, too—as if she wasn't in enough trouble already. Well, he would just have to pay a little visit to this Lieutenant Brown's commanding officer and explain the situation.

He would ride into town first thing in the morning . . . .

John hadn't planned on taking his wife and sister-in-law, or his niece, into town with him today, but Rachel had wanted to do some shopping. How could he deny his wife such a small request? And maybe a trip to town was just what Rachel needed to help take her mind off Samantha. So here he was guiding the flatbed wagon along the narrow dirt road that led into Bear Creek, listening to Rachel and Ruth who were chattering beside him like a couple of magpies over the latest fashions. You could sure tell these two women were sisters . . .

"How much farther, Uncle John?"

He looked over his shoulder at his niece who was seated in the back of the wagon. "We're almost there, Becca."

John drove the wagon down the main street of Bear Creek toward the mercantile store. He still couldn't believe how much their little town had changed just this past summer. He knew when the railroad was finished that Bear Creek would become even bigger. The town now boasted of a new grand hotel which included a fancy restaurant. Next to the new hotel was the newly remodeled saloon which had just recently opened and was doing quite the business. There was also a new bank—another blacksmith's shop and livery—a lady's boutique. The mercantile store—which was now called Carter's General Store—carried just about everything a person could ever imagine. A new sheriff's office was under construction. They had added another room to the school. And the new church would soon be completed. Oh yeah . . . he'd almost forgotten about the old *hurdy-gurdy-house*. It was one of the last remaining original buildings and still set on the far edge of town. John grinned to himself, remembering the time when several angry wives had gotten together and had tried to get the place shut down. 'Course most of the men had voted against it, and there for a while, that particular meeting had caused quite a rift between some happily married couples.

Halting the wagon in front of Carter's General Store, John wound the long reins around the brake handle and hopped to the ground, then turned to help Rachel and Ruth climb down from the seat. After lifting Rebecca out of the back, John casually leaned against the wagon, not wanting his wife to get any suspicions of what he was planning to do, and waited until the ladies had disappeared inside Carter's Store.

John started walking along the boardwalk, meandering his way through the bustling crowd, his long strides carrying him quickly toward the edge of town, where the army camp was located. A person couldn't miss the campsite—enormous as it was—nor did it take him long to find the man he was looking for.

Now standing inside a large tent, John quietly observed the clean-shaven, red-haired man seated behind an oversized metal desk, who was sifting through a stack of papers. If this man was John Lewis, he looked awfully young to be a colonel.

He cleared his throat. "Excuse me, Colonel Lewis?"

"You must be, Mr. Callahan."

It irked John that the man hadn't even glanced up from his work. And it seemed that the colonel wasn't a bit surprised he was here, making John wonder what the lieutenant had told this man, knowing it couldn't have been good. He started to walk forward and stated the obvious, "Apparently you were expecting me."

Colonel Lewis finally looked up and his eyes widened only slightly when he saw the mountain of a man coming toward him. He could already tell that John Callahan was going to be a problem. "Lieutenant Brown described you to a tee."

I just bet he did, John angrily thought. He halted directly in front of the colonel's desk. When the man motioned for him to have a seat, he firmly said, "I'll stand if you don't mind . . . this won't take long."

"Suit yourself."

"I'll get right to the point, Colonel. I came here about one of your men—since you already know who I'm talking about, I won't beat around the bush. I don't like to be threatened, especially on my own property."

"I'll agree that Lieutenant Brown can be a little . . . how shall I say? pushy at times. But we're at war, Mr. Callahan." Colonel Lewis casually leaned back in his chair. "Is it true that you're an acquaintance of Chief Black Hawk?" he bluntly inquired.

"Exactly what is this chief's crime?"

"That would be army business."

"You can't blame a man for fighting to keep what belongs to him."

Colonel Lewis scowled. "We're talking about a heathen, not a man."

"Well, Colonel, there's where we differ, because I'm talking about a man, not a heathen."

"You're beginning to annoy me, Mr. Callahan."

"The feeling's quite mutual."

Colonel Lewis jumped to his feet. "I was hoping we could settle this matter without any trouble . . . evidently that's not going to be the case!"

John wasn't going to bother to mention Chandler, the main reason he'd come here, knowing he'd get no cooperation from this man. "There won't be any trouble, Colonel . . . long as your men stay off my land. I'll see myself out." Without waiting for a reply, he pivoted on his boot heel and strode out of the tent.

His angry strides carried him swiftly through the army camp past dozens of tents, then down the dusty road toward town. As John neared Carter's General Store, his anger turned to fury when he saw Lieutenant Brown standing beside the flatbed wagon, talking with Rebecca. He hurried across the street . . .

"What do you want, Brown?" John demanded, rudely placing himself between the arrogant lieutenant and his innocent niece.

"Uncle John," Rebecca whispered from behind him.

"Uncle?" Jason Brown said, then suddenly burst out laughing.

"What's so funny?" John snapped.

Actually Jason didn't find any thing funny. He just laughed sometimes when he was really angry to hide his emotions, and anger couldn't better describe what he was feeling at the moment. *Whoever would have guessed this lovely young woman was John Callahan's niece.*

"Get in the wagon, Rebecca."

"But, Uncle John . . ."

"Do as I say."

To John's relief, she immediately did as told. Now he moved closer to the lieutenant, so Rebecca couldn't hear what he was saying. "Stay away from my niece, Brown."

Jason held his temper in check. He knew it wouldn't look good, causing a scene in front of the citizens of Bear Creek. There were other ways to deal with the rancher. He turned to the chestnut-haired beauty seated in the back of the wagon, bowing at the waist. "Good day, Rebecca." Then he walked away.

When John noticed the lieutenant was headed toward the saloon, he was tempted to follow the man, but Rachel and Ruth chose that moment to come out of the store. He wordlessly took their packages, set them in the back of the wagon. He helped the ladies into the seat, climbed in beside his wife, picked up the reins and gave them a little jiggle.

As they headed out of town, John could feel his wife's eyes upon him. He never could hide anything from her; she knew him too well. He was debating whether he should tell Rachel about the confrontation he'd had with Lieutenant Brown, because he knew this wasn't the last they'd be seeing of the man. He looked over his shoulder at his niece. He had a gut feeling the lieutenant would be riding out to the ranch again, very soon.

John couldn't help grin when his niece presented him her stiff back. It would appear the docile Rebecca had some spunk hidden beneath that reserved manner after all. He peered straight ahead, urging the team faster.

"Mind telling me what's wrong?" Rachel suddenly said.

John only shrugged in reply.

"Does this have anything to do with that young officer you were talking to?" When he still didn't answer, she bluntly said, "You don't like him, do you?"

John finally looked at his wife. "No, I don't."

Rachel let out a sigh, knowing her husband was going to be furious at her, but he would find out soon enough anyway. "He came inside Carter's Store. I saw him talking to Becca . . . he seemed nice enough so—I invited him over for supper tonight."

"You did what?" John pulled back on the reins, bringing the wagon to a skidding halt. "Well you can just *uninvite* him!" he hollered at his wife.

"I most certainly will not *uninvite* him, John Callahan!" Rachel shouted back. "Had I known you didn't like the man, I never would've asked him over for supper, but what's done is done! Like it or not, Lieutenant Brown will be dining with us this evening!" She leaned back against the seat, angrily folding her arms across her chest.

Grumbling under his breath, John flicked the reins and the wagon lurched forward. The more he thought about it, having Lieutenant Brown over for supper might not be such a bad idea. His lips curled into a sly grin, thinking, a person should always get to know their enemy.

Chapter Twenty-two

Perched behind Morgan on his stallion, Samantha gazed down at the dozens of cone-shaped dwellings that dotted the grassy meadow. The peaceful little valley looked exactly the way it did when Samantha was last here—less than a month ago. She was excited to see Chandler's father again, after all, Chief Running Elk would soon be her father-in-law.

Samantha looked over at Doreen who was seated behind Big Bear. There was still a deep sadness within her pale-blue eyes over Clayton's probable fate at the Kiowas' hands.

"Mmm . . . smell that venison stew," Big Bear remarked, sniffing the air.

"Is that all you think about is your stomach?" Morgan grumbled.

"No." The young warrior looked over his shoulder and boldly peered into the pretty white woman's light blue eyes, adding, "There are other thoughts that occupy my mind."

"Well you can just get those *other thoughts* out of your conceited head!" Samantha snapped.

Big Bear scowled at his oldest brother's betrothed. "You may get away with talking to Graywolf that way, woman, but now that you're here at the village . . ."

"Oh spare me the lecture, Big Bear!"

Morgan threw back his head and laughed.

Big Bear's frown deepened as he nudged his pony forward and slowly started to descend the hillside. He didn't even turn to look if Black Hawk and Samantha followed or not. He was thinking about the young woman riding double with him, who's slender arms were wrapped about his waist, wondering if she had a husband. Even her name was lovely: *Doreen.* It sounded like a gentle breeze whispering through the leaves of a tree. *Doreen.* The young woman really was quite lovely, Big Bear thought, with her long, golden hair, and smooth, creamy skin that looked softer than a rose pedal. Her lips were full and the color of ripe berries. Maybe Doreen did not possess Samantha's unique beauty; neither did she share her sharp-sword-of-a-tongue, to which Big Bear was grateful. Personally, he would much rather have a docile woman. As if to prove his point, he twisted around to look at Doreen, and grinned, when she blushed and shyly lowered her eyes.

Samantha smiled when several children ran over to greet Morgan. They trotted alongside his stallion, chattering excitedly. One of the children said something to her in Cheyenne or Comanche—it sounded the same to Samantha—then they all took off running. When she heard Big Bear burst out laughing, she wanted to know what the child had said.

"Little Deer remembers you, Samantha. He called you the-woman-with-the-temper-like-a-badger." Then Big Bear burst into more peals of laughter.

Now Morgan was laughing. Samantha frowned at both men. "It's not *that* funny!"

"Come on, Samantha, where's your sense of humor?"

"Morgan, you have an odd sense of humor . . . you think everything's funny."

They halted in front of a large tepee that Samantha immediately recognized as Chief Running Elk's. She noticed a black hawk with a wide wingspan had been painted on the buffalo hides, which hadn't been there before, and wondered if Morgan now lived here with his father. She thought whoever had painted the bird had done a beautiful job.

"What should I call you?" Samantha asked Morgan as he lifted her off his horse.

"What do you mean?"

"Should I call you Morgan or Black Hawk?"

"You can call me Morgan." Then, "Come on, let's all go inside."

Samantha smiled reassuringly at Doreen, before ducking through the small opening . . .

Running Elk was seated in the back of the tepee and was working on a new bridle for his horse when they entered. Surprise came over the chief's face when he saw them standing there. He rose to his feet and walked over to greet his sons, and gave Samantha a big hug.

"It is good to see you, daughter," he stated in perfect English. "Where is Graywolf?"

Samantha respectfully remained silent, while Morgan explained to his father what had happened. She hoped Morgan would take her home soon. Though she adored Chandler's and Morgan's father and was happy to see the man, this wasn't a social call. By now her parents were probably panic-stricken wondering where she was . . .

"Aren't you afraid, Samantha?" Doreen whispered beside her.

"You have nothing to worry about . . . these people won't harm you."

"Why did the older man call you daughter?"

"Oh . . . guess I forgot to mention . . . remember my fiancé that I told you about . . . the older man is Chandler's father, Chief Running Elk. The Indian you were riding double with is Chandler's brother Big Bear . . . so's Morgan."

Doreen's eyes widened. "When you told me Chandler was an Indian, I guess it didn't really sink in—until now."

But Samantha was listening to the mens' conversation. "Graywolf will come for his woman," she heard Running Elk say to Morgan.

"How do you know this, Father?" Big Bear asked.

"It is what I would have done as a young warrior."

"Then I will wait, before taking her home," Morgan said.

Samantha wasn't very pleased that her dilemma had just been settled and she hadn't had any say on the matter. Only out of respect for Running Elk did she hold her tongue, but Morgan would definitely hear about it later. *Indian men!* she angrily thought. They were worse than white men, believing that a woman should have no say in anything. Before she lost her temper and said something that might get her into trouble, she needed to get out of there. In as pleasant sounding voice as she could possibly muster, she said to Morgan, "Excuse me, but Doreen and I could really use a bath . . . mind if we take a walk down by the river?"

"I'll take you myself."

Morgan could tell Samantha wanted to argue with him. When her lovely mouth snapped shut, he inwardly sighed with relief. At least Samantha had sense enough to know she wasn't at home on the ranch. Sometimes the woman was too stubborn for her own good.

Morgan quickly shepherded Samantha and her friend outside the tepee. Just as he expected—the moment they were far enough away from the village where nobody would hear—Samantha exploded in a fit of anger, going on about the despicable way that Indian men drove their poor wives like slaves. Morgan burst out laughing when Samantha said that most men were nothing but a bunch of *overbearing jugheads with huge egos.*

"I don't know what you're laughing at, Morgan *Black Hawk* Johnston, you're just as bad! You probably agree with the deplorable way the Indian men treat their wives!"

"Have you ever really taken a good look around you, Samantha? It's not like the women are going hungry . . . they're not beaten or starved—"

"No . . . they just work from dusk till dawn and in between all that they chase after their children and wait upon their men!"

"Men have their duties too." Morgan was starting to feel a little defensive.

"And we all know what those duties are," Samantha sarcastically retorted. "They sit around most of the day gambling with their friends or repairing their precious weapons . . . *gee* . . . I hope they don't strain themselves!"

Both Morgan and Doreen burst out with laughter. When Morgan noticed that Samantha's expression turned angrier, knowing this outspoken woman was capable of starting a war here inside his own village, he could only hope that *Sam* would behave and keep her opinions to herself. Not that it would do any good, he firmly reminded her, "It is the Indians' way of life, Samantha, and as long as you're here, you must accept this."

"You know that'll never happen."

Morgan let out a sigh, and stopped abruptly. "There's the path that leads to the river . . . I'll wait here, while you ladies bathe. If you need anything just holler."

Samantha scowled at him, before following the path through the trees with Doreen. Her arms swinging angrily at her sides, she grumbled more to herself, "I'm surprised the women are even allowed to bathe without the mens' permission."

"Well, here we are." She halted at the edge of the river.

Doreen stood beside Samantha, completely awestruck, staring at the magnificent snow-capped mountain in front of her, which now looked close enough that she could actually reach out and touch it with her hand. A giant waterfall cascaded over the side of a cliff, landing in the crystal clear river below. The late afternoon sun reflected the misty spray, making a rainbow of colors at the base of the mountain. *This place was like a paradise!*

"Beautiful, isn't it?" said Samantha.

Those were Doreen's exact thoughts, but she could only nod in reply. She couldn't speak past the lump in her throat, knowing Clayton would never see this beautiful place.

After Samantha and Doreen quickly stripped down to their undergarments, Doreen gasped, when she saw the ugly jagged-looking scar on the back of Samantha's calf as they waded into the river, that she hadn't noticed before.

"What happened to your leg?"

"I was attacked by a grizzly."

Samantha shuddered just thinking about that horrifying night. Though it had happened several weeks ago, the memory was still fresh in her mind and still terrified her. She could clearly remember that low growling sound—as the huge beast approached her little campsite. "I never knew I could climb a tree so fast," she said in a joking manner to hide her growing fear.

"Unfortunately that grizzly was a faster climber and needless to say—while I was trying to get away my foot slipped on a branch and—that's when it took a swipe at my leg. Everything sort of happened in a daze after that. I remember throwing my knife and," she shrugged, "guess I must've fainted then. Anyway . . . when Chandler and Morgan found me, apparently I was still in the tree, clinging to the trunk. Chandler had to carry me down, but I don't remember that either. And it wasn't until the next morning that I discovered I'd actually hit that grizzly right between the eyes with the blade of my knife." She made a face of disgust and said, "Chandler made a necklace out of one of its huge claws."

"That is absolutely amazing, Samantha." Doreen's eyes were round as saucers. "I would've been scared out of my mind."

"I *was* scared out of my mind," Samantha admitted. She visibly shuddered, and suddenly changed the subject. "I bet Morgan's probably wondering what's taking us so long . . . we'd better hurry."

They finished bathing, then hastily dressed. They were seated on a log, trying to smooth out the tangles in their hair, when Doreen suddenly turned to face Samantha and said, "Do you think Clayton is . . . ?" but she couldn't bring herself to finish the sentence.

Samantha stopped braiding her hair and turned to Doreen. She knew exactly what Doreen was trying to say. "I wish I knew," she honestly replied. "There is a good chance that Clayton might've . . . maybe he escaped the Kiowas."

Tears scalded Doreen's eyes but she blinked them back. "Not long ago Clayton tried to talk me into leavin' Billy . . . if only I'd listened to him and not been such a coward, he would still be alive." Then she burst into tears.

"Doreen, if anything did happen to Clayton, it wasn't your fault," Samantha said, trying to console her friend.

"What's the matter with her?"

Samantha looked over her shoulder at Morgan. "Doreen's just upset over Clayton."

Morgan knew the young woman had good reason to be upset over Clayton. It was unlikely the man survived the Indian attack.

Chandler guided Ranger across the grass-covered meadow toward the Indian village, leading the unconscious man behind him. Just as he'd feared, the wound in Clayton's shoulder had become badly infected. Clayton had finally passed out from fever, so he'd tied the man in the saddle to keep him from falling and hurting himself. He'd already tried everything he could think of to bring Clayton's fever down, but nothing seemed to be working.

Chandler spotted the lone Indian riding out to greet him, and immediately recognized Big Bear's magnificent black stallion. He nodded at his younger brother, who guided his horse alongside his.

"Graywolf. Father said you would come."

Somehow that didn't surprise Chandler. Running Elk seemed to have an uncanny sense of perception. "How is Father?"

"I think our Father is becoming more . . . what is the white man's word? *ornery* in his old age," Big Bear replied, a huge smile showing even white teeth. Then, "Who is the man with you and what is wrong with him?"

"His name's Clayton Bradford. Kiowas attacked his cabin . . . he's got an infection in his shoulder from an arrow."

"Samantha spoke of this man," Big Bear said.

"So . . . Samantha *is* here," Chandler muttered more to himself.

"You do not seem surprised."

"Well—let's just say I had a gut feeling she might be here."

"Black Hawk found your woman with the Kiowas and brought her to the village," Big Bear informed him.

"Black Hawk?"

"Oh, I forgot, you did not know . . . it is Morgan's Indian name. Father has asked Black Hawk to be our next chief. I believe Father has finally accepted the fact that he is no longer a young man. But our brother has not accepted yet . . . he is already war chief to a band of warriors . . . he leads them on raids to rid our lands of the white man. They keep taking more and more of our best hunting grounds," Big Bear added bitterly.

Chandler had heard about the young war chief who was wreaking havoc upon the settlers. It didn't really surprise him that this newest chief was his own brother. "Morgan had better be careful . . . the army's looking for him."

"What troubles you, Graywolf?"

Chandler wondered how he could explain to Big Bear that Morgan had given up any chance that he might have had for a better life just to become some war chief for a short while. What would the Indians really gain by chasing away a few frightened settlers when only more would return to take their place. He knew the Indians were fighting a battle they could never win, but how could he make Big Bear understand without sounding like he was siding with the white man. He'd never felt so torn between two worlds; not even all those years ago when he'd first taken the white man's name of Wade Chandler . . .

As they rode through the village, a couple of dogs started barking at them and nipping at Chandler's stallion's hind legs. Ranger finally laid back his ears and kicked at one of the dogs, sending it yelping across the field. Some children ran past them laughing as they chased each other in a game of tag. Standing outside their tepees, stirring what smelled like venison stew in big iron cooking pots, several Indian women looked at Chandler with mild curiosity as he and Big Bear rode past them. He smiled and nodded his head in greeting.

They were now approaching their father's lodge. Chandler's face split into a huge smile when he saw her: he would know that flowing, chestnut mane of glorious hair anywhere! Samantha was talking with a pretty blond whom he assumed had to be Doreen. Clayton had talked a lot about the young woman.

As if sensing his presence, Chandler saw Samantha suddenly whirl around, and then her sky-blue eyes widened with stunned surprise when she saw him; then she was running toward him shouting his name.

Leaping from his horse, Chandler caught Samantha in his arms and lifted her completely off the ground and twirled her around, before setting her back on her feet. Then he crushed her in his arms and gave her a heartfelt kiss, not caring who was watching . . . until he heard a female giggling behind him. With a sigh, he reluctantly set Samantha away from him. He noticed her cheeks were flushed with embarrassment from his display of affection and couldn't help grin.

Samantha stammered as she introduced her friend to Chandler. "Doreen, this is . . . Chandler's my fiancé . . . the man I was telling you about."

"I already guessed that," Doreen said, giggling.

So this was the young woman whom Clayton had spoken so fondly of, Chandler thought to himself. From what he'd gathered from his and Clayton's conversation, Doreen had no idea that Clayton was in love with her. It was probably best that way, considering it was highly possible that Clayton would not survive . . .

"I brought a friend of yours," he informed Doreen.

"A friend?"

"Clayton."

"Clayton's alive!" Doreen shrieked excitedly. "Where is he?"

It struck Chandler odd that the woman didn't inquire about Billy Baxter—the man was supposed to be the girl's fiancé. "Big Bear took Clayton to Wise Owl's tepee. Clayton has an infection in his shoulder where an arrow struck him. I found him at the cabin, along with the other man Billy Baxter. Billy was killed by the Kiowas," he bluntly stated, figuring it would be better just to come out and say it instead of beating around the bush.

"Will Clayton live?" Doreen wanted to know. She wished she could feel something over Billy's demise, but she didn't.

Chandler wasn't sure how the girl was going to take that bit of news . . . apparently she felt something more for Clayton than just a friend, like Clayton had led him to believe. He looked toward Samantha for help. She seemed to read his mind . . .

"Clayton's not good," Samantha said.

Chandler nodded.

Doreen stood by the tepee's entrance, afraid of what she might find. After a while, she finally mustered the courage to duck through the small opening. It took a few moments for her eyes to adjust to the darker interior, before she saw the still form of a large man lying on top of some thick buffalo hides. She knew at once that it was Clayton. She'd been hoping that he wasn't as bad as Chandler had made it sound. Her eyes welled with tears as she slowly walked toward Clayton, dropping to her knees at his side. In the dim light, she could see the many cuts and scrapes covering his handsome face and bare chest. Clayton looked so deathly pale, Doreen thought, wondering if that was normal for what he'd been through. She reached out to gently brush back some hair that had fallen across his forehead. It frightened Doreen when he didn't even stir. Closing her eyes and bowing her head, she began to pray to God, asking Him to spare the life of the man whom she loved with her whole heart . . .

"Doreen?"

Her eyes flew open at the sound of Clayton's voice. "Oh, Clayton! Please don't die and leave me all alone!" Then she burst into tears.

"Shh, Dory, don't cry."

When Doreen felt his hand touch her on the cheek so tenderly, she cried even harder. The poor man was obviously in a lot of pain, yet, as usual, he was trying to comfort *her*.

Clayton couldn't hold back the tears filling his own eyes, thinking, *fate had once again robbed him of happiness.* Now that Billy was finally out of the way and he stood a fighting chance with Doreen, he probably wouldn't live. He had nobody to blame though but himself. He should have taken Doreen and got away from Billy long ago . . .

"Oh, Clayton, it's all my fault you got hurt," she sniffled.

"That's not true . . . don't ya dare go blamin' yourself."

"But if I'd left Billy when you asked me, none of this would've happened."

"It's not your fault, Doreen, and don't you . . ." Clayton broke into a fit of coughing and lay back upon the buffalo robes. When he'd caught his breath, he said in a low tone of voice, "If anyone's to blame . . . it's Billy." He tried to sit up, but was just too weak.

"Dory?" he rasped. "Could I have a drink of water?"

Doreen hurried to get Wise Owl.

Chandler and Samantha casually strolled alongside the river, stopping to admire what was a breathtaking sunset. The brilliant shades of red and gold that streaked across the horizon caused the nearby snow-capped mountain to glow with a pinkish-orange hue. Chandler was observing the eagle circling high above them in the cloudless sky, while Samantha was mesmerized by the graceful doe and her fawn that cautiously walked down to the river to drink. She noticed how the mother's ears constantly twitched, alerted to any unwanted predator that could possibly harm her young; she would sometimes raise her head to sniff the air.

Now Chandler was watching Samantha, wondering if she had any idea of just how beautiful she looked, the way the setting sun seemed to bring out the red and blond highlights in her knee-length hair, causing the rich mane to sparkle like spun gold. He saw her lips twist into a pout when the doe and her fawn suddenly darted away.

"It's a warm evening, care to go for a swim?" he asked her.

"The last time we went for a swim—which wasn't far from here, if I recall—I believe you dunked me."

"And, as I recall, I was only trying to cool your temper." Chandler saw her frown and hastily added, " 'Course that particular argument was all my fault."

"Are you suggesting it was mine?"

"I wouldn't even consider it."

"Now you're being sarcastic."

"I'm only teasing, Samantha. Why are you always so dog-gone defensive?" Chandler asked in a slightly raised tone of voice.

"You don't need to shout!" she hissed.

"I wasn't shouting. *Now* I'm shouting!"

"Look, Chandler, I don't wanna fight with you," she calmly said.

"That would be a first."

"It's not all *my* fault we can't seem to have a simple conversation," she said more angrily.

"I guess it couldn't possibly have anything to do with your confounded temper, or the fact that you're about as stubborn as a two-headed mule!"

"Well you won't have to put up with my *stubbornness* any longer!"

When Samantha tried to brush past Chandler, he grabbed hold of her upper arm. She glared at the offensive hand that was preventing her from leaving. "I would suggest you release me!"

Abruptly Chandler let go of her, then he walked away without a backward glance.

Turning to face the river, Samantha stared at the sparkling surface in the dwindling light, while silent tears rolled down her cheeks. Much as she hated to admit it, Chandler was right. She knew she had a terrible temper and couldn't seem to control it.

"Samantha?"

So Morgan wouldn't know she'd been crying, Samantha quickly swiped the tears from her eyes, before turning to face him.

Morgan could tell that Samantha was on the verge of tears. He wondered what she and Graywolf had been fighting about but didn't ask. He figured if she wanted him to know, she would tell him. Still, he couldn't stand to see her this way. Even though he knew it was a mistake, he held out his arms, and Samantha walked straight into them, then burst into tears.

He gently crooned, "It can't be that bad. . . ."

Quietly seated upon a buffalo robe inside his father's tepee, Chandler's thoughts were completely absorbed by a certain honey-colored haired beauty who had the face of an angel and a temper like a grizzly with a thorn in its side. It seemed like he and Samantha could never agree on anything . . . were always having disputes about something. Why did she have to be so dang-blame stubborn? "What am I gonna do with her," he mumbled under his breath.

"Did you say something?" Running Elk asked.

"What? Oh—I was just thinking out loud."

"Is something wrong with your stew . . . you have not touched your meal?"

"I'm sure it's good—it's just that . . ." Chandler shrugged. "Guess I'm not real hungry."

"What is troubling you, Graywolf?"

"Nothing you can help me with, Father."

"Are you having problems with your woman again?"

Running Elk's insight into what was bothering him should not have surprised Chandler. "That is putting it rather mildly. But how did you know?"

"Your woman is not with you, and you have been . . . what is the white man's word? . . . brooding, since you have returned from your walk. You have not touched your meal. And you look like you have just lost your best friend in battle." Running Elk grinned. "It was not very hard to guess."

"And now that we're on the subject of *my woman*—I don't know what to do about her. Father, I have never known a woman more stubborn or independent . . . once Samantha sets her mind to something, there is no reasoning with her. Even when she's proven wrong, she still thinks she's right."

"Samantha sounds no more stubborn than you, Graywolf," Running Elk chuckled.

Chandler frowned at his father. He wasn't *that* stubborn. Then, again, now that he thought about it—he could be a bit . . . well . . . maybe unreasonable at times.

Morgan didn't know how much longer he could stand there holding Samantha in his arms, while she cried on his shoulder. Being this near to her was a mistake—yet he could not seem to help himself—but trying to hold his passion in check was becoming nearly impossible. When Samantha innocently tightened her grip around his waist, he inwardly groaned. *For crying out loud, he wasn't made of stone. There was only so much a man could take.*

Gently unwinding her slender arms from around him, Morgan reluctantly set her away, wondering if he would ever get over this woman. He was going to talk to his brother, because the faster he got Samantha home, the better. And if it meant getting caught by the army, it couldn't be as bad as the tremendous pain he now felt in his heart.

Chapter Twenty-three

Samantha and Doreen waited outside Wise Owl's tepee, while Chandler checked to see how Clayton was doing. For some reason Chandler had decided to leave for home this morning and they planned on taking Doreen with them, but Doreen refused to leave without Clayton, and Samantha felt she couldn't just ride away from the village and leave her new friend behind. And apparently Morgan was going to accompany them, against Chandler's fierce warning . . .

"Couldn't you talk Chandler into waiting until Clayton's better?" Doreen asked.

"I could try, but Chandler's determined to leave for home today."

"But if Wise Owl says that Clayton can't be moved . . ."

"Why don't we just wait and see what Chandler has to say."

Chandler emerged from Wise Owl's tepee then. Samantha noticed his expression was inscrutable as always. Dressed completely in buckskins this morning, with his shoulder-length hair braided the way it was, she thought Chandler looked as ferocious as some of the other warriors in the village. Her eyes locked with his as he approached her and Doreen.

"Wise Owl says Clayton can't be moved for several more days." Chandler held up his hand for silence when Samantha started to say something. "I know Doreen won't leave the valley without him, so other arrangements have been made when Clayton's better."

"What other arrangements?" Samantha demanded.

"I was getting to that," Chandler snapped in reply. "When Clayton's well enough to travel, Big Bear and some of his friends will escort him and Doreen to the nearest fort, and they can go wherever they want from there."

Doreen jumped to her feet. "May I see Clayton?"

Chandler nodded. "He's awake."

Running Elk stood outside his tepee, gazing into the handsome face of his eldest son. He hugged Graywolf tightly; then he hugged Black Hawk. "Your mother would be so proud of the men you have become," he told both of his sons.

Now he turned to the lovely young woman standing at Graywolf's side. "I have something for you, daughter." He handed Samantha the medallion necklace. "It was Graywolf's mother's. I know Singing Wind would have wanted you to have it."

"Oh, Running Elk, it's beautiful!" Samantha gushed. She touched the shiny, gold medallion lovingly, before pulling the necklace over her head. "I will treasure this gift always." Then she threw her arms around the older man's neck.

Running Elk chuckled. "I am pleased you like it."

"I remember my mother wearing this," Chandler remarked as he fingered the gold medallion resting close to his woman's heart.

"It's beautiful, Samantha," said a soft, feminine voice.

Samantha turned to Doreen. "I wish you and Clayton were coming with us."

"Me too. I'll write you just as soon as me and Clayton are settled." She blushed prettily and whispered, "Clayton asked me to marry him."

"Congratulations, Doreen, but I'm not surprised. And don't you worry . . . you'll be perfectly safe staying with Running Elk until Clayton's on his feet." Samantha hugged her friend. "I'm sure gonna miss you, Doreen."

"I hate to interrupt, ladies," Chandler cut in, "but we do need to get going . . . it's a long ride back to the ranch." Besides, he hated long good-byes.

"Big Bear, if you decide to take Father's place as chief, do not let it go to your head," Morgan teased his younger brother as he mounted his horse.

"I am deeply troubled by your lack of faith in me, Black Hawk," he replied in the same teasing tone, which got a laugh out of Running Elk.

Chandler lifted Samantha onto the back of his stallion, then he swung on behind her. With a last farewell to his father and Big Bear, he nudged Ranger forward. Morgan followed alongside them. Samantha turned to wave at Running Elk and Doreen as they rode away. She hoped that Clayton and Doreen would be happy together, and hoped to see them again someday.

As they rode out of the peaceful, little village and slowly cantered across the grassy meadow, Samantha suddenly began to feel a little melancholy. It was sad having to part with her new friends and family. Well . . . Running Elk and Big Bear were practically family. Plus she would miss this beautiful valley.

Chandler's arm tightened around Samantha's waist as they followed the narrow path that led up the hillside. When they reached the top, Morgan and Chandler halted their horses, then sat there, admiring the breathtaking view below . . .

"It won't be long before the white man takes this land as well," Morgan bitterly spat.

Chandler knew exactly how his brother felt. When Morgan suddenly swung his horse around and rode away without a word or so much as a backward glance, Chandler followed a short distance behind, sensing his brother's need to be alone.

"Morgan sure is taking a risk coming with us," Samantha remarked.

"He knows the risk he's taking, but he wanted to be there for our wedding. I told him it wasn't necessary, but you know how stubborn Morgan is."

"Guess that means we're still getting married?"

"Unless you've changed your mind?"

Samantha twisted around to look at Chandler. "I haven't changed my mind. But we're not getting married until the end of the month . . . a lot can happen till then."

Chandler wondered what she meant by *a lot can happen till then*, but didn't say anything.

When they stopped that evening to make camp, Morgan volunteered to go hunting for some fresh meat. In truth, it was more of an excuse for him to get away. He was beginning to think that coming along on this trek was a bad idea. Being constantly around Samantha—watching her and Graywolf together—was proving to be much harder than he thought. He grabbed his rifle, then headed into the nearby forest.

While Chandler looked after the horses, Samantha figured the least she could do was get a fire going and put on a fresh pot of coffee. When that chore was done, she took a cake of soap from Chandler's saddlebags, along with one of his clean flannel shirts (she hoped he wouldn't mind), then hurried toward the river to wash off the day's dirt and grime.

Finding a secluded spot, Samantha quickly shucked out of her clothes, leaving on her camisole and pantalets, picked up her soap, then she waded into the river. It was almost the middle of September and it still felt like summer. And this evening felt even warmer than usual, so the water was refreshingly invigorating, especially after such a hard day in the saddle. She took her sweet time washing and rinsing her knee-length hair.

Samantha was enjoying herself so much, she never paid any attention to the possible dangers that could be lurking about . . . until it was too late.

It appeared out of no where.

Samantha stood frozen in place at the sight of the huge grizzly as it suddenly splashed into the river from the opposite side of the shore. Her entire body began to shake with mounting fear as that day of the bear attack flooded Samantha's mind. *Was she about to relive that horrible nightmare all over again?* She opened her mouth to scream, but nothing would come out. So she just stood there, now shaking so badly that her knees were actually knocking together. Samantha didn't dare move as she watched the enormous animal carefully sniff the air. She knew the instant the grizzly bear spotted her. Her eyes now wide with terror, she tried to take a step back, but her wobbly legs refused to function.

"Don't move, Samantha," a familiar voice suddenly said behind her.

"Chandler, I'm . . . scared."

"I know. So am I."

Samantha could hear Chandler moving through the water, then she felt a pair of strong arms slip firmly around her waist. She nearly collapsed with relief against his broad chest. Now Chandler was slowly pulling her backwards with him toward the shore.

"Don't say a word . . . just listen," he whispered against her ear. "When I tell you, I want you to run like the wind and *do not* look back . . . no matter what happens."

"What about you?"

"Samantha, just this once do as I say!"

Her terrified gaze still glued to the grizzly, Samantha was too afraid to argue. As they drew closer to the shore, the animal seemed to ignore them. It splashed around in the water in search of food. Then, without warning, the grizzly let out a loud angry roar as it stood up on its hind legs. *Now the monster was headed right for them!*

Before she knew what was happening Samantha suddenly went sailing through the air and landed safely on the river bank in a thick carpet of grass. Slightly dazed, it took Samantha a moment to realize that Chandler had thrown her out of harm's way, taking the brunt of the grizzly's fury upon himself. She heard him shout, "*Run, Samantha!*" just before the giant beast struck him with its mighty paw.

Springing to her feet, Samantha ran screaming Chandler's name, barely able to see where she was going through her frightened tears, as she raced to get her knife. She scrambled about like a madwoman, trying to find her boots, while the grizzly's thunderous roars—along with Chandler's screams of pain—filled her ears. She had just found her knife and was racing to Chandler's rescue when a loud gunshot echoed through the air.

Then everything went silent.

Halting in her tracks, Samantha watched Morgan carrying the lifeless form of the man she loved toward camp. Knowing there was no time to waste, that Chandler might need her, she suddenly snapped to her senses. She dressed in a hurry, pulled on her boots, then her feet took flight over the ground after Morgan.

Chandler was lying upon his bedroll beside a cozy fire with Morgan bent over him, trying to remove his shirt, when Samantha approached the campsite. She gasped when Morgan rolled Chandler over on his stomach and she saw the long bloody gashes that covered most of his back, and his upper left shoulder looked mangled. Morgan's expression only confirmed what she already knew: it wasn't good.

"Samantha, get me a canteen and hurry!"

Samantha's legs felt like rubber as she trotted over to the pile of saddlebags and grabbed the fullest canteen, then carried it back to Morgan. Her chin began to quiver, and tears rolled down her cheeks. She couldn't bear to see Chandler this way . . .

"I'm going to need your help, Samantha."

She wordlessly dropped to her knees beside Morgan.

"It could've been worse if Graywolf hadn't been wearing his buckskin shirt," he told her. "I want you to thoroughly cleanse the wounds. While you're doing that, I'll see if I can find some herbs that'll help fight infection and keep his fever down." He rose to his feet. "He's going to need some stitches in that shoulder, but I'll worry about that later. You should be safe here until I get back." He was already heading toward his horse.

Samantha watched Morgan ride swiftly out of camp, then she turned her attention to Chandler, praying he wouldn't regain consciousness until she was through. Taking a deep breath and letting it out slowly, she immediately went to work. Tearing a clean strip of cloth from her camisole, Samantha saturated the fabric with water from the canteen, then, gently as possible, she began to wash the wounds on Chandler's shoulder, because those looked the worst. She noticed there was a couple of really deep gashes that would definitely need stitching.

Tears filled her eyes, and she blinked them away. She knew if it weren't for Chandler, it would be her lying here instead . . .

"Samantha?"

The sound of Chandler's voice startled her. *Oh the pain she must be causing him!* "Yes, my love," she sniffled.

"My love," Chandler repeated. "I must really be in bad shape."

"Oh, Chandler, how can you joke at a time like this!"

"Who said I was joking?"

"I'm trying to clean your wounds—now lie still," Samantha gently scolded him.

"Is that what you're doing to my back?"

Samantha hoped his sense of humor was a good sign.

The moon was high in the sky when Samantha leaned back on her heels with a weary sigh, having finally completed her task. Through the entire ordeal, Chandler had not once uttered a word of complaint, only a low groan here and there. She wouldn't have blamed him if he'd screamed and hollered the whole time. She lightly brushed her fingers against Chandler's smooth cheek. He'd been quiet for so long, she wondered if he might have passed out again. It would be a blessing if he did . . .

Hearing a horse's nicker, Samantha looked over her shoulder. She watched Morgan dismount, grab his saddlebags and walk toward her. She frowned when she noticed the bottle of whiskey he carried in his hand.

"How's Graywolf?" he asked, dropping his saddlebags on the ground.

"I've had better days," came a muffled-sounding voice.

Morgan squatted beside his brother. "I'm surprised you're even conscious."

"I wish I weren't."

"That's a funny looking herb you're holding," Samantha said, scowling at Morgan.

"The whiskey's for his back . . . it'll help with infection. I couldn't find the proper herbs. This firewater will also help numb the pain when I stitch his back. And *I'm* gonna need some in order to do the stitching. Any more complaints, woman?"

Samantha's frown deepened.

Morgan took a long swig, then handed the bottle to Samantha. "Be sure Graywolf drinks enough of this."

Samantha wasn't sure how much was enough, but she held the bottle of whiskey, while Chandler took several swigs. She watched Morgan remove a small leather pouch from his saddlebags. She blanched when he pulled out a needle and some thread.

"This is where you should leave," he told her.

"And what if you need my help?"

"Samantha, do as Morgan says." Chandler gave her a reassuring smile.

Samantha could tell that it took a lot of effort for Chandler to speak—she wouldn't make it worse for him by arguing. Wordlessly she handed Morgan back the bottle of whiskey, then walked over to a nearby hollow stump and plopped down. She could see Chandler's handsome features grow taut with pain, as Morgan began to stitch the deep gashes on his shoulder. He showed no other sign of the agony it must be causing him. She didn't know how Chandler endured it. The pain had to be excruciating, yet he didn't utter a sound.

After Morgan was finished, when he poured some whiskey over Chandler's back, Samantha saw his face suddenly pale and then his eyes closed. Unable to watch any longer, she stood and walked over to check on the horses, needing something to occupy her mind . . .

Morgan was grateful when his brother finally passed out. He knew pouring that whiskey over Graywolf's back probably hurt worse than the stitches, but it was something that had to be done to help prevent infection. After carefully applying some healing salve to his wounds, he covered his back with a clean piece of cloth. There was nothing else he could do for now.

Getting to his feet, Morgan stretched the muscles in his aching back. When he noticed Samantha was nowhere in sight, he was just about to go look for her, when he heard somebody was trying to sneak up behind him—and those footsteps sounded way too heavy to be Samantha's. He stood there, statue-still, the hairs on the back of his neck warning him of imminent danger, mentally berating himself for leaving his weapon by his saddlebags.

"I'm unarmed." Morgan raised his hands in the air, then slowly turned around.

"Keep those hands where I can see 'em, Indian," the man gruffly ordered. He motioned with his gun. "What's wrong with your friend?"

"Bear attack," Morgan curtly replied.

"I'll get right to the point. I own a small ranch not far from here . . . some Indians stole several head of cattle . . . you know anything about that?"

"Mister, do you see any cows?"

In the dappled moonlight, Samantha could barely make out the mens' silhouettes, though she could see enough to tell there was a man holding Morgan at gunpoint. She could hear their voices were raised in a heated discussion, but she couldn't understand what they were saying. Removing the knife inside her boot, on silent feet she made her way closer to the men, ducking behind the trunk of a tree . . .

"I already told you, mister, I don't know anything about your cows!" It infuriated Morgan that this rancher naturally assumed he was guilty just because he was Indian!

"I oughtta shoot ya where you stand for lying!"

"Then shoot!"

Morgan stiffened when the rancher leveled his gun, pointing it directly at his chest. He was thinking that maybe he shouldn't have been so quick to lose his temper when he heard a slight hissing sound and then the man suddenly cried out in pain.

Although Morgan knew firsthand just how good Samantha was with a knife, he'd just witnessed something extraordinary. Samantha had hurled her knife, knocking the weapon from the rancher's hand faster than he could have drawn his gun. It was still hard to believe, even though he'd seen it with his own eyes. His admiration for this incredible woman had just increased even more. He walked over and snatched the man's gun off the ground, tucking it safely inside the waistband of his pants; then he picked up Samantha's knife and handed it back to her. "You're amazing, Sam."

"Twas nothing."

"Lady, you cut my hand!" the rancher loudly complained.

"Mister, you were about to shoot me and you're whining about a little cut!" Morgan furiously hissed. "Our Indian women wouldn't make this much of a fuss!"

"I wasn't really going to shoot ya! I was only tryin' to scare you into telling me where to find my cattle!"

"And I told you I didn't take your lousy cattle! Where's your horse?" Morgan growled.

"It's back there," the man said, nodding over his shoulder.

"Morgan, what are you going to do with him?" Samantha wanted to know.

"I'm going to put him on his horse and send him home. What did you think I was going to do . . . scalp him?" Morgan laughed when the rancher suddenly paled.

Seated beside the cozy fire, Morgan had been quietly observing Samantha who sat vigilantly at his brother's side, the tender way she held his hand in her lap. He wondered if Graywolf knew just how lucky he was to have such a woman . . .

"Morgan!"

The frantic way Samantha had said his name brought Morgan instantly to his feet. In two long strides he was at his brother's side, squatting beside Samantha. He touched his brother's forehead: it was just what he'd been dreading.

When Morgan removed the cloth that covered Graywolf's back, it was easy to see that the deepest gash on his left shoulder was red and angry looking . . . a definite sign of infection.

"Morgan, what should we do?"

"First—we'll need to boil some water and let it cool. Then we'll apply warm cloths to the wound . . . that should help draw out the infection."

"Chandler's not going to die . . . is he, Morgan?"

"No." But he wasn't so sure.

"I'll heat some water."

While Samantha rummaged through the saddlebags, looking for something she could use to heat the water, Morgan thoroughly disinfected the blade of his knife with whiskey. Before Samantha returned, he worked quickly to draw out all the pus from Graywolf's wound. It worried Morgan that his brother didn't even flinch a muscle when he lanced the infected gash with his knife.

After Samantha had the hot packs ready, she handed Morgan one of the cooled cloths, and watched him lay it across Chandler's infected shoulder. With Chandler lying on his stomach, Samantha helped Morgan remove his buckskin britches. Then, finding a bowl and filling it with cold water from the river, she began to sponge bathe Chandler's exposed arms and legs, hoping it would help bring down his fever. As Samantha carefully bathed his muscular thighs, she tried not to pay any attention to his well-muscled bottom—though that part of his anatomy was covered with a breechcloth.

All through the night Morgan and Samantha took turns applying warm compresses to Chandler's infected wound. They also took turns sponge bathing his feverish body with cool cloths, and forced him to drink as much water as possible. Whenever Samantha looked at Chandler, her eyes would fill with tears, because, despite the warmth of the night, his teeth chattered constantly and he shivered with chills.

It wasn't until the next morning when Chandler's fever finally broke, and the infection was now under control. Her energy completely spent, Samantha fell asleep sitting up with her head resting on her bent knees. She did not awaken when Morgan gently lifted her in his arms and carried her over to her sleeping mat . . . .

Samantha yawned and stretched; then her eyes fluttered open. Suddenly she sat up straight and looked over at Chandler. Miraculously, he was propped against his saddle—and he was smiling back at her. Though there were dark smudges under his eyes, his skin no longer had that sickly pale color. A huge smile split her entire face.

"How do you feel?"

"You mean—other than the throbbing pain in my shoulder?" he teasingly replied.

Her smile widened even more. *He had a sense of humor—that was a good sign.* Rising, Samantha hurried over to Chandler and touched his cheek. He felt cool. She noticed that Morgan had bandaged his shoulder. She glanced around the campsite. "Where's Morgan?"

"He went hunting for some breakfast."

"I just can't believe how much better you are this morning. Last night—there for a while, I thought . . ." Samantha couldn't even say it.

"Come a little closer, woman, and I'll show you just how much better I really am."

"Oh, Chandler," Samantha giggled.

They both turned at Morgan's approaching footsteps. The rifle tucked under his arm, he carried two large pheasants in his hand. He walked directly over to Samantha and wordlessly dropped the birds on the ground at her feet.

"What am I supposed to do with those?" she asked, frowning.

"What do you think you're supposed to do with 'em?"

"If I knew . . . would I ask?"

Snatching the pheasants off the ground, Morgan walked away, grumbling under his breath, "The woman can throw a knife like a warrior, but she can't skin a couple of little birds."

After breakfast, while Samantha walked the short distance to the river to wash their dirty dishes, Morgan and Chandler got into a heated discussion. Morgan wanted to wait at least a full day before continuing their journey, because he felt that his brother needed more time to regain his strength. But Chandler insisted that he was well enough to travel *now.* So far Samantha hadn't interfered, though she did agree with Morgan. She thought it comical that Morgan had to practically hog-tie the stubborn man to keep him on his bedroll, and would only allow Chandler short walks to the nearby forest to take care of his private needs.

By that evening both Morgan and Samantha had had enough of Chandler's foul mood. Samantha was actually grateful to Morgan when he finally announced in frustration, "Okay, Graywolf, you win . . . we'll leave first thing in the morning." He then looked at Samantha and seriously added, "And here I thought it was *you* who was so cotton-pickin' stubborn."

"Maybe I've been a bad influence on him," she saucily retorted.

Morgan threw back his head and laughed.

Chandler scowled at them.

That night Samantha lay curled up on her bedroll, smiling from ear to ear, while her eyes secretly remained fastened on Chandler just a few short feet away, who was fast asleep upon his own bedroll. She was absolutely elated that he'd managed to make nearly a full recovery, and in just a day. She couldn't seem to take her eyes off him. She noticed how the firelight caused feathery-looking shadows to flicker across Chandler's handsome features, the way his long lashes rested upon his smooth cheeks . . .

Samantha gasped when Chandler's eyes suddenly flew open. She frowned, when she noticed the amusement dancing in their depths. Mortified that he'd caught her watching him like some *lovesick spinster*, she rolled over on her side and pulled the blanket over her head.

Chapter Twenty-four

The Callahan ranch was quiet as Samantha, Chandler, and Morgan rode their weary mounts through the yard with only the bright moonlight to guide their way. Samantha was happy to see Gilda grazing inside the main corral. She was curious if the chestnut mare had found her own way back home from Billy Baxter's cabin—or maybe if one of her father's cowpunchers had come across Gilda while out on the range.

As they came to a halt in front of the huge, steepled-roof barn, Samantha knew at once that something must be wrong when she noticed there was light seeping through the cracks around the wide door. Thinking something might be wrong with Daisy, she hastily slid from Chandler's stallion and hurried forward, quietly slipping inside the barn. But what she found was her parents seated on a bale of hay, and they were laughing as they watched old Suzie's colt trotting around on the hay-strewn floor, kicking up its hind legs. She let out a sigh of relief.

When her father turned and saw her, the next thing Samantha knew she was being squished in between both of her parents. They were hugging her so tightly, she could hardly breath, but she didn't mind. Her voice sounded muffled when she asked, "What are you two doing out here at this hour of the night?"

John set his daughter away from him. "Your mother and I couldn't sleep, so we came out to check on the colt. I knew Chandler would find you."

"Pa, what are you doing?"

"I'm looking for injuries."

Samantha rolled her eyes. "There aren't any injuries."

"Good. Then I won't have to beat Chandler to a pulp."

Though her husband had said it in jest, Rachel still gave him a disapproving frown. "Where is Chandler?" she asked.

"Right behind you."

They all turned at the sound of Chandler's voice.

"Morgan, it's not safe for you to be here," John immediately warned him. "I'm not so sure that you should be here either, Chandler. The army's been sniffing around the place . . . they're looking Morgan . . . they found out somehow that he was working for me. A lieutenant by the name of Brown came by the other day . . . showed me a Wanted poster—and I must admit, Morgan, my wedding picture didn't turn out that good. That lieutenant sees you here, he'll recognize you as Chief Black Hawk on the spot, especially dressed that way. You stick out like a sore thumb too, Chandler. You both should change your clothes."

"I'll worry about all that later," Morgan replied.

"You should worry about it now." John said no more about it, knowing it would do him no good. He looked directly at Chandler. "Did you have any trouble?"

"With Samantha involved . . . what do you think?"

John couldn't help grin. "I know what you mean."

"You should be ashamed of yourself," Rachel admonished her husband.

"Come on, Rach, you know I was only joking."

Only partly listening, Samantha's eyes were on the colt as it trotted back and forth, shaking its head. She smiled. The frisky little fella reminded her of that first day when her father had brought Daisy home. She'd been just a little girl . . .

"Can we keep her, Papa? Can we?" Samantha couldn't contain her excitement. She'd been praying for her very own pony.

"I reckon so," her father answered, playfully ruffling her hair.

"Who'd wanna ride that ugly nag," James said.

"You take that back!" Samantha folded her arms across her puffed-out chest, glaring at her younger brother. "She might be ugly, but I bet she can run faster than your old horse."

James burst out laughing. "That ugly old nag?"

"James, Samantha, that's quite enough," John gently scolded both his children. "If you're going to bicker, go back inside the house."

When her father turned his back, Samantha stuck her tongue out at her brother. Then she ignored him and kept her eye on the little filly prancing back and forth inside the corral. "Can I name her, Papa?" she eagerly asked.

"She's your pony, Samantha—you can name her whatever you like."

"Then I'll call her Daisy—cause Daisies are pretty flowers. And I think she's beautiful. Don't you, Papa?"

"I guess beauty's in the eye of the beholder," John said, chuckling.

"What's that mean?"

"You'll understand someday. . . ."

Samantha smiled in remembrance. She hadn't understood her father's words until she was much older. It was true, Daisy wasn't much to look at. She was a color you couldn't exactly describe—sort of a light brownish gray and, because the mare was so terribly swaybacked, most people laughed and pointed. Then, to her family's complete shock and surprise, something remarkable happened: they later discovered the little mare could run like the wind. To this very day, there hasn't been another horse that could outrun her.

Snapping out of her reminiscent thoughts, Samantha giggled when the colt nudged her hand and then suddenly bolted away. She couldn't wait until Daisy had her foal, which wasn't due until next spring, wondering if it would take after its mother and run like the wind. Chandler insisted the colt would take after its father—Ranger.

"It's going to take me a little time to have everything organized and ready for the wedding by the end of the month," Samantha heard her mother say to Chandler. After overhearing his comment to her father, she sarcastically suggested, "Maybe Chandler would like to reconsider marrying me . . . since I'm so much trouble."

"Samantha Callahan, shame on you," Rachel chided her daughter. "Chandler doesn't really think you're a lot of trouble . . . he was only teasing."

"I'm not so sure," Samantha grumbled to herself.

"Look," Morgan interrupted, "I don't mean to break up the party, but—Rachel, do you think you could take a look at Graywolf's back?"

"What's wrong with his back?" she asked.

"It's nothing, Rachel," Chandler said.

"He was attacked by a grizzly," Samantha informed her parents, now feeling a little guilty. In all the excitement, she'd forgotten all about Chandler's injuries. When she noticed her mother's face had paled considerably, she thought it best not to say anymore about the incident. Giving her mother the gruesome details would only upset her more.

"Take off your shirt," Rachel ordered Chandler.

"Please, there's no need to fuss."

"Wade Chandler, you take off that shirt this instant and let me take a look at your back."

"But . . ."

"Young man, either you take off that shirt or I will."

With a sigh, Chandler eased out of his shirt and turned around. Hearing Rachel's gasp was just the thing he wanted to avoid. "My back doesn't even hardly hurt anymore." Though his shoulder did still bother him quite a bit.

"I don't know how you're even standing with a back like that," he heard Rachel say, sounding almost on the verge of tears. "I'll send John for the doctor . . ."

"There's no need for a doctor." Chandler turned back around, pulling on his shirt.

"Then I insist you come inside the house where I can properly look after those wounds."

Chandler looked toward John for help, but obviously he wasn't going to get any help from him. He glared at his brother for opening his big mouth. Morgan only shrugged and grinned.

In spite of a long night, Samantha woke early the next morning. She didn't want to meet Aunt Ruth and Cousin Rebecca looking like a dirty ragamuffin, so she grabbed a clean change of clothes and her lilac-scented soap, then headed for the bathing room. Her family was lucky to be able to enjoy the modern conveniences an indoor bathroom offered, and she couldn't wait to take advantage of the huge, porcelain tub.

After a long, soaking bath, Samantha hurried back to her bedroom. She sat at her dressing table and, as she began to run a brush through her wet, tangled hair, she thought about the last time she'd seen Aunt Ruth. She'd been just a little girl, and the only thing Samantha could recall about her aunt, was that she looked an awful lot like her mother; unfortunately, she didn't remember much about her cousin Rebecca either.

Samantha descended the wide staircase, and headed toward the kitchen. She could hear a woman's laughter that sounded so much like her mother and knew at once that it must be her Aunt Ruth. Samantha stopped just inside the doorway, taking a moment to observe the attractive woman sitting at the kitchen table, talking with her mother . . .

When Ruth noticed the lovely young woman propped against the doorway, her eyes began to fill with tears. Although she had not seen Samantha since she was a small child, she would have known her anywhere. Wordlessly rising from her chair, Ruth walked over and threw her arms around her niece, hugging her tightly. She then set her away so she could get a better look at the grown woman now standing before her.

"I'm glad that man of yours brought you home safe and sound. You have your father's eyes," Ruth remarked in a voice filled with emotion.

Samantha instantly liked her aunt. "Ma talks so much about you."

Ruth's delicate brow arched toward her sister. "Does she now?"

"Don't worry, Ruthie. I never told her anything she shouldn't hear. Come sit down, Samantha, and eat your breakfast before it gets cold."

Ruth winked at Samantha, who grinned back at her. They both walked over to the table and took their seat. "How's Chandler this morning?" Samantha inquired of her mother as she began to dish her plate with fried potatoes and link sausages.

"Other than a stiff shoulder, he says he's fine. Most men would not have survived a grizzly attack like that, let alone be up and about already. Morgan did a good job stitching Chandler's shoulder . . . it's healing very nicely. When he came in for breakfast this morning, I told him he should still be taking it easy, though I doubt that he is."

"Chandler was lucky Morgan was there, or it could've been much worse. He shot that bear before it had a chance to do any real damage." Samantha shuddered to think what might have happened if Morgan hadn't been there.

"I thank God that nobody was seriously hurt," Rachel commented.

"Aunt Ruth, where's Rebecca?"

"Becca isn't used to getting up quite this early. By the way, I met your Chandler. What an impressive young man . . . very handsome, too . . . so was his brother, Morgan. If I were you, I'd hurry and marry the man before he gets away."

Samantha wondered if her aunt would feel the same way if she knew Chandler had been a full-fledged Cheyenne warrior not very many years ago and had probably raided several white settlers' farms (though Chandler had never actually admitted doing such a thing), and that Morgan was a war chief who's Indian name was Black Hawk and was wanted by the army.

"Chandler and I are planning to marry at the end of this month."

"And I plan on helping your mother with all the wedding preparations."

"Say, Aunt Ruth, where's Uncle Bernard?"

Samantha noticed the strange look that passed between her mother and aunt, before her aunt replied, "Bernard couldn't get away from his business." Her gaze swung from her aunt to her mother. "I suppose being a lawyer—Uncle Bernard's probably kept pretty busy." She really became suspicious when her mother suddenly changed the subject.

"Samantha, did I mention that James and Sarah spent the night here last night? They stayed in your brother's old room. I'm sure Sarah's awake by now. When you finish with your breakfast, you ought to go on upstairs . . . maybe Becca's awake too . . . they'll both be so thrilled to see you."

"Actually I'm already finished." Samantha quickly drained the last of her coffee. She scooted out of her chair, walked around the table to give her aunt a big hug, then she pecked her mother on the cheek, and hurried from the room.

Sarah was seated in the rocking chair, staring out the window, when Samantha entered the room. The moment Sarah saw her, she let out a squeal and leaped out of the chair and grabbed hold of Samantha in a crushing hug.

Samantha giggled. "I'm glad to see you too, Sarah."

"James told me this morning that you and Chandler got back late last night . . . I figured you'd still be sleeping."

"I needed a bath worse than sleep."

"I heard what happened to Chandler."

A picture of the huge grizzly coming across the river toward her and Chandler flashed through Samantha's mind, and she shivered. "He's doing a lot better."

"I'm glad."

"So—what do you think of my Aunt Ruth?" Samantha was curious to know.

"I just adore your aunt, Samantha," Sarah replied. "She looks so much like your mother . . . don't you think?"

"Yeah, she does."

"Aunt Ruth may look like your mother, but she's . . . how should I explain . . . a bit more outspoken than Rachel." Sarah laughed. "I'm sure you'll see what I mean."

"What about Rebecca?"

Sarah shrugged. "I really don't have much of an opinion yet."

At Samantha's disgruntled expression, she hurried to say, "I don't mean she's hoity-toity or anything like that. Rebecca is . . . well . . . she's a very feminine replica of you."

Now Samantha was frowning. "What's that supposed to mean?"

"You'll see."

Samantha changed the subject. "You wouldn't happen to know anything about a Lieutenant Brown that's been coming around the place?"

"I know he's taken an interest in your cousin Rebecca, but I don't think the feeling's mutual."

"Pa never mentioned that—"

Just then somebody knocked on the door. After Sarah hollered "come in" an elegantly dressed young woman entered the room. As she moved across the carpeted floor, her silky, emerald gown swished about her small, slipper-clad feet. *This must be her cousin Rebecca,* Samantha thought. Now she understood what Sarah had meant by her cousin was a feminine replica of herself. It felt strange looking into another face that was strikingly similar to your own. Her hair was darker though—more like a chestnut color—the thick mass hung way past her hips. She wore it pulled back away from her face with a satin ribbon that matched the color of her gown.

Samantha glanced down at her own attire, suddenly feeling very drab in comparison. She had so wanted to make a good first impression—but she hadn't expected her cousin to look like she'd just stepped off the front page of a fashion magazine.

"Cousin, Samantha . . . I'm so glad you're okay."

Samantha stood there, dumbfounded, while Rebecca threw her arms around her, hugging her tightly. What surprised her even more than Rebecca's unexpected show of affection, was the strength the girl had in those skinny arms. When her cousin finally let go, Samantha was actually at a loss for words—she simply couldn't think of a thing to say. Her eyes followed Rebecca as she turned with the graceful beauty of a ballerina and floated over to Sarah, giving her a quick hug. It crossed Samantha's mind that this poor girl will never survive the next few weeks here, other than that, she wasn't really sure what to think of her city cousin just yet.

"You must've had a terrifying experience," Rebecca said as she plopped down on the edge of James's old bed. "I'd be out of my mind, if something like that happened to me."

Samantha started to say something, but Rebecca went on in a rush. "Aunt Rachel said I looked a lot like you, Samantha . . . guess it's true, huh? I bet if we were dressed alike and wore our hair the same way, nobody could tell us apart from behind."

Sarah giggled. She could tell by the expression on Samantha's face, she wasn't sure what to make of her flamboyant cousin.

"I was about to head out to the barn to check on Suzie's colt," Samantha finally interrupted, unable to get a word in edgewise. "I'm sure Sarah won't mind keeping you company . . ."

"May I come with you?"

"I suppose, but—you should change your clothes first."

"Is there something wrong with what I'm wearing?"

Samantha looked at Sarah, who was trying hard not to laugh. "No—I guess not."

As Samantha and Rebecca walked across the yard toward the barn, Samantha wondered how the girl could walk over such hard, rocky ground wearing *sissy-slippers*. Dressed in that fancy silk gown, her city cousin looked so out of place on a ranch . . .

"I can't wait to meet your fiancé," Rebecca remarked.

"You'll probably meet Chandler this evening . . . Watch your step, Rebecca," Samantha warned her as they entered the barn.

"Call me Becca."

Becca, Samantha mouthed the name behind her cousin's back.

After their eyes had a chance to adjust to the dimmer light, Rebecca suddenly let out a shriek of delight, when she spotted the colt. The loud noise frightened the skittish animal and it bolted clear across the barn. Rebecca's laughter sounded melodious as she hurried after the colt across the hay-strewn floor with an outstretched hand. Samantha watched her chase the colt around the barn in her shimmery silk gown. It looked so ridiculous, she couldn't help but grin.

"I thought I'd find you here."

She turned at the sound of her mother's voice.

"Lieutenant Brown's here to see Becca," Rachel announced. She was beginning to understand why her husband didn't like the young man.

"Excuse me, Aunt Rachel, did you say Jason is here?" Rebecca was walking toward them.

"Yes, dear. He's waiting for you on the veranda."

"Would you mind telling him, I'll be right there?"

"Certainly, dear."

Samantha waited until her mother was out of the barn, before turning to her cousin. "What do you know about this lieutenant?"

"I haven't known him long enough to know very much . . . why?"

After what her father had told her, Samantha wondered if this lieutenant might be using her cousin to gain information, but kept her suspicions to herself. "Just curious."

"Won't you come with me, Samantha? I'd like you to meet Jason."

"Yes . . . I think I'd like to meet this—Lieutenant Brown."

Chapter Twenty-five

"So what brings the army to Bear Creek?" Samantha bluntly asked the lieutenant. She couldn't understand what her cousin saw in the man. He might be handsome—she'd give him that—but the man's ego was so big, it greatly detracted from his looks.

"Please, call me Jason. And why would such a beautiful woman, Miss Callahan, inquire about such trivial matters?"

Samantha let out an unladylike snort. *Beautiful woman indeed*, she thought sarcastically. This man had no idea who he was talking to . . .

Jason's gut feeling told him that Samantha Callahan knew something alright. Now . . . if he could only win her trust. Several men in town had recognized the sketch on the Wanted poster that Jason knew as Chief Black Hawk, claiming the Indian had worked for John Callahan; surely all those men could not be mistaken. But—before he could accuse Callahan of any crime, he had to first prove the allegations, and, because he knew he was wasting his time trying to glean information from John Callahan himself, he was hoping he could get somewhere with the rancher's niece—or maybe even his daughter. If he could only capture Black Hawk, he was sure to get that promotion—of that, Jason was certain. Then he could transfer to just about any place he wanted, and women would practically throw themselves at his feet; not that they didn't already do so. Jason smiled to himself at the thought of either one of these lovely ladies fighting for his affection. And why shouldn't they? He was young and handsome with a promising career. What woman in her right mind wouldn't want him . . . ?

"*Lieutenant?*"

"I'm sorry . . . what did you say?"

"I said why shouldn't a woman inquire about such matters?"

"Exactly what matters are you referring to?"

Samantha impatiently snapped, "Why the army punishes men who are only trying to feed their families! Isn't that no less than what you would do, Lieutenant? And would you not protect land that was rightfully yours if somebody was trying to steal it?"

"Miss Callahan, how dare you sit there and . . ."

"Jason, would you care for some lemonade?" Rebecca quickly interceded. She could tell that Samantha had pushed the lieutenant too far, if his angry expression was any hint. Although she had to agree that Indian matters were probably best left to the men, she had to admire the way her cousin had boldly spoke her mind. She wished she had that kind of spunk.

"Yes, Rebecca, lemonade sounds lovely." Jason was grateful for Miss Smith's interference. He'd come awfully close to telling Samantha Callahan exactly what she could do with her opinions, which would have been a terrible error on his part. In the future, he would have to keep control over his temper.

"Would you help me, Samantha?" Rebecca asked as she rose to her feet, hoping to lure her cousin away from Jason before a worse fight developed.

"If you don't mind, Becca, I think I'll just keep Mr. Brown here company." Samantha had purposely used the word *mister*, refusing to acknowledge the man's military status. And it got the results she thought it would; the man looked furious enough to hit her.

When Rebecca stood there looking at her, Samantha knew she was worried about leaving her alone with the lieutenant. She teasingly said, "Don't worry, Becca, I'll go easy on him."

Jason waited until Rebecca had entered the house and closed the door. "So, Miss Callahan, am I to assume then, you believe that savages should be allowed to roam free?"

"Don't all men deserve freedom . . . Indians included?"

"I don't count savages as men!"

"I wasn't talking about savages!" Samantha hissed. "Apparently then, you believe that only white men deserve freedom!"

"In case it has escaped your mind, it's the Indians that keep harassing innocent white folks, so are we to just stand by and do nothing?" Jason furiously spat.

"But the Indians would not be harassing white folks, if we would stay off their land and let them live in peace!" Samantha angrily retorted. "Because of men like you, Mr. Brown, the Indians are given no other choice but to fight!"

"I'll pretend I didn't hear you say that!"

"Why pretend . . . you heard me loud and clear!"

"Is there a problem here?" a deep voice suddenly interrupted.

"Chandler," Samantha said, jumping to her feet.

Jason, too, rose out of his chair. This man's face seemed awfully familiar . . . at least from what he could see of it underneath his wide-brimmed Stetson. He was sorely tempted to knock the hat off the gentleman's head, so he could get a clearer look at his face.

"I don't believe we've been properly introduced," he said to the man.

"I already know who you are."

"Have we met before?"

"No," Chandler curtly replied.

"Are you sure?"

"I think you'd better leave, Lieutenant!" Samantha was afraid that Lieutenant Brown would soon figure out why Chandler looked familiar to him.

His eyes still focussed on the tall, mystery man, Jason spoke to Samantha. "Miss Callahan, would you be so kind to tell Rebecca I said good-bye and that I'll call on her another day?" Without waiting for a reply, he bounded off the veranda and sprinted toward his horse.

Chandler eyed the lieutenant suspiciously, while he mounted and rode away.

Hearing the back door open, Chandler turned and saw a lovely young woman step outside the door, carrying a tray which held a pitcher of lemonade, along with some glasses. She carefully placed the tray on a small table. He knew at once that this was Rebecca, Samantha's city cousin from Boston. *Boy . . . could you ever see the family resemblance.*

The young woman's hair—a little darker than Samantha's—was a wealth of rich chestnut waves that hung past her narrow hips. A pair of light brown eyes, warm and kind, blinked back at him.

"You must be, Chandler." Rebecca stretched out a hand. She hadn't expected her cousin's fiancé to be as tall as a mountain or so devastatingly handsome. She was discovering the men in this part of the country were entirely different from the men back home. "I'm Samantha's cousin, Becca. It's a pleasure to finally meet you."

Chandler gently shook her hand. "The pleasure is all mine."

"What happened to Lieutenant Brown?" Rebecca inquired.

"He said to tell you good-bye and that he would call on you some other day," Samantha informed her cousin. She then let out a sigh. "I suppose I should apologize for being so rude to your friend."

"There's no need to apologize." Rebecca handed Samantha a glass filled with fresh cold lemonade. "Would you care for some lemonade, Chandler?"

"No thank you, ma'am."

"Call me Becca, please."

Chandler nodded and smiled. "Becca."

"Well—if you'll both excuse me, I told my mother I would help her and Aunt Rachel prepare the evening meal." She then disappeared inside the house.

"I like your cousin," Chandler remarked to Samantha, the instant the door closed behind the young woman.

"Becca seems nice enough."

"It's amazing . . . how much you and your cousin look alike."

"And speaking of looking alike—did you see the way Lieutenant Brown was watching you, Chandler?"

"I saw."

"You look enough like Morgan to be his twin . . . that lieutenant will eventually figure out why you looked so familiar. By the way, where is Morgan?"

"Here he comes now."

Following Chandler's line of vision, Samantha saw Morgan with her father, striding across the yard toward them. There was a none-too-happy expression upon her father's face, Samantha noticed. It wasn't hard to guess that he must have already heard about the lieutenant's visit. As both men drew closer, she could hear her father trying to persuade Morgan to return to the village, and Morgan emphatically refusing to leave . . .

"I *will not* run from some conceited lieutenant who wants to further his career by capturing Black Hawk." Morgan stepped up onto the veranda beside Chandler and added, "Besides, if I leave now, I could be endangering the entire tribe. I'm sure the good lieutenant already has his men watching your place . . . probably as we speak."

"I hadn't thought of that," John said more to himself.

"I would rather stay and face the man," Morgan went on to say. "But I don't want to cause you or your family any trouble either. Maybe it would be best if I leave—"

"Don't you dare leave here because you think you might cause my family problems. You're welcome to stay for as long as you want."

"You truly are a good friend, John."

"Need I remind you, dear brother, that you're in a whole heck of a lot more trouble than I am—*Chief*. The worse the army will do to me, is toss my hide on the nearest reservation. Do you know what they'll do to you, if you're caught?"

"That's *if* they catch me," Morgan disputed.

"And if you stay here, that's likely to happen."

"Please, Graywolf, let me do this my way."

"I think I have the perfect solution!" Samantha suddenly declared. "What if Lieutenant Brown *thinks* he's captured Chief Black Hawk?"

"What are you talking about?" John asked.

"Chandler and Morgan look enough alike to pass as twin brothers, so—don't you think it's possible the army just might give up the search for Black Hawk if they arrest the wrong Indian?"

"Are you suggesting we should let Brown arrest Chandler?" John tried to clarify.

"The army won't be able to hold Chandler . . . once they discover they've got the wrong man," Samantha hastened to explain. "And I bet Lieutenant Brown will be so humiliated, we'll never see hide nor hair of the man again."

Morgan burst out laughing. "How did you manage to come up with an idea like that?"

"You got a better idea?" Samantha angrily replied.

"Wait a second." John rubbed his chin thoughtfully. "You know . . . crazy as Samantha's plan sounds, it just might work."

"And what if this so called *brilliant plan* doesn't work out that way?" Morgan argued. "Personally, I doubt it's likely the army will stop searching for Black Hawk just because they happen to arrest the wrong Indian. And I don't think embarrassing this lieutenant will stop him from coming back here . . . if anything, it'll make the man more determined than ever before to prove himself. Then my brother would have risked his identity and more-than-likely be forced on some detestable reservation, all for nothing."

"I agree with Morgan," John intervened. "I say we give this matter some more thought, before we make a final decision."

Seated at the supper table across from Morgan, Rebecca quietly observed this very interesting and handsome younger brother of Chandler's through a veil of lashes. There was no mistaking that Morgan Johnston was full-blooded Indian like Chandler—but where Chandler was garbed in the same western style clothes that the other cowboys wore, Morgan was dressed in cream-colored buckskins with his blue-black hair hanging over his broad shoulders nearly to his waist in two long plaits, looking like he'd just come back from a raid.

Rebecca watched the way Morgan's large hand ever-so-gently gripped the delicate coffee cup and then slowly brought it to his lips. It was so hard for her to believe that this man—who had such impeccable manners—could possibly be some war chief that the army was looking for—according to her cousin Samantha . . .

Morgan found it amusing, the way Rebecca was ogling him. But there probably wasn't very many Indians roaming the streets of Boston. He'd noticed the chestnut-haired beauty when she had entered the dining room. She looked so much like Samantha, he had been instantly drawn to her. Morgan had never seen a more beautiful woman. And oh, how he would love nothing better than to run his fingers through all that rich, glorious mane of hair. Rebecca's large, brown eyes, with those long, sooty lashes, reminded him of a frightened doe.

When she lifted her lashes and looked directly at him, Morgan winked at her. He grinned broadly, when he noticed her blush.

Rebecca inwardly groaned, mortified that Morgan had caught her watching him. She wanted to leap out of her chair and run from the room. She anxiously glanced around the table, wondering if anybody else had noticed; the man might as well have stood out of his chair and announce in front of everyone that she'd been watching him like a hungry tigress. He was still looking at her with that smirking grin. Rebecca wished she was as bold as Samantha, then she might have gotten up the nerve to walk around the table and slap that smirk clean off his handsome face . . .

"What's the matter with you, Becca?" Ruth whispered to her daughter. "You've hardly touched your food. And your face is flushed . . . are you all right?"

"Yes, Mama."

Hearing Morgan chuckle, Rebecca lifted her face and scowled at him.

Samantha leaned back in her chair, grinning. Unless she was mistaken, there seemed to be some kind of attraction between Morgan and Rebecca. She wondered if anybody else had noticed. Her eyes moved slowly around the table, until they came to rest upon the tall man seated in the chair beside her. Samantha frowned. Obviously the only thing Chandler was paying any attention to was the platter of food in front of him. Her brows knitted together in annoyance, as she watched him shovel several bites of food into his mouth.

"You might take the time to chew," she whispered in his ear.

Chandler threw back his head and laughed.

"Let us all in on the joke over there, Samantha," John said. "What's so funny?"

With all eyes now on her, Samantha self-consciously stammered, "I . . . a . . . was just commenting to Chandler about . . . about his appetite."

"There's nothing funny about that," John's tone was serious.

Every person sitting around the table burst out with laughter, except for Chandler.

"Stop picking on the poor man, John," Rachel scolded her husband, trying to keep a straight face. "There's nothing wrong with a healthy appetite."

"Then Chandler is one of the healthiest men I know," James couldn't resist.

More hoots of laughter.

"I'm still recovering from my wounds and I need the extra nourishment," Chandler said in his defense.

"I wonder who can eat more, Chandler or Sarah," this from John. He chuckled when his daughter-in-law blushed. "It's okay, Sarah, at least you have a good reason to eat so much."

"John Callahan, you should be ashamed of yourself."

"Now, Rach, Sarah knows I was only teasing her."

"You think this is bad, Pa, you should see her at home. She never stops eating."

"James!" Sarah gasped.

John burst out laughing. "It's okay, Sarah. You're among family here, and we got plenty of food, so you can eat as much as you want." Chuckling, he tossed his napkin on top of the table, and scooted out of his chair. "Any of you men up for a game of poker? I think Amos and Ernie's got a card game goin' out in the bunkhouse."

"I'm right behind ya, Pa." James hastily pecked his wife on the cheek, then followed his father out of the dining room.

"You comin', Graywolf?" Morgan asked as he got to his feet. "Or are you going to use your wounds as an excuse to stay here with the womenfolk?"

Chandler scowled at his brother as he pushed back his chair. "I'm comin'."

After the last man had ducked through the arched doorway, Ruth remarked, "You know . . . it's amazing how quickly men can clear a room. And notice how much more quieter it is now."

The ladies had a good laugh.

"Would anyone like more coffee?" Rachel asked.

"I would."

Rachel filled her sister's cup, then set the coffeepot back on the table. "Samantha, now that you're safely home and Amos and the boys are back—if we all pitch in—I can't see any reason why we couldn't have everything ready for your wedding by this weekend. That is, if you don't mind getting married a little sooner than planned?"

"Aunt Rachel, I'd be glad to help with whatever needs to be done," Rebecca happily volunteered. "I'm pretty good with a needle and thread."

"That's good to know, Becca," Rachel said with a smile. She looked to her daughter. "Well, Samantha, what do you say?"

"I suppose I could be available this weekend," she replied in a teasing tone. "But I probably should confirm it with Chandler first."

She seriously added more to herself, "With all the problems we've had, he might've changed his mind about us getting married."

Samantha found Chandler inside the barn, forking some hay to old Suzie and her colt. She noticed he was moving a little stiff. Personally, she thought Chandler should still be in bed taking it easy, but there was no convincing the stubborn man. He looked over his shoulder, and smiled, when he saw her.

"What a pleasant surprise," Chandler said, straightening and leaning on the pitchfork.

"How would you like to get married this weekend?" Samantha blurted out. "It was my mother's idea," she added at his shocked expression. "Look—if you'd rather wait . . ."

"I just wasn't expecting to hear you say that. Sounds to me like you're the one who's a little hesitant."

"It's not that."

"What is it then?"

Samantha let out a long sigh. "I always manage to get into trouble . . . you said so yourself—and as much as I hate to admit it, it's true. I also heard what you said to Ernie the other day . . . how much you sympathize with my father."

Chandler burst out with laughter.

"I don't see what's so funny!"

"I was only joking, Samantha."

"It didn't sound like you were joking."

Leaning the pitchfork against the wall, Chandler moved closer to Samantha and took her angelic face into his big hands; then he ever-so-tenderly placed a kiss upon her lips. "Don't you know by now—how much I love you?" When he saw tears glistening in her brilliant blue eyes, his throat tightened with emotion. "If you ever doubt anything about me, Samantha Callahan, never doubt that I love you."

"Oh, Chandler!" She threw her arms around him and hugged him tightly. She heard him grunt in pain and immediately let go of him. "I'm sorry . . . I forgot about your back."

"It's okay."

"Maybe you should have Ma take a look . . ."

"My back's fine, Samantha. It's just still a little sore . . . nothing to worry about."

"Am I interrupting something?" a masculine voice said behind them.

Chandler whirled around. "Dang it, Morgan! Can't you warn a person when you're there?"

"I'll try to make more noise the next time."

Samantha wondered how long Morgan had been standing there—not that she and Chandler had done anything wrong—she just felt a little embarrassed that Morgan had witnessed her and Chandler in a very private moment.

"I'd better get back to the house," Samantha announced. She scowled at Morgan, then turned and strode out of the barn door.

"Has anybody ever told you, you have the worst possible timing!" Chandler snapped.

Morgan only shrugged in reply.

As Samantha burst through the front door, she collided with her aunt. "Oh, Aunt Ruth, I didn't see you! I'm so sorry . . . ! Are you okay?"

"There was no harm done," Ruth replied, rubbing her smarting backside. "I have plenty of cushion in the spot where you got me—though you might check the door for damage."

Samantha couldn't help grin.

"What's the hurry, dear?"

"Aunt Ruth, did you ever have . . ." Samantha suddenly snapped her mouth shut.

"You'll have to be a little bit more specific than that." Sensing there was something troubling her niece, Ruth wordlessly walked over and slipped an arm around her shoulder, then herded the girl toward the parlor.

Once inside the room, Ruth closed the door behind them. There were a pair of matching leather chairs positioned in front of the stone fireplace, so she sat down in one of the chairs, then motioned for Samantha to sit in the other. Then she folded her hands in her lap, patiently waiting for her niece to take her seat.

After a while, when Samantha still hadn't said anything, Ruth decided she would start the conversation. "Did you and your young man have a fight, dear?"

Samantha shook her head.

"Then what could possibly cause such a look of despair on such a beautiful face?"

"Oh, Aunt Ruth, I'm just so afraid that . . . that Chandler . . . that he might . . . maybe we shouldn't get married."

"Why would you say such a thing?"

Rising, Samantha began to pace back and forth. "I can't even cook for crying out loud. The only thing I know how to do is . . . is chase cows around a field." She stopped and turned to face her aunt. "I'm nothing like Becca, Aunt Ruth. It's so obvious that Becca will make some man a good wife someday. What kind of wife will I be to Chandler?"

"I doubt Chandler cares whether you can cook or not."

Samantha folded her arms across her chest and seriously said, "Have you ever seen him eat?"

Ruth pressed her lips together to keep from smiling, and patted the chair next to her. "Have a seat, dear." She was pretty sure what was really bothering her niece was simple wedding jitters, so she thought that maybe a funny story would help take the girl's mind off her fears. "Did your mother ever tell you . . . ?" she started to say, then shook her head. "No . . . I don't suppose Rachel would."

"Tell me what, Aunt Ruth?"

"Just thinking about it makes me laugh."

"Please, tell me what you're talking about?"

"First, Samantha, you have to promise me that you will *never* utter a word to your folks. They would both have my head if they found out I told you."

"I promise."

"What happened was quite embarrassing." Ruth giggled and added, "Looking back now, the whole situation was rather hilarious . . ."

"Aunt Ruth!" Samantha was becoming more exasperated.

"Okay . . . let's see . . . where should I start . . . ? Well—your mother and I were still living at home with our parents when this happened. Rachel was engaged to John, and I was about to marry your Uncle Bernard. I had some last minute shopping to do, so Ma and Pa had taken me into town that day—and I remember how blatantly your mother had insisted on staying home. None of us knew at the time that Rachel had invited John over . . ."

"Maybe you shouldn't be telling me this, Aunt Ruth."

"Nonsense," Ruth said with a wave of her hand. "Besides, I'm not going to give you every little detail . . . what happened could happen to anybody." She quirked a brow and added in a teasing tone, "Even to someone as prudish as your mother."

Samantha giggled.

"Let's see, where was I . . . ? Oh, my folks had taken me into town to do some shopping. I got done got a lot quicker than anticipated, so we came home quite unexpectedly. We had just pulled up in front of the house and was still seated in the carriage when . . . how can I delicately put this?" Ruth paused, then said, "Your father—in his haste to get out of the house—jumped through your mother's bedroom window, wearing nothing but his underdrawers."

Samantha gasped.

"I should stress at this point that nothing happened. But if you could have seen the look on your grandfather's face, Samantha, as we sat there in that carriage, watching John running to his horse in his underdrawers." Ruth started to laugh. "And this is the best part yet . . . your father had to ride through town that way—in broad daylight."

Suddenly peals of laughter filled the room. Samantha could easily picture in her mind, the way her father must have looked, trotting down the main street of town. By now she was laughing so hard, she clutched at her stomach.

"For the longest time, John was known around town as *Mister Godiva*," Ruth said, laughing.

Samantha howled with laughter, wondering how she would ever look at either of her parents without bursting out laughing.

Chapter Twenty-six

The next morning at the breakfast table, Samantha would snicker and cover her mouth, whenever her mother or father would even look at her. She was having difficulty just keeping a straight face. After a while, her Aunt Ruth tried to cover for her strange behavior by telling everybody some silly joke. But when her father innocently asked her to pass him the 'buns', it was finally Samantha's undoing. She suddenly burst out with peals of laughter.

"All right, Samantha . . . what's so funny?" John demanded to know. "You've been sitting over there, cackling all morning. I'm surprised you haven't laid an egg."

Everybody sitting around the table all had a big laugh over that, except for Rachel, who eyed her daughter suspiciously. "Young lady, have you been in your father's liquor cabinet?"

Samantha sobered immediately. That her mother could even think she might have indulged in her father's liquor wasn't funny. "*No*, I have not. May I please be excused?"

"Not until you tell me what's going on."

"But, Pa . . ."

Ruth cleared her throat. "Maybe I should explain."

John raised a curious brow toward his sister-in-law. If she was involved, then anything was possible. "Well, Ruth—I'm waiting."

"I told Samantha about the *Godiva* story," she matter-of-factly replied.

Rachel gasped. "Ruthie, you didn't!"

"Everyone leave the table at once!" John suddenly bellowed. Fighting to control the anger in his voice, he more calmly added, "Except for *you*, Ruth."

"Naturally."

"And *you*, young lady, stay in your seat," John firmly told Samantha when she started to get out of her chair.

"Pa, how about letting us in on the little family secret?" James was grinning from ear to ear.

"Don't you have a ranch of your own?" John snapped.

"John!"

"Then let the boy stay, Rachel! I'm sure James would get a kick out of what he might hear!"

Rachel turned to her son. "I agree with your father . . . you and Sarah should leave the room. Morgan, Chandler, Rebecca, would you mind giving us a little privacy?"

"Come on, Sarah," James said to his wife as he helped her out of her chair. "I think we'd better disappear for a while."

Morgan and Rebecca quickly followed James and Sarah out of the room, but Chandler stubbornly remained in his seat. Leaning back in his chair, he looked at his soon-to-be-father-in-law, casually folding his arms across his chest.

"If this involves Samantha, I'm not going anywhere," he finally remarked.

John frowned, but he didn't say anything.

It was Rachel who began to question her sister. "Surely, Ruthie, you didn't tell Samantha the *entire* story, did you?"

"Yes, pretty much."

"But why?"

"The girl needed a bona fide laugh."

"And I'm sure she got one!" John hissed.

"Will somebody please tell me what's going on?" Chandler finally asked.

"Never you mind, young man," Rachel told him.

"Oh, come on now, Rachel, John . . . there's no need to get yourselves all worked up over something that happened years ago." Ruth started to laugh as she added, "You can't deny, it is rather funny, when you think about it."

John scowled at his sister-in-law. "You would think it's funny."

There was complete silence at the table then. Chandler looked questioningly at Samantha, who bowed her head, refusing to look him in the eye. Suddenly Rachel burst out laughing. Now John was laughing; and so was Samantha and Ruth. The way everybody was acting was driving Chandler crazy. "Will somebody please let me in on the joke?"

When Rachel noticed that glint in her husband's eyes, she nearly screeched at him, "John Callahan, don't you dare!"

Later that afternoon, Morgan questioned Chandler about John and Rachel's curious behavior at breakfast that morning. Unfortunately, Chandler couldn't tell him a thing. He'd tried getting an answer out of Samantha, but she wouldn't even discuss the matter.

"Have you ever noticed that whenever there's trouble, Samantha is always involved in some way or another?" Morgan commented.

"Well, this time, I think she's only *indirectly* involved." At Morgan's burst of laughter, Chandler frowned. "Let's just see how well you do with Becca?"

"What's that suppose to mean?"

"It *means*—I saw the way you were ogling Rebecca at breakfast this morning. I'm surprised you didn't get down on your knee and ask for the girl's hand in marriage."

"Strictly out of mild curiosity, what do you think Rebecca's answer would have been?"

"So you *are* smitten with Becca," Chandler said, grinning.

"I won't deny I find her attractive."

"Attractive, huh? Well—let's just hope for your sake that Becca's nothing like the rest of the Callahan family."

"I know what you're getting at, Graywolf. For your information, Rebecca might look like Samantha, but that's where their similarities end."

"Trust me on this, Morgan. There's bound to be a temper hidden somewhere beneath that meek-and-mild demeanor."

"Don't be confusing Rebecca with that hot-tempered *wildcat* you're about to marry. Speaking of the wildcat . . . here she comes," Morgan said with a nod.

Chandler turned and watched as Samantha rapidly shortened the distance between them. He noticed the swiftness of her stride, the determination in her expression.

Something was wrong . . .

"Lieutenant Brown's here again," Samantha announced.

"I don't believe it!" Chandler hissed. "Better hide inside the barn, Morgan, before he sees you." He saw his brother's eyes harden. "Don't you dare try anything stupid . . . I mean it, Morgan. I'll personally get rid of Lieutenant Brown myself, so don't you dare show your face outside that barn till I say!"

"I'm not going to hide like some coward every time that man comes here!"

"For now you have no other choice!"

"Please, Morgan," Samantha then tried to reason with him.

"Oh, alright."

Chandler waited until his brother was safely inside the barn, then he angrily whirled and started walking toward the house. Samantha practically had to run to keep up with him. She was beginning to have some serious doubts about her plan—it was only a matter of time before Lieutenant Brown figured out that Chandler looked like the drawing on his Wanted poster—maybe that was the reason he was here. There were many details about her so called 'brilliant plan' that she hadn't taken in consideration . . .

"Where is the lieutenant?" Chandler wanted to know.

"He's on the veranda . . . Becca's with him."

Seated in a chair beside Rebecca, Samantha glared at Lieutenant Brown. It infuriated her, the way the man interrogated Chandler like some common criminal.

"I never did catch your full name . . . Chandler, isn't it?"

"I never gave it."

Jason swore he was looking at Black Hawk—this Indian looked exactly like the one in the drawing—but he couldn't be absolutely certain. According to the information he was given, Black Hawk was said to be somewhere in his early to mid-twenties, whereas this man was more likely in his early thirties. Then something occurred to Jason: maybe this man was Black Hawk's brother? He looked enough like the Indian in the drawing to be his twin.

"How about I just call you, Chief." Jason hadn't meant for that to slip out—not yet.

Samantha shot to her feet. "How dare you!"

"Why are you here, Brown?" Chandler angrily inquired.

"I came here to see Rebecca. I guess I should apologize for my remark."

It was on the tip of Samantha's tongue to tell this man what he could do with his *fake* apology, but a look from Chandler snapped her mouth shut. She dropped back down in her chair.

Rebecca was beginning to see the real Lieutenant Jason Brown, and she didn't like what she saw. She didn't appreciate him using her for an excuse to come by the ranch to snoop around, because it was so obvious that's exactly what he was doing. *Samantha had been right about him all along! Well, he wasn't going to get away with it . . .*

Rebecca rose to her feet. "Now that you've seen me, Lieutenant, I think you should leave." She felt a sort of smug satisfaction when she saw the look of surprise that came over Jason's handsome face. He hadn't expected her to turn him away—the man really did have an ego.

Fighting to control his inner rage, Jason slowly got to his feet. "Maybe I was wrong to assume that you were a lady . . ." The punch came out of no where, knocking Jason clear off the veranda and he landed on the hard ground as pain exploded in the left side of his cheek. He sat there, rubbing his throbbing jaw, glaring at the Indian.

"If I were you, Brown, I would get on my horse and ride out of here, before I really lose my temper!" Chandler was so furious, he was shaking. And it was taking every ounce of his self-control not to physically attack him again.

"That was real stupid, Indian," Jason said through gritted teeth, getting to his feet. "I could have you arrested for what you just did!" he furiously spat, brushing the dirt off his britches.

"Try it, Brown, and you'll answer to me," came an ominous warning behind him.

Jason swung around. "You're sticking your nose where it don't belong, Callahan!"

"Get off my property, before I have my men escort you off!"

"My commander will hear about this!"

As John stood there watching the man mount his horse, he hollered out, "If I ever catch you anywhere near my niece again, I'll shoot first and ask questions later!"

"I'm so sorry, Uncle John."

"This isn't your fault, Rebecca," John firmly told his niece, before turning to Chandler. "You know Brown will be back and he won't come alone the next time. I think you and Morgan should leave here immediately. You boys could stay out at the cabin for a while. I don't think the army will find you there."

"Please, Chandler, do what Pa suggested," Samantha urged him. "We can postpone our wedding a little longer."

"I can't speak for Morgan, but I'm not going anywhere." Then to Rebecca, he said, "Would you mind telling my brother the lieutenant's gone . . . he's in the barn."

Not caring whether her father heard, Samantha angrily turned on Chandler. "I don't want to be a widow before I'm even married!"

"I *will not* run from that arrogant, glory-seeking lieutenant!"

"Then you give me no other choice, Chandler, but to call off our wedding until you come to your senses!"

"Then you might as well call it off indefinitely, because I won't change my mind!"

John finally intervened. "Samantha, I know you're getting too old for me to tell you what to do, but for once hold that sharp tongue of yours!"

"But, Pa . . ."

"No buts, young lady! I'm beginning to think that I was wrong to allow you so much independence! After all, a woman has her place!"

"Does she now?" came an angry female voice.

John hadn't heard his wife step outside the door. She stood there, fists planted on her hips, a stern expression on her face. "Now, Rachel, I only meant that . . ."

"I know exactly what you meant, John Callahan! I came out here to tell you that your lunch is ready! If anybody needs me, I'll be in the kitchen . . . where a woman belongs!" Rachel then hiked up her skirt and stormed back inside the house, slamming the door behind her.

Samantha giggled. "You were saying, Pa?"

"It's all your fault your mother's mad at me." John scowled at Chandler when he burst out laughing. "I wouldn't laugh if I were you . . . your turn's comin'."

Rebecca stood inside the barn, listening to the sound of Morgan's laughter, as he ran a brush over the colt's back. It was hard to believe that a man as big as Morgan could be so gentle. He was dressed in a western shirt and a pair of jeans today, though he still wore his knee high moccasins. She had to admit that Morgan was even more handsome in buckskins; somehow he looked out of place wearing white men's clothes. He wore his long, coal-black hair in a queue that hung way down his back, which she found very attractive.

She covered her mouth and giggled, when the colt suddenly bolted away, and the sudden movement caused him to trip over his own feet.

Morgan got up, brushing bits of hay off his pants. "So . . . did you have a nice visit with Lieutenant Brown?"

Rebecca started walking forward. "He's gone. Chandler sent me here to tell you."

"Your *beau* sure didn't stay very long."

"He's not my beau."

As Rebecca halted in front of Morgan, her head automatically tilted back to compensate his extreme height. At this close proximity, she noticed that he had the most beautiful eyes. They were so dark, she could actually see her own reflection mirrored in their depths. And what a woman wouldn't give for those long lashes . . .

They silently gazed into each others' eyes for quite some time. And for a moment there, Rebecca thought that Morgan wanted to kiss her, then he suddenly brushed past her and strode out of the barn without a word or a backward glance . . .

Morgan's long strides carried him swiftly toward the house. He wondered what Rebecca would have done if he had pulled her into his arms and kissed her, like he'd wanted to. Since they barely knew each other, it would have been highly improper, though he'd never been real concerned about proprieties. But Rebecca was probably a stickler about such things, and more than likely would have thought he was no better than a heathen, like so many other people did. A true gentleman would never take such liberties with a lady. *So maybe he was no gentleman*, Morgan thought bitterly.

Graywolf and John were standing on the veranda, Morgan noticed, with their heads locked together in what appeared to be a very serious conversation, so naturally he assumed those solemn expressions must have something to do with Lieutenant Brown. The man was turning out to be a real thorn in his backside . . .

"What's the problem?" he asked, climbing the few steps to stand beside his brother.

"Maybe you'll listen to reason, Morgan," John said. "I think you and Chandler should leave here immediately and stay out at the cabin for a while. Brown will be back with more men . . . you can count on it. Who knows, Bad-Boy-Brown could be rounding up some men as we speak. By the way, Chandler, I suggest you forget about Samantha's plan . . . that crazy lieutenant arrests you, they're liable to throw away the key."

"I already thought of that."

"Maybe if the army can't locate Black Hawk pretty soon, they'll pull up camp and leave town, because I doubt they'll want to stick around through the winter."

"What do you think we should do, Graywolf?" Morgan respected his brother's opinion.

"I say, if we don't see this thing through now, we'll just have to fight the lieutenant another day. But it's you, Morgan, who stands to lose the most." Chandler shrugged and added, "If you want to leave, I'll go with you . . . whatever you decide is okay by me."

"John, what will happen to you if I'm caught here?" Morgan wanted to know.

"I suppose, the worst that could possibly happen, I could be arrested. But I'm not worried about that. I'm willing to take the risk . . ."

"Well I'm not."

John put a comforting hand on Morgan's shoulder. "Son, whether you like it or not, you've become part of this family, and family sticks together, no matter what. What if it was the other way around—" John challenged, "what would *you* do?"

"Tell me then, John, if you thought your mere presence could possibly endanger others, would you not leave?" Morgan countered. "And what of your wife and daughter? If something happened to you, what would become of them?"

John did not respond.

"Graywolf will remain here, but I will leave tonight," Morgan announced with finality.

"I said I'm coming with you . . ."

"No! This is where you belong, Graywolf."

The back door slamming shut drew the mens' attention. Samantha folded her arms across her chest, her angry gaze narrowing on Chandler. "Why is it that men treat women like they have no intelligence . . . especially Indian men? Wade Chandler, don't you think I should be included on decisions that could affect my future as well as yours?"

"But you're the one who suggested that I leave in the first place."

"That's not what I'm talking about!"

"Then what exactly *are* you talking about?"

"If this is the way that it's going to be after we're married then . . . then I'm not so sure that I want to marry you!"

"Samantha!" John angrily intervened. "That kind of talk is uncalled for!"

"Pa, you don't understand . . ."

"No, I'm afraid I don't!"

"Neither do I!" Chandler snapped at Samantha. "And you know—the more I think about it, woman, you're just too darn argumentative for my taste!"

"Then I assume you'll be leaving!"

"You assume correctly!"

"Good." Without another word, Samantha whirled and stormed back inside the house, slamming the door shut.

Samantha ignored the curious stares from her mother and Aunt Ruth who were sitting at the table as she hurriedly crossed the kitchen. She raced up the wide stairway to her room, closing the door behind her, where she burst into tears. She walked over to look out the window toward the barn, wondering if Chandler would really leave. Part of her was hoping he would, while another part of her was afraid he wouldn't . . .

Her bedroom door suddenly crashed open. Samantha looked over shoulder surprised to see both of her parents standing in her room. Her father was wearing an angry scowl, glaring at her; her mother just looked confused.

"Please go away."

"Not until you tell me, what's gotten into you, Samantha?" John angrily retorted.

"John, maybe . . ."

"Stay out of this, Rachel!"

"I didn't mean all those awful things I said, Pa," Samantha suddenly cried. "It was the only way I could think of to get Chandler to leave the ranch. You know if he stays here, Lieutenant Brown will arrest him . . . Morgan too, if he decides to stay."

"John, what is Samantha talking about?"

He let out a sigh. "Guess I'd better explain."

Rebecca stared out the kitchen window, trying to memorize every detail about Morgan's handsome profile, while he spoke with his brother Chandler. She had overheard them talking about leaving the ranch, possibly tonight. If it was true, she may never see Morgan again, because she and her mother would be heading back to Boston soon and it would probably be years before they would ever return for a visit. Though she had just met Morgan and it was still far too soon to understand exactly what it was that she felt for the man, she wanted the chance to explore these new feelings.

Even if she was betrothed to another, Rebecca thought with dread. Just thinking about Albert caused her stomach to churn. He was her father's partner in the law firm. It was her father who had promised Albert her hand in marriage; she'd had no say in the matter. Rebecca personally couldn't even stand the sight of Albert Smythers. For one thing, he was much older than she, but it was Albert's extremely domineering personality that she loathed. He was always trying to boss her around and they weren't even married yet. Rebecca wanted nothing to do with the man, yet she could not go against her father's wishes. *Or could she?* Her engagement to Albert was something she would have to discuss with her mother.

Of course it was quite possible that she and her mother could end up staying here in Bear Creek—on a permanent basis, Rebecca mused. Though that would mean there'd be no chance for a reconciliation between her parents, and she didn't want that; but neither was she ready to leave this place just yet.

Rebecca looked over her shoulder at her mother. It was good to see her smiling again. She had not seen her mother this happy for a long, long time and she certainly didn't want to spoil that happiness. She was still contemplating whether to tell her mother that she knew all about her father's mistress. In fact, Rebecca had known about Bell for quite some time now . . .

"Our tea's ready, Becca," Ruth said, setting the teapot on the kitchen table.

Rebecca moved away from the window and walked over to sit at the table across from her mother. She took a sip of tea from the delicate, rose-painted cup.

"This place is so peaceful, I think I could live here forever," Ruth remarked.

"What about Papa?"

"What about him?"

"I don't think Papa would like it here."

"And I couldn't expect him to give up his business."

"You mean he couldn't give up Bell," Rebecca suddenly blurted out.

Ruth gasped, spewing tea all over the table. "How did you . . . ? Her eyes narrowed into angry slits. "Who told you about bell?" she demanded to know.

"Mama, I swear sometimes you and Papa seem to forget that I'm no longer a child. I've known about Bell for years."

Ruth's brows shot up in surprise. "Then you've known about the woman longer than I have." She waved a hand. "How long your father's been with Bell, it doesn't really matter. And now that you know about the woman . . ." Ruth let out a sigh. "I guess you might as well know the rest. There's been other women in the past."

Now it was Rebecca's turn to look surprised. "Mama, then how could you stay with him?"

After a period of silence, Ruth informed her daughter, "Well—now that you mentioned it—guess you might as well be the first to know that I've decided to leave your father. This wasn't an easy decision, Becca. But your father has been promising me for years that he would stop seeing other women, and obviously that is a promise he will never keep."

"You should have left him long ago," Rebecca gently told her mother.

"Look, Becca, you mustn't let this come between you and your father. He loves you, dear, and I don't want anything to interfere with that."

Personally Rebecca thought her father loved his law firm and Albert more, but she kept her opinion to herself. Though she did say,

"Papa could sure take a lesson from Uncle John about how to treat his wife."

"Yes, he certainly could," Ruth agreed. "Your Uncle John is quite a man. He hasn't changed a bit after all these years."

"Oh, I wouldn't say that," came a baritone voice.

Ruth's eyes swung toward the doorway. She blushed seeing her brother-in-law standing there, knowing he'd heard what she said. Rachel stood beside him, laughing.

"I appreciate the compliment, Ruth," John said, grinning. He started across the floor. "If you ladies will excuse me." He winked at his sister-in-law, before exiting out the back door.

"I can't believe your mother's blushing," Rachel whispered to Rebecca as she sat in an empty chair at the table. "That's something you don't see every day."

Rebecca giggled.

"Honestly, Ruthie—must you swell my husband's head?"

"There isn't a vain bone in John's body. Now if he were anything like Bernard, you would have to spoon-feed the man's ego on a daily basis. John probably only needs a small bite now and then."

Rachel and Rebecca burst out laughing.

Chapter Twenty-seven

Rebecca watched the handsome Indian as he cantered the black stallion across the field. Leaning against one of the wide pillars that supported the covered front porch, her eyes remained fixed upon on Morgan, until he was hardly more than a moving speck. Already her young heart felt like it was breaking . . .

"Morgan will be back, Becca."

"He didn't even say good-bye, Samantha," she sniffled.

"You care about him, don't you?"

"Yes, I do . . . very much." She swiped away the tears that started to fall. "I thought Chandler was supposed to go with Morgan?"

"Against my father's advice, he decided to stay." Samantha wasn't sure why Chandler had changed his mind, but she was glad that he had. "Say—I'm riding over to James and Sarah's in the morning . . . would you like to come along?"

"I would love to, except . . ."

"What?"

"I can't ride."

"We just happen to have a mare that's so gentle, you don't have to know how to ride."

Rebecca smiled. "Then it sounds like fun."

"We'll be leaving pretty early in the morning."

"Then I'll hit the hay right after supper."

Samantha grinned at her cousin. Since Rebecca had been here, she'd managed to pick up some of the cowboys' lingo.

As Samantha lay in bed that night, her disturbing thoughts were on Chandler. He should have gone with Morgan. Now she feared for his safety. Lieutenant Brown was a desperate man, and at this point he would probably settle for any Indian who even remotely looked like Black Hawk—which made Chandler a sitting duck—considering he looked enough like Morgan the man could just about be his twin. Why the sudden change of heart when he'd been so adamant about leaving with Morgan earlier that day? she wondered. Knowing Chandler the way she did, he probably meant to face the lieutenant on his own.

After such a sleepless night, Samantha was finally beginning to feel a little more invigorated as she and Rebecca cantered their horses across the grassy meadow. The troubled dreams that had plagued her mind the previous night about Chandler, now seemed silly. Samantha had just about convinced herself that she was worrying over nothing when she saw the long column of men riding toward them.

Her eyes narrowed on the young lieutenant leading the way. "Well he certainly didn't waste any time," she angrily spat, pulling back on the reins.

Rebecca halted beside her. "What should we do?"

"Find out what he wants." Though Samantha already had a pretty good idea what would bring the lieutenant out to the Callahan ranch at this hour of the morning.

"It's a good thing Morgan left when he did," Rebecca remarked.

"And Chandler should've gone with him," Samantha muttered more to herself.

Watching Lieutenant Brown's approach, Samantha noted the man's smug expression. She sat up straighter in the saddle and squared her shoulders, refusing to be intimidated by this man. She immediately informed him, "You're on Callahan property," the moment he halted his horse in front of her.

Ignoring the woman's sarcasm, "Good day, ladies," Jason cheerfully greeted them. He politely tipped his hat to Rebecca. "And it's especially nice to see you, Miss Smith," then he gave her his most charming smile.

Rebecca frowned at him.

Jason tried to conceal his irritation. "Where are you ladies headed?"

"In case you didn't hear me, Lieutenant, you're trespassing on Callahan land," Samantha more loudly stated. "So say whatever's on your mind, then get off our property!"

Some of his men began to snicker.

"Silence!" Jason shouted over his shoulder.

His head snapped back around. "Very well, Miss Callahan." So far Jason had managed to keep his temper under control, but this rancher's daughter was pushing him to his limits. He wasn't used to people telling him what to do, 'specially some pushy woman who acted more like a man. "I'm headed to your house to arrest Black Hawk."

"Is this some kind of sick joke?" Just what Samantha had been dreading.

"I assure you, it's no joke. And you can stop pretending you don't know what I'm talking about, Miss Callahan. I believe you introduced him as your—*fiancé*."

"You mean Chandler?" Samantha said incredulously. "Chandler's no more Black Hawk than you are—Lieutenant." She grinned to herself with smug satisfaction when several of his men burst out with laughter.

"The next man who even opens his mouth will be placed on permanent guard duty!" Jason spat venomously. Then to the Callahan woman, he hissed, "I'm not here to argue with some silly spoiled rancher's brat!"

"There's no need to be insulting, *Mister* Brown," Samantha tauntingly retorted. "Besides, Chandler isn't at the ranch." Which was true, thankfully. He'd gone into town with her father to pick up some supplies . . . naturally she wasn't about to divulge that bit of information. The lieutenant must've left town before Chandler and her father had gotten there.

"I'll just have a look for myself!"

"You'll be wasting your time, Lieutenant."

"Chandler really isn't there, Jason," Rebecca added in a pleading tone, hoping he would take her word for it and just go away.

"*You* I believe, Rebecca, but me and my men will hang around the ranch until he returns." Jason nudged his horse into a walk. "Good day, ladies," he threw over his shoulder as he rode past them.

Samantha waited for the long column of soldiers to ride by, before turning to Rebecca. "I've got to ride into town and warn my father and Chandler. Do you think you could find your way to my brother's place on your own?"

Rebecca nodded, trying to hide her fear. After all, she wasn't very familiar with this part of the country, nor its hostile inhabitants.

"If you keep riding in this same direction—maybe another few miles—" Samantha told her, "you'll eventually run straight into the house . . . you can't miss it. When you get there, tell James what's happened . . . he'll know what to do."

"Be careful, Samantha."

"You too, Becca."

Samantha spurred her mount into a full gallop toward town. As she raced across the meadow, panic was already threatening to take hold of her, knowing Lieutenant Brown would be waiting at the ranch to arrest Chandler, the moment he showed his face. *She just couldn't allow that to happen!* Leaning over the horse's neck, she urged the little chestnut mare to go faster. *Dang!* If only she'd ridden Daisy she would have been half way to town by now.

John gulped the rest of his whiskey, slammed the empty glass down on the table, and looked seriously at Chandler, who was seated across from him. "This is all my fault; if anybody's to blame, it's me. I gave Samantha way too much free rein. When you two get married, Chandler, I'm afraid that you might be in for a rough time for a while. She can be quite a handful."

"You're not telling me nothing I already don't know."

A dark brow rose. "You haven't changed your mind about marrying her, have you?"

Chandler threw back his head and laughed heartily. "What's the matter, John . . . afraid you might still be stuck with the tyrant?"

He frowned. "It might've crossed my mind."

"I'm well aware of your daughter's . . . independence," Chandler said, laughing.

"That's putting it rather mildly. You can be honest about what you really think."

"I was," Chandler chuckled. "And no, I haven't changed my mind."

"Brave man." John quickly drained another glass of whiskey.

Glancing around the spacious room, Chandler smiled to himself. This was the place where it had all began . . . where he'd first laid eyes on Samantha . . . where he had accosted some drunken cowpoke (Ralf—he couldn't remember the man's last name) for putting his hands on her. Why it seemed like only yesterday when the *spitfire* had stepped through those same swinging doors and . . .

"I don't believe it!"

"What's the matter?" John said.

"The result of what can happen when too much free rein has been given!"

"What are you talking about?"

"Look behind you."

Twisting in his chair, John muttered an oath under his breath, when he spotted his daughter meandering through the crowded room toward them. "Samantha Callahan, you can just turn around and march yourself right back out of here at once!"

"I came here to warn Chandler, Pa . . . Lieutenant Brown and a bunch of soldiers are waiting at the ranch to arrest him."

John was already out of his chair and heading toward the batwing doors. Chandler grabbed hold of Samantha's arm and hurried after John.

They were getting close to the ranch and by now Samantha was nearly panic-stricken with worry, because Chandler insisted on "meeting his enemy head-on" and stubbornly refused to listen to reason. *Men and their foolish pride!* Samantha inwardly raged. Well, she wasn't about to just sit back and do nothing, while the man she loved was thrown behind bars by some egotistical maniac. Throwing Chandler a look of determination, Samantha nudged her horse at a faster pace to catch up with her father . . .

"You can't let Chandler ride to the ranch."

John shrugged. "I've already tried to talk him out of it."

"Then you'll just have to change his mind!"

"And what do you suggest I do, Samantha? Chandler is a grown man—I can't force him to do something against his will."

A delicate brow rose in challenge. "Can't you?"

John frowned at his daughter. "Young lady, haven't you learned your lesson yet about interfering in a man's business? I don't agree with Chandler anymore than you do—but this is his decision."

"But, Pa . . ."

"Besides, having Chandler arrested to humiliate Brown . . . wasn't that *your* bright idea?"

"It was a bad idea," Samantha grudgingly admitted. She turned deploring eyes upon her father and said, "Please, Pa. Can't you think of something?"

"Oh, all right," John grumbled.

"What are you going to do?"

"Just keep your mouth shut and follow my lead."

Suddenly halting his horse, John swung out of the saddle. He then stooped over and picked up his horse's front leg, then pretended to poke around the hoof. He was feeling mighty guilty for what he was about to do.

"What's wrong, John . . . horse go lame?" Chandler asked, dismounting.

It was the last thing he said.

"Ouch!" John bellowed, grasping his throbbing hand. "The man has a jaw like a piece of iron!"

"I hope he's still alive," Samantha angrily complained as she bent over Chandler to examine the side of his bruised face.

"Look—this was your idea."

"I didn't know you were going to knock him senseless. Now what?"

"Scoot over," John ordered. He proceeded to remove Chandler's belt, then turned the unconscious man over onto his stomach and started to slash his wrists together.

"Pa, what are you doing?"

"What's it look like I'm doing?"

"But . . ."

"Didn't you ask for my help, Samantha?"

"Yes, but . . ."

"This was the only thing I could think of to do."

John leaned back on his heels to study his handiwork. "That oughta hold the giant. Sorry 'bout that, Chandler." Rising, he hefted the big man over his shoulder—which was not an easy task—then carried him over to his horse and tossed him over the animal's back.

"What am I suppose to do with him?" Samantha wanted to know.

"Take him to James's place and keep him there, and don't untie him either."

"How long am I supposed to keep him like this?"

"Until I say otherwise!" John impatiently snapped as he swung into the saddle.

"Pa, where are you going?"

"The lieutenant and I are gonna have ourselves a little chat."

"Pa, wait!" Samantha shouted at her father's departing back, but it did no good.

Snatching up Ranger's reins, Samantha mounted her horse, then turned toward her brother's ranch, leading the unconscious Chandler behind her. Already serious doubts plagued her mind, wondering if she'd done the right thing. Chandler was going to be furious with her—and probably at her father too—for interfering again. But they were only trying to protect him.

Just as James's ranch house started to come into view, Samantha heard Chandler groan and then a thunk quickly followed. She looked over her shoulder to find Chandler lying sprawled out on the ground. Immediately jerking back on the reins, she climbed down from the saddle and hurried back to help Chandler to his feet.

"Are you okay?" she asked, taking hold of his arm.

"Don't touch me!" Chandler shouted at top of his lungs. He got to his feet and held his bound wrists out toward her. "Untie my hands this instant, Samantha!"

"I can't do that."

"I said untie my hands!" he thundered.

Samantha had never seen Chandler this enraged before, and actually took a leery step back away from him. She'd expected him to be angry, but . . .

"Pa told me not to untie your hands."

"Since when do you ever do what you're told?" he vehemently spat.

"Chandler, if you would just let me explain . . ."

"If I were you, I wouldn't say another word!"

As Chandler took a step toward her his pants dropped past his knees to pool at his feet. Samantha pressed her lips together to keep from busting out laughing.

"You and that . . . that iron-fisted father of yours are both lunatics!" he shouted in a rage.

"My father saved your blasted hide!" Samantha shouted back defensively.

"I don't see how knocking me out and tying my hands . . ."

"Because it was the only way my father could stop you from riding into Lieutenant Brown's trap, which is exactly what you would have done!"

Now that Chandler understood that John (in his own way) had only been trying to help, most of the anger went of him. "Where is your father?" he more calmly inquired.

"He went to confront Lieutenant Brown."

"John shouldn't have done that!"

"Pa knows what he's doing!"

"Untie my hands, Samantha! I mean it . . . I'm not joking!" Again Chandler stretched his bound wrists out to her.

She stubbornly folded her arms across her chest. "If you promise not to attack me, I'll help you with your britches, but I won't untie your hands."

"Did you stop to think that your father could be riding into the same trap that was meant for me?" Chandler thought to mention, hoping to put a little fear into her.

Samantha frowned. "We're going to my brother's," she suddenly announced. "James will know what to do. Now—shall I help you with your pants or not?"

"Do it!" Chandler hissed.

Retrieving a small length of rope from her saddle, Samantha secured Chandler's pants about his waist, ignoring his verbal warning that she would have to untie his hands sooner or later and when she did that she'd better get out of his way.

"Do you need some help getting back on your horse?" she asked.

Chandler glared at her.

Leading Chandler's horse behind her, Samantha continued toward her brother's ranch. She could see Rebecca standing on the front porch of the big two-story house: there was an urgency in the way she waved her arms high over her head; this was no greeting—something was wrong. She halted, then swung down from the saddle. She hastily looped both horses' reins around the hitch rail, while Chandler threw his leg over Ranger's head and dropped lightly to the ground.

"Becca, what's wrong?" Samantha hurried up the steps.

"Jason was here this morning with an entire troop and searched the premises . . . Maybe I shouldn't ask, but—why are Chandler's hands tied?"

"It's a long story. Let's go inside."

Chandler hopped up on the porch. "Yes, let's do go inside . . . hopefully James isn't as crazy as his father and sister."

Samantha rolled her eyes.

Rebecca waited until Chandler and Samantha were seated at the table, then she plopped into an empty chair. "What Jason neglected to tell us this morning, Samantha, was that he already had orders from a Colonel Lewis to search your ranch and this ranch. Jason believes that either Uncle John or Cousin James is harboring 'the enemy'. The instant they left here, James rode over to your place and I haven't seen him since. Poor Sarah took to her bed, the whole thing upset her so much."

"That sneaky slimy snake!" Samantha hissed.

"Then James isn't here?" Chandler questioned.

Rebecca shook her head. "Now will somebody please tell me—why are Chandler's hands tied behind his back?"

"Oh, please, let *Sam* explain this one," Chandler sarcastically said.

Samantha let out a long sigh, before trying to make some sense out of why her father had bound Chandler's hands—starting from the time they'd left the hurdy-gurdy-house. The way Samantha told the story, Rebecca personally thought what Uncle John had done to Chandler was rather comical. But there was nothing funny about the obvious tension brewing between Chandler and her out-spoken cousin.

"We can't leave his hands tied, Samantha."

"*Finally,* there's a sane person in the family," Chandler angrily said.

"Sanity has nothing to do with . . ." Samantha suddenly snapped her mouth shut when she realized that she was about to insult herself. "Never mind."

"As we sit here socializing, that gloating lieutenant is presenting your father with papers, Samantha, ordering him to allow those soldiers to search his property. Trust me, I know how John's going to react."

Chandler stood out of his chair, turning his back. “Now untie my hands.”

“I can’t.”

“Haven’t you been listening to a word I’ve said?” he snarled over his shoulder.

“My father’s not that stupid!”

“Stupidity has nothing to do with the man’s temper!”

“Pa told me *not* to untie your hands and I trust he knows what he’s doing!”

“Now, let me tell you precisely what *I’m* going to do. I’m going to let Brown arrest me . . . Let me finish!” Chandler hissed when Samantha started to open her mouth. “I happen to know something about the white man’s laws . . . I’m not entirely ignorant! The moment this colonel realizes they have the wrong man, he’ll have no other choice but to let me go.”

Chapter Twenty-eight

"Like I said, Lieutenant, Chandler's not here." John had had just about enough of this presumptuous lieutenant constantly meddling in his privacy. "Now take your men and get off my land."

"I've got my orders, Callahan." Jason thrust the paper under his nose. "This here says I have every right to inspect your property."

John didn't even glance at the paper; he could care less what it said. Peering over the top of Lieutenant Brown's head, he eyed the soldiers standing at attention a short distance away, speaking in a low tone of voice, so only the lieutenant would hear. "You know—one of these days, I'm going to catch you without that uniform on."

"Is that a threat, Callahan?"

"Take it any way you like."

"Pa?"

"Stay out of this, James," John firmly told his son, then his piercing blue eyes swung back to the "still wet behind the ears lieutenant". This young man had absolutely no respect for his elders. Well, John thought, Mr. Brown was about to find out just how they did things here in Bear Creek. "So what's it gonna be, Lieutenant? Will you leave peacefully on your own, or should I call my men?"

Jason knew he would have a battle on his hands if he tried to take this man into custody, yet the temptation was strong to put John Callahan in his place. Then he remembered his commanding officer's warning: Colonel Lewis had given strict orders that they had to catch Black Hawk on John Callahan's property or they didn't have a case. He believed the Indian wasn't here . . . least at the moment, so he really had no choice but to back down—for now.

Suddenly twirling on his boot heel and marching toward his horse, "Let's go men!" Jason shouted in command.

John kept a close eye on the lieutenant and his men, while they all mounted their horses and rode away. He did not trust the army man one bit and said as much to his foreman who was now approaching. "Amos, find Ernie. Tell him to take some of the boys and follow our—*uninvited guests.* I want to know exactly where they're going."

"You got it, boss." Amos then hurried away to do John's bidding.

"Wha'd'ya think, Pa?" James asked.

"This isn't the last we've seen of Jason Brown, is what I think."

Chandler guided the wagon along the narrow dirt road that led toward the Callahan ranch. After some coaxing and pleading from Rebecca, Samantha had finally given in and removed his bonds. He surreptitiously watched Rebecca who sat beside him on the seat, thinking she was quite the lady. And she definitely had a way of bringing the best out of Samantha.

Beside Rebecca sat James's wife, Sarah. Chandler was completely unaware of just how much the bumpy ride was affecting this passenger, until Sarah suddenly hollered out for him to stop the wagon. Which he did without question. Sarah covered her mouth with her hand as she quickly climbed down from the seat and then jogged a short distance away where she promptly proceeded to empty the contents of her stomach.

Samantha halted her horse beside the wagon. "Maybe I should go see how Sarah's doing?" she commented to nobody in particular.

"Sounds like she's still busy," Chandler said.

"Maybe we should leave her alone unless she asks for help," Rebecca suggested. "How long does morning sickness usually last anyway?"

Samantha shrugged. "Heck if I know."

"Well don't look at me," Chandler said, frowning at Samantha. "I know nothing about that kind of thing."

She nodded her head. "Here comes Sarah."

Immediately Chandler jumped to the ground and hurried around to the opposite side of the wagon to give the poor woman a helping hand. Sarah offered him a faint smile as he lifted her into the seat. He thought she looked a little peaked around the gills, but figured it was nothing to worry about. Anybody who'd lost their breakfast the way Sarah just did, probably wouldn't look so good either.

After Chandler climbed back into his seat beside Rebecca, he picked up the reins and gave them a little jiggle. When the wagon lurched forward, he heard Sarah groan. He tried his best to miss the worst of the deep ruts in the dirt road, but sometimes hitting a bump here and there could not be avoided. He wondered if Samantha would have this problem; he knew a lot of women did. In his mind Chandler could easily picture her cradling their own infant son or daughter in her arms, and it brought a smile to his lips.

Chandler turned his head to look at Samantha riding her horse alongside the wagon, and his smile widened. She rode with her back perfectly straight, with her thick, knee-length plait dangling past the horse's belly. He thought Samantha had never looked more beautiful . . .

"Someone's coming," Rebecca announced.

Looking straight ahead, Chandler squinted his eyes against the bright sunlight. He could see several men on horseback riding toward them. Unfortunately, at this distance, he couldn't determine who they were.

"I think it's Ernie—and some of the boys," Samantha said.

Chandler now recognized Ernie's horse, and some of the others. He wondered what would bring them this far from the ranch. Samantha's thoughts matched his own.

"I wonder what they're doing out here?" he heard her say.

Chandler halted the wagon. "We'll soon find out."

Ernie and the boys were almost to them. Ernie stopped his horse directly in front of the wagon, nodded at Samantha, then tipped his hat politely toward Rebecca and Sarah, before explaining, "We've been tracking Lieutenant Brown and about a dozen troopers. They left the ranch maybe an hour or so ago . . . we've been following them ever since. Sorry to say that we lost 'em."

"We haven't seen anybody," Chandler informed him. "Was there any trouble?"

"Nothing John couldn't handle." Ernie removed his hat, wiped his brow with the sleeve of his shirt, and repositioned his hat. "You're lucky, Chandler, you weren't at the ranch." His eyes swept the horizon. "They must've rode off in another direction."

"Lieutenant Brown and his *merry men* were at James's place this morning," Samantha then informed Ernie.

"So we heard from James." Ernie looked seriously at Chandler. "You'd better watch your back where that lieutenant's concerned. I'm sure I don't have to tell ya that it's not safe for you to be hanging around John's place right now. That crazy lieutenant won't rest until Black Hawk's behind bars, and I don't think I need to remind you, Chandler, ya look enough like Morgan to be his twin."

"So I've heard."

"Save your breath, Ernie. He won't listen to me either." Samantha turned her head and narrowed her angry gaze on Chandler.

Ernie and the boys laughed.

It was late afternoon when Chandler halted the wagon in front of the Callahan ranch house, wrapped the long reins around the brake handle. His eyes lingered upon Samantha for a moment as she rode on toward the barn, before alighting from the wagon. He hurried around to the other side to lift Sarah and Rebecca to the ground. After thanking him, Rebecca then took hold of Sarah's arm, who still wasn't looking so good, and escorted her toward the house.

"How's your jaw?"

Chandler turned at the sound of John's voice. His soon-to-be-father-in-law was casually leaning against the wagon with his muscular arms folded across his broad chest. James stood beside him, grinning from ear to ear. Chandler surmised that John must have told his son what had happened. "How's your fist?"

John's lips curled into a smile. "I'd forgotten how hard your jaw was." The only other time he'd ever punched Chandler—was when he'd rescued Samantha from the Indians and had brought her back in tattered clothes and wearing a huge bandage on her leg. He'd taken one look at his daughter and started swinging. His knuckles had been sore for quite some time. The whole thing now seemed rather comical.

"Have you given any more thought about leaving here while the gettin's good?" he asked Chandler. "That lieutenant will be back . . . mark my words."

"I won't run, John."

"Who's asking you to run, Chandler? Go to your father's village. I bet that army camp will be gone . . . less than a month from now. When it's safe for you and Morgan to return, I'll send Ben and Will to fetch you back."

It hadn't struck Chandler, until just then . . . *this was his home—this was where he now belonged.* Which made him even more determined to see this thing through, or he would be constantly looking over his shoulder. "Unless you're ordering me off your property, John, I'm not going anywhere."

"Then I guess we'll do this thing your way."

"And it looks like Chandler will be getting that chance sooner than he thought," James suddenly said. "Look who's coming."

Following his son's line of vision, John hissed, "I don't believe it!" Several army men on horseback were headed their way, and you couldn't miss the man out in the lead. "That lieutenant just won't give it a rest! He's like a . . . a human barnacle!"

"I want you to stay out of this, John . . . this is my fight."

"Sorry—but this is personal now, Chandler."

The instant Lieutenant Brown halted his horse, John walked over and grabbed the man by the front of his shirt, jerking him out of the saddle, then drew back his arm and let loose with a powerful punch that toppled the lieutenant like a tree being felled, knocking him out cold before his head even hit the ground.

John was ready when two soldiers immediately stepped forward to apprehend him. He simply hooked a man under each arm and then slammed their heads together, rendering both men unconscious. James and Chandler decided to join the melee by grabbing himself a man, and the fight was on. It was approximately four to one odds in the soldiers' favor as fists connected with tender flesh. But soon, those odds began to change, when one of Brown's men after another crumbled to the ground.

A punch that came out of nowhere dropped John to his knees, and as he started to get to his feet, another man leaped upon his back. But the much smaller man was no match for John. He twisted with a jerking movement and easily tossed his light burden through the air like a pesky fly. Regaining his balance, from the corner of his eye John noticed a couple of men attack his son at once. Like a crazed grizzly bear he charged forward and plowed his head into the nearest man, sending him crashing to the ground. He was just about to go after the other soldier when a loud gunshot suddenly split the air.

The fighting immediately stopped.

John frowned when he saw his wife standing there with a rifle in her hand. "I ought to shoot every last one of ya!" she shouted in a furious rage. "Grown men fighting like a bunch of adolescent boys! You should all be ashamed of yourselves!"

"Rachel, put that rifle down!" When John started to take a step forward a bullet grazed the ground directly in front of his boot. "Woman, are you crazy?"

"Stay right where you are, John Callahan! Not a man better move!"

They didn't.

Rachel motioned with her rifle. "You there, young man, may explain what's going on."

"That man over there," the soldier said, pointing a finger at Chandler, "is under arrest. And your husband attacked our commanding officer . . ."

"John attacked Lieutenant Brown?"

"Yes, ma'am."

"If my husband attacked him, then I'm sure he had good reason."

"Be that as it may, ma'am, your husband interfered . . ."

"Never mind that. I want to know what are the charges against Chandler?"

"He's Chief Black Hawk . . . wanted by the army."

"Young man, I don't know where you got your information, but this man's name is Wade Chandler. You can verify that with the sheriff in town, if you don't believe me. There is absolutely no way that Chandler could possibly be this chief you're talking about."

"That may be true, ma'am, but we still have our orders to bring him in."

"Then do what you must, Corporal," Chandler said, stepping forward. "But leave this family alone."

"Chandler, what do you think you're doing?"

"Rachel, you and John have already done enough. Now please put that rifle away, before you get into trouble."

"No! Wait!" a female voice suddenly cried out.

Chandler swung around at the sound of Samantha's voice. He *did not* want her to see him arrested and taken away like some common criminal. "Go back inside the house!"

"Samantha, do as Chandler says!" John knew that his hot-tempered daughter would only make matters worse, especially for Chandler.

Rachel quickly handed the rifle to her husband, then she grasped hold of her daughter. "Listen to me, Samantha," she whispered. "Let's go inside the house . . . can't you tell that Chandler doesn't want you to see this. Even if they put him in jail, I promise you, your father and I will do everything in our power to get him released."

"And what if you can't?"

"Then we'll send for Uncle Bernard. Listen to me—if you try to interfere now, you'll only cause more trouble for Chandler."

Samantha knew her mother was right. "Can I at least tell Chandler good-bye?" she hollered at the soldier who seemed to be in charge.

"Make it quick."

Samantha walked over to stand in front of Chandler. She could tell he was wearing his Indian face. Reaching up on her tiptoes, she tenderly kissed his cheek. He just stood there, staring straight ahead, refusing to even look at her. Tears blurred her eyes. Suddenly she turned and raced toward the house . . .

Slamming her bedroom door closed, Samantha hurried over to the window, shoving the lacy white curtains aside. They already had Chandler on his horse, and had tied his hands behind his back. As he quietly sat there, statue-still, staring straight ahead, power seemed to radiate from his body. Samantha knew she was looking at Graywolf the Cheyenne warrior, and she couldn't help but feel proud of him. She shivered. Chandler must have made a fearsome sight in his day. Knowing what the man was capable of, she bowed her head and said a silent prayer, asking God to protect him and keep him from losing his temper.

As they led Chandler away, Samantha could clearly read the defiance on his handsome face. She stood there, watching him, until he was completely out of sight.

After a while, Samantha turned away from the window, walked over to her bed and collapsed upon it. The tears started then, rolling steadily from her eyes. Snuggling her cheek against her pillow, she closed her eyes. . . .

Chapter Twenty-nine

"John, what you're proposing to do is crazy," Rachel argued. "I care about Chandler just as much as you, but you just can't ride into that army camp and demand his release. That colonel's likely to throw you inside the *hoosegow* right alongside Chandler, and then what will we do? So would you please wait for Bernard and let him handle this?"

"The army's not going to wait around for some high-priced Boston attorney to defend an Indian who they believe is some troublemaking war chief."

"If you're going to insult Bernard, John, please keep your voice down," Rachel whispered. "Ruthie and Rebecca might hear you."

"I was only stating a simple fact. Besides, I'm sure that Ruth's opinion of Bernard is . . ."

"John, please."

"Okay. Far as I'm concerned the subject of Bernard is closed," he said in a lower tone of voice. Then, "Now let's figure out what we're going to do about Chandler. I don't think you realize, Rachel, just how much trouble he's in. If Chandler's found guilty, the army could very easily hang him."

"That's absurd! They have the wrong man!"

"The whites want justice; the army won't care if they have the wrong man."

"But—surely the colonel will have no choice but to release Chandler once they discover they have the wrong man?"

"I wouldn't count on it."

"Oh, John, what are we going to do?"

"I can tell you this—I w*ill not* allow the army to hang Chandler. I'm just not sure how to stop them, if it should come to that."

"What should we tell Samantha?"

"Nothing . . . for now."

Her father's words "*they could hang Chandler*" flashed through Samantha's mind as she turned away from the kitchen doorway and tip-toed back down the hall, then out the front door. On the covered porch, she stopped and took several deep gulps of air, trying to get control over her emotions, which were now churning with fear and dread. "Come on, Samantha, you've got to get hold of yourself," she muttered to herself. "It won't do Chandler any good if you fall apart now." *She had to get Chandler out of that jail, but how?*

Samantha began to pace back and forth, along the wide-covered porch that ran the entire length of the house, trying to formulate some kind of plan in her mind. Suddenly twirling on her boot heel, she marched down the porch steps and strode toward the corral to catch and bridle herself a horse. *Somebody at that army camp was going to listen to what she had to say, or she would personally make sure that Lieutenant Brown rued the day he ever came to Bear Creek!*

Just on the outskirts of town, Samantha pulled back on the reins, then sat there, staring at the huge army camp, thinking, what an eyesore, with its numerous canvas dwellings dotting the grassy meadow. She noticed that despite the vastness of the camp, there was hardly a man in sight. Samantha was wondering which tent might be Lieutenant Brown's commanding officer's, when she happened to notice a tent that was larger and slightly different from the other tents. Remembering the Indians—how the chief's tepee seemed to always stand out from the others—she figured it was worth a try.

Samantha guided the bay gelding over to a stand of trees across from the army camp, and dismounted, looping the reins around a low-hanging branch. As she crossed the dirt road toward the campsite, she began to feel a little apprehensive, thinking that maybe she shouldn't have come here alone—but it was a little too late to worry about that now. When Samantha saw two men (whom she guessed were guards) disappear inside a small, wooden shed, she suddenly ducked behind a tree. She had the gut feeling that she'd just found Chandler.

While Samantha intently watched the little shed for any sign of Chandler's presence, anger filled her at the thought of him being locked inside that tiny four-by-four cell. Plus, there wasn't a single tree or a bush of any kind around the shack that might offer some sort of shade from the relentless sun to the inhabitant. She continued to stand there, keeping a close vigil, becoming more and more angrier with each passing minute. She couldn't imagine what it must be like to be caged like some wild animal. *Was Chandler okay?* Samantha wondered. *Maybe at this very moment, he was lying on the ground, unconscious, from lack of food and water.* She tried not to let her imagination get the best of her.

Samantha became more alert when the door opened. One of the soldiers stepped outside and, when Chandler duck through the door behind him, Samantha breathed a sigh of relief. But her relief didn't last long, because Chandler's hands were bound behind his back and the other soldier kept gouging him in the back with his rifle. Strange as it sounded, she'd never felt more proud of Chandler than she did at that very moment, the way he towered over the other two men and walked with the grace of a panther.

Samantha instantly became suspicious when the two men forced Chandler into the back of a flatbed wagon that had been parked near the small shed. She became outraged when one of the soldiers used the butt of his rifle on the back of Chandler's head. She saw him slump forward, and then the soldier pushed him backward with his booted foot. It took everything inside Samantha to stay hidden where she was and not run to Chandler's rescue. There was nobody else around she could call for help—not that she trusted they would help her anyway—so it was up to her to find out where those men were taking Chandler.

Remaining a safe distance behind the wagon, Samantha followed the narrow dirt road that led out of town, praying the two soldiers would not notice her. This stretch of land harbored few trees where a person might hide. So far, she'd been lucky. Once Samantha had panicked when she thought the men had spotted her, but they had only stopped to take care of a private need. They had traveled maybe a couple of miles, then brought the wagon to a sudden halt.

Again Samantha lucked out. She quickly nudged her horse behind a nearby copse of trees, and sat there, wondering what the men were up to. Samantha soon had her answer when she spotted a lone rider swiftly crossing the field. Her brows furrowed in suspicion when she recognized Lieutenant Brown's buckskin stallion. He halted beside the parked wagon, briefly spoke with the other two men, then rode away in a hurry in the direction he'd just come.

When the wagon started forward again, Samantha lagged even farther behind, trying to keep out of sight. It didn't take a real genius to figure out that whatever these soldiers were planning to do with Chandler was not going to be good. Her mind was in a constant state of turmoil. There were two of them and only one of her; and they had rifles, where she had only a small knife for a weapon. *Not very good odds, indeed.*

Samantha knew another moment of panic when the wagon veered off the main road and disappeared into a small grove of trees, until an inner voice warned her, "*You have to remain calm.*" Samantha nudged the big bay to a faster pace. At the edge of the thicket, she slid from her horse, hastily looped the reins around the limb of a tree. Her heart pounding against her chest, she proceeded on foot, cautiously making her way through the brush, ducking limbs as she moved forward. She could hear the men talking, and could see the wagon through the trees. She hit the ground when one of the soldiers turned around, then laid there, statue-still, praying he didn't notice her. When Samantha heard the men resume their conversation, she let out the breath she'd been holding. She lifted her head a little off the ground to make sure that it was safe to proceed—both men seemed preoccupied. She got to her hands and knees and then crawled steadily forward, until she reached the wagon . . .

When Samantha saw Chandler lying in the back face-down and saw the blood on the back of his head, furious rage filled her. She glared at the two soldiers sitting in the wagon seat. Their backs were toward her, and they were talking and laughing like nothing was out of the ordinary. She figured they were just waiting for Chandler to regain consciousness, so she hid behind some nearby bushes to wait.

The moment Chandler barely stirred, both men simultaneously jumped down from their seat and hurried to the back of the wagon. Rage flowed through Samantha's veins as they roughly took hold of

Chandler and forced him to stand. It was obvious that he was badly hurt, for he swayed slightly, yet he somehow managed to stay on his feet. Samantha gasped, when one of the soldiers punched Chandler hard in the stomach, causing him to doubled over in pain. Seething with fury, she remained concealed behind the bushes, knowing it would do neither her or Chandler any good if she lost her temper and did something stupid.

Now the two men seemed to be arguing about something, so Samantha listened very carefully to the heated conversation . . .

"I thought you said that we were just going to drive the Indian a short distance from town and then release him?"

"Lieutenant Brown has a better idea."

"I don't like this, Will."

"I don't remember asking for your opinion, Dewayne!"

"But Colonel Lewis said . . ."

"Lieutenant Brown happens to disagree with the colonel!" Corporal Jones snapped. "And for your information, so do I!"

"But if we get caught, it's us they'll be hangin'!"

"If we do as the lieutenant said, it'll look like an accident and no one will be the wiser!"

"I still don't like this, Will . . . it isn't right."

"Touch that man and I'll sing like a canary!" Samantha had stepped away from her hiding place and was pointing an accusing finger at both men.

"What the . . ."

"I would advise you to point that rifle in a different direction . . . Corporal Jones, wasn't it? I should warn you, anything happens to me, or him," Samantha said with a toss of her head toward Chandler, "and my father will have your hide, Corporal, piece by piece. And, I might add, with the help of just about every rancher in Montana. . . ."

Through a hazy and clouded mind Chandler thought he could hear Samantha's muffled voice. She sounded angry. And she seemed to be arguing with somebody . . . which was nothing new . . . but . . . somehow . . . this seemed different. For some reason, he was having trouble concentrating. His legs felt like rubber; and his head was pounding like a drum. And he couldn't seem to get his senses about him . . . ?

"So what do we do now, Will?" Dewayne wanted to know.

"Shut your mouth, so I can think!" Corporal Jones angrily hissed.

Lieutenant Brown had promised him a fair amount of money for his part in this and he wasn't about to back down—for any reason. He'd known better than to trust Dewayne and had tried to warn Brown, but the man wouldn't listen. And if Dewayne was unwilling to do away with a heathen savage who was bent on harassing innocent white folks, he wouldn't even consider harming a meddling woman. In fact, Dewayne will probably try to intervene . . .

But what harm could one woman possibly do? William tried to rationalize. Then suddenly the woman's identity dawned on him . . . remembering where he'd seen the beauty. She was that rancher's daughter . . . what was his name? . . . John Callahan. William remembered the girl's father well. John Callahan was the kind of man that if he ever found out about this Indian's 'accident', he would demand a full investigation and wouldn't stop until he got one. Maybe he should try to scare the woman first, but if that didn't work . . .

"Miss, if you had a brain in that pretty head of yours, you'd turn around and leave this place and forget what you saw here today."

"I'm afraid I can't do that, Corporal. So why don't you release my fiancé . . ."

"Did I hear you right? This man is your fiancé?"

Samantha's chin rose a notch. "Yes, he is."

Stunned by the young woman's confession, Corporal Jones stood in silence, glaring at the Indian, his features contorted into an evil sneer. After a brief period, he looked back at the woman and announced with disgust, "Then you shall join your—*fiancé*."

"Now hold on, Will . . ."

Corporal Jones swung the rifle toward his partner. "I'll give you a choice, Dewayne—either you tie that Indian to the wagon and we do like Lieutenant Brown said or I'll shoot ya where you stand." He sneered and added suggestively, "I'll personally take care of the woman myself."

When Dewayne just stood there, Will pulled back on the trigger. "I haven't come this far, Corporal Smith, to turn back now."

Samantha watch as the man called Dewayne secured a rope around Chandler's waist, who was still swaying on his feet. When the man began to tie the other end of the rope to the wagon wheel, it was now becoming horrifyingly clear what they intended to do. *They were going to drag Chandler!* She charged forward . . .

"Stop right there, little lady, or I swear I'll shoot him!" Corporal Jones turned the rifle on Chandler and shouted, "I mean it!"

Samantha stopped in her tracks. "You can't do this!"

"Oh yes I can," Corporal Jones calmly replied.

"Will, please let these people go," Dewayne tried to reason with him. "And let's just forget this whole thing ever happened. . . ."

While the men argued, Samantha was forming a plan in her mind. She prayed with her whole heart that she wouldn't miss, asking God to guide her hand. Because Chandler's life depended on her accuracy. She hadn't felt this kind of fear since the grizzly attack. Her heart was pounding inside her chest and her whole body was trembling. What she was about to do would take every ounce of skill she possessed and then some. Sweat was beginning to form on the palms of her hands, which she hastily wiped off on her pants. If her hands were the least bit moist, she would never be able to get a good enough grip on her knife.

By now Chandler was well aware of what these soldiers were planning to do to him. He furiously spat at Corporal Jones, "I don't want her to see this! At least have the decency to cover her eyes, so she doesn't have to watch!"

"No!" Samantha frantically screeched. With the corporal now looking at her oddly, she said the first thing that came to mind, so the man would not become suspicious. "I'm afraid of the dark." She held her breath. If he covered her eyes, she would never be able to save Chandler!

Corporal Jones shrugged. "Suit yourself." He started toward the prisoner. "Better say your lasts rights, Indian."

The thought of what these men might do to Samantha, gave Chandler a sudden burst of strength and he strained harder against the rope binding his wrists. Unfortunately, it wasn't enough to break free. He ceased struggling, knowing he was just wasting his energy. His eyes sought and held those of Samantha's. He didn't want her to see him dragged on the ground like some animal. "Samantha, please turn around."

She sadly smiled in return.

"Maybe I misjudged you, miss," Corporal Jones snickered. When the woman only glared at him, he shrugged and muttered under his breath, "Whatever your reason for wanting to watch, makes no difference to me."

His lips twisted into an evil sneer, Corporal Jones raised his rifle in the air. "Ready to meet the great spirit, Indian?"

Chandler said nothing.

When the rifle went off and the team of horses bolted forward, Samantha moved with the speed of a honed gunslinger. In the blink of an eye she reached inside her boot and then sent her knife sailing threw the air, severing the rope on the wheel.

As Chandler stood there, completely stunned by what had just happened, a bullet whizzed past his head. Samantha charged at Corporal Jones headfirst and caught the man hard in the mid-section, sending them both toppling backwards to the ground. The corporal had lost his grip on the rifle and was struggling to reach it. But Samantha was quicker. She rolled to her feet and snatched the weapon off the ground before either man could grab it. Now holding the rifle on Corporal Jones, she ordered the man called Dewayne to cut Chandler free. Which he did in a hurry. Then, while Chandler proceeded to lash both mens' hands and feet together, she continued to hold the rifle steady.

After they were both secure, Samantha dropped the rifle and ran straight into Chandler's outstretched arms. "Oh, Chandler, I was so afraid!"

"You're truly a remarkable woman, Sam." Chandler held Samantha tightly in his arms, breathing in the clean, fresh scent of her hair. He suddenly realized how foolish he'd been to argue with her over things that didn't matter . . .

Samantha leaned back to look at him. "It was just a lucky shot."

"Then you're one of the luckiest women I know."

"I found you didn't I," she replied with love shining in her brilliant blue eyes.

"Excuse me!" Corporal Jones cut in sharply. "But if you two lovebirds are finished, I would like to know what you plan to do with us?"

"If I were you, I'd keep my mouth shut!" Chandler hissed.

"I was only following orders . . ."

"I speak perfect English, Corporal! I heard Colonel Lewis give you specific orders to take me to the Callahan ranch . . ."

"I meant I was following Lieutenant Brown's orders."

"I might be an Indian, but I understand the white man's laws. You purposely disobeyed a direct order from a much higher commanding officer. I know what you're trying to do and you can save it, it won't work."

Corporal Jones was obviously furious, but he said nothing.

"What *are* you going to do with them?" Samantha asked curiously.

Wordlessly Chandler retrieved Samantha's knife and he cut the rope off both mens' ankles; then he removed their boots and tossed them far into the bushes. "In case you boys haven't figured it out yet, you'll be walking back to camp—barefoot. Be careful of the snakes. I hear they're pretty aggressive this time of year." He nearly burst out laughing at Jones's panic-stricken look.

Samantha touched Chandler's arm. "I thought you should know . . . the other man . . . Dewayne . . . he did try to help you."

"He was still part of it. And what I'm going to do to them is much more humane than what they were planning for me."

Samantha couldn't argue with that. What Chandler said was true.

"I suggest, Corporal, that you and Dewayne get started," she heard Chandler say. "It's a long walk back to camp."

"Wait a minute, you mean you're just going to let Corporal Jones go?" Samantha said incredulously. "I didn't want you to hurt him, but you should at least have the man arrested."

"It's his word against mine, and they're not going to take an Indian's word over one of their own kind!" Chandler bitterly replied.

"But I'm a witness!"

"You've heard what Colonel Lewis thinks of John. Do you think they would take the word of his daughter?"

"But . . ."

"Forget it, Samantha. Besides, my way's better." Chandler picked up the rifle and handed it to her. "Keep an eye on our friends, while I unhitch the horses from the wagon and turn them loose. You do have a horse?" he asked.

Samantha nodded. After Chandler walked away, her eyes narrowed on Corporal Jones. "If I had my way, mister, I would tie your sorry hide to that wagon and do to you what you were going to do to him." She would never really do such a thing, but he didn't know that.

A short while later, Samantha and Chandler were headed toward the ranch, riding double on the bay gelding. Samantha smiled to herself when she thought about the two men they had left behind, and the way that Corporal Jones was hollering at them at the top of his lungs as she and Chandler rode away. Her smile widened even more, remembering how both men had looked, standing there, in nothing but their long underwear. Not only had Chandler gotten rid of their boots, he'd also taken their clothing.

"How long do you think it will take them to walk back to camp?" Samantha inquired.

"Without their boots or," Chandler chuckled, "proper anatomy covering . . . depending on the elements of nature," he added, glancing toward the horizon at the setting sun, "they might make it back to camp some time tomorrow."

"Well I hope Corporal Jones gets bit by a scorpion or worse."

"What could be worse than that?"

Samantha grinned mischievously and replied, "*Where* he gets bit."

Chandler threw back his head and laughed. "Even I couldn't be that cruel. Remind me never to do anything to make you that angry."

"I doubt you could ever do anything to make me that angry."

"I sure hope not," he mumbled more to himself. Then, "You know—when I was a young boy living in my father's village, I remember hearing stories about this old warrior . . . can't seem to remember the man's name . . . Stalking Wolf, I think . . . anyway . . . it was rumored that he could split a blade of grass at several paces with his hatchet in his youth."

"Even I couldn't do that," Samantha said, totally impressed.

"Have you ever tried?"

"I think I know my limits."

Samantha felt so carefree at the moment, relieved to have Chandler back at her side, she halfheartedly joked, "We should just keep riding . . . till we reach your father's village."

"We could even get married Indian style," Chandler played along. "There's nothing more romantic than sleeping under the stars."

"Sounds wonderful," Samantha agreed.

"It is."

Twisting around to look Chandler in the eye, Samantha's brow rose questioningly. "Sounds like you know from experience?" She hated sounding like a jealous female, but she couldn't help herself. When he didn't answer, "Well?"

"I never claimed to be a virgin, Samantha."

"So . . . just how many *starry nights* are we talking about?" she angrily snapped, sitting up a little straighter, her eyes narrowing into furious slits.

"More than I could possibly count," Chandler sarcastically replied. That wasn't true, but he didn't appreciate her accusing tone.

"I should've known you were a . . . a . . . Casanova!"

Chandler shook his head in disbelief. Only a short time ago, this woman had risked her own life to save him—now she was tongue-lashing him for something that had happened way before he even knew her name.

"And furthermore . . ."

"Now just hold on a daggone minute!"

"It sounds to me like one woman won't be enough for your . . . your animalistic appetite!"

"You can't be serious?"

Samantha folded her arms and stared straight ahead, refusing to say another word.

Shading her eyes against the setting sun, Rachel stood on the front porch with a troubled expression on her face, watching the two riders slowly approach the house. Although she was relieved that her daughter had finally returned home safe-and-sound—and had even somehow managed to get Chandler out of jail—she was not very pleased with Samantha for taking off without telling anybody where she was going. Since early that morning, her husband had been out searching for Samantha and he hadn't returned home yet.

"I need to talk to Pa," Samantha told her mother as she swung her leg over the horse's head and dropped to the ground.

"Your father's not here. He's still out looking for you."

"I'm sorry."

"As well you should be, young lady," Rachel said in a scolding tone. She then smiled at Chandler. "Welcome home."

"Rachel," he said, dismounting. "It's good to be home."

"How did you manage to get out of jail so quickly?" She then frowned at Samantha, and added, "Or should I ask."

"Well, I didn't break Chandler out at gunpoint, Ma—if that's what you're asking?"

"Imagine my relief."

"I wouldn't say that just yet."

"What do you mean?"

"That's what I need to talk to Pa about."

"Let me explain." Chandler then relayed the whole story to Rachel, leaving nothing out, especially the heroic efforts on her daughter's part, ending with, "If it wasn't for Samantha, I wouldn't even be here. I owe her my life." He slipped an arm around Samantha's shoulders, hoping she still wasn't angry at him. At least she didn't flinch . . . maybe that was a good sign.

"That's quite a story," Rachel commented. She then kissed her daughter on the forehead. "I'm very proud of you, Samantha—that was a very brave thing you did." *And dangerous*, Rachel thought. She inwardly said a quick prayer, thanking God for protecting her daughter. And Chandler too. "I bet you're both hungry. Come on . . . let's all go inside the house . . . I have supper ready."

Chapter Thirty

John angrily flicked the reins, prompting the team of horses at a faster pace. He glared at the man sitting next to him in the seat, dressed in a fancy silk suit with his polished shoes. *What did Ruth see in Bernard?* John wondered. *And why did he ever agree to let Ruth send for the egotistical man in the first place? What could he have been thinking?* Because it was obvious that his brother-in-law had not changed one little bit after all these years; except that Bernard seemed even more arrogant than he remembered. John was seriously tempted to stop the wagon and throw Bernard out on his conceited hide. *Let the man walk the rest of the way to the ranch!* Or, better yet, he ought to turn the wagon around and head straight back to town—send Bernard back to where he came from, on the very next stage. Besides, now that Chandler was out of jail, there was no reason for him to stay.

John looked over his shoulder at Ruth, seated in the back of the wagon. He still couldn't believe that Bernard had actually had the audacity to insist on riding up front, forcing his own wife to ride in the back. John was surprised the *prissy runt* didn't carry around his own red carpet to walk upon. Shaking his head in disgust, the *pansy* won't survive one day at the ranch, he angrily thought.

He turned back around, now clutching the reins so tightly in his hands that his knuckles turned white. *What was wrong with Ruth? Why did she allow Bernard to treat her in such a disrespectful manner?*

If it wasn't for his sister-in-law, he would reach over and knock the *pathetic peacock* clean off his perch.

Several silent and tense miles later, John finally brought the wagon to a sudden halt in front of the house. He immediately hopped down from his seat to assist Ruth, knowing Bernard would not lift a finger to help his own wife. He noticed that Ruth would not even look at her husband—from embarrassment no doubt, John thought. He was mighty tempted to tell Ruth right then and there in front of Bernard, that she and Rebecca were welcome to stay at the ranch for as long as they wanted, providing she got rid of her husband.

"So this is the big ranch house I heard so much about," Bernard remarked, stepping down from his seat. "How quaint." He then walked to the back of the wagon to retrieve his suitcase. "I'll take this in myself . . . it's pure leather and very expensive."

Ruth was mortified that Bernard was acting even more like a snob than usual. She secretly knew it was because her husband was extremely jealous of John and always had been, although he would never admit it. Now comparing the two men, Ruth could easily understand why Bernard had always envied John Callahan. John was more of a man than her selfish, conceited husband could ever dream of being.

"This way, Bernard," Ruth coolly announced.

John angrily paced back and forth inside the kitchen. "Somebody ought to teach that *dandy* upstairs some manners and how to treat his wife!"

"John, please keep your voice down." Seated at the table, Rachel shuffled through the pages of an old magazine. "I don't want Bernard to hear . . ."

"I hope he *does* hear!" John thundered.

"Bernard can't help that he's always been—well-to-do."

John whirled to face his wife. "Is that what you call it? Why I could buy Bernard with my petty cash and you don't see me acting like some . . . some pompous back end of a mule."

Rachel giggled.

"You wouldn't be laughing if you'd been with us on the ride home," John said, scowling.

Letting out a sigh, Rachel leaned back in her chair, looking at her husband. "Ruth wants to try and save her marriage, and we should help her."

"If you really want to help your sister, try talking some sense into her."

"I honestly don't know what to do, John. From what Ruth has told me, Bernard sounds worse than ever. And from what you've told me only confirms it." Rachel decided that she might as well tell her husband about Bernard's indiscretions—he was bound to hear about them anyway—and it probably should come from her. She bluntly informed him, "Bernard's been having an affair and it's not the first time."

"Why that no good philandering . . . ! Then I really don't understand Ruth!"

"I don't understand either, but we have to abide by her wishes."

"Then keep Bernard out of my way, Rachel. You just gave me even more reason to thrash the man within an inch of his life. I never cared for Bernard when I first met the man and I like him even less now."

"What's all the yelling about?" Samantha asked as she entered the kitchen. She walked over to the table and plopped into a chair, before saying, "Aunt Ruth and Uncle Bernard are having a shouting match of their own. I could hear them from my room."

"Your mother and I were just having a disagreement."

Samantha arched a brow at her father. "Isn't that basically the same thing?"

"Don't you have a stall to clean or a horse to brush?"

"I can take a hint." She stood out of her chair.

"Where's Rebecca?" Rachel thought to inquire.

"She went outside."

"The poor child."

"You think that's bad . . . I heard Uncle Bernard hollering at Aunt Ruth that he wanted to stay at a hotel in town," Samantha quietly stated.

"Let him stay in town!" John hissed.

"What's going on?" Samantha wanted to know. With both her parents glowering at her, "I'll be outside," she said, then hurried from the room.

Samantha found Rebecca seated on the front porch steps. She quietly closed the door behind her. "Mind if I sit here with you?"

Rebecca spoke as she scooted over to make room for Samantha, who dropped on the step beside her. "My mother was hoping us coming here would maybe snap my father out of . . . that maybe he would change. But if you ask me, nothing will ever change the man. You know what I think the problem is? My father doesn't love my mother anymore—who knows, maybe he never did. I don't think Bernard Smith loves anyone but himself."

"I'm sure he loves you, Becca."

"If my father truly loved me, he wouldn't be forcing me to marry Albert . . . that's what my parents are fighting about."

"Albert?"

"Albert Smythers. He's my father's partner in his law firm."

"Smith and Smythers . . . that could get confusing," Samantha joked.

"There's nothing funny about Albert," Rebecca seriously said. "My father believes that Mr. Smythers is going to be rich and powerful someday . . . that's why he wants me to marry the old geezer. That's all my father cares about . . . is money. It doesn't matter that Albert is twice my age and I can barely tolerate the man." She blinked back tears. "My father told me that Albert will be here, day after tomorrow."

"Albert is coming here . . . at the ranch?"

Rebecca nodded. "Oh, Samantha, what am I going to do? I don't even want to speak to Albert, let alone marry him."

"Your father can't force you to marry the man, Becca."

"You don't know my father."

"What about Aunt Ruth? What does she say?"

"Mother's on my side . . . not that it matters, because my father will get his way. You see, I was promised to Mr. Smythers on my sixteenth birthday. 'Course I never took it serious . . . guess I should have . . . at any rate—Albert was promised my hand in marriage when I turned twenty—that was a couple of months ago. Apparently, Mr. Smythers is getting impatient. Mother says it's because Albert is an old prune who's looking for a young flower."

"Sounds like something Aunt Ruth would say," Samantha said, laughing.

Seeing how desperate her cousin was, she let out a sigh. "Becca, you're past the age where your parents can tell you what to do."

"You don't understand, Samantha, I'm not independent like you. Neither do I have the courage to stand up to my father." Without another word, Rebecca suddenly rose to her feet and turned and hurried inside the house.

The next morning John was at his wit's end where it came to Bernard. He couldn't even stand to be in the same room with his brother-in-law. So he had been more than relieved when Ruth announced over breakfast that Bernard had decided to stay at the hotel in town, claiming that the guest room was causing him to feel claustrophobic.

"Claustrophobic my . . ."

"John!"

"Sorry, Rachel, but Bernard is beyond pathetic!"

"I understand your anger, but think of Ruth before you say something you might regret. Besides, he'll be gone soon. More flapjacks, dear?"

"No—I think I've had enough."

Rachel knew it was Bernard that John was referring to. Speaking of the devil, she thought, when the man suddenly appeared inside the kitchen doorway.

"I'll need someone to take me into town," Bernard curtly announced.

"I'll get one of my men to take you immediately," John gruffly replied.

"I would appreciate it."

"May I get you anything, Bernard?" Rachel asked. "Perhaps some breakfast? Or maybe a cup of coffee?" Then for her husband's ears only, she added, "Or perhaps a sound thrashing?"

John burst out laughing.

Bernard looked at John curiously. "No, thank you. If you don't mind, I'll just get my things and be on my way." Then he turned and walked away.

Rachel could hear Bernard's heels clicking on the hardwood floor as he headed down the hallway toward the stairs. "I've never met such a loathsome man," she angrily said.

"I liked the thrashing idea," John chuckled.

"I wasn't joking."

"I'd be happy to thrash the man good before he leaves?"

"If it wasn't for Ruth, I would thrash him myself!"

"I always knew you had a violent side," he teased.

"This isn't funny, John."

"Well—guess I'll go get *Prince Charming's* carriage ready." He scooted away from the table and, a moment later, slammed out the back door.

Rising, Rachel began to clear away the breakfast dishes, wondering how her sister could stay married to such a selfish man. *How unhappy Ruthie must have been all these years*, she thought sadly. If only she had known the truth about Bernard, she would have sent for her sister and niece long before now.

When Ruth entered the kitchen and Rachel saw her sister's red, swollen eyes, she wanted to thrash Bernard all over again within an inch of his miserable life. "There's more to the reason why Bernard wants to stay in town, isn't there? I don't buy the claustrophobic excuse."

Ruth let out a shaky sigh. "Bell's coming with Albert."

Rachel gasped. "Bernard's bringing his . . . his . . . *mistress* here?"

"She'll be staying at the hotel in Bear Creek. But that doesn't bother me as much as the other."

"What other?" Rachel questioned her sister. *What could possibly be worse?*

"Bernard still insists that Becca marry Albert."

"Ruth," Rachel firmly said, grasping her older sister by the shoulders. "You can't give into Bernard anymore, especially where Becca's concerned. What's happened to you, Ruthie? You used to have more spunk."

"I've often wondered that same thing myself." Ruth walked over and dropped wearily into a chair, suddenly feeling completely defeated and just plain worn out. "I've stayed with Bernard all these years, because—because I thought Becca needed her father."

"But she's a grown woman now, Ruthie."

"I haven't loved Bernard in years," she confessed. "Maybe it's my fault he strayed."

Rachel walked over and sat in a chair across from her sister. "That's utter nonsense. I've seen the way Bernard treats you . . . why you didn't divorce the man long before now is beyond me. I don't want to sound like I'm trying to tell you what to do, but—if you do decide to leave Bernard, I want you to know that you and Becca are welcome to stay with us for as long as you want . . . indefinitely if need be."

After a brief discussion with Samantha, John decided to drive Bernard into town himself. As he waited in the wagon for his brother-in-law, he fought to keep control over his temper. It didn't surprise him that the man would force his daughter to do something against her will: but marry a man twice her age? That seemed cruel, even for Bernard.

The longer John sat there in the seat, waiting, the angrier he became. He felt more disgust for his own brother-in-law than he did for Lieutenant Brown. Rebecca was his niece and he would have his say on the matter of 'Albert Smythers' and Bernard had better well listen!

When John saw Bernard step outside the front door, he looked straight ahead, afraid his brother-in-law would see the fury in his eyes, fury he could no longer hide. He heard Bernard set his suitcase in the back of the wagon, then he climbed into the seat beside him. If Bernard was the least bit suspicious why John was driving him to Bear Creek, he didn't say.

Wordlessly John flicked the reins and the wagon rolled forward. They had traveled maybe a mile or so away from the house, when he suddenly pulled back on the reins, bringing the wagon to a complete stop, then turned to face Bernard.

"Thought we could have us a little talk, man-to-man."

"About what?" Bernard questioned, already becoming suspicious.

"About the deplorable way you treat your wife for starters."

"How dare you . . ."

"I would advise you to keep your mouth shut, Bernard, until I'm through speaking!" John furiously spat. He wasn't surprised when Bernard's mouth instantly snapped shut. "I'll get right to the point and I'm going to be perfectly blunt so there's no misunderstanding. If you ever treat Ruth in a disrespectful way or even raise your voice to her in my presence again, you'll answer to me. When you leave Bear Creek and if Ruth goes home with you, there's not a whole lot I can do about it then. The other thing I'm going to warn you about—keep *Albert Smythers* off my property and away from Becca."

"You have no right . . ."

In the blink of an eye John reached across the seat and grabbed Bernard by the front of his silk shirt and pulled him close to his face, so they were almost nose-to-nose. His voice was low when he spoke, but it still held a threatening tone. "I would advise you to heed my warning, Bernard, because I never repeat myself. Do we understand each other?"

Bernard could only nod in reply.

"Good." John then released Bernard. He picked up the reins and gave them a jiggle, and they proceeded toward town like nothing ever happened.

Neither man spoke another word.

As Samantha crossed the yard toward the barn, she felt that somebody was watching her. She looked over her shoulder, but nobody was there. She finally shrugged it off and told herself that she was being silly, before entering the barn.

When the colt came dashing out of a stall, Samantha laughed out loud. Holding out her hand, she slowly approached the frisky animal, not wanting to frighten it. "We still need to think of a name for you yet, little fella," she softly crooned.

Suddenly sensing she was no longer alone, Samantha whirled around. Her eyes widened in alarm when she saw the silhouette of a tall, muscular man hidden within the shadows, leaning against the wall near the wide door, then narrowed in recognition. "Wade Chandler! Can't you make noise like normal people?"

He pushed away from the wall and sauntered toward her. "I'll be sure to make a lot of noise, next time. Something wrong?"

"I never dreamed my family could be so messed up."

"Meaning your Uncle Bernard?"

"I'd rather not admit that man's my uncle. I can't believe what he's doing to my aunt. And he's forcing Rebecca to marry some man in his firm who's twice her age."

"Speaking of your uncle, I saw Bernard and your pa driving away from the house in the wagon a little while ago."

"I thought Ernie was suppose to take Uncle Bernard to town," Samantha muttered more to herself. Then, "Pa must've decided to drive him into town for a reason. What I wouldn't give to be a little bird perched on the side of that wagon about now."

"Danged if you ain't a hostile woman," Chandler said, chuckling.

Samantha gave an unladylike snort.

"And you have such a way with words." He laughed when Samantha scowled at him. "Oh—I almost forgot what I came in here for. I was just wondering . . . care to try again next weekend? . . . to get married, I mean."

"Has it occurred to you yet that every time we plan to get married, something always goes wrong? I'm beginning to think, maybe we should take the hint."

"Are you saying you don't want to get married?"

"No . . . but maybe we should consider eloping," Samantha suggested. "Why didn't I think of that sooner?" she gushed with excitement. "It's the perfect solution."

"Are you serious?" Chandler wasn't so sure about this.

"Of course I'm serious."

"What about your parents and your Aunt Ruth and cousin Rebecca? I would think they would what to be present on the most important day of your life. And I doubt that John would appreciate some man running off with his daughter."

"But you're not just any man, Chandler," she teased.

"I still don't think it's such a good idea."

"I don't see why not . . . it may be the only way we ever get married." Samantha frowned and added, "Unless *you* have changed *your* mind?"

"You know better than that."

"My parents could always throw a reception for us later," she hurried to say. "You know, Chandler—the more I think about it—this just might be the answer for everyone. My poor mother has enough to worry about . . . what with Aunt Ruth and Uncle Bernard . . . a big wedding is probably the last thing on her mind right now. And if we did elope . . . if you want . . . we could get married tomorrow."

"Now that idea I like." Chandler let out a loud whoop of joy as he picked Samantha up in his arms and swung her around, before setting her back on her feet.

Chapter Thirty-one

"Elope!" John thundered from inside the bunkhouse at his daughter. "Are you crazy? Do you have any idea how much your mother's been looking forward to throwing you a big wedding? If you and Chandler elope, it'll break her heart!"

"I bet this was all your idea!" he then shouted at Chandler.

"Actually, it was my idea," Samantha informed her father in mounting irritation.

"You watch your tone, young lady!"

"I'm sorry, Pa . . . it's just that . . . that I honestly thought if Chandler and I eloped, it would be less of a burden on everyone . . . with everything that's happened lately."

"Eloping's out of the question," John stated with finality. "And I don't want to hear another word about it!"

Before she said something she might regret, Samantha turned and stormed out of the bunkhouse, slamming the door behind her. As she marched toward the house, she started to feel a little guilty for leaving Chandler at her father's mercy, but it couldn't be helped. When Samantha spotted the man in uniform standing on the front porch, she stopped in her tracks, grumbling under her breath. *Just what she needed was a confrontation with Lieutenant Brown.* She seriously considered turning around and running in the opposite direction, but he'd already descended the steps and was coming toward her.

Samantha planted both fists on her hips, and angrily spat, "You've got your nerve showing your face here, Lieutenant! I can't believe they didn't throw you inside that four-by-four cell for what you tried to do to Chandler! I will personally have a talk with your commanding officer . . . let him know what kind of man you really are!"

"It would be your word and that Indian's word against mine, Miss Callahan." Jason's lips twisted into a mocking sneer as he added, "Now—who do you think Colonel Lewis will believe?"

"Dewayne will tell the truth."

"That just happens to be the reason why I'm here," he haughtily retorted. "The little stunt that you and your Indian sidekick pulled cost me a good man."

"What are you talking about?"

"On their way back to camp, Dewayne stepped on a snake . . . poor man," Jason said, shaking his head in a feigned gesture of sadness. " 'Course Dewayne would still be alive if only he'd been wearing his boots."

"I beg to differ with you, Lieutenant. Dewayne would still be alive if he and that crazy sidekick of *yours*—Corporal Jones I believe was his name—had taken Chandler home like Colonel Lewis had ordered them to do." Samantha saw surprise and then anger register inside Lieutenant Brown's eyes. "You didn't know I knew, did ya? I guess Corporal Jones forgot to mention that I'd heard from his own lips what you did."

"It doesn't matter."

"We'll see," Samantha replied in the same snide manner. "If your men, Lieutenant, hadn't been trying to do away with Chandler and making it look like an accident, nothing would've happened to Dewayne. So I'm sorry to say that I don't have a whole lot of sympathy for the man. It's just too bad that it wasn't Corporal Jones who got bit."

"I ought to have you arrested right along with that Indian!" Jason angrily hissed. Then in a sudden calmer tone, he said, "The reason I came here today . . . it would look much better if your fiancé were to turn himself in."

Samantha angrily folded her arms across her chest. "For what?"

"For the death of Corporal Dewayne Smith—"

"You can't be serious!"

"—as soon as I can prove that Indian was the cause, even though it was done indirectly. I'm sure I'll be back to arrest him—so you can tell the Indian that he'd better not try to run. I'll be watching his every move and I'll shoot him on sight if he tries to leave."

"Why don't you tell me, yourself."

Jason whirled around. His lips twisted into a mocking grin when he saw Wade Chandler standing there. "Guess I already did."

When Chandler took a step toward the man, Samantha jumped in front of him. "Can't you see he's just taunting you . . . ? Listen to me, Chandler! If Lieutenant Brown had any cause to arrest you, he would have done so. Obviously, he hasn't," she added, glaring at the lieutenant.

"What's going on here?" an angry voice intervened.

"Pa!" Samantha had never been so glad to see anybody in her life.

John's long strides quickly closed the distance between himself and Lieutenant Brown. "I thought I told you to stay off my property."

"I'm here on official business, Callahan."

"You know what you can do with your "official business", Lieutenant."

Jason figured he'd probably pushed his authority far enough—besides, he felt confident that once the colonel considered all the circumstances regarding Corporal Smith's unexpected demise, he would find the Indian guilty.

"Do not leave this ranch, Mister Chandler," Jason said in a warning tone. Then he turned on his boot heel and marched toward his horse.

"Isn't what that lieutenant's doing considered harassment?" Samantha said to her father.

"Not as far as the army's concerned."

"What should we do, Pa?"

John looked seriously at Chandler. "I would stay off the range for a while, if I were you. I wouldn't put it past Lieutenant Brown to shoot you in the back, if he got the chance."

"I'm not afraid of the man, John."

"Chandler, please do what Pa says."

"I won't live that way . . . constantly looking over my shoulder," Chandler snapped at Samantha. "Besides, your father needs every man working on that fence to get it done before winter sets in."

"I can take your place."

"You'll do no such thing!"

"You can't stop me!"

"But *I* can," John interceded. "And I agree with Chandler."

"I was working alongside the men way before Chandler ever came into the picture," Samantha argued with her father.

"We didn't have some *lunatic lieutenant* watching our every move then! I mean it, Samantha! I'd better not catch you out on the range . . . end of discussion!" Without another word John strode toward the house.

"At least your father can still control you," Chandler remarked with a chuckle.

Samantha suddenly turned on him in a furious rage. "It certainly won't last forever, I assure you!" she hissed. "You should have taken my side!"

"I wasn't on your side!" Chandler shouted back.

"You never are! All you men stick together!"

"That's ridiculous! You're just angry because you didn't get your way!"

"Now look who's being ridiculous!"

"I oughtta take you over my knee!"

"You wouldn't dare!"

Chandler's dark brows shot straight up at the challenge. "Wouldn't I?" Without warning his hand snaked out to grab hold of Samantha and then he scooped her up in his arms and tossed her over his shoulder like a sack of potatoes and strode across the yard.

"Put me down!" she screamed at the top of her lungs.

He didn't break stride.

"I mean it, Chandler . . . put me down this instant!"

When he refused to stop, Samantha finally hauled off and punched him in the back with her fist. He retaliated by bringing his hand down hard upon her backside. "Ouch! How dare you strike me you . . . you savage . . . !" Samantha let out a loud screech of surprise when she suddenly went sailing through the air and landed with a big splash in the horses' trough. Her arms and legs flailing wildly, she gasped from the shock of the ice-cold water as she struggled to stand up, but a strong hand held her firmly in place. "Let me out of here!"

"Not until you calm down!"

"I despise you!" she furiously hissed.

"You're unbelievable!" Chandler immediately let go of her and rose to his feet.

Angrily swiping her drenched hair out of her face, Samantha stepped out of the trough and vehemently spat, "If I had a gun right now, I would shoot you myself and save Lieutenant Brown the trouble!" The instant the words were out of her mouth Samantha regretted them, but it was too late to take them back now. *Oh why couldn't she control her own tongue!* She noticed that Chandler's handsome face had gone white, and she knew how much those words had hurt him. She inwardly winced when his eyes suddenly turned cold and then he walked away without even a backward glance.

Samantha just stood there, watching Chandler's departing back for several long moments; then she was racing after him. Her wet boots swished noisily over the hard ground as she hurried toward the corral where he kept his horse, her only thought was to find Chandler and tell him how sorry she was. *But surely he must realize she hadn't meant what she said, that she had only spouted off in anger . . .*

Samantha halted in her tracks when she saw Chandler was already leading Ranger out of the corral. She wanted to call out to him, but pride kept her mouth shut, as he swung onto the stallion's back and then took off at a full gallop toward town. If he wanted to leave then let him. But as Chandler gradually disappeared out of sight, she couldn't stop the tears that began to roll down her cheeks. He probably couldn't wait to get away from her, she thought miserably, and who could blame him.

Her shoulders slumping in defeat, Samantha turned and started walking back toward the house. She couldn't get the pained expression on Chandler's face out of her mind; nor could she forget the way his eyes had turned stone cold when he looked at her. *She hadn't meant what she said! Oh would she never learn to control her terrible temper!*

Samantha paced nervously back and forth under the wide-covered porch that ran the entire length of the front of the house, occasionally glancing across the field, though it was too dark to see anything. Chandler had not yet returned, and she was becoming nearly frantic with each passing minute. *What if Lieutenant Brown ambushed Chandler?* she wondered. She wouldn't put anything past the man, especially after his visit this afternoon. And, now, if anything happened to Chandler, it would be all her fault, because he never would have left the ranch in the first place if it hadn't been for her: then visions of Chandler lying hurt on the ground began to flash through Samantha's severely troubled mind. Suddenly she quit pacing to turn and stare silently into the darkness, mentally saying a prayer to God, asking Him to keep Chandler safe.

She heard the front door open and close, then Rebecca was standing beside her. "I'm sure Chandler will be back, Samantha, after he's had some time to cool off."

Samantha turned to Rebecca. "But how much time does Chandler need to cool off? He's been gone most of the day, while I've been stuck here worried out of my mind," she grumbled more to herself. "Oooo . . . when I see him, I'll . . ."

"You'll do nothing," Rebecca chastised her. "Remember?"

"Yes, I remember . . . how could I forget? My temper is what caused this whole mess!" Now Samantha felt guilty for snapping at her cousin. "I'm sorry, Becca."

"It's okay. I know you're just worried about Chandler."

Samantha needed something else to occupy her mind before she went crazy. "What do you think will happen with your parents?"

"I wish I knew. Sometimes I get so angry at my father I could just spit in his eye!" then Rebecca quickly covered her mouth.

Samantha burst out laughing. "It looks like some of my bad influence has finally rubbed off on you, dear cousin."

"It does appear that way, doesn't it," Rebecca said, giggling. "My father would bust a seam if he heard me speak that way. And so would Albert . . . Samantha! I just had a brilliant idea that I think just might discourage that old *sour puss*. Would you help me?"

"You know I will, Becca, but Pa already warned Uncle Bernard to keep Albert away from you, so I doubt you have anything to worry about."

"You don't know my father very well, Samantha. When he wants something bad enough, nothing stands in his way. If I know my father as well as I think I do, he'll be bringing Albert by the house real soon."

"Then Uncle Bernard has more guts than I thought," Samantha mumbled under her breath.

It was well into the early morning hours when Samantha was suddenly awakened with a start. Tossing aside the covers, she got out of bed and padded over to the window. Relief instantly washed over her when she saw Chandler sitting on Ranger in the yard, thinking, he must have just returned from town. Needing to see for herself that Chandler was okay, she whirled and hurried from her room.

Outside on the front porch, Samantha quickly descended the porch steps and crossed the yard in her bare feet. In the bright moonlight, she could see Chandler was still seated on his horse, and was slumped slightly forward. Instantly becoming panic-stricken, Samantha started to run, ignoring the small rocks poking the bottom of her feet. Now almost to Chandler, she heard him moan, and then he leaned over and fell off his horse, landing on the hard ground with a bone-jarring thud.

Samantha screamed Chandler's name as she dropped to her knees beside him. Gently rolling him over on his back, she nearly gagged when the strong smell of whiskey hit her nostrils with such force that it just about took her breath away.

"You're drunk!" Samantha angrily hissed and shot to her feet.

Suddenly Chandler burst out laughing, then began to slur some words to a tune she didn't recognize. Both fists planted firmly on her hips, she snapped, "Get up, you cad!"

"Is that you, Sam?" Chandler hiccupped. He tried to sit up and then fell back sprawled out on the ground and slurred, "Sam, Sam, oh where—for art thou," hiccup, "Sam." Then he laughed uproariously as if he'd just told the funniest joke.

"How dare you, Wade Chandler!" Samantha angrily shouted. "While I've been worried sick all night, you went into town and got drunk!"

Struggling to a standing position, Chandler staggered on his feet, while pointing an accusing finger in Samantha's direction. "Don't you use that," hiccup, "tone of voice—with me ever again, woman." He started to walk toward her.

Samantha rolled her eyes when Chandler tripped over his own foot and hit the ground. Now he was crawling toward her on his hands and knees, mumbling something about *vindictive women.* If it weren't for the fact that she was so angry, she would have burst out laughing at the picture he made. Grumbling under her breath, Samantha stepped over to Chandler and helped him to his feet. Figuring a good dousing of cold water was just what he needed to sober him up, she steered the drunken man toward the nearest trough: ironically they were headed for the same trough where Chandler had dunked her the previous afternoon.

"Where are you taking me, m'lady?" he slurred.

"You'll see," she replied with a smirking grin.

The moment they stopped, Samantha started to feel guilty for what she was about to do, but told herself that it was for Chandler's own good, before giving him a mighty shove. His arms flailed like a windmill, then, as he started to fall backwards it was just an automatic reaction to reach out and grab hold of Samantha for support, who let out an ear-splitting scream as they both splashed into the trough. Chandler gasped from the frigid water and instantly sprung to his feet, automatically taking Samantha with him. She lost her grip around his neck and dropped to the ground at his feet on her backside.

"Why'd you do that?" Chandler roared.

Samantha slowly got to her feet, rubbing her smarting rear end. "You were drunk and I was trying to sober you," she angrily replied.

"Well maybe I didn't want sobering!"

Shivering in the cool night breeze, with her saturated knee-length hair plastered to her body, her teeth chattering uncontrollably, Samantha finally exploded in fury. "Do you have . . . any idea of what I . . . what I've been through tonight? I thought you were hurt . . . or . . . or worse!"

"That coming from someone who wanted to shoot me!"

"You know I didn't mean that!"

"Then why did you say it?"

"I'll discuss this with you when you're more reasonable!" As Samantha tried to brush past him, Chandler grabbed hold of her arm and jerked her around to face him.

"We'll discuss it now!"

Samantha couldn't understand why Chandler was so angry at her—after all, she wasn't the one who came home rip-roaring drunk. And she wasn't about to stand out here in the cold and argue with the man. "Get your hand off me." She had clearly emphasized each word.

"Is that all you two ever do is fight?"

Both Chandler and Samantha whirled around at the unexpected but familiar voice. In the dappled moonlight, Samantha could clearly see Morgan's tall form leaning against the corral, though his face was hidden in the shadows.

"You're not supposed to be here," Chandler said.

Morgan pushed away from the fence and started to walk toward them. "Is that any way to greet your favorite bother?" he teased.

"How long were you standing there?" Chandler inquired suspiciously.

"I've never seen anything more comical than when you and Samantha landed in that trough," Morgan said, coming to a halt. "It's a good thing I wasn't an enemy meaning to do either of you harm. You should have heard me coming, Graywolf."

"Samantha and I were just having a little disagreement."

"We're always having disagreements," Samantha mumbled under her breath.

The corner of Morgan's mouth lifted into a lop-sided grin. "You know—I've heard somewhere that it's healthy for married couples to argue. If that's true, then you and Samantha are going to be the healthiest people in the entire county."

Until now, it hadn't registered inside Chandler's liquored state-of-mind that Morgan had cut his long hair. It now barely reached the tops of his broad shoulders. Not only that, he'd also shed his Indian garments and had donned western-style clothes: a pair of blue jeans hugged his long, muscular legs, and he was wearing a short-sleeved red-and-white-checked flannel shirt. And, instead of a leather headband, a black Stetson covered his head. But he was still wearing his knee high moccasins.

"What did you do to yourself, Morgan?" Samantha had asked the question.

"It was Father's idea. He figured if I was going to be living with the white man that I should look more like one." Casually pushing his hat back, Morgan grinned at Samantha. "And while we're on the subject of attire, what are you doing out here in your . . . unmentionables?"

Samantha gasped, suddenly crossing her arms over her chest. She'd completely forgotten that she was only wearing her nightgown. Whirling, she trotted toward the house without another word to either man.

Morgan turned to his brother. "This I gotta hear."

"Forget about Samantha—I gotta a question of my own. Why did you leave the village when you know it's not safe for you to be here?"

"I decided to come back and face my enemy." Morgan shrugged and added, "Besides, Father said you were in trouble."

Chandler sarcastically wondered which of his *troubles* their father might have been referring to: Samantha or Lieutenant Brown. "A lot has happened in your absence."

"I haven't been gone *that* long."

"Long enough—for around here."

"This wouldn't have anything to do with the reason why Samantha was outside in the middle of the night in her undergarments, would it?" Morgan's grin had broadened.

"Why is it that my problems always seem to amuse you?"

"Only *that* particular problem. Our father gave me some advice for you about Samantha: you can't fight fire with fire."

Chandler frowned. "What exactly is that supposed to mean?"

"It means—you two seem to ignite each other's temper."

"Now tell me something I don't know."

"Then if you realize what the problem is—"

"And what do you suggest I do, Morgan . . . let Samantha have her way on everything just to keep peace?"

"Are you having second thoughts about getting married?"

Running a hand through his shoulder-length hair, Chandler honestly admitted, "I don't know. Seems like I can't do anything right where that . . . fire-breathing woman's concerned."

Morgan threw back his head and laughed.

"You think it's funny?"

"You wanna know what I really think, Graywolf? You're just going through what a lot of grooms go through just before their wedding. I think you and Samantha will be fine—once the deed is done."

Chandler wasn't so sure if it was simple wedding jitters that was bothering him. "Where's your horse?" he asked, deciding to change the subject.

"I turned it loose inside the corral."

"Why don't we sleep in the barn tonight, so we won't disturb the men in the bunkhouse."

As they started walking across the yard toward the barn, Chandler explained to his brother all that had taken place in the short time he'd been gone. He described how Samantha had rescued him from Lieutenant Brown's partners in crime, how he'd forced both men to walk back to the army camp minus their clothes and boots, and how Lieutenant Brown was now trying to blame him for the death of Corporal Dewayne Smith.

"It wasn't your fault the man stepped on a snake," Morgan remarked.

"I know that . . . providing Corporal Smith really did step on a snake."

"You suspect foul play?"

"I would never be able to prove my suspicions anyway."

"Which is?"

"I'd bet my last dollar that either Lieutenant Brown or Corporal Jones had something to do with Corporal Smith's sudden demise, but I'm sure they covered their tracks well."

"What are you going to do?"

"There's nothing I can do." But Chandler was going to keep his eyes and ears open.

They entered the barn, and Chandler shut the door behind them. Then, feeling his way along the wall, he found the lantern and lit it. With the soft-glowing light to lead the way, they crossed the hay-strewn floor. Chandler saw the colt laying on some hay in the far corner of the barn; its mother standing close by. The colt was nearly big enough to put outside in the pasture where it could graze with the other horses and cattle. Setting the lantern on the ground, Chandler sat down on a bay of hay. His mind was still a little fuzzy from the bottle of whiskey he'd consumed earlier; and he was starting to get a headache.

Morgan straddled the bale across from his brother. "Samantha must love you very much to risk her life the way she did," he said after a brief period of silence.

"And I love her more than my own life, if that's what you're wondering?"

"What then?"

Chandler let out a heavy sigh. "She's too . . ."

"Independent?" Morgan offered.

"There's a difference between being independent and mule-headed stubborn."

"Which reminds me. Big Bear said to tell you—if Samantha ever becomes too much for you to handle, you can always bring her back to the village."

"As if he could handle the *wildcat* any better," Chandler grumbled. "Besides, I would never put the tribe through that kind of trouble."

Morgan busted out laughing. "Speaking of trouble—mind telling me why you and Samantha were arguing—why she dunked you in the horse trough, and why she was running around in a flimsy nighty?"

"I went into town and got drunk."

"Is that all?"

"Isn't that enough?"

"You wouldn't happen to be feeling a little guilty about something, dear brother?"

"What do you mean?"

"Come on, Graywolf . . . I bet I could just about narrate what happened tonight. You and Samantha had an argument, which is the reason you went into town to get drunk in the first place—that's conclusive enough. While you were at the *hurdy-gurdy house*—you were with another woman . . . a woman who's name you can't seem to remember or what you might've done with her . . . am I close?"

Rising, Chandler began to pace back and forth. "You're close enough—but I think her name was—Rose." He turned to face his brother. "If Samantha ever finds out—"

"I would definitely hide that knife of hers," Morgan chuckled.

"Maybe Samantha stabbing me in the back is what *trouble* Father was talking about."

Morgan burst out in uproarious laughter. "I don't think that's the kind of trouble Father meant." Then he teasingly added, "Although he didn't really say."

Chandler scowled at his brother. "You just wait . . . your turn will come. I suspect your heart already belongs to a certain young woman—which is part of the reason you came back, though you would never admit it. Need I again remind you, little brother, Rebecca has the potential of possessing the Callahan temper."

"Don't you think comparing Rebecca to Samantha, is like comparing a . . . a dove to a rattlesnake? And besides, who says my heart belongs to any woman."

A challenging brow rose, then a lopsided grin lifted the corner of Chandler's mouth. "Then maybe this would be an appropriate time to tell you about Albert."

"Who's Albert?"

"Like I said, Morgan, a lot has happened in your absence."

For the umpteenth time Samantha got out of bed, padded over to the window and looked toward the barn. She could still see a faint light was shining from inside, and wondered what Chandler and Morgan could be talking about. Above the horizon the night sky was just starting to lighten, telling Samantha it would soon be dawn. Turning away from the window, she padded back to her bed, pulled the covers over her head, and closed her eyes. But, now, wide-awake, she knew she would not be getting any more sleep this night.

With a sigh, Samantha tossed the covers aside and swung her bare legs over the edge of the bed; then rising, she tiptoed over to the door and listened carefully. The house was still silent, so nobody was up yet. Grabbing a clean change of clothes from her chest of drawers, she headed to the bathing room. A long soaking bath was just what she needed . . .

When Samantha returned to her room, she sat in the chair at her dressing table and looked in the mirror. There were dark circles under her eyes, but there wasn't a whole lot she could do about them. Reaching for the hairbrush, she began to brush the tangles from her freshly washed knee-length hair, deciding to leave it unbraided this morning, allowing the thick mane to flow down her back, just the way Chandler liked it.

Anxious to get started on her morning chores, she quietly left her room.

Inside the barn, Samantha forked some hay to old Suzie, and gave the mare some extra oats. Meanwhile, the little colt had trotted over to Samantha to investigate what she was doing. Now that the colt was more used to her and wasn't so jumpity around people anymore, he was almost becoming a nuisance. She giggled when the colt nudged her with his velvety nose.

"We still haven't given you a name yet, have we, little man," Samantha crooned, patting the colt's fluffy coat. "How about calling you Frisky . . . you like that?" When the colt shook his head as if to answer "no", she burst out laughing. The loud noise spooked the little animal and it bolted away.

As Samantha turned to leave, she spotted something lying on the hay-strewn floor, so she walked over to pick it up. *What would a woman's fancy lace handkerchief be doing in here?* Samantha wondered. She was certain it didn't belong to her mother; and it definitely was not hers. She didn't think it belonged to Aunt Ruth or Rebecca.

Then she noticed there was a letter "R" neatly stitched in one corner. And the hanky smelled like cheap perfume. Her blue eyes narrowed in anger when another reality struck her. Evidently getting drunk wasn't the only thing that Chandler had done last night.

Clutching the silk hanky tightly in her fist, Samantha strode across the barn.

Chapter Thirty-two

Samantha stood staring out her bedroom window, still contemplating on whether she should confront Chandler about the woman's handkerchief. She wondered if it might be best to wait and follow him the next time he rode into town. Yet—at the same time—if Chandler was seeing another woman—did she really want to know?

Her dismal thoughts were temporarily disrupted when a woman's musical laughter drifted through her open window. Her eyes caught sight of Morgan and Rebecca. The two of them were standing close together under the big oak tree, talking and laughing. They looked so happy together, Samantha thought to herself, and she wondered if Chandler ever looked at her the way that Morgan was now looking at Rebecca.

Thinking about Chandler brought a frown to Samantha's lips. She hadn't seen him yet this morning . . . no doubt he was inside the bunkhouse, probably still sleeping it off, she angrily mused. Then, as if she had somehow conjured the man up in her mind, Chandler emerged from the bunkhouse. Her piercing blue eyes followed him as he crossed the yard toward Morgan and Becca. Jealous daggers shot from her eyes. She suddenly came to a decision.

Walking over to her dressing table, Samantha snatched up the delicate, lacy handkerchief and tied it around her neck. She looked at herself in the mirror: the hanky was in plain sight; even a man in a *drunken stupor* couldn't miss it.

Samantha then walked out of her room and, like a soldier marching into combat, she stomped down the stairway, and slammed out the front door. Outside on the porch, she stopped long enough to draw in a deep breath and let it out slowly, trying to maintain control over her raging emotions; then she continued down the porch steps and marched forward, her arms swinging angrily at her sides with each long stride she took.

As Samantha approached the small group, Chandler smiled, when he noticed her. But, then, that welcoming smile quickly turned into a concerned frown. *Good!* she inwardly fumed. *He should be concerned!* Though Samantha was sorry that Morgan and Rebecca would have to witness the confrontation, but it couldn't be helped.

She halted directly in front of Chandler and sarcastically snapped, "Lose something?"

His jaw muscles twitched slightly, but he said nothing. In even a bolder attempt to get a reaction out of Chandler, she yanked the handkerchief off her neck and held it out to him. "I think you'd better give this back to its rightful owner."

When Chandler still didn't utter a word, she angrily hurled the hanky at his moccasined feet, and furiously spat, "When were you planning on telling me about your little tryst, Chandler—*after* we were married?"

"That's my handkerchief, Samantha," Rebecca softly said. "I must have dropped it."

Samantha's face visibly paled at Rebecca's words as she stared into Chandler's hurt-filled eyes. *What could she say?* Sorry seemed like such an inadequate apology. Once again, she had allowed her temper to get the best of her. She should have trusted Chandler, or at least should have given him a change to explain. Before she accused him of anything, she could have first confirmed with Rebecca that the hanky wasn't hers or Aunt Ruth's. But the handkerchief had smelled like cheap perfume, so naturally she'd thought the worse. She started to reach out with her hand, then suddenly turned and fled toward the house.

"Let her go, Chandler!" Rebecca shouted, grabbing him by the arm. When she saw the pain in the man's eyes, she almost felt sympathy for him. *Almost.*

"Why did you lie, Becca?" Chandler wanted to know.

"To protect Samantha."

"You might have just made a bad situation even worse, although it's my own fault."

"You'd better tell Samantha the truth, Graywolf," Morgan said.

"And just what is the truth?" Rebecca snapped at Chandler.

"Honestly? I'm not sure . . . I was too drunk."

"A likely excuse! Do you have any idea of what you've done, Wade Chandler . . . !"

Morgan listened while the woman—whom he'd claimed to be as gentle as a dove—verbally reprimanded his older brother on the evils of infidelity. His "little dove" could definitely hold her own, Morgan thought with a wide grin. The words shot from her mouth like a flaming arrow—and when he heard the docile Rebecca use the phrase, "A despicable, no-good, philandering Casanova!" he finally burst out with laughter.

Rebecca whirled on Morgan. "And you . . . you're probably just like your brother!" She then lifted her skirt and stormed off toward the house.

Morgan watched her stiff, departing back with a stunned expression. "What did *I* do?"

"Don't ask me. You're the one who compared Samantha's soft-spoken cousin to a . . . a dove, wasn't it? I did try to warn you."

"She's almost as temperamental as—your *betrothed*."

"Well don't look at me."

Suddenly Morgan threw back his head and laughed heartily.

Inside her bedroom, Samantha paced back and forth, while carefully listening to every word Rebecca had to say. When she heard her finish with "I'm sure there's a reasonable explanation how that hanky got inside the barn" Samantha stopped pacing and turned to look at her cousin. "Don't you dare defend Chandler, Becca. There's only one explanation I can think of . . . how that woman's handkerchief got there." She then walked over to the window and shoved the curtain aside.

"Are they still out there?" Rebecca asked.

"They haven't budged an inch."

"I'm sorry I lied to you, Samantha . . . do you forgive me?"

"Of course I forgive you, Becca," she replied, still staring out the window. "I understand why you said the hanky was yours. I probably would've done the same."

"Won't you at least listen to what Chandler has to say?"

Samantha turned away from the window to face her cousin. "Drunk as he was last night, I doubt he can even remember the ride home—let alone anything else." She walked over to her bed and plopped down on it. "I don't know, Becca—maybe Chandler and I shouldn't get married . . . we seem to argue most of the time and now—this."

"Don't you love him?"

"I'll always love Chandler," Samantha didn't hesitate to answer. "Unfortunately, love doesn't necessarily guarantee a good marriage. Now that Chandler's been with another woman, I don't think I can forgive him for that—or ever trust him again."

"But you don't know for sure that he *was* with another woman."

"Did he deny it then?"

No response.

"I didn't think so."

"But, Samantha—isn't forgiveness part of what love's all about?"

"Oh, Becca, it's not that easy."

The door suddenly opened and Ruth peeked her head inside the room. "I'm sorry to interrupt you girls, but—Becca, your father's here and Albert came with him," Ruth informed her daughter. "Albert is waiting for you on the veranda, dear, but I would be happy to tell him you're not feeling well?"

The corners of Rebecca's mouth lifted into a mischievous grin. "That's okay, Mama. Tell Albert I'll be right down." The instant the door closed behind her mother, she turned to Samantha and said, "I need your help."

A short while later, Rebecca was descending the wide-banistered staircase. She paused at the bottom step, listening to her parents' raised voices coming from the parlor. Tempted as she was to barge into the room and tell her father what she thought of him, she continued toward the kitchen, thinking this was something her parents had to work out . . .

Inside the kitchen, Rebecca lingered at the back door, mustering the courage to step outside and face Albert. Squaring her shoulders, she opened the door, frowning, when she spotted Mr. Smythers sitting in one of the chairs beside the picnic table. He was dressed in his usual attire—a ruffled white shirt and silk suit—and he was dabbing at his sweaty brow with a silk handkerchief. No doubt Albert wasn't used to the late September climate here in Montana, which was much warmer and humid than back home. He looked quite uncomfortable, but she could feel no sympathy for him. In fact, the sight of Albert made Rebecca want to gag. She angrily slammed the door shut behind her.

Albert twisted around in his chair, and rose to his feet. "Rebecca?" he said incredulously.

"It isn't polite to stare, Albert."

"What have you done to yourself?"

"They're called pants, Albert." Rebecca then hooked her thumbs inside the waistband of the tight leather pants she'd borrowed from Samantha and swaggered toward an empty chair, purposely taking long, manly strides. She then flipped the chair around and straddled the seat like a man. She nearly burst out laughing, the way Albert just stood there, staring at her with his mouth wide open. "Careful, Albert, you might catch a fly."

"Is this some kind of sick joke, Rebecca?"

"Whatever do you mean?"

"Don't play coy with me."

"I'm not trying to play anything, Albert."

Reaching inside his shirt pocket, Albert pulled out an expensive cigar, lit it, then leaned back in his chair. After taking several puffs, he angrily said, "I tried to warn your father about letting you come to this dreadful place, but Bernard wouldn't listen to me."

"Figures you would find this place dreadful. Personally I find it—wildly exciting."

"I'm not sure what you mean by wildly exciting," Albert grumbled more to himself.

Rising, Rebecca sauntered over to Albert, reached inside his shirt pocket and pulled out one of his expensive cigars, placed the thing in between her front teeth, then stood there, patiently waiting for Albert to light it.

"Okay, Rebecca, I'll play along with your little ruse."

After Albert lit the cigar, Rebecca sauntered back to her chair and straddled it like a man, then quietly sat there, puffing away on the cigar, pretending to enjoy it, when the smoke was actually causing her to feel a little nauseous.

"This rebellion of yours is no longer funny."

"I'm not trying to rebel!" Rebecca snapped. "You make me sound like a willful child!"

"Look, Rebecca, I came here to tell you that your father has arranged for us to get married in town . . . day after tomorrow. I wanted to tell you the good news myself."

"I don't want to marry you." *There! It was finally out in the open.*

Albert leaned forward. "What did you say?"

"I said I don't want to marry you."

"It's a little late for . . ."

"I never consented to marry you, Albert . . . you and my father made that decision for me. And now, well—I'm way past the age where my father can tell me what to do."

"I knew you coming here was a huge mistake!"

"Why, because I'm finally making a decision on my own?"

"We've been planning this wedding for over two years, Rebecca!"

"No, you and my father have been planning this wedding!"

"It's because I'm so much older than you, isn't it?" Albert was determined to marry this woman. Her elegant beauty alone would further his career in the near future. After they were married, he was planning on quitting her father's law firm and getting into politics, and Rebecca was just the kind of wife he needed at his side.

"Please, Albert, just accept the fact that I don't want to marry you." The furious look Albert then gave her actually frightened Rebecca.

Albert threw down his cigar and shot to his feet. "Have you met someone else?" he demanded in a jealous rage. "Answer me, Rebecca!"

She stood out of her chair. "Albert, please . . ."

"Is there a problem?" a loud voice sharply cut in.

Rebecca whirled around. "Uncle John," she said with relief.

"Rebecca, who is this man?"

"Forgive my bad manners, Sir," Albert immediately apologized. The last thing he wanted to do was anger Rebecca's uncle. "I'm Albert Smythers . . . Rebecca's fiancé."

John was infuriated at Bernard for bringing Albert here after he had warned his brother-in-law to keep the man away from Rebecca. He had to restrain himself from physically picking Albert up and tossing him off the veranda. "I couldn't help but overhear part of your conversation, Albert, wasn't it?"

Albert could feel tiny beads of perspiration breaking out across his forehead. Bernard never told him Rebecca's uncle was as tall as a tree. "Look . . . if I've offended Rebecca—"

"Well let's find out," John said in a matter-of-fact tone. He turned to his niece and said, "Becca, did this man offend you?"

Albert looked so scared, Rebecca wanted to laugh. She couldn't remember anybody ever intimidating Albert Smythers this way before. But, then again, he'd never met her Uncle John. Rebecca stifled a giggle as she replied, "He hasn't offended me yet." She didn't miss the look of relief that came over Albert's flushed face.

John turned back to Albert. "Let's keep it that way."

Albert didn't need to be told twice. "Tell your father, I'll be waiting for him in the buggy," he said to Rebecca. Then he stepped off the veranda and quickly disappeared around the corner of the house.

"Did you see the look on Albert's face?" Rebecca remarked to her uncle.

"A face I'll not soon be forgetting, that's for sure."

Rebecca burst out laughing.

"Out of mild curiosity, why are you dressed like a gunslinger?" John asked his niece.

"I was trying to annoy that—stiff old goat."

"Sounds like something Samantha would do."

"I guess some of her positive traits are starting to wear off on me," Rebecca proudly stated.

"I'm not exactly sure I would call *those* particular traits positive."

"What a terrible thing for a father to say." A look of amusement twitched the corners of Samantha's mouth as she closed the back door.

"I could have said a lot worse." Then, "I'd better get back to work." John threw over his shoulder as he walked away, "Stay out of trouble, Samantha."

"You know, Becca—it's a sad thing when your own father doesn't trust ya," Samantha innocently commented.

Rebecca would have laughed at her cousin's remark had it not made her think of her own father. "Which reminds me, I still need to have a little talk with mine."

"Want me to go with you?"

"I appreciate the offer, but—this is something I should have done a long time ago."

Rebecca stood at the parlor door, listening to her parents arguing. It really wasn't anything out of the ordinary, the way her father was yelling at her mother. This time, however, she wasn't about to do nothing, while her mother took the brunt of her father's anger. After all, they were arguing over her. She turned the doorknob and boldly entered the room.

"What is this, Rebecca, some kind of joke?" Bernard demanded, the moment he saw her. "Go change those ridiculous clothes at once!"

Rebecca slammed the door shut. "No!"

"What did you say, young lady?"

"There's nothing wrong with the clothes I'm wearing."

"You see, Ruth!" Bernard angrily bellowed, waving a hand through the air. "I told you it was a bad idea to bring an impressionable young woman to this uncivilized land! Not counting that . . . that *barbarian* your sister's married to!"

"Uncle John has nothing to do with this!" Rebecca shouted back. "Oh, by the way, Father, before I forget—Albert's waiting in the buggy."

"Whatever for?"

"I suppose he's upset because I told him the wedding's off."

"You did what?" Bernard roared. "Do you realize what you've done? Albert's your security for the future, Rebecca! Someday he's going to be a rich man!"

"Then *you* marry him!" Rebecca snapped.

Bernard headed toward the door. "Ruth, talk some sense into your daughter, while I try and straighten this mess out with Albert!"

"Not so fast, Bernard." When her husband turned around, Ruth's chin went up a notch, determined not to back down from him, this time. "If Becca doesn't want to marry Albert, then there will be no wedding, and if you won't tell that *old coot*, I will!"

"Do you know what you're saying?"

"Something I should have said long ago!" Ruth turned to her daughter and calmly said, "Becca, leave us at once . . . there's something

I want to say to your father in private. And close the door behind you."

"Are you sure, Mama?"

"I've never been more certain about anything in my life. Go on now, dear."

Ruth held her tongue, until her daughter was completely out of the room, before turning to face her husband. "I've put up with your philandering nearly our entire marriage and I'm not doing it any longer. As far as I'm concerned, Bernard, you can have your harlots, including the most recent one that's staying with you over at the hotel."

"How dare you speak to me this way!"

"It's no more than you deserve! This time, when you go back to the hotel, you can tell Bell that she has my blessings where you're concerned! Now leave, before I have John throw you out! You remember him? the *barbarian* my sister's married to!"

"This isn't over with, Ruth!" Bernard furiously spat as he headed toward the door. "Remember what I said I'd do if you ever tried to leave me?"

"That threat doesn't work anymore, Bernard . . . Rebecca's a grown woman. I can finally be free of you—now get out!"

The instant Bernard left the room, Ruth grabbed hold of a nearby chair for support. She had never stood up to her husband that way before. Although it had felt absolutely wonderful, her entire body was shaking. When the door opened behind her, Ruth stiffened, thinking that Bernard had returned.

"Are you okay, Ruthie?"

Ruth looked over her shoulder at her sister. "Never been better."

Rebecca stood beside the corral, dangling her arms over the top rail, watching her father and Albert drive away in the buggy. She wondered if her mother told her father she was leaving him—it was probably for the best, because her father would never be faithful. But even in spite of the trouble between her parents, Rebecca felt like a heavy burden had been lifted from her shoulders. She should've told Albert a long time ago she wouldn't marry him. Now she wouldn't have to constantly worry about *proprieties*; nor would she have to listen to one of Albert's lectures on how important it was that his future wife learn proper etiquettes. *Proper etiquettes indeed!*

"Did you see the look on your father's face?" Samantha commented beside her.

"I saw."

"Aunt Ruth must've given Uncle Bernard the boot."

Rebecca grinned to herself. That's what she liked most about her cousin Samantha—her outspokenness—the way she bluntly said what was on her mind.

"Well, well, here comes the *gruesome twosome*," Samantha grumbled under her breath.

Rebecca followed her cousin's line of vision and saw Chandler and Morgan were walking toward them. "Samantha, you're going to have to face Chandler sooner or later."

"Then let it be later."

"At least give the man a chance to explain about the hanky."

"He should have a pretty good explanation by now . . . he's had all morning to think of an excuse."

"I don't think Chandler would deliberately lie," Rebecca argued.

"Maybe."

"Good day, ladies," Morgan politely stated. He quirked a brow toward Rebecca. "Need a light for that thing?"

Rebecca had forgotten all about the cigar she was still holding between her fingers. She slipped it inside her shirt pocket and firmly replied, "No."

"Who was the man with your uncle?" Chandler asked Samantha curiously.

"That was Albert."

"Albert," Morgan repeated the name, then burst out laughing. So *that* was the competition his brother had warned him about.

"What's so funny?" Rebecca wanted to know.

"Nothing," Morgan said, shaking his head.

"So where did the hanky come from, Chandler?" Samantha suddenly blurted out. She knew this wasn't the best time to broach the subject, but she was too angry to care.

"You certainly don't beat around the bush, do you?"

"You know me better than that."

"Sometimes I think I don't know you at all."

Samantha folded her arms across her chest. "And just what's that supposed to mean?"

"If you two don't mind, I think Becca and I will get out of harm's way." Morgan held out his hand to her and said, "Shall we go for a walk?"

"That might be wise," Rebecca agreed, tossing a worried look toward Samantha.

Chandler watched Morgan and Rebecca for several long moments, before turning to face Samantha. "For whatever it's worth, I'm sorry."

"It's not worth much if you don't even know what you're apologizing for."

"If you're asking me how that hanky came into my possession—I have no idea." Chandler let out a long sigh and ran both his hands nervously through his shoulder-length hair. "After our little disagreement yesterday . . ."

"One of many disagreements, I might add."

"Will you let me finish!" Chandler snapped. "Look . . . long story short—I went into town and got drunk—obviously that much you already know—and I honestly can't remember much after that."

"How convenient!" Samantha hissed.

"I'm telling the truth!"

"You must have some idea who that hanky belongs to!"

"I don't know . . . maybe someone named Rose. Look, Samantha, I know what you're thinking and nothing happened."

"If you can't remember . . . how do you know nothing happened?" she angrily countered.

"I just do."

"I'll tell you what I *do* believe . . . I'm sure nobody was pouring drinks down your throat!"

"So what do you want me to say?"

"I don't think there's anything you can say!" Samantha blinked back tears gathering behind her eyes. She jerked away from Chandler when he tried to put his arm around her.

"I'm truly sorry, Samantha. I never meant to hurt you."

Hearing Chandler's soft footsteps walking away, Samantha turned to watch him, until he disappeared inside the bunkhouse.

Chapter Thirty-three

The next morning Samantha was suddenly awakened by what sounded like a small herd of horses thundering over the ground. Leaping out of bed, she hurried over to the window and shoved aside the curtain. Her eyes widened in stunned surprise. It looked like the entire cavalry was running rampant around the ranch. She also noticed there were several men leading Chandler from the bunkhouse.

Wondering what Lieutenant Brown was trying to pull now, Samantha dressed in a hurry, and rushed from her room. She flew down the wide-banistered stairway and out the front door, then vaulted off the porch and ran toward a group of men who already had Chandler in shackles. She furiously approached Lieutenant Brown.

"What do you think you're doing?" she shouted at the top of her lungs.

"I suppose you'll find out soon enough, Miss Callahan. Wade Chandler assaulted a white woman in town last night."

"That's impossible!"

"We have the young woman's complete testimony and she described the Indian to a tee," the lieutenant informed her. He then pointed an accusing finger at Chandler and snarled in a hateful tone, "He's a dangerous criminal!"

"That's a lie!" Samantha screamed.

"You have no business on this property, Lieutenant!"

Samantha whirled at the sound of her mother's voice. "Ma! Now this *ego maniac* is accusing Chandler of . . . of assaulting a woman! He would never do such a thing!"

"Lieutenant, when my husband finds out . . ."

"Your husband, pardon me, ma'am, has no say over army matters. And the Indian you're trying to protect . . . we have the young woman's testimony."

"Then she's lying!" Samantha cried. "Chandler would never hurt a woman!"

"Well, Miss Callahan, Rose says different!"

"I would like to speak to Chandler in private!" Samantha demanded.

"He's not going anywhere, so I suppose it can't hurt." Lieutenant Brown threw over his shoulder, "Watch him men!" as he walked away.

As Samantha stood watching Chandler, she instantly recognized his Indian face. He was now Graywolf, full-blooded Cheyenne warrior, and it was hard to say what he might do. She could tell that his muscles were taut like a bowstring about ready to snap; and his dark eyes were secretly observing everything around him. She could only pray he wouldn't try anything that would get him into even more trouble.

Samantha slid her arms around Chandler's waist. "I'm so sorry this is happening again." He didn't even blink, but continued to stare straight ahead. "I want you to know that I don't believe what Lieutenant Brown said about Rose."

This finally got a reaction out of him. "Rose?"

"Apparently it's the name of the woman you supposedly assaulted last night."

So the woman who'd given him all those drinks, her name was Rose . . . that much Chandler could remember. Even though he couldn't remember anything else, the woman was lying. He focussed on Samantha's brilliant blue eyes, looking so trustingly up at him. He could read her so well. "Stay out of this—I already have enough to worry about."

"When my father gets back . . ."

"I doubt even John will be able to get me out of this mess."

"I hate to break up the little party, but I have a job to do," came Lieutenant Brown's taunting voice behind Samantha.

"Move away from me, Samantha," Chandler gently urged her.

Not caring who was watching, Samantha wrapped her arms around Chandler's neck and stood on her tiptoes to kiss him good-bye. "Don't forget that I love you," she whispered for his ears only. His eyes softened when he looked at Samantha, then, once again, he was staring straight ahead, wearing his Indian face.

There was nothing Samantha could do, but stand there and watch, while Chandler was roughly hoisted onto the back of a horse, and then Lieutenant Brown led him away. The rest of his men immediately followed. No longer able to hold back the tears, they rolled silently down Samantha's cheeks. When she felt her mother's arms go around her, she covered her face with her hands and burst into tears.

"I know Chandler didn't touch that woman and we'll prove it somehow. I don't know how we'll do it, but we'll find a way," Rachel added, gently patting her daughter's head. "Now here comes Morgan, so pull yourself together, dear."

"What did they charge Graywolf with this time?" Morgan wanted to know. His eyes were drawn to the heavy cloud of dust being churned up by the horses' hooves in the distance. If he'd had any idea they were going to arrest his brother, he never would've stayed in the barn, but would have gladly confronted the lieutenant himself.

"Lieutenant Brown claims Chandler assaulted a woman," Rachel informed him.

"Graywolf would never do such a thing!" Morgan angrily spat.

"That's what I said, but they wouldn't listen," Samantha sniffled.

"Morgan, do you think you could find John?" Rachel asked hopefully.

"I'll find him."

"When you do, tell him what's happened."

When Morgan started to walk away, he heard Samantha call out, "Wait! I'm coming with you." He whirled around. "You're staying here!"

"Samantha, I think you should listen to Morgan," Rachel added.

"Ma, I can't stay here and do nothing."

"Then promise me, you'll be careful?"

"Now hold on a second—"

"Morgan, please . . . if I stay here I'll go crazy."

"Come on then," he grumbled, already headed toward the corral to fetch his horse. *Dang blam stubborn woman!*

Samantha and Morgan had been riding for over an hour and there still was no sign of her father or Amos or Ernie or any of the cowpunchers who might know where to find him. There was still so much ground to cover yet; her father could be just about anywhere. The longer she and Morgan rode over the grassy terrain, the more frazzled her nerves became. While they were on some wild goose chase, anything could be happening to Chandler.

"It wouldn't surprise me if Lieutenant Brown is somehow behind this whole thing," Samantha angrily declared. "Maybe he and this Rose are . . ."

"Rose?"

"That's the name of the woman who Chandler supposedly assaulted." Samantha frowned suspiciously. "Do you know her?"

Not sure what his brother had told Samantha about the night he'd gotten drunk, Morgan shook his head. "Well, whatever her name is—she's lying."

"That's what I tried to tell Lieutenant Brown, but of course he wouldn't listen. The man's had it in for Chandler from the very first moment they met."

Morgan was only partially listening, because he was trying to remember what Graywolf had told him about Rose, which wasn't very much. The woman had insisted on buying Graywolf a drink, and had brought him several throughout the evening. He couldn't seem to remember much after that first drink, which Morgan found peculiar, considering his brother could practically drink an entire bottle before the whiskey affected him. Graywolf couldn't even recall what the woman looked like—except that she had hair so blond it was nearly white and she had worn a lot of paint on her face. Morgan wondered why some white woman would buy his brother so many drinks?

What Samantha said made sense. In fact, the more Morgan thought about it, this Lieutenant Brown was probably the person behind whatever happened to Rose that night . . . if anything even really did happen to her, but . . . more likely the woman was lying. He only knew one thing for certain: he would be paying *Rose* a little visit . . .

Morgan pulled back on the reins, and turned to Samantha as she halted her horse beside his. "Do you think you could find John without me?"

"I suppose, but—where are you going?"

"I'm gonna pay Rose a little visit."

"Are you crazy, Morgan?" Samantha suddenly shrieked, becoming panic-stricken. "Lieutenant Brown is still looking for Black Hawk, remember? You go into town and he sees you . . ."

"That's a chance I'm willing to take."

"Chandler wouldn't approve."

"You got a better idea?"

"Actually paying Rose a little visit isn't a bad idea, Morgan."

"Forget it, Samantha!"

"Will you just listen!"

"Your father would skin me alive and so would my brother!"

"Need I remind you if they find Chandler guilty what the outcome will be—because I doubt that it's possible for an Indian to get a fair trial. Somehow we have to prove that Chandler didn't assault that woman, or he could very easily spend the rest of his life in prison—or worse."

"Okay . . . I'm listening . . . what do you have in mind?"

"We're almost to my brother's place . . . I'll explain then," Samantha said. Without waiting for a response from Morgan, she nudged her horse into a slow canter.

James anxiously paced inside the kitchen, trying to decide what to do. This only proved what he'd suspected all along—Jason Brown was an extremely dangerous man and a force to be reckoned with. He also knew his sister well and, unless he could change her mind, Samantha would go into town without him. He stopped pacing and turned to face her.

"I think we should let the sheriff handle this."

"That's a good idea," Morgan agreed.

"Lieutenant Brown will tell Sheriff Sanders the same thing he told us—that this is army business."

"Chief Black Hawk might be army business," James argued, "but what supposedly happened to Rose is Bear Creek's business."

"You still don't get it, James!" Samantha hissed in frustration. "This is about some crazy lieutenant who's determined to see Chandler behind bars. And whether the man truly believes that Chandler's Black Hawk or not—who knows for sure. But I do know that Lieutenant Brown hates Indians that much—even if it means lying to get what he wants."

"I still think the smartest thing to do is to go to Sheriff Sanders."

"And say what, James? That we suspect some lieutenant in the army is trying to frame Chandler? I'm sure the sheriff will believe us," she sarcastically added.

"I think you underestimate the man."

"I don't. And we're wasting time arguing."

James threw his hands in the air. "I give up." He looked to Morgan. "Maybe *you* could talk some sense into her."

"Already tried."

"This is crazy, Samantha." James began to pace once again. "If Pa finds out I went along with this . . . this harebrained idea of yours—"

"What Pa don't know won't hurt."

"Why must you always be so stubborn," James mumbled under his breath. He turned to look at his wife; Sarah hadn't said a word this whole time. It was her way of telling him this decision was his alone. "Okay, Samantha, let's get this over with."

She was already scooting out of her chair.

James walked around the table and pecked his wife on the cheek. "Promise you won't worry while I'm gone?"

"How can I worry if you're with Samantha?" Sarah replied with a teasing grin.

James frowned at his wife. "Don't encourage her."

Sarah giggled.

"Let's go," James told his sister, "before I change my mind."

Just outside of town, James and Samantha guided their horses into the trees, and dismounted. Samantha handed James her reins, then retrieved an extra flannel shirt inside her saddlebags, deciding the larger shirt would hide her curves much better than the one she was wearing. As she stepped behind some bushes to change, she started thinking about her plan, trying to determine if there were any flaws and, quite frankly, the only "flaw" she could think of was her brother. If her plan was going to work, James could not interfere: she needed him as a witness.

Figuring that now might be an appropriate time to recount a very important part of her plan, Samantha hollered out from behind the bushes, "Remember, James—absolutely under *no* circumstance are you to lift a finger to help me—unless things get out of hand."

"You could be messing with fire, Samantha," James yelled back at his sister. "I have a bad feeling about this—brilliant plan of yours."

"You know I'm perfectly capable of taking care of myself, James," Samantha reassured her brother as she hastily finished buttoning her shirt. "You're worrying over nothing."

"Did it ever occur to you, big sister, that you're just a little overconfident?"

"Look . . . I'll be extra careful . . . you just keep your ears and eyes open."

"I intend to."

After carefully tucking her knee-length hair under her hat—which wasn't an easy task—Samantha looked down at her snug-fitting jeans, thinking they would have to do, before stepping out from behind the bushes.

"Well?" she asked her brother.

"Turn around," James said.

Samantha did as told.

"I don't know . . . maybe . . . providing nobody recognizes you . . . I guess you might be able to pass as a young man. But a *very* young man who hasn't even started shaving yet," James added skeptically. "I still don't understand why you won't let me do this?"

"Because you don't look vulnerable enough."

"Chandler looks about as vulnerable as a grizzly bear and Rose approached him."

"I can't explain . . . I just have a gut feeling."

"I have a gut feeling too," James reminded his sister for argument's sake.

"Please . . . let's not fight about this."

As Samantha mounted her horse, she spoke to her brother. "Now remember, James . . . wait a while before you follow me. I'll find a table where you can sit close enough to hear our conversation."

"I'll be as close as a flea on a dog."

"James, please don't blow this."

"And what if you can't entice this Rose to talk to you?"

"Isn't it her job to talk to the customers?"

James rolled his eyes. He wasn't about to try and explain that one to his sister. "You'd better get going." *Before I change my mind and put a halt to this crazy idea of yours!*

Samantha nudged her horse toward town. Already she was starting to tremble inside; and her palms were sweating. This might be her only change to prove Chandler's innocence and she was afraid that something would go wrong. Riding steadily down the dusty street of town, she noticed the boardwalks were filled with people going about their daily business. Samantha was now getting close to the hurdy-gurdy house. She took a deep breath and then let it out slowly, trying to calm her nerves. Halting outside the shabby-looking building, she slid gracefully from her horse and looped the reins around the hitch rail. She paused for only a moment, before stepping through the swinging doors.

Casually looking around the spacious room, Samantha located a small table in the back, then, hooking her thumbs inside her pants pockets, she sauntered across the room, trying to remember to walk like a man, keeping her eyes turned away from the only other customer in the place as she passed by him. She dropped heavily into one of the empty chairs, *in a manly fashion*. The man was watching Samantha, but she ignored him, hoping he would leave her alone. She kept her eyes glued to the swinging doors, nervously drumming her fingers across the top of the table, wishing her brother would hurry.

Thinking it might be best to look as inconspicuous as possible while she waited for James, Samantha rose and went to the bar to buy herself a drink. While she stood there waiting for the bartender to finish with his task, several men entered the premises. Samantha stiffened when she recognized one of the men: he'd been with the group of soldiers that had arrested Chandler earlier that morning. *And he was heading toward the bar!* Though it was doubtful the man would recognize her disguised this way, she quickly lowered her hat to hide her face.

"May I help you, young man?"

It took Samantha a few moments to realize the bartender was speaking to her. "Yes, sir," she blurted out, forgetting to lower her voice. She noticed the curious expression on the bartender's face and started to stammer, "Gimme a . . . a . . ."

"Well spit it out, boy, I haven't got all day!"

"I'll have a whiskey."

"Glass or bottle?"

"A glass please."

Samantha then dug some money out of her pocket and slammed it on top of the counter, mumbling under her breath, "Mean old goat."

She grabbed the glass of whiskey as soon as the bartender set it in front of her, then hurried back to her table. She continued to watch the batwing doors for her brother, praying the soldier wouldn't notice her. Wearing a man's flannel shirt and with her hair tucked underneath her hat, surely he couldn't possibly recognize her. Samantha's eyes swung toward the large table where the soldier was playing cards with the small group of men. She watched him stand out of his chair and walk back over to the bar. He was talking with the barkeeper and, when she happened to overhear the name Rose, she listened very carefully to the conversation . . .

"Would you mind telling Rose that Willy's friend is here?"

"She's busy!" the bartender snapped.

"Well—when she *isn't* busy, tell her Corporal Biggins would like to see her."

"Yeah, I'll tell her."

Her eyes followed the corporal as he walked back to his table and sat down in his chair. He said something to the other men, and they all burst out laughing. Shifting nervously in her chair, Samantha was beginning to wonder what was taking her brother so long, thinking he should have been here by now. She fidgeted with the glass of whiskey in front of her, unconsciously took a big swallow, then began to cough and sputter. Samantha could feel her cheeks grow warm from embarrassment when the men sitting at the large table laughed uproariously. She tried not to panic when she saw Corporal Biggins stand out of his chair and was now walking toward her. She lowered her eyes as he approached her table.

"Care to play some poker, kid?" he asked.

"No thank you, mister," Samantha replied, remembering to lower her voice.

"Suit yourself."

A short while later, Samantha was utterly shocked by the man and woman who stepped through the swinging doors. *Uncle Bernard!* He was with a petite, dark-haired sultry beauty who was hanging possessively onto his arm as he escorted her across the room. *The woman must be his mistress!* Samantha inwardly gasped. *What was her name . . . ? Bell.* Her furious gaze narrowed on the lovey-dovey couple as she watched her uncle help the young woman into a chair, then he seated himself across from her.

Samantha's hand wrapped tightly around her glass and she quickly downed the rest of her drink, then choked back the cough. When she saw the bartender walk over to her uncle's table with a couple of drinks, it became rather obvious that this was not the first time her uncle and his mistress had been here. If it wasn't for the fact that she couldn't risk a scene, Samantha would have marched right over there and give her uncle a piece of her mind. *How dare he do this to her Aunt Ruth!*

As Samantha continued to wait for her brother, she periodically would look over at her uncle and the dark-haired woman. Much as she hated to admit it, Bell was incredibly beautiful. Not that Aunt Ruth wasn't beautiful in her own way—it was just that this much younger woman had a kind of sultry beauty that probably most men would find irresistible. Her olive complexion was smooth and flawless. Her large, doe-like eyes were framed with long, sooty lashes. She looked absolutely stunning in her silk emerald-colored gown, the way her pitch-black hair was swept into a loose bun. Though Samantha did think the woman looked ridiculous sitting in such a shady establishment dressed like some heiress.

Hearing loud catcalls drew her attention back toward the men seated at the large table. They were watching a buxom woman with hair so blond it appeared almost white as she slowly descended the stairs. Her generous hips swayed enticingly with every step she took. There was a provocative smile upon her full red lips. And Samantha knew without being told that this woman was Rose: maybe it was because of the rose-colored dress she was wearing. If you could call what she was wearing a dress. Because there wasn't much to the garment; it barely covered the woman's backside, while the top part of the dress exposed way too much cleavage.

Samantha could feel her cheeks burn from embarrassment when the woman stopped at her table and said, "I've never seen you in here before . . . you knew in town, honey?"

"No, ma'am," Samantha replied in as low tone of voice as possible.

Her suspicions about the woman's identity was confirmed when she heard Corporal Biggins holler out from across the room. "Hey, Rose! Get your pretty behind over here!" As Rose walked away swishing her ample hips, Samantha wondered how the woman could appear so relaxed after just supposedly being assaulted.

Suddenly her brother was standing by the swinging doors, looking around the room. It took James only a moment to notice her. From underneath the brim of her hat Samantha watched her brother as he walked over to the table directly across from her and dropped into a chair.

Staring straight ahead, she whispered, "What took you so long?"

"You told me to wait a while."

"I didn't mean all day."

"Find out anything yet?" James inquired, ignoring his sister's sarcasm.

"The blond woman . . . over at the big table . . . that's Rose."

"You sure?"

"I'm sure."

"Is that Uncle Bernard over there with a woman?" James asked.

"It's him," Samantha said in a disgusted tone.

"So it's true then . . . he does have a mistress."

"Look, James, could we worry about that later . . . right now we're here to help Chandler."

"Okay—don't get into such a snit."

"Wouldn't you agree that corporal Rose is talking to, are pretty well acquainted?" Samantha asked.

"It appears that way."

"His name is Biggins and he just happens to be a friend of Lieutenant Brown's," she informed her brother.

"How interesting."

"That's what I thought."

It repulsed Samantha, the way Rose was sitting in the soldier's lap with the man's face practically shoved into her chest. "I hope he suffocates."

James chuckled. "But what a way to go."

"I wonder what Sarah would say if she heard that," Samantha angrily grumbled.

"I was just joking."

Shortly after sunset the room rapidly began to fill with men. It seemed like every wrangler from town was here, including some Samantha had never seen before. She was feeling more apprehensive as the room became overcrowded with men; she was even having second thoughts about her so called plan. Samantha was just about to suggest to her brother that maybe they should leave when she noticed Rose approaching her table.

"What should I do?"

"Stay calm," James whispered.

That was easy for him to say! Samantha thought.

"This seat taken, cowboy?" Rose practically purred.

Ignoring her brother's laughter, Samantha shook her head.

"Buy me a drink?"

Samantha wondered if she agreed, did that mean she was supposed to go to the bar and buy the woman a glass of whiskey or what?

Rose thought the cowboy sitting across from her was awfully cute, but young. She wished Corporal Biggins hadn't asked her to find out what she could about the young man, because that probably meant trouble. But Silas claimed the kid seemed familiar for some reason and it was driving him crazy, so here she was . . .

"What about that drink, cowboy?"

Out of the corner of her eye, Samantha could see that her brother was motioning toward the woman and shaking his head up and down. "Oh . . . yeah . . . sure," she stammered in reply.

"You don't talk much, do ya, honey? I guess you're just shy." Rose hunched across the small table to add seductively, "That's okay . . . I like the shy ones better." Then, "I'll go get us those drinks." She gracefully rose from her chair and sashayed toward the bar.

Samantha glared at her brother who started to snicker. "It isn't funny, James."

"This was all your idea—*Sam*. Gee . . . I wonder what Chandler would say if he knew his competition was a *hurdy-gurdy gal*." Then he burst out laughing.

"Shhh . . . someone might hear you!" Samantha angrily hissed.

"A gun could go off inside this place and nobody would notice, loud as it is in here."

"I just don't want to take any chances, James. Now be quiet . . . here comes Rose."

Samantha forced a smile on her face as the woman placed a drink in front of her, then sat back down at the table with her own.

"Drink up, honey. By the way, I'm Rose. And what should I call you?"

"Sam."

"Well, Sam, are you from around here?"

"Yes, ma'am." Samantha took a sip of whiskey and tried not to pucker her face.

Rose closely watched the young man, thinking, small as he was, the sleeping powder she'd put in his drink should quickly take effect, making the rest of her job a whole lot easier. She thought about her last job. It had been quite a chore getting the big Indian up those stairs. Rose still felt guilty about what happened after that, but she'd only done what Will had ordered her to do. She'd learned the hard way never to question the man; she still sported an ugly bruise on her cheek that she kept concealed with lots of face paint. It hadn't taken her long to realize Corporal Jones was insane; that first night they'd spent together revealed a controlling egotistical maniac. She wished she'd never set eyes on Corporal William Jones, though the man could be quite charming when he wanted to be; unfortunately, it was all an act.

Rose wondered why Corporal Jones hated Wade Chandler so much. Though it was no secret how he felt about Indians. Hatred had oozed from William's very pores, Rose remembered, the moment the handsome Indian had stepped through the swinging doors that night. Personally, she had liked Chandler and had hated having to trick the man to get him to her bedroom, and then had claimed he'd assaulted her. She never would have even considered doing such a thing, but William had threatened her.

She hoped that Corporal Biggins wouldn't ask her to do anything worse than question this young man, because he seemed like such an innocent kid.

"Here's to you, Sam," Rose said, raising her glass in the air. Then she quickly downed every last drop of whiskey.

Samantha had a curious feeling about Rose: she was certain the woman was hiding something. She took another sip of her drink, wondering how anyone could drink this awful stuff without gagging. She stifled a yawn, leaned back in her chair, glancing around the crowded room. Once again, her eyes narrowed on her uncle who was still sitting with his mistress, their heads close together in quiet conversation. Samantha wondered what they could be talking about. *Oh what she wouldn't give to walk over there and give them both a piece of her mind!* But she was here for a far more important reason, Samantha reminded herself, and she couldn't blow it now, not when she was this close.

She turned her attention back to Rose. Was that curious expression on the woman's face concern? She covered her mouth and yawned, suddenly feeling a little sleepy.

"Are you okay, Sam?"

"I'm—just tired."

Rose frowned. The young man's voice—it had sounded more *feminine*. She shook her head, thinking maybe she'd had a little too much to drink, then shrugged it off. Sam's eyes were starting to flutter, Rose noticed. So the sleeping potion was already taking effect. Wanting to get this ordeal over with, she suggested, "Would you like to come upstairs to my room and lie down for a while?"

"I . . . a . . . well . . . a . . ." Samantha stammered, trying not to panic. She was suddenly feeling strangely light-headed, and was unable to control her own tongue. *What on earth was wrong with her?* she wondered. From the corner of her eye Samantha could tell that her brother was vigorously shaking his head in a negative manner . . . *What was he trying to tell her? And why was she feeling so confused . . . ?*

"Here . . . let me help you, honey," Rose offered as she scooted out of her chair.

"Excuse me?" James said, immediately rising to his feet. He moved over to his sister and helped her out of her chair. "I know Sam here, ma'am, and I don't think his wife would appreciate him going to your room."

"His wife?" Rose didn't think the kid looked old enough to have a wife.

"Apparently, Sam must've forgotten to mention that. I'll just take him home where he belongs!" James added in an angry tone.

"You can't tell me what to do!" Samantha snapped.

"What happened to his voice?" Rose wanted to know. *Something was going on here?*

Clamping a hand tightly over his sister's mouth, James hastily explained, "Well . . . when Sam here gets excited, his voice changes . . . runs in his family . . . so I heard." He whispered in Samantha's ear,

"Stop fighting me, before we get caught." That finally seemed to get her attention. She ceased struggling, and he let go of her.

This time Samantha remembered to disguise her voice. "I'm so glad you stopped me from doing a foolish thing a . . . Billy." Then, "Forgive me, ma'am, but—much as I'm tempted, I am a married man. I'd better go home now."

Something still wasn't right here, Rose thought, before reminding Sam, "Most of the men in this place are married." There was something peculiar about this kid . . .

"My wife . . . a . . . Daisy-May . . . she'll take a skillet after my head if she ever finds out I've been to your room."

James rolled his eyes. *Daisy-May? Was she kidding?*

Rose shrugged noncommittally. "Maybe some other time."

"Come on, Sam, let's get you home." James grabbed hold of his sister's arm and pulled her toward the batwing doors. Once they were safely outside, "Daisy-May?" he blurted out, then burst out laughing.

The cool evening air seemed to revitalize Samantha and, with her renewed energy, came her temper. "How dare you, James Callahan!" she snapped. "Now I'll never find out the truth!"

"If I hadn't intervened, how would you have explained to Rose about your . . . your slight gender problem, Samantha?" he angrily retorted. "Or should I say *Sam!*"

"How would she have known?"

"How would she have known?" James repeated incredulously. "Why do you think Rose wanted you to go to her room?"

"To take a nap or maybe talk," Samantha innocently replied. Then her cheeks started to turn crimson when realization suddenly sank in of what she'd almost gotten herself into. "That's disgusting! She didn't even know me!"

James burst out with uproarious laughter.

"When you're through cackling, little brother, maybe you can help me come up with a different plan? How are we going to get back inside there now and question Rose without drawing attention to ourselves?"

"We're not."

"I beg your pardon?"

"Look, Samantha, going back in there tonight is out of the question. We'll just have to think of something else." James practically threw Samantha onto the back of her horse, slapped the reins in her hand, then mounted his own. "Besides, Pa's probably home by now, so you'd better start thinking about how you're going to explain your absents."

Grumbling under her breath, Samantha spurred her horse and galloped after her brother. As they both hightailed it out of town, she knew that James was right, that they couldn't have gone back in there tonight. But a new plan was already beginning to form in her mind as she kneed her horse into a faster pace.

Chapter Thirty-four

Samantha had gone to bed several hours ago, but she couldn't sleep. Seated in a chair with her arms wrapped tightly about her legs which were drawn against her chest, she continued to stare out her bedroom window into the darkness. She thought about Chandler locked inside that tiny cell . . . how hot in had been today . . . if anybody had even bothered to give him a drink of water . . . now he was probably shivering from the cold night air . . . probably weak from hunger, too. A single tear slid down her cheek. They had planned to be married by the end of September, which was only a few short days away, and she definitely had her doubts if their wedding would ever take place. There always seemed to be some kind of catastrophe or another preventing her from becoming Chandler's wife, and now she was starting to think that maybe they weren't meant to get married.

Samantha wondered why Rose would lie about Chandler? Could she possibly be in cahoots with Lieutenant Brown? Considering Rose's line of work, the woman had seemed nice enough. At least she hadn't struck Samantha as the kind of woman who was vindictive, or would deviously lie to hurt another. Yet, that's exactly what she'd done—but why? And what about this . . . what had she heard Rose call the man? oh, yes . . . Corporal Biggins . . . could he somehow be involved?

Starting to feel a little chilled, Samantha unfolded her legs and walked over to grab a blanket off the bottom of her bed, wrapping it around her shoulders as she padded back to the chair, dropping heavily into the seat. While the days could still sometimes get downright hot in late September, the nights were usually quite chilly.

Gazing out her window, Samantha wondered if anyone had thought to bring Chandler a blanket. She closed her eyes and began to pray, asking God to watch over the man she loved, and she also asked Him to change her father's mind so she could accompany him into town in the morning. It would give her the perfect opportunity to sneak away and talk to Rose. Unfortunately, her father was angry with her for taking matters into her own hands (James had warned her about confronting Rose) so she doubted he'd even allow her out of her room.

With a weary sigh, Samantha rose and slowly padded toward her bed. She had to try and get some sleep—more than likely tomorrow would be another long day.

Inside his tiny four-by-four cell, Chandler paced back and forth, trying to keep warm. The only blanket he had was thread bare, but danged if he'd ask for another! He shouldn't even be here in the first place and, at the moment, he thought that if he could get his hands on that blond-haired woman responsible for him being here, he wasn't so sure he wouldn't do exactly what she'd accused him of.

His only contact with the outside world was the tiny window he was now standing before. His fingers tightened around the iron bars as he gazed up into the starry night sky, wishing he was anywhere but here. When his belly rumbled with hunger again, he thought about the hard biscuit the guard had brought him earlier. Hungry as he was right now, even a hunk of stale bread was beginning to sound appetizing.

As Chandler began to pace once again, he thought about Samantha at home, who was probably sleeping by now, he figured. And, if so, was she dreaming about him? Chandler wondered. If he closed his eyes, he could easily picture Samantha standing before him, her knee-length hair surrounding her slender body in glorious chestnut-colored waves, her brilliant blue eyes looking up at him adoringly, shining with love . . .

Chandler stepped over to the window again and grabbed the bars tightly in his hands. He didn't think he could stand it in here much longer. They wouldn't even let him out long enough to relieve himself.

He could still hear Lieutenant Brown's mocking laughter when the man had handed him a jar for that particular function—which was even more humiliating. Just for spite, he was tempted to throw that jar at Brown the next time he saw the man. For the first time since they put him in this dreadful shed, a slow smile curled Chandler's lips. . . .

Sitting quietly at the kitchen table, Samantha watched the morning sky gradually lighten along the horizon. She'd hardly slept a wink last night, so worried was she over Chandler, and had been up for several hours already. Within minutes she saw the sky start to change into a pale pink color, a while later it was a dazzling reddish-orange, then, finally, a brilliant shade of crimson. The sunrise was always a beautiful sight to behold and Samantha never tired of looking at it. Then, after a short time, the cloudless sky was a sapphire blue.

Samantha had a fresh pot of coffee brewing on the stove and had prepared her father's favorite breakfast, because she wanted him in the best mood as possible when she told him about an idea she had. She heard a creaking sound on the staircase as somebody descended the steps, then she heard the familiar clomping of her father's boot heels as he walked the short distance along the hallway toward the kitchen.

"Good morning, Pa," Samantha cheerfully greeted her father when he entered the room. She stood out of her chair and headed toward the stove. "Have a seat, Pa. I'll get you some coffee—and your breakfast is ready."

John seated himself at the table, watching Samantha suspiciously. "Did the world suddenly come to an end?"

"Why—whatever do you mean?"

"Come on, Samantha, I know you better than that."

Samantha ignored her father's sarcastic remark as she placed a large platter of flapjacks before him, along with a container which held some creamy butter and a small pitcher of warm maple syrup. "I hope they're the way you like 'em."

John almost burst out laughing he could so easily read his daughter. "Forget it, Samantha, you're not going with me."

"But, Pa . . ."

"Did you think these flapjacks would miraculously change my mind?"

"I guess I was hoping that . . ."

"Well you can just forget whatever it is you have in mind, young lady."

"But I promise I won't interfere."

"Now you know as well as I do, Samantha—you won't keep that promise," John said between mouthfuls of food. "I'll talk to Sheriff Sanders . . . he'll get to the bottom of this."

"He couldn't find the bottom of a barrel," Samantha grumbled.

John chuckled. "I'm sure he can locate this woman and question her."

Samantha let out a sigh. "I already talked to her."

His fork stopping in mid-air, John looked sternly at his daughter. "Why didn't you tell me this last night?"

"You didn't ask me that . . . you only asked . . ."

"Samantha!"

"Oh alright, I suppose I should've mentioned it."

"So . . . where did you find this mysterious woman?"

"How 'bout I bring her to the sheriff's office and . . ."

"Samantha Callahan!"

"Okay . . . she works at the brothel."

Samantha braced herself for the shouting that was sure to follow, but it never came. Instead, her father simply said, "So what'd you find out?"

"She's lying, Pa."

"Did she tell you that?" John questioned.

"Well . . . no . . . not exactly."

"So what *exactly* did she say?"

"Not much."

"We're gonna need a lot more evidence than that, Samantha."

"Pa, if I could go back to the brothel . . ."

"No way!"

"But . . ."

"Going back to that 'house of ill repute' is out of the question, Samantha, and I won't hear another word about it! You let me handle this from now on and I mean it!"

"Will you ever stop treating me like a child?"

"After you're married," John muttered under his breath, "then you're Chandler's problem."

"What an unfatherlike thing to say."

John stood out of his chair and was already heading for the back door. "Tell your mother I might not be home till late tonight." He abruptly turned and said, "Remember, Samantha—stay out of this," before slamming the door shut behind him.

Samantha knew it would have done no good to argue with her father. She would wait for a while, then ride into town to talk to Rose and pray that she wouldn't get caught. Chandler could be an old man before Sheriff Sanders found out anything.

Rebecca entered the kitchen then, heading directly over to the stove. "Why the long face?" she asked as she poured herself a cup of coffee.

"Because I'm twenty-one years old and my father still treats me like a child."

"I know the feeling."

As Rebecca sat in the chair across from her, Samantha noticed she was wearing the leather pants she'd given her and a short-sleeved flannel shirt. Her hair was braided in a long, thick plait that hung past her rear end, instead of swept up on her head in the latest style. And she was even wearing one of her old suede hats.

"You're staring," Rebecca said. "Do I look that bad?"

"No, of course not. Just different."

"Personally, I like my new look."

"I may prove to be a bad influence on you yet," Samantha said, frowning.

"If it wasn't for you, I never would've had the courage to stand up to Albert."

There was a brief period of silence, then, "Becca, how would you like to ride into town with me this morning?"

"Uncle John didn't change his mind, huh?"

"No. And I'll go crazy just sitting here. I have to be doing something to help Chandler. My father will just have to understand."

"Something tells me Uncle John's going to be furious."

"Yeah, I know. But I'll worry about that later."

Samantha and Rebecca had mounted their horses and were just about to ride away when a sudden shout from Morgan stopped them in their tracks. Samantha looked over her shoulder, frowning, as Morgan quickly closed the distance between them.

"Just where do you think you're going?" he demanded to know.

"Does my father have you spying on me now?"

"He asked me to keep an eye on you."

"Becca and I are going for a ride."

"Where?"

Samantha's frown deepened. "That, Mr. Johnston, is none of your business."

"It is, until your father tells me otherwise."

"Oh alright!" Samantha angrily snapped. She knew she might as well tell Morgan the truth—he'd probably follow them anyway. "We're headed to town."

"Your father warned me you'd try something like this." Morgan pushed back his hat. "John knows you pretty well."

"If you want to come along—fine! If not, get out of my way!"

"Samantha," Rebecca gently scolded, "Morgan's only doing what Uncle John asked him to do."

"I'm going to town to question Rose and you're not going to stop me!" Samantha hissed at Morgan. Without another word, she spurred her horse forward.

When Samantha heard the sound of a horse's hooves behind her, she looked over her shoulder and smiled at Rebecca as she pulled her horse up alongside hers. "I would understand if you'd rather spend the day with Morgan, Becca. You might stay out of trouble that way," she muttered more to herself.

Rebecca giggled and teasingly replied, "I'm hoping to keep *you* out of trouble."

They both had a laugh over that.

As Samantha and Rebecca trotted down the dusty street of Bear Creek, Samantha kept a close vigil out for her father. When she spotted his horse tethered outside the sheriff's office, they took a quick detour around the back of the building. By the time they reached their destination, Samantha was convinced that Rebecca never should have come with her. Halting in front of the shabby-looking building, she remained perched upon the back of her horse, her eyes fixed straight ahead on the swinging doors before her.

"What's the matter?" Rebecca asked.

"I have a bad feeling about this."

"Well, I'm going inside," Rebecca said, dismounting and wrapping the reins around the hitch rail. "I've never had the opportunity to see in one of these places."

Sliding from her horse, Samantha looped the reins over the hitching post. "Trust me, Becca, you're not missing anything." She let out a sigh. "Well—let's get this over with."

The girls stood inside the darker interior, glancing around the room. *So this was a hurdy-gurdy house*, Rebecca thought to herself. She wasn't sure what she'd expected to find, but it looked like an ordinary saloon. She was surprised that the place clean and well organized. There were dozens of wooden tables arranged in neat little rows. The long mahogany bar glowed with a polished shine; behind it were dozens of glasses stacked on a counter in front of a huge mirror—a variety of whiskey bottles set on a long shelf. Above the bar a deer head stuck out of the wall, and Rebecca swore the large brown eyes were watching her.

Samantha noticed the bartender kept staring at them from behind the mahogany bar. She grabbed Rebecca's arm and hastily escorted her cousin across the room over to a small corner table where they could easily talk without being overheard. Samantha dropped into the chair with her back facing the wall, because from here she could easily see anybody who entered the premises.

When Rebecca heard a woman's amorous laughter coming from upstairs, her eyes caught Samantha's, and both women covered their mouths, giggling. Somebody cleared their throat then, and Samantha turned her head to find the bartender standing beside their table, a disapproving frown upon his face.

"May I help you ladies?" he gruffly asked.

"Yeah. What's all that racket upstairs?" Samantha boldly inquired.

Rebecca gasped.

The bartender, who was obviously embarrassed by the question, whirled on his heel and walked away. Samantha burst out laughing. "I bet he doesn't bother us again."

"I can't believe you'd say such a thing," Rebecca whispered. "So—now what?"

"*Now* we wait," Samantha replied. "I don't hear any more *noises* upstairs . . . my guess is ole Rose will be coming down those stairs pretty soon." Her eyes suddenly widened. "Becca—very casually—turn around and take a look who just walked in."

Slowly, Rebecca twisted in her chair. "I wonder what Albert's doing here?"

Just then a female voice called out "Albert darling" and Samantha and Rebecca turned toward the staircase to see a woman quickly descend the stairs and hurry across the room to greet Albert with a kiss. She hooked her arm through his and they proceeded toward the bar.

"Is that Rose?" Rebecca asked Samantha.

"That's her."

"I hope you haven't been waiting long, Albert," Rose purred. Then, "Charlie, give me a whiskey on the rocks—and whatever Albert's having."

"Right away, Rosy," the bartender cheerfully replied.

"I'm surprised Albert hasn't tripped over his tongue—far as the thing's hanging out," Rebecca muttered under her breath. She watched Albert and Rose take their drinks in hand and then the couple hurried back across the room and hastened up the staircase; then, a moment later, she heard a door slam shut. "Well now—don't that beat all," she commented more to herself.

"Are you okay, Becca? I know Albert's your fiancé—"

"*Was* my fiancé," she corrected. "Maybe now that Albert's found a . . . a lady friend, he'll leave me alone. That might sound a bit uncaring but—" What could Rebecca say. She had never loved Albert. Now, if it had been Morgan she'd seen heading up those stairs with Rose, she would've been fighting mad . . .

"How am I suppose to question Rose now?" Samantha complained. "Obviously, the woman's going to be busy for a while . . . oh . . . Becca, I'm so sorry. That was really insensitive of me."

Rebecca waved her hand. "It's okay . . . really."

There was a short period of silence, then Samantha suddenly said, "Albert's an important attorney, isn't he?"

"He's one of the best." Rebecca was beginning to recognize *that* particular look on her cousin's face. "What do you have in mind?"

Samantha's lips twitched with amusement. "It certainly wouldn't look very good for a prominent attorney in Albert's position to get caught with a woman like Rose . . . if you know what I mean?"

Rebecca giggled.

"I can just read the headlines now," Samantha went on to say dramatically. "Everybody thought that Albert Smythers was a decent man . . . who would have thought the promising attorney from Boston had an infatuation with . . . *painted ladies.*"

Rebecca burst out laughing. "That would be downright mean, Samantha."

"Wouldn't it though."

"I think it's a brilliant idea."

"Then what are we waiting for, Becca? Let's go pay a little visit to Albert."

Samantha and Rebecca scooted out of their chairs and hastened up the nearby staircase. At the top of the stairs, they stopped in their tracks, staring down the long corridor before them, which had rooms on either side.

"What do we do now?" Rebecca asked.

"Well—we could knock on every door until we find the right one."

"Samantha, I'm not so sure we should . . ."

A door suddenly opened then and a woman clad only in a skimpy nightgown stepped out into the hallway. The woman frowned when she saw them. "Are you ladies lost or something?"

"We're looking for somebody," Samantha answered.

"Who?" the woman inquired.

"My fiancé," Rebecca informed her.

"What's his name?"

"Albert Smythers."

The woman's eyes widened in surprise. "Albert never mentioned a fiancé."

"Do they ever?"

"No, they don't." The woman angrily added, "Men can't be trusted."

"That's true," Samantha agreed. "My cousin here wants to confront Albert—so would you mind telling us which room he's in?"

"Albert's with Rose . . . the room over there," the woman motioned with her hand, then she went back inside her room and shut the door.

Samantha turned to Rebecca. "Would you rather wait here?"

"No."

Together Samantha and Rebecca walked the short distance down the long hallway and stopped in front of the door the woman had indicated.

"Well, Becca . . . do you think we should knock or just barge right in?"

"How should I know?"

With a shrug Samantha tried to turn the knob, but found the door was locked. "Looks like we'll have to knock after all." She then rapped on the door several times.

Behind the door they could hear angry muffled voices, then a female's voice called out, "Who is it?" Samantha looked questioningly at Rebecca, but neither women said anything. A moment later, the door opened slightly, and then a blond-haired woman appeared wearing a blanket which was wrapped around her bare shoulders. Samantha immediately recognized Rose. She inwardly groaned when Rose gave her the oddest look.

"Do I know you?" Rose asked Samantha.

"No, ma'am."

"So what can I do for you ladies? Are ya lost?"

Samantha let out a sigh. *Well, here goes nothing.* "I'm here to inform you . . . how can I put this? . . . the man you're—entertaining . . . he's my cousin's fiancé and . . ."

"*Was*," Rebecca corrected her.

"Okay, so he *was* her fiancé . . ."

"What are you talking about?"

"What's going on out there, Rose?" they heard Albert holler out.

Before Rose could answer, Samantha suddenly pushed past the woman and burst her way into the room, pulling Rebecca with her.

"What do you think you're doing?" Rose angrily demanded.

"What the . . . Rebecca!" Albert gasped from the bed, yanking the covers to his chest. "What are you doing here?"

"I was about to ask you the same thing, Albert."

"I think you should close the door, Rose," Samantha calmly suggested.

Immediately the door slammed shut, before she whirled on Albert. "I want to know what's going on here! For starters, who are these women?"

When Albert didn't respond, Samantha gladly informed Rose, "This is my cousin, Rebecca. As I was trying to explain a little while ago, she was engaged to Albert . . ."

"You said *was*," Rose interrupted.

"I did."

"So, if they're no longer engaged, what's the problem?"

"Well—the problem is with Albert." Samantha glared at the man lying on the bed, the covers pulled up to his chin.

"What problem are you talking about?" he angrily wanted to know.

"I'll be a little more blunt, Albert." Samantha stepped closer to the bed. "Gee . . . I wonder what would happen if Rebecca wrote a letter to the board about your . . . certain extracurricular activities?"

"Just what are you getting at?" Albert snapped.

"Simple. I need your services."

Samantha scowled when the corner of Albert's mouth lifted into a lopsided grin. "You're not my type, so you can wipe that silly smirk off your face. I want you to get my fiancé out of jail."

"You must be talking about Chandler."

"Of course I'm talking about Chandler!"

"Yeah, I heard he was arrested. Sorry, but I'm afraid I can't help you."

"You have no other choice in the matter if you want to continue practicing the law. And you can start by questioning this woman here," Samantha said, thrusting a thumb toward Rose. "She falsely accused Chandler of . . . of . . . she knows what I'm talking about . . . ask her!"

"What *is* she talking about, Rose?" Albert asked.

"I don't know what she's talking about."

"You lied about Chandler assaulting you!" Samantha shouted at her.

"Samantha, yelling at the poor woman won't get us anywhere," Rebecca gently admonished her. "Please try to remain calm."

"Wait a second—now I remember where I've seen you!" Rose suddenly declared, pointing an accusing finger at Samantha. "You're that young man from last night . . . Sam, wasn't it? Yes . . . I recognize the face!"

"Disguising myself as a man was the only way I could think of to gain your attention so I could question you about Chandler! Because I know he didn't assault you!"

Rose started to say something and then snapped her mouth shut. Then she covered her face with her hands and burst into tears.

"Is there something you want to tell me, Rose?" Albert said gently. "I am a lawyer . . . if you're in some kind of trouble—"

"Please, Albert, could we talk in private?" she softly replied.

Samantha dropped into a nearby chair, folded her arms across her chest. "If this concerns Chandler, I'm not going anywhere."

"I didn't mean to lie, Albert!" Rose blurted out. "But you have no idea what that man is capable of if you don't do what he says!"

"What man?"

"Unless I miss my guess, she's talking about Lieutenant Brown," Samantha informed Albert.

"Rose, is what she says true?"

Rose nodded.

Albert didn't get the chance to question her further, because just then there was a ruckus outside the door. "Now what," he grumbled under his breath, and arranged the covers more snugly around him.

The door suddenly crashed open and when a tall man stepped inside the room, Albert demanded, "What's the meaning of this, mister?"

"What are you doing here, Morgan?" Samantha angrily snapped. Just when it sounded like Rose was about to confess, Morgan had to spoil it.

"I might ask the same thing about you and Becca?"

"What was that noise outside the door?"

The corner of Morgan's mouth lifted into a lopsided grin. "The bartender and I had ourselves a little disagreement. Now answer my question."

"Rebecca, how do you know this man?" Albert wanted to know.

"That's not important right now," she curtly replied.

"I believe Rose here was just about to reveal the truth about Chandler," Samantha informed Morgan. Then she whirled on Rose and said, "Isn't that true?"

"Well, I . . ."

"I think I've heard enough to get the picture," Albert loudly intervened to prevent Rose from saying something that could innocently incriminate herself. He wanted the chance to question her in private. "Miss Callahan, if you will give me some time, I just might be able to build enough of a case that could get your fiancé out of jail. There will be no need for a letter."

"What letter?" Morgan asked.

"I'll explain everything on the way home," Samantha told him. Then to Albert, "You've got until the day after tomorrow . . . if Chandler isn't out of jail by then or I haven't heard from you, I'll be back."

Albert nodded his agreement.

Chapter Thirty-five

Standing beside the window, Chandler's grip tightened around the iron bars as he breathed deeply of the clean fresh air. The stench inside this place was bad enough to gag a maggot, so he stayed near the window as much as possible. He was famished this morning; he hadn't eaten a morsel of food since the day of his capture, because he refused to eat the stale biscuits they provided him. *How did they expect a full grown man to live on a hunk of bread twice a day?* He closed his eyes, thinking, what he wouldn't give right now for one of Rachel's famous Sunday chicken suppers.

Chandler didn't bother turning around when he heard the door to the shed open, knowing it was just somebody bringing him his morning ration of bread.

"You got a visitor, Indian."

Surprised by the announcement, Chandler looked over his shoulder and saw John standing outside his cell. He stepped over to the iron door.

"They treatin' you okay?" John asked.

"You're not here to get me out by chance, are you?"

"I'm working on it. I brought you something." John reached inside his shirt and pulled out what looked like a folded piece of cloth.

"That wouldn't happen to be a tool I could use to dig my way out of here?"

"No," John chuckled. "This is from Rachel." He carefully squeezed the folded cloth between the iron bars, handing it to Chandler.

When Chandler unfolded the cloth, his mouth instantly began to water as his eyes feasted upon a good-sized helping of Rachel's homemade peach pie. He stuffed a huge bite into his mouth and chewed slowly. "Mmmm . . . this is absolutely delicious."

"Sorry it's a little squished," John apologized. "The young man that brought me here . . . for a minute there, I thought he was going to frisk me. And he probably would have taken the pie, had he found it."

"I would have fought him to the death for this," Chandler seriously said, licking his fingers clean, wishing there was more.

John burst out laughing.

"How's Samantha?" Chandler asked.

"She wanted to come with me, but I said no."

"Good."

"I should mention that I had to practically threaten to lock Samantha in her room to keep her at home." John hoped to cheer Chandler some—the man looked like he could use some cheering. That seemed to do the trick; at least he was smiling. "Oh, before I forget the reason I came here, Sheriff Sanders said he would try and stop by later today to talk to you. Tell him anything you can remember."

"I appreciate everything you've done, John."

"You're not out of here yet, Chandler."

"I still appreciate it."

"We'll get you out of here somehow."

"I don't know how I'll ever repay you."

"You're family now. Or will be just as soon as you marry Samantha."

"You make that sound so urgent. What's the matter, John . . . afraid Samantha might change her mind about marrying me?" Chandler teased.

"No . . . I'm afraid that *you* might change *your* mind."

Chandler threw back his head and laughed.

The door to the shed opened then and the same young soldier who'd escorted John, curtly announced, "Sorry, Mr. Callahan, but your time is up."

"I'll be back soon," John told Chandler.

"Tell Rachel that pie was a blessing."

John nodded, then followed the soldier out the door.

Stepping over to the window, Chandler watched John mount his horse and ride away, until he'd completely disappeared out of sight.

As Morgan, Samantha, and Rebecca rode out of town, Morgan watched his two companions surreptitiously. After a while, and Samantha still hadn't said anything (it was obvious she was trying to avoid him) he accusingly snapped, "Okay, Samantha . . . out with it."

"Out with what?" she innocently replied.

"Why would Albert agree to help Chandler?"

"Let me explain," Rebecca gladly offered.

"Be my guest."

Rebecca turned to Morgan. "Where I come from, Albert is a very important attorney. Samantha and I happened upon a . . . well . . . we discovered that Albert was having a little fling with Rose—the lady back at the . . . well, you know.

"It was Samantha's idea . . . an ingenious plan actually. You see—it wouldn't look very good for a man of Albert's importance to . . . to be caught with . . . with an inappropriate woman . . . if you get my meaning. Samantha simply threatened to write a letter to the board back in Boston, exposing Albert's—*little escapade,* which would have been in all the papers. So Albert really had no choice in the matter."

Morgan burst out with laughter. "Leave it to Samantha."

"I take it then, you approve of our little scheme?" Rebecca asked.

"Most definitely."

They were approaching the Callahan ranch, and Samantha kept shifting nervously on the back of her horse. She knew her father was going to be furious at her for disobeying his orders—again. She was awfully tempted to turn her horse around and skedaddle it out of there, while she still had the chance.

Oh no, Samantha inwardly groaned. *That was her father leaning against the corral.* If he was waiting for her to return, then she was in a heap of more trouble than she'd thought. Now she was seriously considering turning her horse around . . .

"Isn't that your pa over there?" she heard Morgan ask.

"Yes."

"John looks madder than a grizzly. If it'll help any, I'll take full responsibility."

"I'm responsible for my own actions."

"Samantha, I was only trying to help."

"Sorry, Morgan. I didn't mean to sound so . . . ungrateful."

"Maybe Uncle John will understand," Rebecca said hopefully.

Somehow Samantha doubted that her father would understand. She watched him push away from the fence and was now walking toward them. There was no mistake where those piercing blue eyes were directed. Samantha cringed. Her pa looked furious.

"Maybe you should run," Morgan suggested.

"It's too late now."

"Get down from your horse, Samantha," John ordered, reaching for the reins. Wordlessly she did as told. Then he handed the reins over to Morgan. "Would you mind taking care of Samantha's horse?"

"No problem."

"Uncle John, I . . ."

"Your ma's waiting for you inside the house, Becca," he firmly interrupted.

Rebecca gave Samantha a sympathetic look, before nudging her horse after Morgan.

John waited until Morgan and Rebecca were out of earshot, then he whirled on Samantha. "I gave you explicit orders not to leave the house!"

"But . . ."

"But nothin'! You deliberately disobeyed me, Samantha!"

"I only wanted to help Chandler!"

"And I told you to let me handle this!"

"Before you lock me in my room and throw away the key, would you at least let me tell you what happened?"

"Very well," John more calmly replied.

"Long story short, Albert agreed to help Chandler."

"However did you manage that?"

"Let's just say that Rebecca and I caught Albert in a . . . a very compromising position, and we used it to our advantage."

"A compromising position, huh?"

"Please, Pa, don't ask me to explain."

John let out a sigh. "I just hope you didn't make a bad situation even worse."

"How could getting Albert to represent Chandler worsen the situation?"

"I suppose it can't hurt."

"If you'd only trust me more . . ."

"With your past deeds, young lady, I hope you don't want me to respond to that?"

"Now that you put it that way—"

"There's no other way to put it." John held up a hand for silence. "Look . . . we'll talk about this later . . . your mother probably has lunch waiting and I'm starved."

Rachel frowned as she poured her husband some more coffee, then filled her own cup, and set the flowered-porcelain coffeepot back on top of the table. She knew something was wrong with John. He'd hardly spoken a word all through lunch. Now he just sat there in his chair, looking completely lost in thought . . .

She cleared her throat, trying to gain her husband's attention.

Nothing.

"Are you going to tell me what's bothering you?" she finally asked.

"I was just thinking."

"That's obvious enough. So what are you thinking about?"

"What kind of mess Samantha might have gotten herself into this time. Come on, Rachel, you know as well as I do that Albert wouldn't lift a finger to help anyone but himself. Yet your daughter somehow . . ."

"What happened to *our* daughter?"

"Are you going to listen or not?"

"Okay . . . I'm listening."

"Samantha managed to retain Albert as Chandler's attorney . . . shouldn't we be a little concerned about that?"

"Oh, I don't know . . . Samantha does have a good head on her shoulders . . . combine *that* with your determination—I don't think Albert stood a chance." Rachel then inquired, "Didn't you ask Samantha how she did it?"

"She said something about her and Rebecca catching Albert in a . . . how did she put it? oh, yeah . . . compromising position."

Rachel frowned. "What's that mean?"

John arched a dark brow at his wife. "Need I really explain?"

"Oh my."

"Now you understand why I'm concerned."

Morgan and Rebecca stood by the corral, laughing, as they watched Suzie's colt trot back and forth, how the little stud would shake his proud head and kick up his hind legs. Morgan thought that if the colt ever grew into those long legs, he was going to be a runner. The sound of Rebecca's musical laughter brought a wistful smile to his lips. He looked at her, thinking, Rebecca Smith's beauty went far beyond just outward appearance; she was as beautiful on the inside as she was on the outside.

There was something Morgan had been wanting to do for a long time, to reach out and grab a handful of that rich brown mane which fell past her slender hips. The temptation was so strong, he gripped the top fence rail with both hands to refrain himself from doing so . . .

"You're staring."

"Sorry," Morgan said. "Guess I'm just not used to seeing you dressed that way." It was the first thing that came to mind.

"You don't like my new clothes?"

"As a matter-of-fact—now that you ask—I like your new clothes very much," Morgan said in a suggestive manner, and chuckled when she blushed. He teasingly added, "But you still have that Eastern look about ya."

"And what look is that?" Rebecca was frowning.

Morgan pushed back his hat, grinning. "You just look too delicate to be wearing leather pants and flannel shirts."

"I'll have you know there's nothing delicate about me!" Rebecca angrily said. "Good day, Mr. Morgan!" Then she whirled around and marched toward the house.

Morgan stood there, completely dumbfounded, as he observed Rebecca's stiff, departing back, wondering what the heck he'd said wrong. Then Graywolf's words came back at him: *Rebecca was a Callahan and had the potential of possessing the same kind of temper as Samantha.* At the time Morgan had disagreed, thinking there was no way that soft-spoken Rebecca could possibly have a temper like Samantha.

Apparently he'd been wrong.

Two days had passed and when there was still no word from Albert, Samantha feared that Albert wouldn't come through. So her father was going into town this morning to find out what he could; unfortunately, she would not be going with him. Now staring out her bedroom window, Samantha watched her father as he climbed into the saddle and rode away in the direction of town. Though Samantha understood that her father was only trying to protect her—or keep her out of trouble—she wasn't sure which—either way, she felt like he was still treating her like a child. And sometimes you had to be allowed to make a mistake—how else was a person ever going to learn anything?

A knock on her door drew Samantha out of her thoughts, and when she looked over her shoulder and saw Becca enter her room, she still found it so hard to believe that here was the same girl who'd arrived at the ranch just a short time ago, dressed in a fancy silk gown and looking like she'd just stepped off the page of a fashion catalog. Now her city cousin looked more like one of the wranglers.

Samantha noticed the dark circles around Rebecca's eyes and said, "Looks like somebody didn't sleep very well last night . . . let me guess . . . he's tall, dark, and handsome—and goes by the name of Morgan."

"Did I tell you that Morgan said I was delicate?"

"He didn't . . . the beast," Samantha said, giggling.

"I know that sounds funny, but—you don't understand. Translated that means Morgan would never want a *delicate* city girl for a wife . . . he would choose a . . . well . . . more of a rugged woman . . . like you."

"Gee, Becca, you make me sound like an amazon."

"All I'm trying to say is Morgan would choose a strong woman who loves this land the way that he does . . . the way that you love this land."

"You're falling in love with him." It had been more of a statement than a question.

"Yes . . . I suppose that I am," Rebecca sadly admitted. "But Morgan could never love me enough to . . ."

"Did he tell you that?"

"Well . . . no . . . not exactly."

"Then, Becca, how do you know that Morgan could never love you?"

"It's just a feeling." She let out a sigh. "Maybe I do belong with a man like Albert."

"I'll admit that when you first arrived here, I didn't think you'd last a week on the ranch. But I was wrong about you, Becca . . . you've adjusted to our way of life like . . . like you were born here."

"I never want to go back to Boston."

"Then don't."

"But what if my father's right, Samantha?"

"About?"

"That I should marry Albert."

"Can you honestly say you could live the rest of your life married to that—old man? Besides, I have a feeling about you and Morgan."

"You do?"

"I just think Morgan needs a little push."

"Push?"

Samantha began to pace around the room. "Morgan needs to realize that he has feelings for you—and I'm sure that he does." She turned to face her cousin adding, "If Morgan thought he might lose you—"

"What's going through that demented head of yours?" Rebecca was almost afraid to ask.

"Leave this to me, Becca." Samantha was thinking that getting her cousin and Morgan together was just the kind of distraction she needed to help take her mind off Chandler.

"What are you going to do?"

"Just trust me on this," was all Samantha would say.

Later that afternoon Samantha finally caught Morgan alone inside the barn. She stood watching him, while he emptied a large sack of grain into the grain barrel; now he was forking some hay into a stall. Samantha covered her mouth, giggling secretly, before slumping her shoulders and trying to look as depressed as possible, as she slowly moseyed her way toward Morgan, pretending not to notice him.

"You look like you just lost your best friend."

"Oh, Morgan! I didn't see you." Samantha let out a long sigh.

"Okay. What's the matter?" Morgan asked, leaning the pitchfork against the wall.

"Didn't she tell you?"

"Who?"

"Becca."

"Tell me what?"

"Evidently you haven't heard yet."

"What are you talking about, Samantha?"

"Sounds like Becca might be going back to Boston—with Albert no less."

Morgan visibly stiffened. "I thought she decided not to marry that old coot?"

"I didn't say that Becca was going to marry Albert . . . just that she might be going back to Boston with him." Samantha sighed and added, "But who knows—if Becca goes back with Albert, more-than-likely they'll probably get married—sooner or later."

"Where is she?"

"Who?"

"You know very well who I'm talking about!" Morgan snapped impatiently.

"Oh—you must mean Becca?"

"Samantha!"

"Well . . . she was sitting out back on the veranda a while ago . . . she might still be there."

Samantha smiled triumphantly when Morgan whirled around and stormed out of the barn. She had never seen him look so angry; he always seemed to keep his cool no matter what. So . . . Mr. Restraint had a touchy spot after all, Samantha thought with a wry grin. Now she knew she hadn't been wrong about Morgan's feelings for Rebecca.

Morgan's angry strides carried him quickly toward the Callahan house. He couldn't allow Rebecca to leave with that old buzzard of an attorney! She wasn't going anywhere with Albert Smyth or Smythers or whatever his name was! When Morgan came around the corner of the house and saw Rebecca standing on the veranda, he stopped abruptly in his tracks. She looked so beautiful, he thought, watching the way the warm breeze caused her hip-length hair to gently flutter around her . . .

Who was he kidding? Morgan mused. *Rebecca didn't belong here and she certainly didn't belong with him!* What did he have to offer her? not even a proper home. Oh he'd done all right for himself over the years as a bounty hunter and had even managed to save a large sum of money. But all that money could not change the fact that he was a full-blooded Indian and she was a delicately-bred lady.

Suddenly Morgan spun around and headed toward the corral to fetch his horse. His mind was in a turmoil and all he wanted to do was ride into town and get rip-roaring drunk. He wasn't about to allow some glory-seeking white man stop him. And what were the odds that Lieutenant Brown would see him? It was a chance Morgan was willing to take. Besides, he wanted to see what he could find out about his brother.

A short while later Morgan was mounted on his stallion and riding toward town. *Too bad he didn't have his war bonnet with him!* he thought sarcastically. The way he was feeling at the moment, he would have put it on his head and proudly rode into that army camp as Chief Black Hawk. The look on Lieutenant Brown's face would have been worth it. . . .

Samantha hurried toward the house. She couldn't wait to find out what happened between Rebecca and Morgan. But when she came around the corner and saw her cousin wearing a miserable expression on her face—and Morgan nowhere in sight—her hopes began to fade.

"Where's Morgan?" she asked, hopping up on the veranda to stand beside Rebecca—who was now giving her an odd look. "Wasn't Morgan just here?"

"No. But I saw him ride away on his horse a short while ago," Rebecca replied.

"I don't understand," Samantha said more to herself. "Morgan seemed so angry . . . I know he was jealous . . ."

"Samantha, what are you talking about?"

"Never mind that now, Becca. I have a feeling that Morgan's on his way to town—probably to get drunk," Samantha muttered to herself. Then adding, "He shouldn't be anywhere near town." She was now feeling guilty, thinking she never should have told Morgan that little fib about Becca going back to Boston with Albert. But how was she supposed to have known that Morgan would react this way? *You should've known better*, an inner voice scolded her. "Come on, Becca . . . we'd best go find Morgan before he gets himself into trouble." Samantha was already heading toward the barn to fetch a horse. If she could only ride Daisy, she'd probably catch up to Morgan before he got to town. But her father had warned her about running the little mare too fast in her condition. "I hope nobody in town recognizes Morgan and runs and tells Lieutenant Brown."

"But I thought everybody in town was Morgan's friend?"

"Not everybody, Becca."

Chapter Thirty-six

Morgan picked a small table in the far corner of the room, then sat down in a chair with his back toward the wall as was his habit. Uncorking the bottle of whiskey he'd purchased at the bar, he poured a some into a glass, and quickly drained it in one easy swallow. Except for the bartender and himself, there wasn't another soul inside the place this early in the day. Which was exactly the way Morgan preferred it . . . there would be less chance for any trouble.

He reached for the bottle and poured himself another drink, downed it, then immediately refilled the glass again. The way he was feeling at the moment, Morgan almost wished Lieutenant Brown *would* step through those swinging doors, because a good fight was just what he needed to snap him out of this foul mood.

Morgan tried hard to push Rebecca from his mind, but her beautiful face kept appearing before him. He shook his head to clear it. And he tried focussing on an important matter like: why he didn't need a woman complicating his life when it was already complicated enough. Not counting that he liked things just the way they were. He didn't have to answer to anyone but himself. And he could pack up and leave whenever he wanted. He didn't need nor did he want a woman tying him to one place.

Morgan slammed his empty glass down hard on top of the table and, as he poured more whiskey into his glass, he happened to notice the straggly-looking man—whom he'd never seen before—quietly slip through the swinging doors. His curious eyes followed the man as he walked over to the bar. At first Morgan thought the gentleman was probably just some prospector who hadn't bathed in a month of Sundays. When the man casually glanced in his direction, Morgan caught a familiar recognition in those ice-cold blue eyes. And then it suddenly struck him . . . Billy Baxter! *But that was impossible!* Billy Baxter had been killed in an Indian attack! Graywolf himself had seen the notorious outlaw lying on the ground with several arrows sticking out of his chest. *So how could Billy be sitting at a bar having a drink?* He couldn't. The man just resembled the gunslinger, Morgan knew. Still, it gave him such an eerie feeling to see a man with those same kind of disturbing blue eyes. In all his years as a bounty hunter, he'd never come across a more violent man than Billy Baxter. A man like Billy would shoot his own mother!

Morgan noticed the way the gentleman kept looking over at him. So, just in case, he reached underneath the table to position his gun at a better angle. After all, he'd made several enemies over the years as a bounty hunter, so he could never be too careful. Morgan watched the unkempt man grab his bottle of whiskey from the bar and was now walking in his direction.

Without an invitation, the Billy Baxter look-alike plopped down at Morgan's table, which prompted him to ask, none too kindly, "May I help you, mister?"

"Almost didn't recognize ya with yer hair cut short," the man replied, pouring himself a drink.

"Well—now that you know me, mind telling me who *you* are?"

"Ya don't know?"

"Would I ask if I did?" Morgan snapped.

"Look closer."

Morgan thought if he got any closer to the putrid smelling man, he might lose the entire contents of his stomach. "I don't like playing guessing games! Either tell me who you are and what you want, or get your filthy hide away from my table!"

"I'm Bart Baxter, Billy's twin brother."

"I thought those cold blue eyes looked familiar."

Bart's eyes glittered with hate. "I heard ya shot Billy?"

"I might have." Why not take the credit for ridding the world of another vermin, Morgan thought to himself. He saw Bart Baxter's eyes turn even colder and then his hand slowly reached underneath the table. "I wouldn't try that, Bart, if I were you."

Suddenly Morgan's gun was in his hand. "Now, Mr. Baxter, put both your hands on top of the table where I can see 'em."

Bart had just witnessed the Indian drawing his gun faster than he could blink an eye. Now he knew those rumors he'd heard over the years about Morgan were true. Knowing he didn't stand a lick of a chance against the bounty hunter, Bart carefully put both hands on top of the table, as told. There were other ways of settling the score.

"I should still shoot your ugly hide and save the taxpayers' money!" Morgan snarled.

"But that would be against the law," Bart replied with a smug grin.

"Not in my book."

"You killed my brother, Indian! Billy was all the family I had left!"

"Your precious brother would still be alive if he hadn't broken the law! Now get out of my sight, before I really lose my temper!"

If looks could kill Morgan would have dropped dead on the spot from the hate-filled glare Bart gave him. The angry man's chair flew out behind him when he stood, then, without another word, Bart turned and strode out of the batwing doors.

Morgan had an uneasy feeling that wasn't the last he'd be seeing of Bart Baxter. Pouring the remainder of whiskey into his glass, he raised his drink toward the bartender, who was still staring at him, then drained the glass in a single gulp.

Morgan frowned when he noticed Rebecca's and Samantha's head appear over the top of the swinging doors. What were they doing here? he wondered. Samantha wasn't even supposed to leave the property . . . 'course when did anything like *rules* ever stop the mule-headed woman. Samantha preceded Rebecca through the double doors, and now they were walking toward him.

"Thought we'd find you here," Samantha remarked, dropping into an empty chair.

Rebecca sat in the only other chair, but said nothing.

"Don't you ever do what you're told?" Morgan snapped. "You shouldn't be here!"

"Neither should you!" Samantha snapped back at him. "Might as well order us something to drink . . . looks like we're going to be here for a while."

"You're not ordering nothing, since you and Rebecca are leaving!"

"Not unless you're coming with us!"

"I'm not ready to leave just yet!"

"Maybe we should leave Morgan alone, Samantha," Rebecca softly intervened.

"Now that's the most intelligent thing I've heard either of you ladies say." Morgan then chastised Samantha. "You should know better than to bring Rebecca to a place like this."

"For your information, Morgan Johnston, Samantha couldn't have stopped me!" Rebecca angrily said, crossing her arms over her chest. "And to think I was stupid enough to . . . oh . . . just never mind! I don't know what I thought!"

Morgan threw back his head and laughed. Apparently Miss Smith had a lot more spunk than he'd given her credit.

"Please come home with us, Morgan, before there's trouble," Samantha pleaded.

"Trouble," Morgan said incredulously. "From what my brother's told me and from what I've witnessed with my own eyes, woman—it's *you* who trouble seems to follow. Besides, I can't leave just yet," he hastily added. "I'm waiting to speak to Rebecca's old flame."

"Albert is coming here?" Rebecca wanted to know.

Morgan nodded.

"So what did he find out about Chandler?" Samantha asked.

"I haven't had a chance to talk to Albert yet . . . that's why I'm waiting."

"Well, I wish he'd hurry and get here."

"Albert already *is* here," Morgan informed Samantha. Then he glanced up at the ceiling and said, "I believe he's with Rosy." He watched for Rebecca's reaction—and was relieved when she seemed completely unaffected by the blunt announcement. That would mean she must not care about Albert—least not in that way.

"Speaking of Albert . . . here he comes." Samantha nodded toward the stairway.

Morgan twisted around in his chair, and frowned, as he watched the frail-looking Easterner descending the steps. He wondered how Rebecca's father could have even considered an old man like that as husband material for his only daughter.

Albert looked surprised when he spotted them; then his face reddened from obvious embarrassment as he crossed the room to their table. "I was just on my way to see you, Miss Callahan," he said. "I didn't expect to see you here—or you either, Rebecca."

"I could say the same thing about you, Albert."

His brows drew together in a scowl.

"So what'd you find out about Chandler?" Samantha was anxious to know.

"Actually, it was much easier than I thought . . . just a minor technicality."

"So—is Chandler getting out of jail or not?"

"The army can't hold him." Albert checked his pocket watch and said, "Mister Chandler is probably being released as we speak."

Samantha rolled her eyes. "Well why didn't you say so?"

"I just did."

"I suppose I should thank you, Mr. Smythers." Samantha stood out of her chair. "Come on, Becca. Are you coming with us, Morgan?"

"You think for one moment I would allow you to run around town unescorted?"

"I could say the same thing about you."

"That you could," Morgan chuckled.

"I'll probably be going back to Boston day after tomorrow," Albert said to Rebecca. "I would like to stop by the ranch and see you before I leave."

"Sure, Albert, if you like."

"Now can we please go get Chandler." Samantha was already heading toward the batwing doors to get her horse.

Just outside of town, across from the army camp, Samantha dismounted, then stood there impatiently waiting for Morgan and Rebecca to do the same. She could hardly believe that Chandler would be going home with them. One thing Samantha could say about Albert Smythers, the man was good at his job. She watched Morgan gently lift Rebecca from the saddle, and then he looped both horses' reins around a low-hanging branch.

"You ladies wait here, while I go inquire about my brother."

"Morgan Johnston, you must be completely out of your mind!" Samantha's hands flew to her hips as she added, "You can't go traipsing into that army camp!"

"With my hair cut and dressed the way I am, do you really think that any of those soldiers is going to recognize me as Chief Black Hawk?"

"Well . . . no . . . I suppose not, but . . ."

"Then wait here like I said."

Samantha frowned at Morgan's departing back as he crossed the dirt road. He was probably right, but she still didn't like it. Morgan may not look very much like the infamous war chief anymore, but he still looked Indian . . . that might be all it will take to draw unwanted attention, and she didn't want to take any unnecessary risks, not with Chandler's freedom at stake. There was no reason why she couldn't have gone to inquire about . . .

"Do you think Morgan will have any trouble?" Rebecca asked.

"I hope not."

"He sure didn't seem very happy to see me today, did he?"

This was just the kind of distraction Samantha needed to take her mind off Chandler. "Don't let that discourage you, Becca. If you could have seen the look on Morgan's face when I told him you were going back to Boston with Albert. Morgan was absolutely consumed with jealousy."

"Of Albert?"

"Don't look so shocked. Albert's no handsome prince, but—you were engaged to the man, even though it was Uncle Bernard's doing."

"Then you think Morgan truly cares about me?"

"Of course he cares, Becca. If it helps any—for the longest time I thought that Chandler couldn't stand me and I had good reason to believe that. He didn't have a very good opinion of me . . . actually I think his exact words were "a spoiled rich brat".

Rebecca giggled.

"It took Chandler a while to realize that I was just a little—stubborn." Then, "I wonder what's taking so long," Samantha muttered more to herself.

"Patience is not one of your better virtues either," Rebecca teased her. "Hey . . . don't look now . . . here comes Morgan . . . I wonder why Chandler's not with him."

"What happened?" Samantha hollered out at Morgan.

"They already let him go," he replied, slightly out of breath. "Since we didn't see him in town, my guess is he's on his way home."

"On foot?"

"I doubt they loaned him a horse."

"Then what are we waiting for?"

By the time Morgan lifted Rebecca into the saddle and handed her the reins, Samantha was already mounted on her horse, waiting. He swung onto the back of his stallion, then they were heading back toward town.

Chandler wasn't sure how long he'd been running, but his legs were beginning to cramp, and there was a dull ache starting in his side. The blazing sun caused sweat to pour from his body, and he was awfully thirsty. He had to slow his pace a bit. Apparently being caged inside that tiny cell had left him a little out of shape. He thought that after everything the army had put him through, the least they could've done was loan him a horse—or somebody could have given him a ride home.

He wondered how Samantha had managed to get Albert to represent him? Then, again, knowing Samantha the way that he did, why should it surprise him? And, whatever he thought of Albert personally, he was indebted to the man.

The rumbling in his stomach reminded Chandler that he hadn't eaten a bite since that peach pie John had brought him. The first thing that Chandler was going to do when he reached the Callahan ranch was ask Rachel to make him some of her famous fried chicken for supper. His mouth began to water just thinking about it.

Hearing a horse's hooves coming up behind him, Chandler slowed to a walk, hoping he could get a ride the rest of the way to the ranch. When he turned his head toward the scruffy-looking gentleman who rode up alongside him, there was a brief flash of familiarity when he looked into a pair of cold blue eyes . . .

"Lose your horse, mister?" the man asked him.

Chandler looked straight ahead. He had a bad feeling in his gut about this man and wished he had some kind of weapon. He kept on walking as he curtly replied, "Nope." Then from the corner of his eye he saw the man draw his gun and heard the click of the hammer.

"Hold it right where you are, Indian."

Chandler stopped and turned to face his enemy. "What do you want?"

"Keep those hands where I can see 'em."

"I don't have a weapon."

"Just do as you're told!" Bart snarled.

"I don't have any money," Chandler said, raising both hands in the air.

"I'm not after your money. You resemble a bounty hunter named Morgan enough to be his twin. You his brother?" Bart grumbled, "I didn't expect to get an answer," when the Indian didn't say anything. "Two men couldn't possibly look that much alike and not be brothers."

"Who are you, mister?"

"Name's Bart Baxter."

Billy Baxter's brother! Chandler wondered what this man wanted with Morgan. "Thought I recognized the ice-blue eyes."

"So—you've heard of my brother Billy."

"Who hasn't."

"Start walkin', Indian, and stay in front of me," Bart motioned with his gun.

Knowing he had no other choice in the matter, Chandler did as told. His eyes darted back and forth across the narrow dirt road as he walked forward, thinking, the odds were definitely not in his favor, especially if Bart was anything like Billy. After looking into Bart Baxter's cold blue eyes, he had his doubts the man was any different than his vicious outlaw brother.

Chandler was beginning to figure out what was happening here. For whatever reason, Bart was going to use him as bait to lure Morgan. He had to think of a way to save his brother. Then an idea suddenly came to mind! At least it was worth a try!

"If you're looking for Morgan, he's nowhere around these parts," Chandler hollered over his shoulder at Bart Baxter.

"I oughtta shoot ya for lyin'!" came his furious reply. "It just so happens that I saw yer brother in town earlier today. Almost didn't recognize him though, with all his hair cut off."

Chandler knew that Bart was telling the truth, because how else could the man have known about Morgan's hair. "So what are you planning to do?"

"You'll find out soon enough, Indian."

Bart ordered Chandler into the small thicket just a short distance up ahead. If memory served Chandler correctly, there was a watering hole there. He could already taste the cool liquid trickling down his parched throat . . .

Through the trees Chandler saw the pool of water glistening in the bright sunlight. He walked a little faster, dropping upon the grassy shore to his knees, then, using his hand, he hastily scooped some water to his mouth. After drinking his fill, Chandler removed his shirt and then he splashed some water over his face and chest. He hadn't had a bath in days, but this was better than nothing. At least he felt human again.

"Sit down over there," he heard the order from behind him.

Chandler pulled on his shirt as he walked over to the tree where Bart had indicated, and nearly collapsed upon the ground. He felt about as weak as a kitten—mostly from lack of food. Plus, he'd just run several miles when Bart Baxter had overtaken him—though without any kind of weapon the outcome probably would have been the same.

"Put yer hands behind yer back, Indian."

In his extreme weakened condition, Chandler knew he didn't stand a chance against the much smaller but wiry man. He leaned forward and allowed Bart to lash his hands together; then Bart wrapped another rope around his chest and secured him to the trunk of the tree. Chandler glared at the man as he walked over to his tethered horse to grab his saddlebags. Bart then got a small fire going, and made a fresh pot of coffee.

Chandler happened to notice a flat rock lying on the ground near his foot. A portion of the edge looked thin and jagged. If he could somehow manage to get hold of that rock, it just might be sharp enough to cut through the rope binding his wrists. So, while Bart was busy throwing together some lunch, Chandler easily loosened the rock with his foot. Now the hard part would be getting it in his hand. Keeping the rock concealed underneath his moccasined foot, he began to slide it over the ground toward him. It took a little maneuvering, but Chandler finally managed to move the rock close enough to his back where he could grasp hold of it. He almost had the rock in his hand . . . just a little further . . . *there! He got it!*

Hearing horses coming through the trees, Chandler wanted to call out a warning to the unsuspecting visitors—who were probably stopping at the watering hole to water their horses—but Bart already had his gun drawn and was pointing it toward the trees, and he feared a shout from him would prompt Bart to start shooting.

When Chandler saw his brother emerge through the trees, immediately followed by Samantha and Rebecca, fear like he'd never felt before came over him. And there was nothing he could do but sit there, helplessly watching, while Bart held them all at gunpoint.

Bart instantly recognized Morgan Johnston and stepped over to his captive and held the gun to his head. "Drop yer weapon, bounty hunter," he shouted at the top of his lungs. "Then get down from yer horse real slow or yer brother here gets it! You women do the same! Every one does as I say . . . nobody will get hurt!"

Chandler hoped that *just this once* Samantha would do as told without an argument, that she wouldn't resist in any way. Because the man holding a gun to his head was as crazy as his brother Billy; Bart Baxter wouldn't give a second thought about shooting a woman. Chandler let out an inward sigh of relief, when Samantha wordlessly slid from her horse, followed by Rebecca—who looked scared out of her mind.

Morgan, very carefully, reached for his gun and dropped it on the ground, then dismounted. He snapped, "Now what, Baxter?"

"You!" Bart hollered at Rebecca. "Find a rope and tie Morgan's hands behind his back. And if ya don't tie them proper, he won't have a brother." Bart then pressed his gun more firmly against the Indian's head to emphasize his words.

"Do as he says, Becca," Morgan urged her. "There's a rope on my saddle . . . use that."

Blinking back tears of fright, Rebecca hurried to Morgan's horse and hastily grabbed the rope from the saddle horn and hurried over to Morgan. Her hands were shaking so badly, she was having trouble winding the rope around his wrists.

"I'm sorry I have to do this," she whispered behind him.

"It's okay, Becca," he replied in a low tone of voice. "Don't worry, we'll get out of this mess somehow . . . just be sure you get that rope on tight."

"Quiet over there!" Bart snarled at them.

"She's just scared, Baxter . . . give her a break," Morgan angrily shouted back.

When Rebecca was finished, Bart, holding his gun steady on Morgan, walked over to check the rope. Satisfied, he then motioned for Rebecca to take a seat on a nearby log. Now Bart turned to Samantha and ordered her to put some more wood on the fire. She folded her arms across her chest, refusing to budge.

"Woman, I said put some more wood on the fire!"

So this man was Billy Baxter's brother, Samantha thought. *No wonder his eyes had seemed so familiar*. She wondered why Bart Baxter wanted more wood on the fire? It didn't matter—he could find his own blasted wood. "Do it yourself!"

"What did you say?"

"Are you deaf, mister?"

The next thing Samantha knew she was sprawled out on the ground, her jaw throbbing with pain where Bart had struck her. It had happened so fast, she never saw it coming. It reminded her of the time that Billy had punched her; he had moved quicker than greased lightning. She now had her answer: Bart Baxter was every bit as cold-hearted as his brother. There would be no reasoning with the man. . . .

"You'll regret that, Baxter!" Chandler furiously thundered as he worked the sharp edge of the rock faster against the rope in a frantic attempt to free himself. He could feel blood oozing from his wrist, but he didn't care.

Samantha's jaw was smarting something awful, but she didn't think it was broke; at least she could still move it. She struggled to her feet, then, squaring her shoulders, she stepped directly in front of Bart Baxter. "Is that the best you can do?"

This time when Bart struck Samantha she hit the ground so hard that it actually knocked the breath from her lungs. Now Bart was shouting at her to get up. Though she was tempted to remain where she lay, pride would not allow her. Sometimes Samantha questioned her own sanity; for she must be plain crazy to enrage a man like Bart Baxter. Stifling a groan, Samantha raised upon her arms and pushed herself to her feet. Behind her, she could hear Rebecca sobbing, and Morgan trying to sooth her with comforting words, which only seemed to fuel Samantha's fury toward Bart even more . . .

Chandler recognized that particular look in Samantha's piercing blue eyes and worked feverishly to loosen the rope just enough to slip his hands through. He strained with all his might, but he couldn't even budge the rope.

Morgan now wished he would've shot Bart Baxter when he'd had the chance. And what jury would have convicted him—Indian or not? After all, Bart had threatened his life—the bartender had witnessed it. He should have at least escorted Bart to the sheriff's office, then none of them would be in this predicament. Morgan had assumed Bart would leave town; he never dreamed the man would pull something like this. He tugged furiously at the rope that bound his wrists, thinking, whatever happened it would be all his fault.

When Samantha found herself looking down the barrel of Bart Baxter's gun, what was going through her mind was: *now she and Chandler would never marry . . .*

Chandler became enraged when he saw Bart level his gun at Samantha. Taking a deep breath, he struggled frenetically at the rope binding his wrists, straining and pulling with every bit of strength he possessed. The rope suddenly snapped in two and Chandler yanked at the other one around his waist, lifting it over his head. Ignoring the cramping pain in his legs, he was on his feet in an instant and charging toward Bart Baxter like a raging bull. He hit Baxter with everything he had, sending them both crashing to the ground; then, jerking Bart to his feet, he threw a punch that sent the man sailing through the air.

Bart didn't get up.

Chandler caught Samantha as she flew into his outstretched arms and he crushed her hard against his chest, kissing the top of her head. Her arms tightened around his waist, then they stood there, clinging to each other. After a while, Chandler set Samantha away from him.

"Are you okay?" he asked.

Samantha nodded. "And you?"

"I'm fine."

"Would somebody cut me loose?" Morgan snapped impatiently.

Wordlessly Samantha reached inside her boot for her knife, walked over to Morgan and began to slice through his bonds. Meanwhile, Chandler snatched Bart's gun off the ground and slipped it inside the waistband of his pants, then proceeded to lash the unconscious man's hands together.

"Has anybody seen Becca?" Samantha said as she slipped her knife back inside her boot.

"Becca! Where are you?" Morgan called out, glancing around.

"I'm over here," came a female's voice from behind some nearby bushes.

Praying that nobody would know that she'd gotten sick, Rebecca finished wiping her mouth off with the sleeve of her shirt, before stepping away from her hiding place. For the first time since arriving in Bear Creek, Rebecca wanted to go home. Morgan had tried to tell her that she didn't belong here—apparently he was right.

Sensing something was terribly wrong with Becca, "Chandler, why don't you and Morgan take Billy's brother to the sheriff's office," Samantha suggested. "You can take Becca's horse and we'll ride double on mine. We'll meet you back at the ranch."

Chandler reached out to touch the horrible bruise on the side of Samantha's face, before gently kissing her on the cheek. He was tempted to beat Bart Baxter within an inch of his miserable life! He lifted Samantha onto the back of her horse, handing her the reins. And as he lifted an awfully quiet Rebecca on behind her, he thought the woman looked a little rough around the edges, but figured after what she'd been through that it was probably just nerves.

"If you and Becca hurry, you can make it home before dark."

Samantha rolled her eyes. "Wade Chandler, you're beginning to sound like my father."

"I'll take that as a compliment," he replied with a lopsided grin.

"I didn't mean it as a compliment."

"Just be careful."

Rebecca turned and waved to Morgan as they rode away, then she looked straight ahead, trying hard to concentrate on the rugged beauty surrounding her, forcing what had happened out of her mind. Though it didn't seem to be working. Rebecca thought people were sure different out here . . . some of them no better than *barbarians!* . . . no wonder they called this part of the country the *Wild West!* She couldn't remember ever being so terrified . . .

"You wanna tell me what's wrong, Becca?"

There was a brief period of silence, then, "I was so scared, Samantha . . . I got sick back there. I don't belong here and I . . . I'm thinking about going home."

"What happened back there, Becca, could've happened to anyone."

"It wouldn't have happened to you."

Samantha looked over her shoulder at her cousin. "What? You don't think I ever get scared? I get scared plenty."

"You're just saying that to make me feel better."

Samantha decided to try a different approach. "I know you love Morgan. And if you leave now, he'll go back to his people and you'll lose him for good. You have to keep on fighting, Becca."

"I'm not sure how to do that."

"You already *have* been doing it . . . Morgan just can't see it."

Rebecca frowned thoughtfully, not really sure what Samantha was talking about. "Do you think you could teach me how to throw a knife?"

"You're not going to stab Morgan, are you?" Samantha teased.

"No," Rebecca giggled.

"I'm not sure why you wanna learn, but—I'd be happy to teach you. We'll start first thing in the morning." Suddenly anxious to get home, Samantha kneed her horse into a slow canter.

Chapter Thirty-seven

True to her word, bright and early the next morning, Samantha woke her cousin and, after a quick breakfast of toast and coffee, the girls eagerly headed to the barn where Rebecca would have her first knife-tossing lesson. But teaching Rebecca how to throw a knife was proving to be a lot more difficult than Samantha had anticipated. And after a few hours of constant practice, she was beginning to wonder if her cousin could hit the broad side of a barn with a boulder. Once Rebecca had somehow managed to hurtle the knife behind her, claiming the blade had slipped out of her hand. Samantha couldn't help but feel a little leery, and now stood farther away from her cousin's *lethal arm.* Still, she had to give Rebecca credit for pure determination.

"No, Becca, don't jerk your arm," Samantha said, walking toward her. "Remember, you have to let the knife flow smoothly out in front of you. I'll show you again." *Very carefully* she removed the knife from Rebecca's hand.

"I'm that bad, huh?"

"You'll get better." Though Samantha wasn't so sure. "Now watch, Becca." She grasped the handle lightly. "You have to hold the knife in your hand—like this," she patiently instructed her cousin. "Remember, not too tight—and not to loose . . . just so." Samantha now looked at the target she pinned on the wall; drawing back her arm, she then sent the knife flying swiftly and smoothly through the air, hitting the target precisely in the middle.

"I'll never be able to do that," Rebecca muttered, completely amazed.

"Sure you will."

"How'd you learn how to do that?"

"Amos taught me, and I practiced a lot."

"Were you as bad as me, when you first started?"

"You're not going to learn over night, Becca." Samantha didn't have the heart to tell her cousin that a blind man could do better.

"How about before I'm an old woman?"

"Maybe," Samantha laughed. "How 'bout we quit for the day and start fresh in the morning—so you don't become too frustrated and quit?"

"I think I'll keep practicing, if you don't mind?"

"Try not to stab yourself."

"Very funny," Rebecca said, frowning at her cousin's departing back.

Now with more determination than ever, Rebecca focussed on the target Samantha had hammered on the wall. She gripped the handle of the knife loosely in her hand (the way Samantha had showed her) then, drawing back her arm, she suddenly released the knife and sent it hurtling through the air—but, instead if hitting the target the knife hit the wall cockeyed and then it spun around the barn like a boomerang and landed in an empty bucket with a loud clang.

Hearing a burst of laughter behind her, Rebecca whirled around. "How long have you been standing there?"

"Long enough to know to keep out of your way," Morgan said, chuckling.

Rebecca angrily marched over to the bucket to retrieve the knife and then she walked back to stand in front of the makeshift target—to try it all over again.

"What are you doing?" Morgan wanted to know.

"What's it look like I'm doing?"

"Trying to wound yourself?"

Rebecca glared at Morgan over her shoulder. "Samantha's been teaching me how to throw a knife, and I'm just practicing. Or I was, before you interrupted me."

Morgan thought women were the most peculiar creatures. "Any particular reason why you want to learn how to throw a knife?"

To impress you, Rebecca thought to herself. "Just something to do, I guess." Again she threw the knife at the target—this time the blade hit the wall the wrong way and the knife bounced back at her and landed on the ground close to her foot.

"Maybe you should find another hobby?" Morgan seriously suggested.

"How does she do it?" Rebecca grumbled to herself as she reached over to snatch the knife off the hay-shrewn floor.

"I've often wondered that myself," Morgan admitted. "The way Samantha can use her knife—I've never seen anything like it. Did she ever tell you about the time her father almost got bit by a rattler and how she killed the snake with her knife, from several yards away?" Rebecca shook her head negatively. "Graywolf was there . . . said he saw the whole thing with his own eyes. Apparently—just as the snake was about to strike John—Samantha threw her knife and actually pierced the reptile's head to the ground, faster than my brother could draw his gun."

"That's absolutely amazing," Rebecca said in awe.

"Graywolf once told me . . . their best warrior could not compete with Samantha."

Morgan wondered what was it about Rebecca Smith that pulled at his heartstrings? He used to think it was because she resembled Samantha so much, but he now knew that wasn't true. He was completely enchanted by this young woman from Boston—mens duds and all, Morgan thought grinning to himself. And he wanted Miss Rebecca Smith for his own. He never dreamed of finding a woman he would want to spend the rest of his life with. *But was that what he really wanted?* Morgan then wondered. *To settle down and get married?* He had his answer when he tried to picture his life without Rebecca. And he knew she was strongly attracted to him. It was there, in her warm brown eyes, the way she was looking at him.

Right then and there, Morgan came to an important decision: he was going to ask Rebecca to be his wife. True, they hadn't known each other very long, but some couples started their marriages with less than that. Then Morgan thought about what Rebecca's father would say when he found out that his only daughter had married an Indian. He certainly didn't want any problems with his in-laws. But his brother was Indian and Samantha was white? Morgan tried to rationalize in his troubled mind. But Rebecca was different from Samantha; she'd been pampered and protected her whole life.

He then thought about what he had to offer Rebecca: nothing; not even a decent home. And she deserved so much better than what he could ever give her. If Rebecca went back to Boston, she would eventually marry a man who could give her the finer things in life; if she married him, she would probably come to resent the day she ever met him. And *that* was a risk that Morgan was not willing to take. He couldn't stand the thought of Rebecca possibly growing to hate him someday for ruining her life.

No, Morgan finally concluded, Rebecca should go back to Boston where she belonged. And after Rebecca left Bear Creek, he would return to his father's village . . . where *he* belonged!

"Guess I'd better get back to work." He politely tipped his hat and walked away.

Rebecca's confused gaze followed Morgan as he strode out of the barn. For a moment there, she thought he was going to kiss her—but apparently he'd changed his mind. She sensed that Morgan liked her—maybe even a lot—but she just didn't have that much experience with men to be sure. *Then fight for him!* Samantha's words came back to haunt her, loud and clear. Unfortunately, Rebecca didn't know how to go about getting Morgan to see that she wasn't a delicate Easterner, that she could easily handle surviving here in this rugged country—with him.

The next morning Bernard stopped by the Callahan ranch in a last attempt to persuade Rebecca to return to Boston with him. Inside the parlor, Rebecca sat stiffly on the dark leather sofa, watching her father pace around the room. Albert sat beside her with that smug expression on his face, and she had an overwhelming urge to slap him. She felt like screaming at Albert that even if she did decide to go home, she would never marry him.

"Have you come to your senses yet, Rebecca?"

"And what about mother?" she questioned her father.

Bernard stopped pacing and turned to face his daughter. "She can come home if she wants."

"How noble of you, Father. I bet you wouldn't leave your harlot behind."

"Rebecca!"

"Well it's true!"

"Where did you learn such kind of talk?" Albert demanded to know.

Rebecca whirled on him. "Why don't you mind your own business, old coot!"

Albert gasped.

"Rebecca!" Bernard angrily snarled.

The door to the parlor suddenly opened and Ruth entered the room. "I thought I heard your contemptuous voice, Bernard," she said, closing the door behind her. "What's Albert doing here?" She glared at the arrogant attorney. She was glad that Albert got Chandler out of jail, but she still couldn't stand the man.

"He's here with me . . . we won't be long."

"Father's leaving on the afternoon stage," Rebecca informed her mother. "He wants me to go with him and Albert."

"Is that what you want to do, Becca?"

"No."

"Then have a good trip, Bernard," Ruth bluntly told her husband. "You too, Albert."

"I'm not leaving my daughter here in this . . . this country filled with barbarians!"

Ruth let out an unladylike snort. "If you're so worried about your daughter being around barbarians, keep that *old buzzard* away from Becca!"

"Ruth!"

"Now see here, Mrs. Smith, I resent that!"

Ruth swung around to face Albert. "You think I don't know why you want Becca to go home so badly! If you think my husband's going to force Becca to marry you, think again! I would never allow my daughter to marry the likes of you! Unless that's what Becca wanted, but I would hope my daughter has better taste!"

"That's enough, Ruth!" Bernard furiously hissed.

"I said no more than what that *buffoon* you call a partner deserved!" she shouted back.

"You're still my wife, Ruth, and a wife's place is with her husband!"

"Not if that wife has to share her place with her husband's mistresses!"

Bernard's face turned red with rage. He never should have allowed his wife and daughter to come here! His entire future was at stake! If Albert didn't marry Rebecca . . . ! Besides, he knew Albert would make a good husband, that at least his daughter would never want for anything—so his intentions weren't entirely selfish. But he could clearly see that to get his way in this matter, he was going to have to swallow his pride and placate his wife.

"What if I gave you my word, Ruth, I'll never see Bell again?"

"You've been giving me that empty promise for years, Bernard, remember? Now leave—and take that *old vulture* with you!"

Albert shot to his feet. "Now see here, madame!"

"Is there a problem here, Ruth?" None of them had heard John enter the room. He stood there, towering over Bernard and Albert, his muscular arms casually folded across his broad chest.

Ruth was filled with relief to see her brother-in-law. "I don't think there's a problem, John, but I'm not sure. *Is* there a problem, Bernard?" Ruth knew her husband was angry beyond words, but he would never stand up to John.

"Albert and I were just leaving."

Bernard angrily brushed past John with Albert close on his heels. A moment later, they all heard the front door slam shut. John looked at his sister-in-law. "I assume this means that you and Becca will be staying on at the ranch?"

"Yes . . . I suppose it does. If that's okay with you?"

"My home is your home, Ruth. You should know that."

"Thank you, John. I could never ask for a better brother-in-law."

"I'd better get back to work while my head can still fit through the door."

Ruth looked at Becca, and they both burst out laughing.

Samantha and Chandler stood watching the colt run around the corral on its long, spindly legs, laughing. Periodically the little stud would stop abruptly and kick up his hind legs. Now it was trotting over to them and stuck its velvety nose over the top rail of the fence.

"I guess the little fella needs some attention," Samantha said, giggling.

"Are you ever going to give the "little fella" a name?" Chandler asked.

"You have any suggestions?"

"With legs like that he's going to be a runner . . . how about calling him Thunder?"

"I'm saving that name for Daisy's colt."

"You know—that mare is just a freak of nature . . . there's no logical explanation why she should run like the wind—so makes you think Daisy's foal will be a runner?"

Samantha shrugged. "I just do."

Chandler rolled his eyes.

The colt darted away, and Samantha turned to Chandler. "I sort of brought you over here for a reason—where we would be away from prying ears," she confessed. "I didn't want to take a chance that somebody might overhear . . . there's something I want to talk to you about."

"Sounds serious."

"Well—I suppose that depends on how you look at it. Ma gave me the idea . . . how would you like to get married next weekend?" Samantha rushed on to say, "Trust me, I would understand if you declined, considering every time we plan to get married some kind of catastrophe takes place. Maybe we should take the hint," she muttered to herself.

Chandler looked away for a moment so she wouldn't see his grin. "I think us getting married is a good idea . . . the sooner the better. How about tomorrow?"

"Shouldn't we at least wait until the bruises on my face are better? I'm hoping by next weekend they'll be faded enough they won't be as noticeable. I wouldn't want our guests to think my husband-to-be is already beating me."

Taking Samantha by the shoulders, Chandler playfully teased her. "Bruises or no bruises, we're getting married next weekend, woman, and that's an order."

"Yes, master," Samantha giggled.

"That's better. I like it when you're more . . . obedient."

"Then enjoy it while it lasts."

"I'll say," an unexpected voice said.

Chandler and Samantha both whirled around. "Pa!" Samantha shrieked. "How long have you been standing there?"

"Long enough." John laughed when Samantha's cheeks flushed from embarrassment. "Your mother needs your help in the kitchen."

"But . . ."

"I can still order you around, young lady . . . you're not married yet."

"Oh, very well."

John waited until his daughter was out of earshot, then turned to Chandler. "I didn't want Samantha to hear this, because I wanted it to be a surprise. I was beginning to think I'd never get it completed in time for the wedding—what with all the postponements," John added more to himself. "But I think your house will be done in time."

"House?" There was a look of confusion on Chandler's face.

"It's your and Samantha's wedding gift."

"You built us a house?" Chandler said incredulously.

"Well you sure didn't expect to live with me, did you?" John teasingly replied.

"But how . . . ? when . . . ?" Then it suddenly occurred to Chandler. "So that's what you and the boys have been doing for the past several weeks?"

John grinned.

"I don't know what to say." Chandler was touched beyond words by his soon-to-be-father-in-law's overwhelming generosity.

"There is nothing *to* say . . . you're part of the family now, son. Now—let me give you a little hint about the house. From the living room window you have a clear view of the pond."

"Oh, John, that area of the ranch is Samantha's favorite place."

"I know. Plus, it's a fairly good distance away from here."

Chandler through back his head and laughed.

"I was only joking about the last part," John chuckled. Then, "I've been holding my breath, hoping Samantha wouldn't ride over there, and now that you know, it'll be your job keeping her away until the wedding. Oh, by the way, there's plenty of room for another house." He arched a dark brow adding, "I'm assuming Morgan and Rebecca will be getting married soon."

Staring out the kitchen window, wondering what she could do different to win Morgan's affection, Rebecca was only halfheartedly listening to her mother and her aunt Ruth, who were chattering away like a couple of magpies, while preparing the evening meal. At least Morgan had seemed mighty pleased that her mother had decided to make Bear Creek their permanent place of residence. *That was a good sign, wasn't it?*

Morgan suddenly appeared on the back veranda, and Rebecca wanted to run out the door and throw her arms around the man and tell him how she felt—since he couldn't seem to take a hint. But a proper lady did not do such things, or so she'd been taught from a child. *Samantha wouldn't allow something as silly as that keep her from the man she loved . . .*

"Becca?"

She looked over her shoulder. "Yes, Mama?"

"Why don't you take that nice young man outside some of this fresh lemonade?"

Rebecca's entire face split into a radiant smile. This was her mother's way of telling her that she approved of Morgan. She quickly took the glass of lemonade from her mother's hand, then exited out the back door.

Morgan shot to his feet when he noticed Rebecca standing there. She shyly held the glass out to him and said, "I hope you like lemonade." His fingers lightly brushed against hers as he took the glass from her hand.

"It's my favorite," Morgan said with a nod of thanks. Although he could certainly use something a bit stronger than lemonade at the moment. He wanted to take Rebecca in his arms and kiss her until she was breathless and a stiff drink might give him the courage he needed. He guzzled the lemonade and set the empty glass on a nearby table.

"Care to go for a walk?" he asked, before he lost his nerve.

"I would like that very much," Rebecca replied with a huge smile.

As they strolled around the ranch, Morgan spoke to Rebecca about what he could remember growing up in an Indian village. She listened with keen interest, while Morgan recounted some childhood stories about himself and Chandler, whom he still referred to as Graywolf. He told her about when he was yet a small boy, how he'd gotten separated from Graywolf on a hunting trip—how several days later a kindhearted elderly white man had found him wandering alone in the wilderness—and that it was Samuel and his wife Martha who'd loved and raised him as their own son. The Johnstons had given him the name of Morgan and had taught him the white man's tongue. Rebecca noticed that Morgan was much more reluctant to share his days as a bounty hunter; the only thing he would tell her was that he'd taken up the gun after two white men had brutally murdered Samuel and Martha Johnston, his adoptive parents. She felt it was probably best not to pressure Morgan—that maybe he would talk more about his bounty hunting days when he was ready.

"You said your real father was a chief?"

"Why? Does that bother you?"

"Of course not. Why should it?"

"Because most white people think the Indian is beneath them," Morgan replied bitterly.

"Not where I come from," Rebecca assured him. There was a slight pause. "You never said anything about your real mother—"

"Singing Wind died giving me life."

Rebecca stopped walking and turned to face him. "I heard that usually a son will take the place of a chief. Chandler's not going anywhere . . . does that mean you might eventually return to your father's people to lead them?" She didn't mention that she knew he was Black Hawk and was already war chief to a bunch of renegades.

"I haven't decided yet," Morgan honestly replied. His dark eyes held Rebecca's questioning gaze. "It depends on a certain young woman."

"I don't know what you mean."

Morgan peered deeply into Rebecca's warm brown eyes. If he wasn't mistaken that was love he saw shining within their depths. Or maybe it was just wishful thinking? he wasn't sure. Unable to resist the urge to kiss her any longer, his head bent slowly toward hers and he gently brushed his lips against her velvety soft cheek . . .

When his warm lips touched hers, Rebecca's arms instinctively went around Morgan's neck, and she kissed him back. His arm tightened around her waist and the kiss deepened. Her legs suddenly felt like butter left out in the sun too long and it was a good thing that Morgan was holding her or she would have collapsed at his feet. Rebecca shivered as he kissed her along the neck, whispering her name.

Then he said something that completely shocked her. She leaned back, blinking up at him, thinking, surely she must have heard him wrong . . .

"Did you . . . did you just ask me to . . . to marry you?" Rebecca stammered.

Morgan shrugged and grinned. "I guess I did. So—what's your answer?"

On the verge of bursting into tears, Rebecca tried to push away from him. "If you didn't mean it, now would be the time to say so."

"Now hold on there, Becca," Morgan said, tightening his grip around her waist. "I wouldn't have asked if I didn't mean it."

She stopped struggling then. "Honest?"

"Honest." After a brief period of silence, Morgan repeated with heartfelt sincerity, "Will you marry me, Rebecca Smith?" Her eyes welled with tears. "I hope those are happy tears," he said, brushing away a single tear that had broke free to roll down a silky-soft cheek.

Rebecca thought she might burst with utter happiness. "Yes—these are happy tears. And, yes, Morgan Johnston, I would be proud to be your wife."

Chapter Thirty-eight

Samantha stood in front of the full-length mirror inside her bedroom, staring at her reflection, while Sarah finished buttoning the long row of tiny pearl buttons on the back of her wedding gown. She could hardly believe that she was about to get married and nothing had gone wrong; even the dress fit her to perfection. If it wasn't for the faded greenish bruise still noticeable on her right cheek (where Bart Baxter had hit her) Samantha would have thought herself beautiful.

She ran a hand lovingly over the satiny gown, knowing her mother had worn this when she'd married her father and had sewn it with her own two hands. With a high neckline and long sleeves that tapered to a ve, the dress was elegantly beautiful. Delicate beads had been sewn around the bodice and were carefully stitched in flowered designs over the lower part of the garment. She tried to twist around to get a look at the back.

"Hold still," Sarah complained.

"Sorry."

The bedroom door opened then and Rachel stepped into the room. Her eyes began to fill with tears when she got a look at her daughter in the mirror. She thought Samantha looked like an angel. "I've never seen you look more beautiful than you do right now."

"Thank you, Ma, but my face—it looks like I got into a fist fight."

Rachel grinned. "I have some powder that'll hide that bruise."

"What's that in your hand?" Samantha asked.

"Oh—I almost forgot. Chandler wanted me to give this to you."

"I wonder what it could be." Samantha took the package from her mother's hand, then, gathering her dress, she walked over to her bed and plopped down on it. Eagerly she tore away the brown paper and opened the box. Her eyes widened in surprise when she saw a small pair of white moccasins.

"Oh, Samantha, they're beautiful!" Sarah gushed.

"Well, try them on," her mother said.

Carefully moving aside her dress, Samantha slipped the moccasins on her feet. "They fit perfectly," she happily announced, wiggling her toes.

"Don't you think those shoes clash with that dress?" a deep voice remarked.

Sarah frowned at her husband. "Those shoes have nothing to do with fashion, James Callahan . . . they're a gift from Chandler."

"So that's where those rabbit hides went to." James burst out laughing at his sister's horrified expression. "I was only teasing, Sam."

"James, you should be ashamed of yourself," Rachel scolded her son. Then, "Well—guess I'd better get back downstairs . . . our guests should start arriving soon and I still have a lot to do. Sarah, I could sure use your opinion on something, if you're not busy?"

"Certainly."

After her mother and Sarah had left the room, Samantha immediately began to question her brother. "Have you seen Chandler?"

"Your groom awaits inside the bunkhouse. He's playing poker with Ernie and the boys . . . they'll take good care of him."

"That's what I'm afraid of," Samantha said, her brows knitted together in a scowl.

James chuckled. "What? You don't trust Ernie and the guys?"

"I trust all those confirmed bachelors about as far as I could throw them—which isn't very far. Now would you please go keep an eye on Chandler?"

"Okay, okay. I'll personally make sure that your *betrothed* is standing by your side this afternoon, even if I have to hold him at gunpoint."

"That's not funny, James."

"I'm only joking, Samantha. You really should try to relax."

"That's easy for you to say."

"If something was going to go wrong, it would've happened by now."

"The day's not over yet."

"Since when did you become such a pessimist?" At his sister's angry scowl, "Okay, I'm going," James muttered under his breath.

After her brother left, Samantha sat at her dressing table with a sigh, and stared into the mirror. Was it just her imagination or was that bruise on her cheek more noticeable? Her cousin entered the room then to do her hair.

"That dress looks absolutely gorgeous on you, Samantha."

"Thanks, Becca."

Rebecca picked up the hairbrush and began to brush Samantha's long hair, noting her forlorn expression in the mirror. "What's the matter?"

"I just keep expecting something to go wrong."

"That's certainly understandable, but—maybe you shouldn't go looking for trouble."

"I never have to look very far," Samantha sarcastically retorted.

Rebecca giggled. "You should see our mothers running around downstairs like there's no tomorrow. I heard Aunt Rachel threaten Uncle John with a broom if he ate another morsel of food before the guests arrived."

"I guess my getting married is stressful on everyone."

"Especially the bride." Rebecca was silent for several long moments. "I wasn't going to say anything yet, but—I have to tell somebody before I burst."

"What is it, Becca?"

"Morgan asked me to marry him."

Samantha shrieked with excitement. "Did you say yes?"

"Of course I said yes."

"Oh, Becca, I'm so happy for you. So when's the big day?"

"We haven't set a date yet," Rebecca said, laughing. "Now hold still, Samantha, so I can finish your hair."

As Ernie dealt another hand around the table, his eyes were fixed on the groom. Chandler looked about as nervous as a caged mountain lion, he thought, grinning to himself. But it was all part of the fun and he had to get in another barb. "You know, Chandler, it's still not too late to change your mind. You could leave now and hightail it back to your father's village."

Chandler frowned at him.

"Then if you insist on going through with it, if you have any trouble keeping that new wife of yours in line . . . come see me."

"Watch it, Ernie, that's my sister you're talking about," James said.

"Are you going to play cards or keep yappin'?" Chandler snapped at Ernie.

"I think my brother's had enough," this from Morgan.

"I'm just having a little fun."

"I'm with Chandler," Amos yelled at Ernie. "Are you playing cards or not?"

"Don't get your rooster tail ruffled, old man." Ernie wasn't bothered in the least. He studied his cards for a moment, and slapped them down on the table in front of him. "I'm out of this hand." He then looked at Chandler and winked. "Don't ya think you should be getting your suit on . . . it is getting about that time."

Chandler angrily tossed his cards on the table, scooted out of his chair, then strode out of the bunkhouse with Ernie's hoots of laughter filling his ears. Outside, he shoved his hands inside his pockets as he started walking toward the barn. Watching the colt always seemed to cheer him up—maybe he would try that. But why should he need cheering on such a day like today? he wondered. Soon, he would finally be marrying the woman he loved more than his own life and he was thrilled beyond words—*wasn't he?*

A sudden movement behind the barn caught Chandler's attention. Removing his gun from its holster, he crept forward on silent feet, staying close to the side of the building. He was pretty sure that was the shadow of a man nosing around the corner of the barn. If that was Lieutenant Brown or any of his followers, he was just angry enough to shoot and ask questions later. He nearly ran into the man . . .

"Father?" Chandler said when he found his tongue.

"Are you going to shoot this old man?"

Immediately holstering his gun, Chandler gave his father a huge bear hug. "I can't believe you're here! How did you find this place? Is anyone with you?"

"Hold on, son," Running Elk said, chuckling. "I can only answer one question at a time." Then he let out a loud whistle.

Chandler smiled when he saw his youngest brother emerge from the trees. Big Bear's straight teeth shone pearly white in his handsome face when he smiled in return. Even though it had not been so long ago since he'd last seen his father and his half brother, somehow it still felt like years. The two brothers clasped hands.

"Are you an old married man yet?" Big Bear asked in perfect English.

"As a matter-of-fact, I'm getting married today."

"Then there's still a chance I could win Samantha for myself," Big Bear teased.

"Here comes Black Hawk," Running Elk announced.

"If we had known you were coming, Father, we would have prepared a feast," Morgan hollered out as he hurried forward. He hugged his father, then pumped Big Bear's hand. "To what do we owe this pleasant surprise?"

"I wanted to see with my own eyes that everything was okay with you and your brother," Running Elk told Morgan. Then, "Graywolf, I hope you will bring my new daughter to our village for a visit the next summer season."

"Are you sure you want me to bring Samantha to the village?" Chandler was remembering what happened the last time his *betrothed* was there—she'd nearly started a war.

Running Elk laughed. "I am sure."

"There's something I need to tell you, Father." Now that Morgan seemed to have everyone's attention, he officially announced, "I have asked Samantha's cousin Rebecca to be my wife."

"Then I will soon be blessed with many strong grandsons."

A huge grin spread across Morgan's face. "I will certainly do my best."

"Congratulations, brother," Chandler said, slapping him on the back.

"Does this cousin have the same kind of fiery temper as Samantha?" Big Bear asked.

"Let's hope not," Morgan seriously replied.

They all had a hearty laugh over that.

"Then you will not be taking Father's place as our next chief?" Big Bear inquired of Morgan.

Morgan was now looking at Running Elk. "I hope that doesn't disappoint you, Father?"

"I know it was never in your heart, son, to be the next chief. I also know that you and Graywolf will be happier here. Big Bear will take my place when the time comes. I only ask that you and Graywolf will bring your families to the village sometimes."

Morgan nodded.

"Big Bear and I must leave now."

"I hope all goes well on your journey, Father," Chandler said. He gave his father a hug, then grasped Big Bear's hand in farewell. He stood by watching, while Morgan did the same, and was shocked to see moisture—which looked suspiciously like tears—in his eyes.

Chandler and Morgan watched in silence, until both men disappeared into the trees. Now Morgan turned to face his older brother. He knew something was deeply troubling Graywolf, which was the reason he had followed him here in the first place.

"You wanna tell me what's bothering you?"

Chandler's eyes held a note of sadness as he explained, "I thought it was the responsibility of taking on a wife that was bothering me, but now I know that's not true." He let out a sigh. "I miss the old way of life, Morgan. And once I marry Samantha, there will be no turning back."

"Unless you can convince her to live in a tepee. Sorry, I shouldn't have joked," Morgan apologized at his brother's scowling expression. "If it helps any, I was feeling the same way—then I tried to imagine my life without Rebecca and . . ." he shrugged.

"I feel the same way."

"And when it's my turn to marry Becca, I hope you'll remind me of what I just said."

"You can count on it."

"Figured as much."

"Well—guess I'd better go get my suit on," Chandler said. Both men started walking back toward the bunkhouse.

With the ceremony about to begin, Samantha stood at the top of the stairway, holding a small bouquet of orange blossoms and daffodils in her slightly trembling hand, while she waited for her father to escort her outside on the veranda where the wedding would take place. She nervously played with the floor-length veil, careful not to move her head around too much; for it had taken Rebecca over an hour just to weave the tiny white rosebuds throughout her knee-length hair, which hung down her back in a thick mass of shiny waves.

Samantha looked over her shoulder when she heard her parents' bedroom door open. She smiled when she saw her father, thinking, he looked very handsome in his dark suit and silk cravat. When he reached her side, Samantha slipped her arm through his.

Gazing down into his daughter's upturned face, John was thinking that it seemed like only yesterday when he'd just taught Samantha how to ride her first pony—now here she was about to get married. Remembering his own wedding day, he said, "You look as beautiful as your mother did, the day she wore that dress."

"Thank you, Pa."

"I hope Chandler realizes just how lucky he is."

"Oh, Pa, what a lovely thing to say."

"I mean to have me as a father-in-law."

Samantha burst out with laughter. Finally, she was starting to relax. "I hope Chandler's sense of humor is as good as yours." They started down the steps. "I want you to know that just because I'm getting married, that doesn't mean you're getting rid of me."

At the bottom of the stairway Rachel's thoughts momentarily took her back as she stood there watching her daughter descend the steps on her father's arm. Seemed like it was only yesterday when Samantha had just taken her first step and here she was a grown woman already. Now both of her children would be married and on their own, and she was about to become a grandmother. Where did the time all go?

Rachel hugged her daughter when she reached the bottom step. "You look absolutely breathtaking," she said, fighting to keep her voice steady. "Well," she sniffled, "we'd better get out there . . . everybody's waiting on us."

Samantha's satin gown rustled softly at her feet as she followed her parents down the long hallway to the kitchen. "I'll escort your mother outside, then I'll come back for you," her father told her, before disappearing out the back door with her mother clutching his arm. Samantha stepped over to the window to look outside and gasped in surprise by what she saw. Her mother and Aunt Ruth had transformed the veranda into an outdoor church. The dozens of chairs that Reverend Peters had brought over from the church were arranged in several neat rows. On the end of each row, there was a large vase filled with colorful flowers. It must have taken every flower in her mother's garden to decorate the place.

Her gaze began to move over the small crowd of family and friends that had gathered on this special day as they took their seats. Samantha noticed that Morgan and Rebecca were sitting together, and seemed to have eyes only for each other. She was so happy for them. Seated on the other side of Morgan was Amos. Samantha smiled, having never seen the older man in a suit and tie before. Amos had been her father's foreman ever since she could remember and was more like a grandfather to her. She was surprised to see that every ranch hand was present today, but especially Ernie, who was a confirmed bachelor and never went to weddings, claiming they were bad luck. And what surprised Samantha even more was the way that Ernie was looking at her Aunt Ruth. Her smile widened, thinking, anything was possible.

Reverend Peters was now taking his place in front of the crowd. There was a smile on his face, and the Bible was open in his hands. Then Samantha's breath suddenly caught in her throat, when she got a look at Chandler, who was climbing the steps to take his place in front of the Reverend. Dressed in a dark blue suit and tie—with his shoulder-length hair pulled neatly back into a queue—he truly looked more handsome than ever before . . .

Samantha heard the back door open and close, then her father called her name. She turned to face him. "You haven't called me *Sam* in quite a while."

John walked over to stand directly in front of his daughter. "You know I love you."

"I love you too, Pa."

He hugged Samantha, kissed the top of her head. After several long moments, he gently set her away, and pulled the veil down over her lovely face. "I guess we'd better get out there, before the poor groom thinks you've changed your mind."

When Chandler saw Samantha step outside onto the veranda, he thought he was looking at a beautiful angel adorned in a cloud of white satin. As she slowly moved toward him to take her place at his side, Chandler could not take his eyes off her. And, as the Reverend Peters spoke the words that joined them together for the rest of their lives, he never once removed his eyes from the vision at his side. It wasn't until he heard the words, "I now pronounce you husband and wife," that Chandler realized the ceremony was over.

"You may kiss the bride," Reverend Peters said with a beaming smile.

Carefully lifting the veil over Samantha's head, when Chandler peered into those bright blue eyes, he was struck by the love he saw shining there. And he knew that no matter what difficulties they may face in the future—or whatever disagreements they might have and there probably would be plenty—he would never want to change a thing about his life.

Taking Samantha Chandler in his arms, he then kissed his new bride with all the love he felt in his heart, while family and friends cheered him on. . . .

"I don't see why we couldn't have waited until after the reception?" Samantha complained.

"Because I couldn't wait until then," Chandler irritably replied.

"So—where are we going?"

"You'll see."

"Could you at least give me a hint?"

"Be still."

"I should tell my father that you're already trying to boss me around."

"Your father gave me permission to turn you over my knee, if you ever get out of hand."

Samantha looked over her shoulder, frowning at him. "I should've ridden my own horse."

Chandler chuckled.

"Would you at least tell me if we're almost there?"

Chandler rolled his eyes as his arm tightened around his impatient wife, and nudged Ranger into a slow canter.

It was several miles later when Samantha finally realized where they were headed, and she wondered why Chandler would be taking her to the pond? But, since he knew it was her most favorite place on the entire ranch, she assumed that he must have arranged for them to honeymoon there. The thought of camping out under the stars brought a dreamy smile to her lips. As they approached the pond,

Samantha was stunned to see a large two-story house nestled among the tall cottonwoods that hadn't been there before. A short distance from the house was a small barn and corral. She squeezed her eyes shut and then opened them again. *Surely she must be seeing things!*

"Is that a house or are my eyes playing tricks on me?" she finally asked.

"It's a house."

"But how . . . ? Who . . . ?"

"Your father," Chandler informed her. "This is where John and the boys have really been since we got back from the cattle drive. Your father told me about the house just the other day. He wanted it to be a surprise."

"I can't believe my father actually built us a house!"

"Your father told me to tell you and I quote, "You've lived with me long enough."

Samantha threw back her head and laughed. It sounded like something her father would say. "I can't wait to see the inside."

Chandler halted his horse in front of the house, then alighted to the ground. He lifted his blushing bride out of the saddle and headed toward the covered porch with her still in his arms. Her bubbly laughter filled the air as he hurried up the steps. . . .

Made in United States
Troutdale, OR
06/28/2023